What People
Hidden

A beautifully told story of a young woman's search for her birth mother. Loosely based on her own journey of discovery, Catherine West infuses a transparency and depth of emotion both **heartrending and immensely satisfying.** I couldn't put it down. Novel Rocket and I give it a very high recommendation.

> —**ANE MULLIGAN**, Sr. editor, Novel Rocket, http://www.novelrocket.com

Takes you on an emotional journey through the life of Claire Ferguson—one of loss, hope, and a promise for the future. Claire struggles through darkness until a sleepy Maine town and its inhabitants show a glimpse of light and rest. Catherine's gift for writing the family saga with emotional power has made her one of my favorite authors. A Catherine West novel is **a must-read.**

> —**LINDI PETERSON**, award-winning author of *Her Best Catch*

A compelling love song of a novel **about finding a true home in a lonely world.** Gifted author Catherine West writes with lump-in-the-throat power to transport you through a family's journey from brokenness to grace. A page-turner full of honest spiritual insight and poignant characters, this luminous story of forgiveness will take hold of your heart and lift its hidden burdens.

> —**ROSSLYN ELLIOTT,** award-winning author of *Fairer Than Morning* and *Sweeter than Birdsong*

Goes beyond the quick fix of discovery and delves into struggles with faith, commitment, complication circumstances, and difficult decisions. **If your family has been touched by adoption, you will want to read this well-told story.**

> —**LORI WILDBERG**, coauthor of *Empowered Parents: Putting Faith First,* speaker, licensed parent-family educator, cowriter of *The Parenting Prose* column in *Marriage Magazine,* team member of The M.O.M. Initiative

A well-told story complete with flawed characters who must deal with their mistakes, heartbreak, and pain. *"I'm not so sure God deals in guilt. If anything, I think he deals in forgiveness."* A lesson for us all.

> —**EILEEN KEY**, author of *Cedar Creek Seasons* and *Sundays in Fredericksburg* (Barbour)

An emotionally mesmerizing drama of the relationships that define and mold a family. A love story on many levels, *Hidden in the Heart* speaks to the heart about the soul-deep experiences of being an adopted child, the value of forgiveness, and the ultimate beauty of love.

—SUE HARRISON, international bestselling author of *Mother Earth, Father Sky*

Hidden in the Heart is a compelling tale of forgiveness, redemption, and hope. Catherine West brilliantly weaves a story that you will leave but will not leave you because it **embodies what we all desire each and every day—the chance to love better than we did the day before.**

—DINEEN MILLER, author of *The Soul Saver*

A thought-provoking story that explores the depths of human despair—and Christ's redemptive, soul-changing power. Full of witty dialogue and poignant examples of faith, Catherine West has captured one woman's journey to find her true self in a way that will touch each mother, daughter, sister, or friend.

—ERIN MACPHERSON, author of The Christian Mama's Guide series

Catherine West's adept prose unfurls moments with the power to change lives, giving us both **the dismay of heartbreak and a call to redemption** in the story of two women who did not know how much they needed each other.

—OLIVIA NEWPORT, author of *The Pursuit of Lucy Banning*

Through her novels, Catherine West asks readers to examine the deeper issues of the heart: how our failures shape our futures, what real faith looks like, and how much heartache can a marriage survive. In *Hidden in the Heart,* West explores the many facets of adoption, writing with **gut-wrenching honesty and yet tenderness** that kept me turning pages late into the night.

—BETH K. VOGT, author of *Wish You Were Here* (Howard Books, May 2012) and *Catch a Falling Star* (May 2013)

Catherine West intricately weaves a story about one family's journey toward truth, healing, and wholeness. *Hidden in the Heart* is **a touching tale** that will leave readers with a sense that, even in the midst of great hurt, God can redeem what's been lost.

—KATIE GANSHERT, author of *Wildflowers from Winter* (Waterbrook Multnomah)

What People Are Saying About
Yesterday's Tomorrow

2011 INSPY Award Winner (Romance)
Finalist, 2012 Reader's Favorite Awards
ACFW Book Club Selection, August 2011

This compelling love story, set against the backdrop of the Vietnam War, transported me through recent history. Cathy West's debut novel is **beautifully crafted and thoroughly engaging!**

—**DEBORAH RANEY**, best-selling author of the Clayburn Novels and *Almost Forever*

Vietnam. The word evokes a myriad of emotions, depending on the hearer's age, knowledge, and experience. I for one remember the Vietnam War era well, having bid farewell to my then twenty-year-old military husband as he deployed for a year to that faraway, dangerous land, leaving me at home to care for two babies in diapers.

Author Catherine West **exquisitely captures the feel of that time and place** in the pages of her amazing debut novel, *Yesterday's Tomorrow*. This book speaks to the very depths of your heart, whether you have any personal recollection of that tumultuous time or not. Get ready for an exciting adventure and a heart-pounding ride as you dive into this page-turning story. No doubt this will be the first of many excellent offerings from this talented new author.

—**KATHI MACIAS**, award-winning author of more than 30 books, including the popular Extreme Devotion series www.kathimacias.com, www.thetitus2women.com

Heartwrenching! Powerful! In *Yesterday's Tomorrow*, Catherine West **spans seas and generations to report on the Perfect Love Who will never let go.** Don't miss this poignant debut novel.

—**PATTI LACY**, author of *The Rhythm of Secrets*

With grace and authenticity, West takes on the difficult setting of Vietnam and **shows how even the most painful history can bring a future of beauty and redemption.**

—**MEREDITH EFKEN**, author of *Lucky Baby*

In her thrilling breakout novel, *Yesterday's Tomorrow*, Catherine West has all-at-once crafted a wonderful story of magnetic cross-appeal for romance lovers, for historical fiction lovers, and for fans of stories of international intrigue spiced around a military setting! From riveting tension starting in the prologue, and through the eyes of Kristin Taylor, an independent journalist covering of the Vietnam War while fighting her reluctant attraction for the ruggedly handsome, Oxford-educated war-photographer Luke Maddox, *Yesterday's Tomorrow* is **filled with action, emotion, and splendid imagery that captivates the reader from the get-go.** As an ex-naval officer, I am grateful that Catherine chose the Vietnam War as the exciting backdrop for this novel. In doing so, she has done a great service to hundreds of thousands of veterans who have shamefully been forgotten over the years, and has admirably brought attention to their sacrifice. I love Catherine's easy-to-follow writing style, am proud to heartily endorse *Yesterday's Tomorrow*, and to be counted as a fan of Catherine West.

—DON BROWN, author of Zondervan's Navy Justice series

Catherine West's *Yesterday's Tomorrow* conveys the bloodstained misery of war without gratuitous violence but with heart-wrenchingly real images that carry the reader breathlessly from scene to scene. Tucked inside and between and around wartime Vietnam with its pungent odors, its lush landscape, its heated humidity, its lost peoples, is a moving love story—both human and heavenly; a story of redemption, of finding Place when the known world is upheaved into the unknown. In and around these vivid images of war, two achingly sad and lonely characters reach out to each other, to God, to friends, and to family, in their struggle to find Home, Love, and Forgiveness.

A beautifully crafted love story with poignantly flawed characters who give this novel a full-to-bursting heart.

—KATHRYN MAGENDIE, author of *Tender Graces, Secret Graces, Sweetie,* Publishing Editor, Rose & Thorn Journal
http://kathrynmagendie.com/

HIDDEN IN THE HEART

"YOU EXISTED BEFORE YOU WERE ADOPTED."

CATHERINE WEST

OakTara

Waterford, Virginia

Hidden in the Heart

Published in the U.S. by:
OakTara Publishers
P.O. Box 8, Waterford, VA 20197
www.oaktara.com

Cover design by Yvonne Parks at www.pearcreative.ca
Cover images © shutterstock.com: girl holding flowers/Mitya
Author photo © Sarah West Photography

ISBN: 978-1-60290-329-6

Hidden in the Heart is a work of fiction. References to real people, events, establishments, organizations, or locales are intended only to provide a sense of authenticity and are used fictitiously. All other characters, incidents, and dialogue are drawn from the author's imagination.

Printed in the U.S.A.

* * *

FOR MY SISTER, PAM.

If I had known this journey would lead me to you,
I would have started sooner.

With praise and humble gratitude
to my Father in Heaven.
You led me every step of the way,
carried me when I could go no further,
and then gave me miracles I did not deserve.

* * *

For you created my inmost being;
you knit me together in my mother's womb.
I praise you because I am fearfully and wonderfully made;
your works are wonderful,
I know that full well.
My frame was not hidden from you
when I was made in the secret place,
when I was woven together in the depths of the earth.
Your eyes saw my unformed body;
all the days ordained for me were written in your book
before one of them came to be.
—PSALM 139: 13-16

Acknowledgments

They say it takes a village to raise a child. It takes a lot more than that to raise a book.

I would like to thank my parents for their love and unwavering support over the years—we were indeed a match made in Heaven. My mother instilled in me a love of reading, a love of words that grew into a desire to write stories. I only wish she was here today to read them.

As always, thanks to my husband, Stephen, for his unconditional love, patience, and encouragement. I love you. This is really happening!

Huge thanks and mad love (just to embarrass them) to my children, Sarah and Christopher, and to my future son-in-law, Randy, for being there every step of the way, and believing in me. You all make me so proud. I could not do this without you.

To my wonderful agent, Rachelle Gardner, thank you for your support and your love for this story! Your input, advice, encouragement, and friendship means more than you know.

A special thanks to my critique partners, Jenness Walker and Lindi Peterson. You are always there when I need you, and I value your feedback so much.

To my ACFW family—I wouldn't be where I am today without this wonderful group of writers. You are all awesome!

To Ramona Tucker and everyone at OakTara, for saying yes. You've made this author's dreams come true!

Yvonne Parks—you're the best cover designer ever! And a great friend!

To all my friends and family in Bermuda and abroad—you never cease to amaze me with the way you support and encourage me. I treasure our friendships and look forward to many more years of fun together!

To my best friend in the world, Lee Anne. For all the phone calls, advice, many tears, and a whole lot of laughter in between. Thank you for traveling this road with me. This one's for you.

1

Claire Ferguson stood outside Baby Gap, unable to look away from the Christmas display. Red velvet dresses and miniature-sized plaid waistcoats. Tiny suede boots, tiny patent leather shoes, tiny colorful striped hats and scarves. Everything was tiny.

Claire stared at a little red dress, her eyes filling as she imagined and wished for the impossible.

People filed in and out of the store, smiling, laughing. Happy. An ordinary day filled with ordinary tasks and lists of things that must be accomplished. She had no such list—just an overwhelming need to pass time quickly on this day that was not so ordinary.

Claire steadied herself and glanced at her watch. Late afternoon. Shoppers jostled by, oblivious to her pain, all in a hurry to get their purchases and conquer the next store in the mall.

If only she had a reason to hurry.

"Have Yourself A Merry Little Christmas" crooned from the mall loudspeakers. Claire bit her lip and cursed Bing.

Christmas would be merry when it was over.

Claire tightened her grip around the numerous bags she carried and slowly moved forward. Her heel slipped on a slick patch of tile. She regained her balance before falling, but the effort shook her and sent her pulse racing.

After walking a bit, her arms began to burn. Her overflowing shopping bags were heavy but gave a sense of accomplishment. She'd gotten out of bed and had the purchases to prove it.

"Claire? Hey...yoo-hoo!" A woman's greeting floated above the noise of the crowd.

Claire lowered her head and rummaged through her purse. She popped a few breath mints into her mouth and chewed as she weighed her options.

Pretend she didn't hear. Pretend to be someone else. Or turn and face the owner of the vaguely familiar voice still calling out her name.

Curiosity won out and Claire turned.

"Hi, Claire! I thought that was you." The woman waved and hurried over. Platinum blonde hair swooshed around her shoulders. "Long time no see. You do remember me, don't you?"

"Um…" No. Claire pushed through the tangled cobwebs in her brain. "Ashley…something? High school?" The woman's Colgate-bright smile never faltered. She could have been on the cover of a magazine. Or a toothpaste commercial.

"Amanda. Barrington." Blue eyes twinkled as though she held some untold secret. "Gosh, it's been a while. How are you? Have time for a coffee?"

"Coffee?" Claire screwed up her nose. Vodka tonic would be more enticing, but whatever. She didn't have anywhere to be. Not really. "Sure."

They settled around a table at Starbucks. Amanda insisted on buying, which was fine with Claire. A few minutes later she sipped an Espresso and managed a smile. "So, Amanda. What have you been up to since high school?"

"Oh, not too much. Busy. You?"

Claire nodded. "Same. Busy. Very busy." Busy not answering the phone. Busy surfing channels. Busy ignoring the whole world.

Amanda stirred another packet of sweetener into her Caffè Misto. "You got married a few years ago, didn't you? You and James?"

A bizarre image of Guy Smiley from *Sesame Street* flashed before her, and Claire wondered what she'd done to win a spot on *This Is Your Life.* She suppressed a giggle. That third drink at lunch probably hadn't been such a great idea. "Yep. Me and James."

"Any kids?"

As if on cue, a mother walked past them pushing a toddler in a stroller. The kid looked her way and released a blood-curdling wail. Claire let out her breath. "Didn't you go to Vassar?"

"Oh." Amanda's pretty smile petered out as she fiddled with the top of her cup. "Yes, but I dropped out. Had a breakdown of sorts."

"Of sorts?" Maybe that was the same as being a little bit pregnant. A ripple of anxiety washed over Amanda's face, and Claire felt a pinch of guilt. "Hey, it's cool. I'm the last person to be throwing judgment around." She pulled at a loose thread on her sweater.

Getting out of bed this morning had been tiresome enough; she hadn't given much thought to her wardrobe. Just grabbed a pair of yoga pants and a long sweater that covered her butt and pushed her feet into a pair of Uggs. She took in Amanda's pristine appearance, fumbled with her hair, and tried to remember whether she'd even brushed it. "Are you…okay now?" Stupid question. Of course she was.

"Oh, yes," Amanda answered too quickly. "Right as rain."

"Funny, that." Claire couldn't stop a grin. "Right as rain. People always complain when it rains, don't they? I mean, what's right about it, really?"

Amanda didn't hide surprise well. She opened her mouth, but no words came. She nibbled on a bran muffin and dabbed cherry lips with a paper napkin. "I heard your mother died. Last year, was it? I'm sorry."

Of course she was sorry. Everybody was sorry. God was probably even sorry.

Claire studied her nails. The pink polish was chipped and faded, most of her nails worn down by her chewing on them. Another habit she couldn't seem to break. "She had cancer. Only lived a few months after her diagnosis."

"I'm so sorry."

"Yup." Claire nodded, still pondering Amanda's mysterious breakdown. She really wanted to ask how the accommodations were at the funny farm, because if things got any worse she might be heading there herself. "So, what are you doing now that you're...*okay*?" Small talk seemed more appropriate.

Amanda perked up at the change of subject. "Oh, a bit of this and that. I'm planning a wedding. I got engaged a few months ago." She waved a hand, a diamond the size of a small country in Africa almost blinding Claire. "When I saw you, I remembered. You were adopted too, right?"

Hot liquid sloshed out of the small hole in the plastic lid, and Claire put her cup down in a hurry. She dabbed at the mess and tried to think what an appropriate response would be. "None of your business" probably wouldn't go over so well.

"Too?" As Claire lifted the top off her paper cup to clean it, the lid on her memory slid off with it. "That's right. You were the only other kid I knew who was adopted. Our mothers were friends for a while, weren't they?"

"When we were in eighth and ninth grade." Amanda's eyes got misty. "I used to love going over to your house; you were so much fun. But then we...drifted apart I guess. You ran with the cool kids. I was a geek."

"Oh." Claire pushed down the lid of her cup and prayed she hadn't been completely horrible to this poor girl who had apparently once been a friend.

"Anyway, I found my birth mother." Amanda sat back, a small smile set in place. "That's what I wanted to tell you. I thought you...would understand."

"Your birth mother?" The words slammed into Claire, went straight for the gut, held tight, and twisted. "No kidding?" She took another sip and hoped Amanda wouldn't notice the tremor in her hand. "How?"

"It wasn't that hard, really." Amanda blinked and gazed across the crowded room. A bizarre heavy metal version of "Jingle Bells" blasted through the speakers and they shared a smile. "I suppose I just got tired of looking in the mirror and wondering. You know?"

3

Boy, did she know. Claire shrugged. "When was this?"

"Two years ago. I talked to my parents first, and they were okay with it. I wrote away for my non-identifying information and next thing I knew, Social Services was calling to put me in touch with her."

"How'd that go?" A slow pounding began in her temples, and Claire swallowed the urge to puke. There was something wrong about this—having this conversation—today, on the anniversary of her mother's death. Amanda of course, couldn't know that. Couldn't know that Claire had, of late, thought of doing the very same thing.

Searching.

Searching for answers. Searching for truth. As if somehow knowing the truth would help her get her life back.

Thoughts of whether or not to proceed had become an obsession.

Maybe her best friend, Melanie, was right. "*There are no coincidences, Claire. Only Godincidences.*" Claire could hear Melanie now. "*It's a sign. You should do it.*"

The only sign Claire wanted to see was the one that said BAR.

She turned her attention back to her long-lost friend and hoped she hadn't missed anything earth-shattering.

"We're not that much alike, and after the first meeting..." Amanda prattled on. "But did you ever think about it? I mean, your mom's gone now and..."

"Me? Oh, no." Claire checked her watch and frowned. She had to meet James for dinner. "Hey, this was great, but...my husband...we have plans."

"Yes, of course. Well..." Amanda foraged in her Marc Jacobs bag and came up with a gold-embossed business card. "Give me a call sometime, Claire. And if you change your mind, about searching, I'm here to help."

"Thanks. It was great to see you."

"Merry Christmas."

"Sure. You have a good one."

Claire waded through the sea of shoppers until she reached the doors to the parking lot and stumbled outside. Cold air brought clarity, and she breathed deeply. She clasped her elbows and willed the trembling to stop, willed the world to stop spinning as she tried to get her bearings and headed in the general direction she hoped she'd parked.

She needed to get out of here. But to what?

Claire stopped walking and stared at the slush beneath her feet. The knot in her stomach pulled tight. James would be expecting her.

He wanted to talk. Again.

Claire had run out of words a long time ago.

She turned and entered the warm building again, scanned the area, and spied a TGI Friday's. It was a bit too early for food, but that didn't matter. She wasn't planning on eating.

Two hours later, Claire peered at her reflection in the bathroom mirror. Maybe she should call a cab. She splashed some water on her face, spritzed a little perfume on her neck, and picked up her bags.

After waiting half an hour for a cab to come into sight, Claire's feet were frozen. She gave up and headed back to her car. It would be fine. She hadn't had that much to drink.

She maneuvered her car down the back roads as carefully as she could. Snow started to fall and got heavier by the minute. Claire shook her head and cursed the snow. Cursed herself for being so stupid.

Staying in bed would have been the more sensible solution.

She'd been doing better. Almost convinced herself she could make it through the holidays. Now all she could think about was Mom, and that stupid conversation she'd had with Amanda.

Pain rushed her with such force she considered pulling off the road to expel the liquid sloshing around in her stomach. She was re-living it all over again. That long, dark night when her world had shattered like a Christmas ornament dropped from the highest branches of the tree.

"She's gone, Claire..."

They all thought death was something you could prepare for. Thought if you read up, prayed up, and clammed up, it would all be okay.

Her father read books and retreated into silence.

James went to church, put them all on the prayer chain, and talked to God.

And Claire ignored it, hoping the day would never come.

But it had, come and gone, and taken her mother with it.

A blast of sirens jolted her back to the present. Her SUV swerved, and she slowed until the vehicle straightened. Obnoxious blue and red flashers intensified the pain in her head. Claire flicked on her turn signal and pulled over. Just what she needed to make a crappy day even crappier.

"Ya better watch out, ya better not cry..." The modern version of the classic blasted from the radio. *"Ya better not pout, I'm tellin' you why..."* The Boss's raspy voice belted out the warning.

Claire almost grinned. *Too late, Bruce. Already on the blacklist this year.*

Through the rearview mirror she watched the officer step out of his vehicle. He sloshed through gray snow, his burly frame shadowed in the setting sun, but she'd recognize that bear-like gait anywhere.

Definitely not Santa Claus.

Why did it have to be him?

Claire shoved her hand in her purse, pulled out her breath mints, and put a few in her mouth, wishing she'd had a second cup of coffee. She chewed quickly and shoved another couple in just before he reached her car.

Robert Ferguson tapped on her car window, a scowl set in place. His dark blue jacket was zipped halfway, his badge glinting. Claire returned the scowl and prayed for an apocalypse. He rapped again, and Claire knew she had no choice. She pressed the button and the window slid down.

"Hello, Claire." Her brother-in-law stepped back and folded his arms over his chest.

A blast of cold air smacked her face as she shifted to face him, tightening her grip on the wheel. "Robert. What a pleasant surprise." Not. She forced a smile and ignored the hammering of her heart.

"You okay?" He studied her in silence, suspicion settling in his eyes.

Okay? She had a wet butt from falling in the parking lot, lived through that strange conversation with Amanda, and had a case of major indigestion, but whatever. "Sure, I'm okay. Sweet of you to ask." Her heart rate kicked up a notch as he let out a sigh.

"Can you turn off the stereo, please?"

"Sure." Claire blinked at the dash and squinted. The silver buttons were so small and they all looked alike. "Ah. There. Better?"

"Where've you been, Claire? You were driving a little erratically."

"Erratically?" She widened her eyes, surprised he knew such a big word. "Oh, back there, you mean? Yeah, black ice. Thought I was done for."

His scowl deepened, forming a crater above the bridge of his nose. "Black ice, huh? You were all over the road. Going too fast, then too slow…I've been following you about a quarter mile. I guess you didn't notice."

"Seriously? Guess I didn't. You know, female drivers. We never check the rearview mirror unless we're putting on lipstick." Her palms grew moist despite the cold air flooding her car.

His bland expression told her he wasn't buying it. "Have you been drinking?" Robert narrowed his eyes, leaning in a little closer.

Claire shook her head and the interior of the car spun. She covered her mouth with one hand and took a minute. "Of course not. I'm not stupid. I wouldn't do something like that."

"Claire," he growled, placing his big hands on the ledge of the open window, "level with me."

There might have been a hint of compassion in his eyes, but it faded too soon. Claire stared at the falling snow and wondered what she'd look like in orange. "I...um...went out for lunch. I might have had a glass of wine. That's all. Really. I'm fine."

"You don't look fine." He took a step back. "Want to get out of the car?"

"No," she squeaked. "Come on, Robby. I just told you, I'm okay. Thanks for checking up on me, though." The back of her neck prickled. He couldn't possibly be serious.

Robert yanked the door open. "Get out."

"Please, Robert. I'm begging you. I'm not drunk. You can follow me home if you want to."

"Get out of the car, Claire." Anger dripped off his tongue, and she knew she'd pushed his limit. Maybe if she pretended to pass out she'd wake up and find this was all some weird dream. Maybe she'd just pass out anyway.

"Claire. Today. If you wouldn't mind."

"I'm coming." She struggled to stand, slipped on the slush beneath her, and he caught her elbow before she fell. The towering pines across the road blurred into one big green snowball, hurtling toward her. She steadied herself and tried to focus on Robert. This was a nightmare. It had to be.

But no, she'd definitely had too much to drink, and now she was busted.

Served her right. There was always a price to pay. But she wished Robert didn't have to be the one to collect.

He barked instructions at her, and Claire tried to follow what he was saying, but the buzzing in her ears made it hard to understand him. And she really had to pee.

"You're a mess," he muttered, eyes blazing into her. "You're going to blow over, you know that, right?"

"Maybe we should skip it then." Claire held out her wrists toward him and smiled.

"Get in the patrol car. I'll drive you home."

"What? You're not going to arrest me? You're actually going to give me a break?" Claire stared in disbelief. "That's...so...unlike you, Robby."

He shifted and put his hands on his hips, his stance wide. "Claire, seriously? I'm trying to be nice here."

"Just spreading a little Christmas joy, huh?" Her eyes landed on the butt of his revolver, his hand dangerously close to it. Tears welled, and one rolled down her cheek into the corner of her mouth.

"All right." He zipped up his coat and propelled her toward the police car. "Let's get you off the road before you kill somebody."

"I don't need your help, Robert." She tried to squirm out of his grip, but he was too strong.

"Do you want me to bring you in, Claire? Honestly, it would be a real pleasure. I'm only giving you a break out of respect for my brother. If you want to throw your life away, fine, I really don't care, but don't take him down with you."

Claire whirled to face him. "Then arrest me! Go on. It's what you're supposed to do anyway, right?" The words flew out before she could stop them. She watched his mouth twitch.

"Get in the car." His glare was enough to silence her into submission.

Claire climbed into the back of the black and white patrol car. It reeked of sweat, cigarettes, and coffee. She leaned her head against the plastic-covered seat and waited. Out of the corner of her eye she saw him retrieve her purse from her vehicle while he talked on his cell phone. Her heart raced as she tried to second-guess him. He wasn't going to arrest her. That was the good news.

Maybe she could get home without her father or James finding out. She'd sleep it off and be fine in the morning.

Done with his call, Robert tossed her purse onto the seat beside her and slammed the door. The car shook from side to side. Claire winced and closed her eyes. She pulled her knees up, resting her boots on the divider as he pulled back onto the road. "Excuse me?" She rapped on the plastic glass between them. "Can you maybe have my car taken home? There's a lot of stuff in there. I just went shopping."

"Before or after you stopped at the bar?"

"Robert!"

"Relax, Claire." He cracked his gum and sniffed. "There's a tow-truck on the way. It'll be impounded. You'll get it back eventually."

"Stop kidding around. You can't do this to me. Come on…"

He slowed at a stoplight along Main. Claire inched down on the seat, searching the faces on the sidewalk. "Where are you taking me? The exit is the other way."

"I know where the exit is."

He hated her. He was going to arrest her after all.

Claire swallowed back nausea and chewed on a torn fingernail. "So, um…how's the family?"

Robert's shoulders stiffened, and he glanced back at her through the mirror. "Claire?"

"Yes?"

"Stop talking."

"Sorry." Claire foraged through the jumbled mess of things inside her purse and came up with a lipstick. Didn't bother checking the color. After applying a generous amount to her dry lips, she smacked them together. Bad idea. Her stomach rolled again, and she popped a couple more mints in her mouth.

When he parked the car at the back of the precinct, Claire glared at the three-story gray building, crumbling in places. She swore it would fall down one of these days. With any luck Robert would be inside when it did.

"You said you were going to take me home, Robert." Claire stared at the back of his big head, watching a fly settle on the short dark hair. Maybe she could smack it for him.

He cleared his throat and she pushed aside the idea.

"You're staying at your dad's house now, right?" he asked.

"Yes."

"That's what I thought. That place is at least a half hour out on the other side of town. That would be going way beyond my family obligations. You can wait here until somebody comes for you."

"Who's coming? Who did you call?" Claire pushed herself out of the car, but he ignored her and escorted her through the back doors. She walked slowly, determined not to slip. Or fall over. They passed a couple of officers in the hall. Claire saw some raised eyebrows, and one of the men let out a low whistle. Wonderful. She'd be the talk of small-town Connecticut within the hour.

Robert stopped outside a small office at the far end of the corridor. He kicked the door with his black boot and it swung open. He walked in and checked out the room. "Take a seat. Nobody will bother you. Unless I tell them to."

Claire's feet wouldn't move. "Look, I can call a cab. I..."

"Nope. You'll stay right here until you sober up."

She marched to the desk, threw her purse down, and turned on him. "You can't just shove me in here, Robert! I know my rights! Which you haven't even read me by the way, and..."

"Claire." He breathed out her name, sounding tired and beyond reasoning. "Sit down, and for the last time, shut up." Fury ran across his face. "I told you, I'm not arresting you. But I should be. You should be thanking me, not yelling at me like you haven't done anything wrong." Robert stood near the door, his eyes softening. "You've got to start dealing with life, Claire. You can't go on like this."

She pushed hair off her face and pinched her lips together. "Where do you get off telling me how to 'deal with it'?" Familiar anger coiled inside her stomach and the dull ache returned. She sank into the chair behind the desk. "First my mother dies; then I have a miscarriage. Why does everybody expect me to 'forget' and 'get over it'?" Claire leaned back and closed her eyes.

"That's not what I meant. But it'd be nice if you started acting more like a mature adult instead of a spoiled, out-of-control teenager."

"Are you done?" She put her head in her hands.

"I'll be back in a while."

"Fine." Claire gazed up at him, unsmiling. "Thank you."

"Sure. Whatever." He slammed the door behind him. The noise reverberated around the small room and pierced through her skull.

Claire rubbed her temples and wondered if she could down a couple of Tylenol without water. Robert was probably enjoying every minute of this. He'd hold court later at his favorite watering hole and regale his buddies of how he finally one-upped his wayward sister-in-law.

It wasn't fair. Since Mom's death, things seemed to go from bad to worse. Her family, her husband, the whole world was against her. Every single day she had to endure some trial.

She slumped down, put her head on the desk, and took a deep breath.

Robert was right, though. This time.

She was guilty. She should have known better than to drink and drive. But once she got started, it was so easy to keep them coming. She only wanted to get rid of the pain. But whatever the amount she'd consumed today, it wasn't enough.

It was never enough.

2

Michelle Hart listened as her secretary took yet another call.

"Ms. Hart's office. No, sir, she's still not available. Yes, I do realize she's the mayor's press secretary...no...we have no statement at this time. No...I don't believe Mayor Harrison is in the building at the moment." There was an audible sigh. "Oh, no, sir, I'm sure they're not talking to the entire city of New York and not you...what was your name again? Yes, I will tell Ms. Hart you called. Have a good night."

Sharlene marched into Michelle's office a minute later, her cheeks puffed out like two apples on the way to ripening. Silver-rimmed spectacles were just about to slip off her nose. "That nasty newspaper reporter called again," she huffed, pushing up her glasses. "For the fifth time. I turned on the answering machine. I will not tolerate profanity."

Picking up a stack of files from the desk, Sharlene glanced at the broadcast coming from the flat-screen on the wall. Her expression changed from anger to pity. "That poor woman." Sharlene rubbed a Kleenex over her bifocals and put them back on, squinting at the screen. "It's bad enough to find out your husband's cheating, but to have it splashed all over the six o'clock news...and right before the holidays. Don't they have little kids?"

Michelle worked hard not to let out a sigh of frustration. Her aging secretary wasn't cut out for this job. "I thought you were headed home." She turned up the volume. Sharlene meant well, but she'd never understand politics. They should discuss her retirement again. Soon.

"On my way." Sharlene moved to the door. "It's been a long day."

"Did I miss it?" Kevin Harrison strode into the office, striped tie askew, his long black coat flapping open.

"Evening, Mr. Harrison. Good night to you both." Sharlene scurried out, closing the door behind her.

"Oh, good, it's still on..." Kevin's eyes went straight to the television. His face blazed from the cold and his obvious excitement.

Michelle smiled, a familiar heat rushing through her at the sight of him—blond hair slightly mussed by the wind, blue eyes sparkling brighter than ever. He was as handsome as the day they'd met five years ago. Maybe even more so. She lifted her chin and waited for him to approach, but he was already absorbed in the broadcast.

"What's he saying?" He shrugged out of his coat, took off his gloves, and flung everything on a chair by the wall.

"Shh...sit." Michelle clasped her hands behind her head and watched New York Senator Barry Whiting walk to the podium and tap on the microphone. A few minutes later he was finished. Literally. And the senate seat was up for grabs.

Kevin smacked his palms together and gave a low chuckle. Victory danced in his eyes and around the room, filling the air with anticipation.

Michelle pressed the off switch and the screen went black. "Well done, Kev. How does it feel to be God?"

Kevin gave a short laugh, strode across the rug, flung open the antique mahogany cabinet, and poured a couple of drinks. He handed her a crystal tumbler and sank into one of the chairs opposite her desk. He polished off his drink in two gulps and met her eyes, a sly smile tugging at his lips. "Not fair. Whiting made his own mistakes, and now he's paying for them. I had nothing to do with it."

"Not directly, of course." Michelle sipped the dark liquid, made a face, and coughed. She hated bourbon. He knew it, of course, but her needs were never high on Kevin's list of things to remember. She put her glass down. "But I'm pretty sure you had a lunch meeting a couple of days ago with your buddy Skip, from the *Times*. And if I'm not mistaken, that's who broke the story."

Kevin waved a hand and went back to the bar. "So what? Rumors have been flying all over town for months. I didn't tell him anything he didn't already know." He poured himself a refill. "So how do we play this? I assume you've been fielding calls?"

She raised her eyes to the ceiling. "For the last three hours. Everybody knows you're going to run for Barry's seat. The question of the day is when will you confirm it?" Michelle reached for her Blackberry. "Next Saturday night you'll host a private dinner at Le Bernardin. Sharlene will send out the invitations tomorrow. I've planned for fifty. You can go through the list. If there's anyone..."

"The governor?"

"Of course. I talked to his wife this afternoon. They were going to Nantucket for a little R and R, but she'll put it off a day."

"Excellent. We'll make the announcement then." The wrinkles around his eyes crinkled with a rare genuine smile. "What would I do without you?"

Michelle grinned and lifted an eyebrow. "Probably still be practicing law in Queens."

His jaw tightened, and the light fled from his eyes. She broke his hard stare, ran her tongue over her bottom lip, and checked her email. Her inbox was flooded again. "You should call Barry. Say something supportive." She looked up and put on a conciliatory smile.

"Right." Kevin mussed his hair and fiddled with the thick gold band of his watch. "Maybe he'll back me—what do you think?"

"He doesn't have a lot of choice." Michelle put down her phone and massaged her temples. For some ridiculous reason, the image of a bedraggled Louise Whiting holding a child by each hand as they exited their home yesterday hounded by the press rankled her. "Do you think his wife will stay with him?"

"Why should I care?" Kevin undid the top button of his navy shirt and checking his own mail. "Listen to you, getting all melodramatic."

Melodramatic? No. Michelle fingered the strand of pearls around her neck. She'd met Louise a few times. Nice girl. Whiting was definitely an idiot. But she suspected Louise had been trained to turn a blind eye. The perfect politician's wife. "I do feel sorry for her and their children. It's not fair that they have to pay for his mistakes."

"Oh, please." Kevin looked up from his Blackberry. "He's getting what he deserves. Infidelity is still a mortal sin in the eyes of the public. At least this year."

"A little hypocritical coming from you, Kev."

"What?" His innocent expression chilled her.

Michelle rubbed her arms and looked away.

"Did you get hold of Felicity?" He glanced at his watch again. "I can't have the kids hanging around this weekend. Too much going on." There was no regret in his eyes as he talked of his estranged wife and children, only a keen glint of what the future now held.

Michelle checked the calendar. "I talked to her this afternoon. The kids were disappointed. I told them you'd make it up to them, so you'd better come up with something pretty cool. Felicity sends you her best regards."

"I'm sure she does." He rose and pushed up the knot of his tie. "I should get going. Sorry, but dinner won't work tonight. I ran into John Fortin earlier today, and we're going to meet for drinks. I've promised him an exclusive. Make sure to seat him at a good table on Saturday. Come by later?"

Michelle swiveled her chair to face the window. The Manhattan skyline projected a yellow glow against the dark night. Large flakes of snow spiraled downward, a hint that the predicted winter storm might be on its way. She watched a couple lights flicker off in the building opposite theirs.

"No. I think I'll stay home tonight, Kev. I want to run through the menu for Saturday and do a few other things."

Like ignore the fact that Christmas was just around the corner.

She swung to face him and smiled at his expression of chagrin. "You should try to get an early night for a change. You're going to need all the rest you can get over the next few months. We'll start working on your speech in the morning."

Kevin grinned as he pulled on his coat, but his face clouded over as he moved toward her. "Look, ah...since I'm going to be running now, we should probably cancel our cruise over New Year's. I've been thinking maybe I should spend more time with the kids..."

"I see." Michelle's heart thudded against her chest. The moment she'd heard of Whiting's situation, she'd been expecting this, but still, after two years with Kevin, it stung.

"Hey." Kevin placed his hands on the arms of her chair, his eyes piercing. "Don't give me that look. You know as well as I do how this has to go down. Let me handle things with Felicity. Once I'm elected, once the divorce is final, everything will be different. You know that, right?"

Michelle managed a nod and forced herself to respond when his lips met hers. His kiss grew more demanding, and for a moment she gave in to the need to be held. Needed. But probably not loved.

She pushed him off and straightened her blouse. "You better go, Kev. Don't want to keep Joe waiting. I'll see you in the morning."

"John."

"What?" Michelle lifted her head and caught a flash of anger in his eyes.

"It's John. From *The Post*. Whatever you do, don't get it wrong in front of him." He turned on the heel of his shiny black loafers and stalked out of her office.

Michelle moved her chair to face the painting on the wall above the long bookcase. She studied the image of the lake, forgotten feelings stretching, daring to emerge from exile.

Life had been simple once. Fun. Good.

Now it was just complicated.

"Knock, knock. Where's the man of the hour?" Belinda Cassidy sauntered in, olive skin glowing from the latest scrub she'd no doubt just had at Clarins. She wore her usual thousand-watt smile and Michelle's Emilio Pucci blouse.

Michelle scowled. "You missed him. And I thought you were going to quit stealing my clothes. We're not in college anymore. You can afford your own."

Her old friend slipped out of her mink coat, lowered herself into the chair Kevin had vacated, and swatted the air, the diamonds on her fingers sparkling. "You left it in the closet when you spent Thanksgiving with us. I couldn't bear to part with it. Call it an early Christmas present. I'll buy you another one, darling. What are you still doing in the office?"

Michelle gave a snort and pulled a tortoise-shell clip from her hair, allowing it to fall against her neck. She twisted her finger around a thick strand. "Just waiting for my personal masseuse to show up, sweetie."

"Sarcasm doesn't become you. You shouldn't be working here at all. Kevin should hire someone else, divorce what's-her-name, and marry you. Especially now."

Michelle grinned. Belinda was in fine form, and they hadn't had drinks yet. "Unlike you, my dear friend, I happen to believe there is more to life than shopping and lunching at The Plaza. I find having a career fulfilling, not to mention necessary. Besides, I like my job."

Belinda's knowing smile inched upward and lit her eyes with mischief. "And you may be moving offices if things go the way your boyfriend hopes they will."

Michelle opened the drawer to her desk and ignored her. "What's going on out there?"

Her friend's low laughter flooded the office. "As you'd expect, the city's buzzing. Word on the street is that Kevin's going to run for Barry's seat. And he'll get it."

"Of course he will." Michelle slammed the drawer shut and gave her a pointed stare. "And you've lived in New York long enough to know where that leaves me."

Belinda waved off the comment. "He's not going to get back together with his wife. They've been separated for two years. They're getting a divorce. Don't be ridiculous."

"Ridiculous?" Michelle shrugged, shutting down her computer. "I'm not being ridiculous. Just realistic. Felicity would take him back tomorrow. You and I both know it, Kevin knows it, half the city probably knows it."

Belinda's full mouth turned downward and Michelle groaned. She should have kept her mouth shut. "Don't start, Belinda."

"Why do you put up with this? You deserve better."

"Do I?" Michelle tried to push off gloomy thoughts. It wouldn't be the first Christmas spent alone. She studied the painting again, marveling at how the long brush strokes captured the pure stillness of dawn. She could almost smell the crisp, pine-scented air.

"Go home, Shel. Go spend the holidays with your folks."

She whirled to face Belinda. "You're kidding, right? How long have we been friends? You of all people know I can't go home. I can't believe you'd even suggest it."

"It's Christmas. Maybe it's time to put the past where it belongs."

"No." Michelle reached across the desk for her laptop, snapped it shut, and slipped it into the slim leather briefcase beside her desk. "If you came here to aggravate me, leave."

Belinda's throaty chuckle filled the office once again. "I didn't come here to aggravate you. I wanted to see if you were free for dinner. I'm sorry. Okay?"

Michelle forced a smile. "Fine. Is Don still out of town?"

"Yes, so you can come and keep me company. And I want to show you the plans for the place in Connecticut. You'll love it."

"Great." Drooling over Belinda's weekend getaway mansion would still be better than sitting home alone, mooning over what would never be. "So you decided to go with that architect firm then, Fergus something?"

"Shephard and Ferguson. Yes. They were highly recommended. We met. Nice young guys. One is the architect and the other runs the construction side of things. Seems like a family affair. The architect's wife was going to do my interior, but…"

Michelle carried the glasses over to the bar sink. "But what?"

Her friend put her coat back on and slung her purse over one shoulder. "She's not working right now. I'm not sure why. Maybe she's sick or something."

"Shame." Michelle grabbed her own wool coat and briefcase and moved to the door.

Belinda caught her arm, compassion shimmering in her dark eyes. "It's going to work out, Shel."

Michelle exhaled and set her jaw. "Unless you've developed a talent for predicting the future, I wouldn't be so sure."

Belinda's smile returned as she gave Michelle's arm a squeeze. "Madame Zelda at your service, my de-ah child." She shot her a wink. "You'll spend the holidays with us. Leave Kevin to plan his empire of dominion over the free world. We'll do our own thing. Maybe even fly off to Vegas. What do you think?"

"Please." Michelle shuddered at the images that particular idea conjured up, but then she smiled. At least Belinda would keep her laughing. "Vegas? Well, life's a gamble, so why not?"

3

Claire lost track of time in the small office. Her stomach protested its emptiness and began to growl. She dozed off for a bit but woke with a start at the thudding of footsteps against the cement floor. She turned toward the door as it opened. Robert stepped into the room, somebody behind him.

Robert nodded her way. "Your ride's here."

Her husband cast a long shadow across the floor. He stood to one side, his hands thrust into the pockets of his beat-up leather jacket. His sandy-brown hair was windblown, his face flushed, his jaw covered in light scruff. Dark circles framed his hazel eyes and told her he still wasn't sleeping. She watched him take a deep breath and let it out.

Claire blinked, unmoving. She ran her fingers through her tangled mess of hair, sobriety having set in some time ago. She hadn't seen James in a couple of weeks. Not since their last argument that had been the catalyst for her throwing her stuff in a suitcase and moving back to Dad's. Then today he'd called, asked her to meet him...and she'd bailed.

Maybe being thrown in jail was her punishment. A punishment she definitely deserved but didn't desire.

Robert held the door open. "Unless you really want to spend the night here, you can go."

Claire hesitated. Staying in this hole-in-the-wall might be better than navigating the forthcoming battle her little expedition would incite.

But she wasn't that crazy.

She reached for her purse and moved to the door, lowering her gaze as she passed Robert. "Thanks," she mumbled.

"Claire?" His low voice stopped her and she turned to meet his stare. His expression softened a tad. "Get some help. If you get pulled over again, you will be arrested. You're putting yourself and everybody else on the road at risk. You're past the point of rational behavior. You're dangerous."

Familiar anger sparked, but she swallowed it down. She wanted to get out of here. "I didn't think I'd had that much. I won't do it again. And I'm sorry." She ran her tongue over her cracked lips and picked up her purse. Neither of them acknowledged her flimsy excuse, but she didn't care.

Claire brushed past them and headed down the hall to the back door Robert had brought her through earlier. James' dark blue Jeep sat in the parking lot. He caught up and marched beside her, hands pushed into his pockets, his mouth drawn in a firm line, the tendon in his jaw pulsing.

Claire sucked in cold air and pulled out her cell phone. "I'm sorry he called you. You can leave. I'll call a cab."

"Oh, that's a good idea. Maybe you should have thought of it a few hours ago." James sent a scathing glance her way as he unlocked the Jeep. "You're unbelievable. Get in. And don't talk to me."

"You sound just like your brother." Claire climbed in on the passenger side and clicked her seatbelt in place.

James slid his legs under the wheel and slammed his door. Then he faced her, eyes blazing. Opened his mouth, shut it again. Shook his head and emitted a low groan. "Driving drunk? It's not like you can't afford cab fare, Claire."

She pushed her shoulders back against the seat. Reality made her blood run cold. "I know."

"You could have killed someone."

"I know."

"Or yourself."

"Yes." Wrapped her car around a tree and it would have been all over. A slight twitch of regret pricked her. "It was stupid. I wasn't thinking."

"No, I guess you weren't. You haven't been *thinking* for a while now."

She pinched her lips and refused the guilt he threw her way. "Are we going to have another fight? Because I'm really not up for it. My head hurts."

"Good." James pounded a fist on the steering wheel. "Did you forget that we were supposed to meet tonight? Or did getting a DUI seem like more fun?"

"He didn't arrest me."

"He should have." James gunned the engine and exited the parking lot.

Claire closed her eyes as he turned onto the road. Maybe if she feigned exhaustion he wouldn't bother talking to her. He slowed down and drove just under the speed limit for once, probably too tempted to pitch the Jeep into a snow bank. The normal thirty-minute ride to the gates of her father's estate took sixty excruciatingly silent minutes.

The Jeep shuddered to a stop outside the front steps. James kept the engine going and fiddled with the heating controls. Then he rested his head against the seat and let out his breath. "Are you still taking the anti-depressant medication Dr. Kay prescribed?"

"Yep. Lot of good it's doing." She glared at the dashboard.

James pressed his hands against the wheel. "Jesus, help me. What am I supposed to do with you?"

Claire raised an eyebrow. Jesus? He wouldn't help. Not that she'd asked lately. She clenched her fists and fought with sorrow. "Do you know what day it is?"

"Yeah. Thursday. What's that got to do with anything?"

Claire waited a minute before she trusted speech. These days her emotions surged too close to the surface. "My mother died a year ago today, James. Two days before Christmas. Remember?"

"Claire…" His voice got thick and gravelly, like he too was going to cry any minute. She shouldn't have let him drive her. Claire gripped the door handle, ready to bolt, but he put a hand on her arm. "I'm sorry. I should have remembered." He took a shaky breath and tightened his grip. "Will you stop this ridiculous behavior? Let's end this stupid separation or whatever you want to call it. Come home. We should be spending the holidays together."

"No." Claire looked out the window at the grand stone house she'd grown up in—such a contrast to the modest but comfortable three-bedroom on Comber that she and James had shared only months ago. "We've been through this. I'm not ready. You keep pushing me, James. I don't want to try to get pregnant again."

Golden shards of light shone from the long windows onto the sparkling snow. Maybe she should reconsider. Being here, her mother no longer inside waiting for her, wasn't any better.

"I don't get you, Claire. I know the miscarriage…" He squeezed his eyes shut. "It's not that uncommon, especially in a first pregnancy. Remember what the doctor said? You were under a lot of stress with your mom's death. I know it hurts, Claire, but it's almost been a year now. I…just want…"

Claire huffed out a breath. "I know what you want. You want to start over. Start again. That's what you're going to say, right? We'll pick up where we left off and play Happy Families like none of this ever happened. Look at me! Do you think I'm in any shape to have a child, James? Do you think I'm in any shape to be the kind of wife you need?"

"Yes." His face remained impassive, used to her incoherent ramblings. "You could be. If you would agree to get help, Claire, to stop this…to…"

He wasn't even listening.

"No." She sniffed, desperate to escape the warm car and searing conversation. "Give it up. You're better off without me, Jamie. The sooner you accept that, the easier this will be."

James locked eyes with hers, definitely paying attention now. "I *won't* accept that. I'm not giving up on you, Claire." He grabbed her wrist and held tight. "You don't get it, do you? I've loved you since the day we met, and I won't stop loving you until I take my last breath. You can shut me out. You can hate me if it makes you feel better. You can even leave town. Disappear if you want. But you can't ever make me stop loving you."

Claire bit down to keep her lower lip from trembling. She stared out the window, taking deep gulps of air. The moon slid from behind the clouds and tossed tiny diamonds across the snow-covered hills that surrounded the house.

James reached over, his hand soft against her cheek. "Say something."

"I...I can't," she stammered, black grief encompassing her. He couldn't mean it. After everything she'd said, all she'd done. "You're right," she whispered, meeting his gaze. "I don't understand it. And I don't deserve it. You should hate me. Why don't you?"

He leaned toward her and brushed her cheek with his lips. The weariness in his eyes told her he was too worn out to argue. "Go on. Try to get some sleep tonight. I'll call you tomorrow. If you need anything…"

"Stop." Claire placed two fingers on his lips. "Stop trying to fix things that can't be fixed, Jamie. Stop trying to be my knight in shining armor." She gave a wan smile. She'd thought her broken heart couldn't hurt anymore.

Wrong again, Claire.

She took in the familiar curve of his face, the way the gold flecks in his eyes sparkled when he looked at her—the hard jaw line, the small dimple that sat in the middle of his chin and deepened when he smiled. Claire moved her trembling hand across his face to touch a stray lock of hair that fell over one eye. "You need a haircut," she murmured.

He caught her hand in his and held it against the side of his face. Sudden warmth flooded her, the feeling so startling and unexpected that she wondered if she was imagining the sensation. Slowly he moved closer. The familiar scent of his cologne reached her nose and almost woke her sleeping soul. When he brought his mouth to hers, she closed her eyes, melting in the comfort of his kiss.

James brushed her lips with his, gently. Once, twice…but before she could put her arms around him and respond, he drew back, a smile flickering across his mouth. "By the way, I should warn you. Your dad got home a few hours ago. I had to tell him where you were. He's a little miffed."

Claire watched the Jeep disappear down the long drive, then trudged up the steps to the house, turned her key in the lock, and pushed open the large mahogany front door. Exhaustion dogging her, she cringed as the door slammed shut against the wind.

Suddenly she was a teenager again, creeping home after curfew.

Her two golden retrievers careened down the front hall to meet her. At least they were glad to see her. She took a moment to pat them, then watched them race away to another corner of the house, sending the Persian rug flying across the highly polished wood floor.

She kicked off her boots and swept her gaze over the foyer, missing the usual Christmas splendor the house was known for. At this time of year the house would be so extravagantly decorated it could compete with any Fifth Avenue department store and win. Mom and her decorator, Miles, Giles or whatever his name was, went to town decking the halls.

Her parents fought each year over the extent of the decorations, which in Dad's estimation multiplied like rabbits, but as in all arguments, Mom had the last word. *"Darling, it's simply the best time of the year, and if my house looks like Saint Nicholas threw up all over it, so be it."*

Mom loved Christmas.

Had loved Christmas.

Claire imagined Heaven, or wherever her mother was, looked pretty spectacular right about now.

She walked to the staircase, so tired it was almost tempting to curl up on a couch downstairs rather than drag herself all the way up to her bedroom.

"Claire. In here." Her father's deep voice stopped her on the second step.

She made a face. So much for sneaking upstairs unnoticed. She crossed the floor to the open double doors on the other side of the foyer, her head pounding. "Hi, Dad."

He stood as she shuffled into the room.

Blue eyes studied her from under thick eyebrows that were starting to match his salt-and-pepper hair. A smile brightened his face for an instant. "Come give your old man a hug."

He held out his arms and Claire moved into them, her eyes stinging as she rested her head against his wool sweater and allowed the tension of the day to fade. He'd only been out of town a week, but Claire had missed him. His smile disappeared as she drew back. Deep lines creased his forehead. "How was your visit to the police station?"

Claire went to the sofa, relishing the way it encased her weary body as she sank in to it. "Robert has to get his jollies somehow, I guess." She massaged her temples with her thumbs.

Her mother's silver service sat on a tray on the long mahogany table in front of them. Dad grunted as he poured coffee from the ornate pot. He handed her a cup, took one for himself, and sat across from her.

"Are you telling me you weren't drinking?"

"I had a few drinks, Dad. It was nothing."

They sipped in silence. Claire inhaled the strong aroma and welcomed the warmth of the hot liquid.

Dad studied her over the rim of his china cup. "I had your car returned. It's in the garage. I'll be holding your keys until further notice."

"You'll be what?" Claire's hand began to shake, coffee spilling over onto the saucer. A drop fell onto her jeans. She put down the cup and saucer and watched the stain spread.

"If I could still ground you, I would," he went on. "But for now, since you insist on living here and not with your husband, I'm asking you not to drive. I can't forbid you to drink, Claire, much as I wish you wouldn't. But I refuse to have you put your own life or anybody else's in danger."

Claire chewed on a fingernail and tried to come up with a mature response. "That's not fair. This is like a house arrest. You can't do this to me, Daddy."

"Claire." He put his cup on the side table and crossed one brown corduroy-clad leg over the other. His hands rested in his lap as he pinned her with the expression he wore when on the brink of giving a lecture. "If you're determined to act like a child, we're going to have to treat you like one. You don't have to stay here, but if you do, those are my rules."

"You don't understand…"

"Oh, I understand plenty." A mask of sorrow cloaked him. He'd been wearing it since the day her mother died. "You think you're the only one who knows about grief, Claire? I've lived through watching the woman I love being overtaken by a disease with no cure. All I could do was stand by and watch her die. I know it was hard on you as well, and then your miscarriage…I can't begin to express how deeply I ache for you, for James, for all of us. So don't tell me I don't understand." His sigh was shaky. "And I'm sorry I haven't been around."

"It's a little late for apologies." Unable to look at him, she wiped away angry tears. Fine and dandy to make her stay home like a prisoner. He'd probably be on the next plane out of here tomorrow. Dad's way of dealing with problems was to simply pretend they didn't exist.

He paced the thick crème carpet, his shoes leaving imprints as he walked.

Silence and sorrow separated them.

Claire glanced around the room. It had been her mother's favorite and somehow offered a measure of comfort. Fine silk curtains of the palest peach hung from thick wooden rods above the long windows. Antique china graced almost every available space on the coffee tables and shelves—English porcelain from the 1700s and pieces from the Ming Dynasty. Eggshell white walls displayed family portraits cleverly blended in between paintings by the Masters—a Van Gogh, her mother's prized possession, a Titian, and other artists Claire could never remember the names of.

She managed to find her voice. "I wish…there were answers. I've been thinking maybe if I could find out where I came from…" She watched a shadow creep across his face and looked down at her feet.

Talking about her adoption with her father would only serve to increase the ever-widening chasm between them.

"It won't help you get better, Claire."

"How *do* I get better, Dad?" Claire raised her head again. He'd always been able to solve any problem she presented him with. Bail her out of any sticky situation.

But the defeat in his eyes told her he didn't have the answer for this one.

"You know what you need to do. Go back to counseling. Go to AA" He stood at the fireplace and put his back to her, staring up at the family portrait that hung over the mantle.

Claire looked upward with some reluctance. Over the years she'd studied that portrait for hours. She picked out the obvious differences in their appearances by habit. Dad's blue eyes and dark hair, almost jet-black in those days, a handsome match for Mom's long elegant nose and aristocratic smile, eyes that wavered between blue and gray depending on her mood. Rich auburn hair waved around a face any model would pay for. And there *she* sat, wedged between her parents, looking nothing like either of them.

Her eyes always caught her attention. Hair color and facial features could be explained away, but anyone with grade school biology under their belt would tell you how rare it was for two blue-eyed parents to come up with a brown-eyed child.

As always, Claire was left to wonder whose eyes those were staring back at her.

4

"**P**ass the stuffing." Robert glared at her across the crowded table. Claire lowered her eyes and pushed the food around on her plate. She was definitely insane. Her very presence here in the Ferguson household on Christmas Day confirmed it.

James begged her to spend the day with him and the family. He and her father joined forces for once and cajoled her into coming. His parents did seem pleased to see her. But now, jammed in between James' youngest sister, Brianna, and her twin, Brian, everyone walking on eggshells and Dad looking at her like she would fall apart any second, the room was closing in.

"Excuse me, Claire? Did you not hear me, or are you ignoring me?"

Claire winced at Robert's obnoxious tone. She couldn't recall the last time they'd had a pleasant conversation, but it was the holidays after all. She'd vowed to at least make an effort.

She counted to ten and tapped her fork against her mother-in-law's best Christmas china. Margaret had brought it over with her from Ireland. Shamrocks intertwined with holly. Green and red. Red and green.

Claire was beginning to loathe those colors.

"She's ignoring me."

Claire studied the red lampshades on the light fixture above the table. Apparently Robert's Christmas spirit had fled the instant she'd entered the house.

"Robert..." James' voice held a clear warning.

"What? No, I'm serious, Jamie. Look at her. She comes here half-tanked, and you're defending her? Give me a break."

Break your face. Claire raised an eyebrow, took a moment to make sure she wasn't about to throw up, then got to her feet. She reached for the big bowl of stuffing and marched over to where he sat.

Surprise crept into Robert's eyes, but a smirk pulled at his moustache.

"It was the stuffing you wanted, right?" With a shaking hand she doled out several heaping spoonfuls onto his plate. "There. Is that good?" She banged down the china dish and grabbed the gravy boat. "Looks like you need some gravy with that." Claire watched the brown sauce trickle over the white china rim, slowly at first and then it gathered speed.

A rushing river of gravy. Cool.

It splashed onto his plate, swirled into a muddy lake, and spilled onto the green linen tablecloth. And then it spilled over onto Robert's lap.

The loud conversation around the table stopped, and the room fell into deafening silence.

"Claire!" Robert jumped out of his seat, a dark stain seeping into his gray flannel pants. "Are you out of your freakin' mind?"

James appeared beside her before she knew he'd moved. "Claire, what are you doing? What's wrong with you?" He pried the gravy boat from her grip.

Claire wrenched her hand from his and realized everyone was looking at her. She trained her gaze on him. "I'm sorry, what?"

"I said, what's wrong with you?" he hissed, his Adam's apple jumping.

"What's *wrong* with me?" She blinked and willed the buzzing from her ears. Drinking a bottle of wine before coming here seemed like a good idea at the time.

James' mother was about to cry. His dad appeared ready to slug someone, probably her. She didn't dare look at her own father.

"Claire, why don't we go into the kitchen? Maybe you need some air." James' sister, Melanie, stood, wearing a frantic expression.

Claire raised a hand.

An infant's cry pierced the air and shattered what was left of her sanity.

"Sorry." Robert's wife shot past her and ran down the hall.

"Sweetheart, would you like to have a wee rest?" James' mother offered. "I could make you a cup of tea." The tremor in her soft voice brought back rational thought, and Claire shook her head.

"No, thank you, Margaret. I don't want to lie down, and I don't want any tea." Claire took a few steps back, tears blurring her vision. "I just want…"

What?

What she wanted couldn't be voiced.

Not here.

Not now.

Maybe not ever.

Claire spun and raced from the room, through the kitchen, and out onto the back porch. She slid through the slush and almost lost her balance, but made it to the far end and down the three steps into the garden.

The frozen river at the end of the property mirrored the condition of her heart. A light snow fell, sticking to her hair and eyelashes. Gray clouds moved across the sky with stealth and loomed over the rooftops of the surrounding homes. Thin wisps of smoke curled from the chimneys.

Claire ignored the cold and took deep breaths, welcoming the frigid air into her lungs. Noise rushed in her ears, and she waited for the bright spots in her eyes to fade. With any luck she could freeze to death.

The screen door squeaked open and banged shut. Her coat fell around her shoulders. Claire gave an involuntary shiver and slipped her arms through the sleeves.

James stood beside her, silent as the winter scene around them. She didn't know whether to be grateful or terrified.

Eventually she swiveled to face him. Her heart began to pound at the anger in his eyes. "I'm sorry," she whispered.

He stared back at her, his expression hard. "You've said that so many times I'm sick of hearing it."

Claire wrapped her coat around her and shuddered. "What do you want from me?"

He took a step back. "Where do you want me to start?"

"Forget it." She moved off, trudging through the snow. Her feet were already numb, the wet stuff sliding through her loafers.

"No, Claire, stop." James caught up with her and grabbed her arm. His blazing eyes gave off the only source of heat in the frigid afternoon. "I've been patient. I let you move out, even though I didn't agree with it. I gave you space. But enough is enough. I want you to get some help. You need counseling. You need AA You need to get your life back."

Claire threw his glare back at him. "I need, I need, I need! Don't tell me what I need! What about you, Jamie? Am I the only one who's screwing up around here? The fact we're barely speaking to each other is all my fault? Oh, wait, yeah, it is." She hardly recognized the shrill laughter that shot out of her, like a subway train whooshing by so fast it takes your breath away.

"Don't." James ran a hand over his ashen face.

"Don't what?" She squinted as the sun appeared through the clouds and tried to warm her. "Do you have any idea what it feels like to be in there, looking at those little kids, seeing Robert and Karen's baby, hearing about Melanie's visit to the obstetrician…everybody looking at me, wondering why I can't pull it together, why we're having problems, why I can't just be normal…do you?" She kicked at the snow, fury boiling and threatening to bubble over.

"Yes, actually I do. I was in there too, Claire. I have to deal with those questions all the time. And I don't have answers."

"Well, neither do I!" She pushed hair out of her eyes and refused to look his way.

"Listen to yourself, Claire," he hissed. "You're so caught up in your own grief that you don't even see me anymore. If you do, you sure don't care."

She raised her eyes to his and saw defeat in them. Her muscles tightened as she clenched her jaw. "It's hard to care about someone who doesn't try to understand how I feel."

"Give me a break." James turned toward the house.

"Then tell me it's not true," she cried. "Turn around and tell me that you know what I'm going through. That you understand. Tell me!" Claire drew in a shaky breath and waited. Her lips tingled with cold, but hot tears sliced her cheeks.

Slowly he swiveled to face her and pierced her with a look that overrode whatever lie he was about to produce. "I can't. I don't." His voice was low, barely audible. "You want the truth, Claire? There it is. I don't understand you. I don't understand the depression. I don't understand the drinking. And I sure as heck don't understand why you've decided you're better off without me. Yes, your mother died; yes, we lost the baby. But life goes on. We can try again. We can..."

"See, that's just it." She shuddered and shook her head. "How many times do I have to say it? I. Don't. Want. To. I can't."

She moved her foot back and forth, shifting snow until she'd created a crater. She stared at the path beneath her, unable to push any further. A stray blade of grass poked up between the concrete tiles, a strange and unexpected sight, a promise of the spring to come and new beginnings.

But not for them.

"I talked to Pastor Black, again last night, after Christmas Eve service." James thrust his hands into the pockets of his leather jacket. "He wondered if you might reconsider coming in for counseling. The two of us together, I mean."

Claire rubbed her nose and watched her breath curl like smoke around her. "Has Pastor Black ever lost a child?"

"I don't know. I don't think so."

"Then he can't help me."

"Claire, if you would..."

"No. You cling to your faith if that helps you. But I don't want it. Not anymore." She managed to look at him, nausea rising. "I couldn't bear it if it happened again, James. I mean, what if it's my fault? What if there's something wrong with me, genetically, something I don't know about?"

His sigh traveled away on the wind as the snow fell around them. The sun escaped the clouds once again and sank lower, covering the rooftops with a soft orange blanket of light. "There aren't any answers, Claire." His voice caught and his hazel eyes shimmered with a hint of tears. He brushed a hand across his face. "It's nobody's fault. Okay?"

"Sure."

Nobody's fault.

A shiver raced through her as she willed her own tears away.

Perhaps one day she'd believe that.

Perhaps one day he'd mean it.

But not today.

* * *

"I can't refill your prescription, Claire." Dr. Kay's brows knit together as his frown deepened.

Claire stiffened, pressed her back against the chair she sat in, and stared him down across the desk. "I'm sorry?" She laced her hands together and tightened her smile. "I'm pretty sure you can. You're the doctor. I'm the patient. I need those pills."

"Claire." His steady gaze made her want to squirm in her seat like a two-year-old. "I had a chat with your husband yesterday. He tells me you're drinking. Heavily."

Her hands trembled. "He doesn't know what he's talking about. We're separated. He's angry." She veered her gaze, not wanting the doctor's pity. Or his suspicion.

"He told me. I'm sorry to hear it." His kind voice almost reduced her to tears. But she wouldn't give him the satisfaction of being able to say, "*There, there, dear.*" "How is James coping?"

"He has a big family. They're supportive." Her jaw twitched at the memory of Christmas. She'd opted to spend New Year's alone, with the dogs and a bottle of Smirnoff.

"They'd be there for you too, Claire," Dr. Kay said, "if you let them."

She gave a short laugh and pushed her hair behind her ears. "I doubt it. They blame me. James blames me. They're right. I should have been more careful. I…"

"Claire, that's completely irrational. We've been through this…"

"I know." Claire twisted her hands together. "It's not my fault."

"It isn't."

"Dr. Kay, you know I need those pills." Why was he doing this to her? Claire forced a smile, really wanting to put her hands around his throat. She inched them under her legs. "Okay, so I have a couple of glasses of wine. I don't think it's that big a deal."

"Claire, you can't have any alcohol at all when you're on anti-depressants. I'd like to see you stop taking the pills altogether. But if you're using alcohol as well...my dear, I need you to be honest with me. Is this a problem?"

"It's not a problem." Claire gritted her teeth and ground the pointed tips of her boots into the faded rug beneath her feet. She met the doctor's eyes and willed him to believe her.

His concerned expression told her he didn't. After a long moment, he nodded. "I think it's time we consider our options, Claire. Perhaps you need to get away for a while. Go somewhere warm. There are several fine clinics I can recommend. Florida, California?"

His words registered, but she didn't accept them. "A clinic? Like rehab or what? You want to send me to some place for crazy people? With shrinks?"

"Now, Claire. Be rational. You're getting worse instead of better. I think you need more than I can offer you here."

Claire wound her thumbs around each other, studying her newly polished fingernails. Pink champagne. An appropriate choice. "I don't know myself anymore," she whispered, raising her head to meet his eyes. Might as well tell the truth. The words choked her, made her sick. "I've become someone I don't like. I do things I'd never have imagined myself capable of. And most of the time I don't even care. How long will it take for me to stop feeling this way?"

"Claire, you must acknowledge that you need help. That's the first step. You *must* get counseling. I think getting away for a while in a safe environment will be what you need. Will you at least consider it?"

Claire turned her head, looked through the open wood blinds that covered the window behind him, and watched traffic creep by. People walked past, bundled up in coats and scarves against the wind. On the other side of the street a young woman pushed a stroller.

"Doctor Kay?" Claire met his eyes and shifted in her chair and set her jaw. "Do you think it's possible that I might have caused the miscarriage?" The thought tortured her, crept into her consciousness no matter how hard she willed it away. "That I have some medical condition we don't know about? Do you think if I...if I found out who my biological parents were...well, do you think that would be a good idea?"

The clock on the white wall ticked out the minutes it took for him to respond. "Have you talked to your father about this?"

A forgotten memory raced through her mind.

"You want to know where you came from? Honestly, Claire. What a silly question. You belong to your mother and me now. That's all that matters. Now run along and play..."

"Yes, Daddy."

Claire fiddled with the slim chain around her neck, rubbing the small gold heart between her thumb and forefinger. "My parents and I never really discussed my adoption. I always felt the subject was off limits somehow. I didn't want to hurt their feelings by asking questions. It's not like I ever needed to know. But now..."

"Claire." Dr. Kay's tone was gentle. He sat forward, studying her with a solemn expression. "It won't solve all your problems."

His words reverberated around the room. Tears stung her eyes, and she fumbled in her purse for a tissue, blew her nose, and nodded. Her heart thumped out a dull beat. "I know that. But I thought..."

"You're twenty-six years old, a grown woman. You don't need anyone's permission to search for your birth family if you want to. As your doctor, I think it would be good for you to know your medical history. But this isn't something you should enter into lightly. You won't have any way of knowing what you're walking into. Frankly, at this point, I don't think you're strong enough emotionally, and I'd advise against it."

Claire pushed back her chair, stood, put on her coat, and grabbed her purse. "Fine. Thanks, Doctor Kay. I'll be in touch."

"Take care of yourself, Claire. And please consider what I said." He rounded the desk and walked her to the door. Claire pulled on a pair of leather gloves over her shaking hands.

"Could you..." She swallowed back the words as the resolute look he wore conveyed his answer. It didn't matter. She could always go somewhere else. Dr. Kay knew her too well. There were other doctors that didn't.

"You'll let me know what you decide? I can make arrangements..."

"I'll let you know." She marched out of the waiting area and out onto the street, almost slipping on the slush-covered sidewalk. Stupid man! No way was she going to some clinic for addicts.

Claire started her car and turned up the heat, air blasting through the vents on the dash. She reached for her Blackberry and punched numbers with her thumb.

"Shephard and Ferguson. How may I help you?" Melanie answered, chipper as ever. Claire pictured her sister-in-law behind the desk of the office where she herself had worked just months ago.

"Put James on."

"Claire. I've been trying to reach you. Steve and I really want you to come for dinner and…" Claire could practically feel Melanie's smile oozing through the phone. Trying to make her feel better. Trying to make it seem like everything was fine when it wasn't.

Trying way too hard.

"I need to speak to James." Claire pulled out of her parking spot, the SUV sliding over the wet snow. Her father had left on another business trip and given her keys back after she swore up and down she wouldn't do anything stupid again. Fingers crossed behind her back.

"When can you come over? Friday?"

Melanie needed to get the hint and leave her alone. Claire had been ignoring her calls for weeks now.

"I don't know, Mel. Maybe. Can you put James on, please?"

"He's not here. He and Steve are on site."

"On site where? Where, Mel?" Claire accelerated as she took the on-ramp for the highway. Melanie's silence turned up the heat of her anger. "Tell me where he is." A bright yellow VW zipped in front of her, and Claire pressed down on the horn.

"Are you driving? You know you shouldn't be on your cell if you're driving. It's illegal."

Claire snorted. "I'm well aware of Connecticut state law, and I don't need another lecture from you. I just need to know where my husband is."

"Oh, he's your husband today, is he?"

"Nice, Mel." Claire winced against the pain and the lights that flashed across her eyes. She clenched the steering wheel and willed her hands to stop shaking. She needed a drink. And needed Melanie to shut up. "Doctor Kay won't give me another prescription." Tears welled and made it more difficult to see.

Melanie let out a sigh. "That's good. You don't need any more medication, Claire. You know that, right?"

"I guess." Claire put Mel on loudspeaker and set the phone on the passenger seat while she searched the glove compartment with one hand. She'd had a small flask stashed in there awhile back. Empty. Where was the closest liquor store? She glanced around and tried to get her bearings. All her thoughts seemed to blend together, like thick syrup oozing out of the bottle, a drop at a time. A car to her right honked as it whizzed by.

Claire jumped, put both hands back on the wheel, swerved slightly, and attempted to get control of her car on the icy road. Attempting to get control of her life might be harder.

Thick snow fell as the sun gave way to dusk. Lights from the cars on the other side of the highway blinded her and made her dizzy. Her head felt as though one of Steve's construction workers was drilling into her brain. "Mel, are you still there? I don't feel so good."

"Stop driving, Claire." Fear laced Melanie's stern tone. "Get off the road. Where are you now? I was about to leave work anyway. I can meet you."

"I'm...on..." Claire drew in a breath and glanced in her rearview mirror as she pulled across two lanes. More honking ensued and brought a fresh wave of panic. "I don't know. I-95. I think I'm going north. There's an exit. I'm getting off." She'd driven this road a million times. Why was it suddenly all so unfamiliar? She slowed her speed and blinked sweat out of her eyes as she turned onto a smaller side road.

A shopping plaza came into view and Claire breathed a sigh of relief. She flicked on her turn signal and pulled into the parking lot of The Olive Garden.

"Claire, are you still there? Are you okay?"

"I'm fine, Mel. I'm parked now. Sorry if I scared you. Listen, I'll talk to you later."

"Claire, wait! Where are you?"

Claire powered off her Blackberry and dropped it into her purse. She pulled down the visor, looked in the small square mirror, and reached for her makeup. She brushed a dab of blush on her cheeks and applied a touch of lipstick.

She stared at the restaurant in front of her and hesitated. The last thing she needed was a DUI arrest. No matter, she'd get a cab this time.

Claire eased herself out onto the snowy pavement and clicked the remote lock on her keys. The car beeped back at her, and she picked her way across icy patches until she reached the sidewalk and entered the warm foyer.

Glancing around, she smiled. The bar was on her right.

5

Michelle checked her speed. They'd made good time, missed the weekend traffic heading out of the city. She pressed a little harder on the accelerator and allowed a smile.

"Thanks for coming with me, Shel." Belinda stared out the window of the passenger seat as they zipped through the countryside. "With Don away again, I didn't really want to drive all the way here on my own. And you know my mom's going to love seeing you. I'm sure she's been cooking for days since I told her we were coming."

Michelle glanced her way for an instant. "It's nice to have a weekend off, Lin. Thanks for forcing me into it."

Reluctantly she slowed the car as they came into town. She loved driving Belinda's Jag. She never drove in the city. Didn't even own a car anymore. If she needed to get anywhere, Kevin insisted she take the limo.

The last few months since Christmas had been an endless stream of meetings, dinners, and fundraising balls. With Kevin in Disneyworld for the kids' spring break, she'd finally been able to catch her breath.

She would have preferred a quiet weekend alone, but if she hadn't agreed to come to Connecticut and accompany Belinda to her appointment with this architect, Michelle knew she'd never hear the end of it.

She drove slowly down Main, tamping forgotten memories. They crept back anyway, a persistent puppy not happy until it got the attention it wanted.

Twenty-six years, but everything looked pretty much the same. She hadn't counted on that. "It's been a long time." She idled at the stoplight and heard Belinda's sudden intake of breath.

"Oh, crap, honey. I didn't think! I'm sorry…"

"It's fine, honest." Michelle pushed up her sunglasses, pushed down emotion, and scanned the area. "Did you say number fifteen? Is it that building there?" She indicated right and maneuvered Belinda's car into the parking spot. "Perfecto. Not a scratch."

"You always were a much better driver than me." Belinda laughed as they got out. She threw a teal Pashmina around her shoulders and adjusted her Gucci shades. "Now, you have to be honest. If you'd rather head back to New York after this, instead of going to see my mom, just say so."

Michelle pulled her lightweight coat around her and glanced down the familiar street. Baskets of bright pink geraniums and blue and white alyssum hung from black lampposts. The buildings still looked old, although the movie theatre had been given a facelift. She'd only spent a few months here, but remembered every detail. Mrs. Gracie had been so good to her.

"I'd love to see your mom. And she's expecting us. Don't be silly."

"Okay. Well, here we are."

Belinda led the way up a long flight of stairs, and Michelle followed her into the offices of Shephard and Ferguson. The interior of the building was refreshingly modern, crisp clean lines and bold colors. Contemporary black leather furniture, sleek, not too over the top. Modern art hung from the walls, the largest spaces taken up with framed architectural drawings. Fresh flowers sat on the glass table in the waiting area. Whoever the decorator was certainly had an eye for detail.

A young woman seated behind the desk in the reception room glanced up with a friendly smile. "Ah, Mrs. Cassidy. You're right on time. How was the drive?" She pushed back her chair and rose, revealing a gently rounding stomach.

Belinda greeted her with her signature double air-kiss. "Lovely. No traffic at all. How are you, dear? You're looking great. This is my friend, Michelle Hart. She's here in Don's stead. She has impeccable taste. Michelle, this is Melanie Shephard. Melanie is married to Steven, the contractor, and her brother is James Ferguson, my architect."

"Nice to meet you." Michelle didn't have a hope of remembering all that, but she extended a hand and the redhead shook it with sincere enthusiasm.

"It's wonderful of you to come." She smiled, blue eyes sparkling. She looked like she was about to say something else but didn't. A frown creased her forehead but then the smile returned. "James is expecting you, Mrs. Cassidy."

She had to be in her last few months of pregnancy. Just starting to feel uncomfortable and unable to sleep well.

Michelle shifted her gaze.

"Can I get you both some coffee?"

Michelle shook her head. "No, thanks. Shouldn't you be at home with your feet up…" What was her name again? "…Melanie?"

Melanie Shephard's laugh was cheerful, and she waved a hand. "Oh, no. I've awhile to go yet. And my mother was overdue with all of us, so we'll see what happens with me."

"I'm sure you'll be fine." Belinda shot Michelle her "I'll head her off at the pass" look and for once Michelle didn't mind. "Is James in his office? Come along, Shel."

She breezed past the desk before Melanie could interject. Michelle smiled an apology and followed her friend down a narrow passageway. Belinda rapped on an open door and walked right in. Michelle lingered outside. Maybe she'd just go down the street and grab some coffee.

"Shelly, are you coming?"

Or not.

She smothered a sigh and went into the office. An attractive man, possibly in his late twenties, stood behind a long metal desk, the glass top covered in plans. Dressed in faded jeans and a button-down shirt, untucked and a little rumpled, he looked more like the contractor.

"Here we are! I hope we're not late." Belinda took off her jacket and indicated the other chair for Michelle. She stayed put near the doorway.

"Not a bit. Nice to see you again, Mrs. Cassidy." He flicked a strand of sandy brown hair out of his eyes, looked past Belinda, removed a pair of silver-rimmed glasses, and stared. "Hello."

"James Ferguson, Michelle Hart." Belinda was all business now, barely giving them time to shake hands. "Okay, show me what you've got."

Michelle moved off to one side, uncomfortable under the scrutinizing gaze of James Ferguson's hazel eyes. She didn't remember people in Connecticut staring so much.

The young man bent over the drawings. In another minute Belinda was crowing over whatever he was showing her. Michelle peered over her friend's shoulder and gave a few enthusiastic oohs and aahs every now and then.

After an hour, Belinda was ready to go. Michelle couldn't wait. The guy was giving her the heebie-jeebies.

"Isn't he a genius, Shel?"

"Very talented. You must give me a card." Michelle smiled effortlessly as the words slipped off her tongue. Schmoozing she could do.

"Sure." He gave her a thin white card and a lopsided grin. "You…uh…work for Senator Harrison, don't you?"

Relief lowered her blood pressure. So maybe he wasn't so creepy. "You follow politics?"

"Occasionally. I thought I recognized you."

Michelle slipped his card into her purse. "I'm on television a lot."

"Well, I love what you've come up with, James," Belinda interrupted. "So exciting to finally be at this stage. We're on schedule to break ground next week, yes?"

Michelle took a look around the spacious office as Belinda yammered, scanning the photographs on the shelves. One caught her eye. A close-up of a young woman with shoulder-length brown hair, bending over a pair of golden labs, the background faded out around them. She edged closer, staring at the gold locket around the girl's neck. A knot twisted in her stomach, and she turned away.

"How's your wife doing, James?" Belinda asked, all tea and sympathy. "Is she back to work now? I hope she didn't have that nasty flu that's going around."

The man shook his head. "No, nothing like that, thank God. She's just...uh...going through a bit of a rough patch. She'll be back to work soon, I'm sure."

Michelle caught the unspoken sorrow in his eyes as they captured hers. The shadows around them said that was not quite the truth.

He held her gaze for a moment, as though looking for something—something she definitely did not possess. "Well." He smiled and turned his attention back to Belinda. "We have a new designer on board now, taking over for Claire, temporarily of course, but I'd be glad to set up a meeting for you."

"Wonderful." Belinda took another card from him. A few minutes later they were heading down the street back to the car.

"So, what did you think? Isn't he amazing? And a good architect to boot!" Belinda's wicked laughter floated on the air.

Michelle stopped walking. "You're incorrigible. Leave the poor man alone."

There it was. Just across the street. But the brownstone building she'd expected to see wasn't there. A florist shop stood in its place. Outside the shop, irises, sunflowers, roses of every color, and fragrant white lilies blended into a vibrant display that made her stop and catch her breath. A bucket full of bright pink and red Gerber daisies captured her attention, threw memories hard and fast.

She shouldn't have come here.

"They closed down about ten years ago." Belinda's voice softened. "Merged all the smaller town offices and moved to a big building in Hartford."

"Oh." Michelle blew air through her lips. A faint buzzing sounded in her ears. If she'd had any inkling this was going to be so difficult, she'd never have agreed to it.

"You all right?" Belinda stood in front of her, her eyes shimmering in the afternoon sun.

Michelle pushed back her shoulders. "Of course I am. Ready to go?"

Belinda tipped her head and applied a layer of lipstick. "Did you ever...you know...wonder?"

"Wonder what?"

"Shel..."

"No." The answer rushed out of her. She let out another breath and steadied herself. *Pull it together, Shel. Leave it alone.*

"What do you think Kevin would say?"

The dull ache in her chest returned. "The question is irrelevant." Michelle unclasped the butterfly clip that held her hair in place, twisted it up again and clipped it tight. She pulled at the belt of her spring coat and redid the knot. "Why are we talking about this?"

"Do you honestly think he'd hold it against you?"

Belinda sounded so innocent that Michelle had to laugh. "Do you honestly think he wouldn't?"

Belinda took off her sunglasses and gave a dramatic sniff that signaled she was on the verge of an emotional outburst. "I think about it every now and then, at the strangest times. Sometimes I wonder how you got through it."

"Please, Belinda. Can you give it a rest?" Michelle balked at the slight edge of hysteria in her own voice. She took a deep, relaxing breath. There was absolutely no point in venturing down that road.

"I'm sorry, Shel. I just thought...maybe we should talk about it."

Michelle took a last look around and shook her head. "There's nothing to talk about." She faltered at the sadness in Belinda's eyes, tempted for a moment to give in, find the nearest coffee shop, and rip the lid off every bit of emotion she'd tamped down and buried someplace deep within her.

So deep she doubted she'd find it.

Instead, she smiled and shook her head. "Come along, Miss Naiveté. Your mother will be wondering where we are." Michelle slipped an arm through her friend's and pulled her toward the car.

Perhaps it had been good to come here and get a brief glimpse into her past, to remember where she had come from.

To remember just how far she'd come. Remember all she had endured, suffered, and accepted in the name of something she now no longer understood.

And to remind herself once again that there would be no going back.

6

Claire paced the sidewalk. She hadn't known for sure where she was headed when she'd gotten behind the wheel that morning. Somehow the car ended up in Hartford. She stopped walking and stared at the sign on the building in front of her.

This was the Hogwarts of her imagination. This place held all her secrets, contained magical mysteries with the power to change everything she knew about herself. But there were no turrets. No black-robed professors or magic wands. No flying owls delivering messages to explain all. Just a plain old glass building, about ten stories high, that housed the offices of The Department of Children and Families.

She wrestled with the idea of actually going in, jumping out of the way as people walked by. She stood close enough to feel the breeze as the doors swung open and closed.

Flowers added color to the scene, purple petunias and green ferns hanging from baskets on the lampposts. Spring was lovely this year. Not that she got outside enough to enjoy it. The past few months had been a struggle. But maybe now...now that she was making an effort to live again...

The sun warmed her face and almost had her believing it was a normal day. But there was nothing normal about it. There was nothing normal at all about standing in front of the place that could possibly change your life.

Claire pushed her fingers through her hair. Her heart was doing some kind of spastic dance that made her want to throw up. It joined forces with a feeling she didn't want to face and shadowed her every move.

She hated that feeling. That incomprehensible need to quench a thirst she still didn't understand. Which really sucked, because she'd been doing so well. It was almost the end of the week and she'd had nothing but Starbucks and San Pellegrino. Kicking back with a bottle of Chardonnay was all she could think of right now. If she closed her eyes, she could almost taste it on her tongue. She shoved the thought aside, chewed a nail, and stared at the building again.

After another minute, Claire moved forward with purpose and pulled open the glass door. Her heels clicked on the tile of the lobby. She tucked her sunglasses into her purse and scanned the directory on the wall, got on the elevator, and leaned against the side while it took her up to the correct floor.

By the time she reached the front desk, she was trembling.

"Can I help?" A woman with skin the color of dark chocolate sat behind the desk. She stared at a computer screen, her monotone telling Claire she probably could care less whether she could help or not.

Claire swallowed and leaned forward. "I hope so. I was adopted, you see, and I'd like my information. My birth certificate. The original one."

"Really." The woman sat back in her chair, unsmiling ,as she gave Claire the once over. She may as well have asked her where the lingerie section was.

Claire shifted and clenched her fingers around the strap of her purse. "Am I in the right place?"

"Yes, you're in the right place." The lady heaved a sigh, stood, and shuffled to the other side of her small cubicle, opened a large file cabinet, and returned with a stack of papers. "Fill these out. Read everything very carefully. Bring it all back in or do it now if you want."

"What is this?" Claire narrowed her eyes at the woman. Surely it wouldn't kill her to be a little helpful.

On the other hand, it might.

"You have to apply in writing for the release of your non-identifying information." The clerk's mouth lifted in a smile. "Takes about six weeks, maybe longer. Wheels of bureaucracy and all that." She cracked a wad of gum.

"And then you'll tell me who my birth mother was?"

"Honey." The sympathetic smile reminded Claire of her kindergarten teacher. *Of course your mother's coming to pick you up. She's just a little late.* But Claire would not be consoled until she caught sight of her mother's car driving into the school's parking lot.

"Is that a yes or a no?"

"Those records are sealed. Depending on what's on file for you, all you get is the identifying information, okay? No names. Stuff like height, weight, ethnicity, and religion of your biological parents. But we can only give that to you if your birth mother gave consent for the information to be released."

"What?" Claire didn't remember reading that on the Internet. "What if she didn't?"

"Well, then…" The woman sank into her chair with a bored expression, as though she had a billion better things to do. "The department has sixty days to conduct a search for your birth mother. She'll be asked to release the information. She has the right to refuse."

"*She* has the right?" Claire inhaled and pinched her lips. Sweat formed on her brow. "What about my rights? Don't I have any rights?"

The woman's dark eyes glazed over, and she turned back to the computer. "Anything else I can do for you today?"

* * *

"I'm going to talk to my father's lawyer." Claire slammed her hand down on the top of the mahogany cabinet. Pain shot up her arm and brought her back to reality. Ugly, harsh reality that said she was nothing to nobody.

"Claire, sit." Melanie guided her over to an armchair. "When did all this happen? Why didn't you tell me?"

"I went to Hartford a couple of weeks ago." Claire hunched in her chair, drew her knees up to her chest, and stared at the empty fireplace. "I don't know why I didn't tell you."

Exhaustion cloaked her. She'd fallen asleep on the couch sometime that Friday night and found Melanie in the room when she woke. "It's like I'm not even a real person, Mel. Like I don't exist. Never existed. S'not fair."

"How much have you had to drink?"

Melanie had a knack for asking stupid questions.

"Not enough." Claire made a push to get up, but Melanie's fierce expression forced her back down. She slumped in her chair again. "Do you know that I can't even get my original birth certificate?"

"You told me. Several times." Melanie poured steaming liquid from a blue ceramic teapot and handed Claire a cup. "Here, have some tea. When did you last eat?"

"I don't remember." Claire shifted in her chair and took the tea. Her tongue stuck to the roof of her mouth. She sipped and they sat in silence. Things started to come back into focus.

"Where's your dad?"

"He went to a show and spent the night in New York. Nice, huh? He gets back…what time is it?" She vaguely remembered seeing Melanie heading down the hall to the kitchen some time ago but couldn't recall letting her in the house. Hours and days molded together.

Melanie glanced at her watch. "It's after midnight."

"Oh." Claire rubbed her eyes. "Saturday. He gets back later today I guess. What are you doing here anyway, Mel?"

"Don't you remember calling me?"

"I called you?"

"Yes. About two hours ago. I couldn't understand what you were saying and told you to go to bed. You kept calling. When Steve put the answering machine on, I guess you tried James. Then he called me. Said you were frantic. I figured I wasn't going to sleep anyway, worrying, so I might as well come here and make sure you didn't do anything stupid."

"James didn't come?"

"Nope. Dropped me off, gave me his key to get in, and told me to call him later."

"Oh." Of course he wouldn't have come. She'd chased him out of her life. Maybe for good this time.

"I'm so tired." Claire blinked, her eyes stinging. The past few days were a blur. Time stopped with the phone call from the DCF. She'd been surprised when they called after just two weeks. But then the caseworker gave her the news. "I can't believe she refused to release the information. It's not like I'm asking for blood or a kidney even. I only want...to know where I came from. I want answers."

Melanie sat in the chair opposite her. Tears shimmering in her eyes, Melanie cradled her belly. "I don't know why she wouldn't allow them to give you anything, Claire. I'm sure she has her reasons."

"I'm sure she's just being a—"

"Claire."

"What?" She shrank under Melanie's sorrowful gaze. "Shouldn't you be in the hospital by now? When's that baby due?"

Melanie smiled. "Any day now, I hope. He or she is taking their own sweet time, that's for sure. I'll be induced on Monday if nothing happens before then."

Claire sat forward and put her head in her hands. The buzz was wearing off, sobriety kicking in. That was the day after tomorrow.

"Claire?"

"I'm okay."

The baby would be here soon. She'd have to see it, see how happy Melanie and Steve were...then she'd have to face James and deal with her own inability to find it in her heart to even think about giving their marriage another try.

"I'm sorry you didn't get the news you wanted, Claire, but I wish..."

"I know. It's okay." Claire raised her head and waited for her nausea to pass. "I'll survive."

"You were doing so well." Melanie nodded, as though she'd made up her mind. "I'm really worried about you. We all are. Will you please get some help? I know you think you can do it on your own, but..."

"No." Claire put down her cup. "I *can* quit on my own. You know I can.

You said I was doing really well."

"You were. *Were*, being the operative word. Claire, you were passed out when I got here and you don't remember calling me."

"A setback."

"Claire..." Melanie's voice quavered. "Please. Let us help you. You don't have to do this alone. You know that, right?"

Claire closed her eyes again.

After her mother died, she'd had trouble sleeping. She hadn't taken anything because of her pregnancy. But then a week after the funeral, she started bleeding. It was over. No more pregnancy.

The doctor gave her a prescription then, to help her rest. Each day got harder, and eventually she found it easier to stay in bed. One drink led to another, blocked out the pain of a loss she couldn't begin to comprehend.

Claire secured the locks around her heart. "I know you mean well, but you can't help me, Mel. Nobody can help me."

"I wish I could."

"I know you do. But you don't know how this feels." Claire stared at her feet and wondered how to explain something she didn't understand. "I don't want to do anything, go anywhere, talk to anyone. This...ache...my chest feels tight all the time. I only want to curl up in bed and cry. Every day. Sometimes I think..." She stopped, waited, listened to the dogs pacing up and down the hall. She wouldn't go that far. Melanie would make James have her committed for sure.

"Claire?" Melanie's voice was gentle, no hint of judgment. "You'll get through this."

Raising her head, she put on a smile. "Of course I will." *Or die trying.* She watched the grandfather clock on the far side of the room. "I'll try again, Mel. Okay? But sometimes it's...nice to not feel anything."

Melanie narrowed her eyes. "If you block out the pain, you'll never accept it, never be able to deal with it. If you continue on the way you're going...I don't want to think about what might happen. I don't want to lose you, Claire."

"Who are you—Dr. Laura now?" Claire laughed, but deep down she knew Mel was right. Just one pill too many or another day thinking she was sober enough to drive. Fear crept over her, teasing, taunting, and whispering incomprehensible thoughts into her ear. "I'm going to find her, Mel. I have to."

Sudden understanding flooded Melanie's face. "I wish you'd stop blaming yourself. If you think finding your medical history will somehow explain..."

"And what if it did?" Claire leaned forward. "You don't understand. I have to know! I have to know that I'm not responsible...or I am. And aside from that, I...I'm curious. I won't lie."

"Has it really bothered you, not knowing where you came from?" Melanie grabbed a chocolate chip cookie and handed the bag to Claire.

Claire took one, the smell too impossible to resist. She wasn't sure she could stomach it but wouldn't risk Mel shoving it down her throat. "I guess if I'm honest, yes, it has bothered me. Each time I'd look in the mirror, I'd wonder. My parents and I look so different." Laughter crept out of her, unbidden. "Remember when I tried to dye my hair the same color as my mom's? She nearly had a fit laughing when she tried to explain that hers came out of a bottle too."

Melanie smiled. "You've never really been able to talk to your dad about your adoption."

Claire nibbled on the cookie. So far, so good. She took another bite and that stayed down too. "I'll have to. He's the only way I'll get answers now. If I petition the court to get them to release my information, he'll find out anyway."

"He's not going to like it."

"I know. But what choice do I have?"

Melanie rubbed her nose with the tip of her finger, her freckles blending together in a frown. "Do you really want to do it, Claire? You don't know what you might be walking into. You don't know who they are, why they gave you up. It may not be a pretty story."

Claire sat back, her throat tight. "I can't stop thinking about it. I know what you're going to say. Dr. Kay said the same thing. Finding them won't fix things. But I..." She waited for Melanie to interrupt, then raised an eyebrow. "You're not stopping me. Don't you want to try to talk me out of it?"

Melanie shook her head. "Claire, you're one of the smartest women I know. I don't think you really believe that finding out your medical history or even connecting with your birth family will change a thing. But if it's something you need to do, for yourself, to help you get through this time in your life, then I think you should."

"Thanks." Claire enjoyed the little victory. It had been a long time since Melanie had taken her side over anything. "I never thought I'd actually get to the point where I'd search. I didn't really know I could."

"How did you even know where to start?"

Claire stifled a yawn. "I ran into Amanda...um something or other, before Christmas. Remember her from school? Anyway, she found her birth mother. She told me to check with Social Services. I have the right to request my non-identifying information. I went to the DCF offices in Hartford and filled out the paperwork."

"And that's when they contacted your birth mother?"

"Yeah. Whoever she is." Claire leaned her head against the chair and closed her eyes. Another hangover was tapping at her temples. Of course the alternative was getting drunk and passing out again. Gaining a few more pain-free hours. But sooner or later the anguish would return.

"I'm sorry, Claire." Melanie's sincerity hung on the words.

Claire pulled at a strand of her hair and studied the fire. She'd brought Mel out here in the middle of the night, in her condition, and her friend was still on her side. What kind of person was she becoming? Guilt and remorse picked up placards and picketed around her heart. "Thanks, Mel. And thanks for coming over. I-I'm really sorry I called you." Claire shrugged. "I thought...I guess I figured this would go differently. I never realized there was no hope of ever getting answers."

"It doesn't seem fair."

Claire nodded, but the reality of the situation drove the point home. "I guess it's perfectly fair if you're on the other side of the fence. And I have to admit, I never considered that."

"Never considered what?"

"That she wouldn't want to be found."

7

Claire shielded her eyes against the Sunday afternoon sun and looked toward the stables. The dogs bounded across the lush green lawn, happy to be outside after intermittent thunderstorms. Spring had firmly settled across the state in splendor, cloaking the grounds in crocuses, daffodils, and tulips. Her sneakers crunched on the gravel path as she walked, rehearsing what she needed to say.

Her father had returned late the previous evening. She'd pretended to be asleep. But she couldn't put this off any longer. She walked past the stalls and breathed in the scent of hay and horses. It had been a long time since she'd come down here. Forever since she'd actually ridden. They'd sold her own horse a long time ago.

Dad stood behind Mojo, his favorite stallion. Hesitation crossed his face as he glanced up and saw her watching him. He gave the horse's rump a pat and moved out of the stall. "Claire. You all right?"

Claire shrugged. "Sure." Melanie still hadn't delivered and would be induced tomorrow. She and Dad had shared a quiet breakfast earlier, with few words. Claire fiddled with the chain around her neck, nerves muddling her thoughts. "Dad, I was wondering if I could talk to you about something."

He came to where she stood, questions in his eyes. "Well, that's interesting. I have something I need to talk to you about as well."

"Okay. You go first, then." Claire slipped her arm through his, and they took the gravel path around the pond. The grounds of the estate buzzed with activity as the landscapers mowed lawns and tended to the flowerbeds. He probably wanted to have her committed. Or send off to Europe—indefinitely.

That wouldn't be so bad. They had Starbucks there, too.

They sat together on the old wooden bench beside the pond. The smell of freshly cut grass hung in the air. Claire inhaled and allowed herself a smile. But the ache in her heart soon returned and shrouded her day in darkness once again.

"I've met somebody, Claire."

She jerked her head around. Despite his serious expression, there was an unmistakable twinkle in his eye. "You what?" Dad's sense of humor was beginning to worry her.

"Her name is Eleanor Jones. We met at a horse show a few months ago—through a mutual friend. She's a widow. We've seen a lot of each other lately. We have a lot of things in common. It's quite remarkable."

"You're not serious," Claire breathed out. "Why haven't you said anything?"

His face paled, as though he hadn't realized what this would mean to her. Then he straightened. "I'm sorry, honey. But I'm going away again tomorrow, and I thought you should know."

Claire couldn't respond. Maybe he'd take the words back, say something else instead. But his agitated expression told her otherwise.

"I'd like to ask her to marry me."

"What?" Claire gripped the bench so she wouldn't fall off it. Sweat formed on her brow. She couldn't speak. She tried to—oh. she wanted to—but the words wouldn't come.

A tinge of annoyance crept into Dad's eyes and Claire turned away. She clenched her hands on the tops of her knees and tried to breathe.

"I don't expect you to like the idea at first, Claire. I know it's kind of fast—it's a shock—for me too. But don't overreact. I loved your mother very much. I always will."

Like the idea? Overreact? Claire's pulse accelerated with every word. The image of her father with another woman galled her. The idea of actually pitching herself down onto the grass and letting go with a full-blown temper tantrum worthy of a two-year-old held some merit. She rubbed her hands on her shorts. "How long have you been seeing her?"

"Not too long. I wasn't sure how to tell you, to be honest." His eyes grew sad, his handsome face getting older by the second. "I wasn't looking for this, Claire. But it happened."

"And now you want to get married? Just like that?"

"Well, not right away, but eventually, yes. She's wonderful, Claire. You'll love her."

Right. Love her like a root canal.

Claire scowled at the grass and focused on a brown leaf. This was so typical. Her parents had always lived this way. They made plans and filled her in after the fact. She was expected to "go with the flow." And she always did.

"Claire?" He pressed her gently and for a moment she feared she would break down in front of him. Claire managed to meet his eyes, the happiness in them undeniable.

She forced a smile and hoped it would suffice. "Great, Dad. I'm very happy for you. When do I get to meet her?"

He chuckled, tension fading from his features. "Soon, honey. When I get back from my trip to Virginia, we'll have dinner or something. Would that be okay?"

"Sure, that'll be fine."

"Wonderful. We'll make plans. So, what did you want to talk to me about?"

Claire hesitated, studying her bitten-down fingernails. "I've decided to search for my birth mother." Her palms grew moist.

Dad stared at her in silence.

Claire sat back, her arms folded across her chest. She tried to gage his reaction, but he had his poker face on. Then all color left his cheeks. He could well be on the verge of having a heart attack. Maybe he'd keel over and die right then and there, and it would be her fault.

"Dad?"

He veered his gaze and stared across the pond, finally emitting a deep sigh. "Well, I'd say that trumps my news." Blue eyes pierced through her, his mouth drawn in a thin line. "What brought this on?"

Claire played with the rings on her finger. "It's something I've thought about for a while. Since…"

His face darkened. "This is about losing the baby, isn't it?" He clicked his tongue, a habit that gave away his frustration. "You didn't do anything wrong, Claire. It simply happened."

Claire pushed herself off the bench and blinked back tears as she walked toward the pond. She made a half circle, then turned back to face him. "I don't know that for sure, Dad. I…have to find out. You've asked me to understand you, accept your decision to move on…now I'm asking you to do the same for me. I need to know where I came from."

He rubbed the back of his neck and studied her. Sun filtered through the trees above them and lit the lines that creased his forehead. The breeze played with his hair. He shook his head. "You *don't* need to know, Claire. There's nothing *to* know. As we told you, we adopted you through Social Services in Hartford. It was a closed adoption. We weren't told who your birth parents were; they weren't told who we were. They said your birth mother was perfectly healthy with no genetic abnormalities in the family to be concerned with. Okay? That's it." A scarlet hue touched his cheeks, and his jaw twitched the way it always did when he was angry.

Claire shook her head, defeat dragging her down. "I went to the DCF in Hartford. They have to have her permission to release my non-identifying information. She refused. They said I could petition the court and…"

"Claire, for heaven's sake, why didn't you tell me?" His frown deepened. "How long have you been stewing on this?"

"I haven't been stewing." Claire swatted at a fly. Guilt rankled her, fueled by the betrayal in his eyes. "And I didn't tell you because I knew what your reaction would be."

"And you did it anyway. Typical." He grunted and made fists with his hands.

Claire summoned fresh courage. "Dad, if you...if you know anything, anything at all, could you please tell me?"

She may as well have beamed across the head with a baseball bat. After an instant, his stunned expression morphed into white anger. She met his eyes and saw them harden.

"This is ludicrous. You have no idea what you're getting yourself into, Claire. You're not well. You're not making rational decisions."

"Stop it, Dad." Anger crept over her, and she clenched her fists at her side. She'd never openly defied her father. They barely argued. But this was something she wouldn't back down on. After weeks of thinking about it, the need to know had intensified into a burning desire, something she *had* to do. She knew she wouldn't rest until she was sure there were no other options.

"I know I'm having problems, I admit that. But I don't need rehab, and I don't need some shrink trying to tell me how to move on. What I do need is to live my own life. To make my own decisions for once, not merely go along with whatever you and James suggest. I've made up my mind. This is what I'm doing. And I'd really love to have your support."

He slapped his knees, his face a display of muted anger. "I'm warning you, Claire. Don't do it. It will be the biggest mistake of your life."

Suspicion knocked at her. "Why? Why don't you want me to do this?" A slow hammering began inside her as she watched him avoid her eyes.

"No good can come of it." He looked down at his feet, winding his thumbs around each other.

Claire laughed softly, reaching for the charm around her neck. She took it between her thumb and forefinger, tried to find comfort where there was none. "You know something, don't you? Something you're not telling me."

He raised his head, his mouth in a tight line. "Of course not. The very idea is ridiculous. I can't support you in this, Claire. Get the notion out of your head. You're only setting yourself up for more heartache."

Anger, pain, and stubbornness pitched a tent and demanded she camp out with them. Claire didn't need much convincing. She pinched her lips and pushed her hands into the pockets of her shorts.

"It's not something you can stop me from doing." Her own boldness shocked her, almost sent her running to the house to begin the grounding she half-expected to receive. A few years ago that's exactly how this conversation would have gone. Claire waited for him to speak. Waited for him to voice the anger he was so obviously trying to put a lid on. He didn't. He was ignoring her. "Did you hear me, Dad?"

"I heard you." He drew one knee over the other, his jaw firm. "And I've told you, I don't want you doing it. Do you understand me?"

"Perfectly. And I'm sorry you feel that way."

"Don't do this, Claire Elizabeth." His voice held a warning tone she'd only heard a few times in her life.

She met his eyes, unflinching. "What? It's okay for you to get on with your life, but I'm not allowed to get on with mine? Is that what it comes down to?"

Exasperation moved over his face. "Not at all. I do want you to get on with your life. But I don't see how going on some wild goose chase is going to help you do that."

"No, I don't suppose you would."

"Fine. Since you're obviously not listening to me, I won't say anymore." He pushed up off the bench and stood, casting a weary glance her way. "When I get back from Virginia with Eleanor, I want to hear you've put this aside."

"Don't hold your breath." Claire folded her arms across her chest, ignored the sting of tears, and focused her attention on the lake. The crunching of his retreating footsteps over the gravel was matched by the thundering of her heart.

* * *

Her father left early the next morning, furious with her, and she was just as angry. She doubted he would ever stop treating her like a child. Much as she wanted to go on a binge, she fought the urge to drink and spent the day huddled under a green afghan, watching movies in the den.

Another storm moved in with more rain, bringing a chill to the air. She stifled a yawn and contemplated going back to bed. She couldn't shut her mind off during the day.

Claire jotted notes on a pad of paper, her mind replaying every possible scenario she could come up with if she ever did find the woman who gave her life. They all came back to the same one—her greatest fear.

She would still be unwanted.

Claire wandered through the big house, the dogs at her heels. She'd had lunch, and it was too early for dinner. She thought about calling some of her old friends, but she hadn't talked to anyone in months. Except Mel.

Mel would be in the hospital. Claire glanced at her watch. The baby might even be here. What kind of friend wouldn't be happy, wouldn't want to know everything was all right? Months ago, that kind of friend would have been her. Now she was somebody she didn't recognize. Somebody Melanie didn't need to hear from.

Her father's study door was open, and Claire stopped outside it. She hesitated, staring at the wood file cabinet behind his desk.

It wouldn't be the first time she'd rifled through those drawers. She'd been about ten, after being teased at school because she didn't know where she came from, when she'd poked around when her parents were out. She'd lived in terror for weeks that somehow they'd find out and get mad at her.

She hadn't found anything then, and as she went through the musty-smelling drawers again, it didn't look like this time would be any different. Just her adoption papers, all the legal documents, and bills from their lawyer, faded yellow papers, exactly where they had been all those years ago. But as she put the thick manila file back in its place, she noticed something she hadn't seen before. A name scrawled at the top of one of the papers.

Kelly.

Kelly who? Was it a first name or a last name? She searched all the files again, hoping to find more clues. An old brochure caught her eye, and she flipped through it. It looked to be some kind of bed-and-breakfast place. *Tara's Place. An old-fashioned country inn on the sparkling shores of Lake Christopher.* Claire scrutinized the glossy pictures, decades old judging by the styles the people wore. *Home-made meals and family fun—spend your days relaxing in the sun.*

Claire grinned. Couldn't get much cornier than that. Maybe her parents had gone there for a vacation. But Dad wasn't the sentimental type. Why would he keep this? Why in the file with all her information in it? She read through it again. *Owners Mac and Jessie Kelly...*

That name again. She searched the back page for the address.

Bethel, Maine.

Claire shivered at the tingling sensation that ran down her spine. There had to be some connection. She sat at the computer, typed in the name *Kelly* into the Google search engine and waited. Results from ancestry.com came up, as well as a bunch of obituaries that didn't seem pertinent.

Claire typed in *Tara's Place.* If it still existed, she'd soon find out.

A link popped up right away. Claire clicked. The colorful pictures were more recent than the ones in the brochure, but it was the same place.

Interesting website. Good design, nice descriptions, not too wordy. She scrolled through the pages, stopping when she got to a brief blurb about the owners, Mac and Jessie Kelly.

Claire peered at the small picture of an older couple, tried to enlarge it but failed. They both had silvery hair and looked to be in their late sixties, maybe seventies. The woman's hair was pulled back off her face in a bun; the man's gray locks waved around his ruddy cheeks. They both wore denim and friendly smiles.

She squinted at the screen, searching for any obvious resemblances, but the picture was too small. Still, it was entirely possible that these people could be her relatives.

Or else she was nuts.

Claire reached for a pad of paper and jotted down the phone number.

Dad needed to give her answers.

A glance at the clock told her his plane would have landed a couple of hours ago. She reached for the phone and dialed his cell.

He picked up at once, probably expecting to have to come back and bail her out of jail. "Claire. Are you all right?"

"I'm fine, Dad. I'm at home. But listen, I need to ask…"

"Claire, please. Not this again." He sounded worn out and very far away.

She ignored the hammering of her heart. "Dad, does the name *Kelly* mean anything to you?"

"Of course not." His reply came too quickly.

Claire frowned at the computer screen. "Well, I've been doing some research and I know that, by law, you and Mom would have to have been given some basic information about my biological parents. If you could just—"

Silence. At last he said, "Since you're clearly not going to give this up, I'll try to tell you what I can remember, which isn't much. But we weren't told much either. Your birth mother was young. A college student, I think. She couldn't afford to keep you. There were no health issues with the pregnancy and no genetic diseases that we were told about. We didn't get any information about your birth father."

"Where was she from? Can you remember that?" Claire gripped the receiver and swallowed a bitter cocktail of anticipation mixed with anxiety. Shaken not stirred.

"Some place up north. Vermont."

"Maine?"

"Let it go, Claire."

"Thanks, Dad. Have a good trip." Claire ended the call and stared at the website for Tara's Place again. The idea wouldn't leave her alone.

Ludicrous.

She picked up the handset again. The implications of making the next call jacked up her pulse and made her a little light-headed. But if she didn't follow this lead, she'd never know.

Claire concentrated on the figures she'd written down and punched in the numbers.

"Tara's Place, Mac speaking."

Claire balked at the gruff voice and her ability to speak vamoosed along with her nerve.

"Hallo? Anybody there?"

"Uh, yes. Sorry. I...uh...I was wondering about booking a room."

"Ayuh."

Claire blinked. "Excuse me?"

"Ayuh. You want to book a cabin or just one room? We don't have many visitors yet—it's early in the season—so you can take your pick."

Claire scanned the website again. The cabins were newly renovated. "A cabin would be great. Maybe next month? Do you have anything available?"

"Ayuh. We have a new cabin available at the beginning of May. For how long, miss?"

Claire tapped her fingers on the desk. How long would it take to uncover the past? "Can we say two weeks and go from there?"

"As you like. Now, I'll take down your information..."

Claire hung up a few minutes later and stared at the phone. She was going to Maine. Probably the craziest thing she'd ever done in her life. She could see it now. *Hi, I'm here to find my birth mother. I think you may have some information that could help me...* She'd better stop drinking altogether.

The shrill ring of the phone made her jump. Maybe the old guy was calling back to say he'd made a mistake, that they were full after all. Claire lunged for the receiver.

"You *are* there. I was starting to think your phone was out."

"James."

"I...uh...I'm coming over."

"What? What's going on?" He didn't sound good. Claire waited for his answer, but all she heard was dial tone.

8

Thunder clapped overhead in conjunction with the doorbell. Claire ran downstairs, the dogs ahead of her, barking. She peeked through the curtain on the side window, flung open the door, and stared at the dripping figure on her doorstep. "You're actually here. I didn't think you were serious."

He pushed back his hood, small rivers of water running off his yellow rain slicker onto the threshold. "Why was your phone busy so long? Don't you use call waiting?"

"I was talking to my father." Claire leaned against the door, feeling woozy. She still hadn't eaten. "What are you doing here?"

He looked over her head, and she watched the light in his eyes go out.

"It's Mel, isn't it?"

"They induced her this morning." His face said it all, tension etched into every crevasse. "She's not doing so well."

"I don't want to hear this." Fear slammed her and she backed away, but he took hold of her arm before she could escape. Claire met her husband's eyes and saw the reality of the situation in them.

"The baby is breach. They'll probably do a C-section. She's scared. She asked if you would come."

Claire struggled out of his grip and gasped for air. "Oh, no." She stumbled toward the stairs and sank onto the bottom step, her hands shaking.

As if it wasn't enough for God to take her mother, then the baby.

Melanie was going to die too.

She heard James shrugging out of his coat and coming to crouch before her. His hands rested on her knees, his touch forcing her to look up and meet his anxious eyes.

"I don't want to do this alone, Claire," he whispered. "Will you please come with me?"

Claire ran a finger across his cheek, wiping away the moisture. "You don't know what you're asking."

"Yes, I do."

"I don't think I can. Jamie, I…" She buried her head in her hands. "I can't go to that hospital, Jamie. Please don't make me."

She'd started bleeding in the middle of the night. As soon as she saw the blood, she knew she was having a miscarriage. They said it was due to stress, nothing she could have done to prevent it. Sometimes pregnancies just had a way of terminating themselves. A few more weeks and she would have made it through the first trimester. They'd done a D&C and kept her in overnight for observation.

Sobs rose and threatened to explode in loud and violent protest. Her chest wanted to explode with them, needed to. But she sucked in air and refused the indulgence. James pulled her close and rested his forehead against hers.

"Okay." His voice hinted of defeat and desperation. "Okay. It's okay. You don't have to. Mel will understand." He rose and turned.

Claire stood, reached out, and took his hand. "I'm sorry. I-I can't."

"I know." James grabbed his coat and yanked the door open. "Stay by the phone."

Claire watched him go, locked the door and went upstairs to the bathroom. Her stomach emptied, she washed her face, popped a couple of pills, and tried to quell the hammering of her heart. James looked so lost, so out of control. She'd only ever seen that look on his face once before...the night she tried not to think about.

Maybe she should go.

"No, no, no." Nausea returned with a vengeance, and Claire put a fist to her mouth. She willed her body to stop trembling and waited for the pills to kick in. Going to that hospital, re-living it all, was more than she could bear.

She stopped outside the closed door of her parents' bedroom. Her father had insisted they share a room, right to the end. Instead of hospice, Mom had spent her final days here at home, in a hospital bed by the window, looking out at the gardens she'd loved.

Claire pushed open the double doors and stepped inside the large room. Dad was a neat freak. Nothing was ever out of place. In the months after Mom's death, he'd organized the packing and clearing out of all her things. Claire hadn't been able to stand it. In the end it had been James, Melanie, and Steve who'd come to help him.

She wandered across to the spacious dressing room, her mother's side now completely empty. Almost. Something on the floor at the very back of the closet caught her eye. Claire bent to retrieve it, her fingers closing over a colorful silk scarf.

She sank to her knees, brought the thin material up to her face, and breathed in the scent of her mother's perfume. Tears stung her eyes as she let out a muffled wail and let emotion have its way.

Sometime later Claire trudged back downstairs, hating the silence of the big house.

In the kitchen she jacked up the volume of the stereo, fed the dogs, and threw a handful of salad greens onto a plate. Toasted a piece of bread and opened a container of black olives. She set everything down on the table and stared at her meager meal. Then she slowly inched towards the refrigerator. An invisible, magnetic force field pulled her toward it. The more she resisted, the stronger the tug grew.

Claire grasped the stainless steel handle, cold metal on her hand. Took a deep breath and yanked it open. The bottles of wine sat where she'd left them days ago, golden liquid glimmering under the bright fluorescent bulb. Untouched.

One glass wouldn't hurt. One glass would actually help.

One glass would get her through the next few hours.

Claire wrestled with conscience, determination to do the right thing, and a desire that overpowered both.

Tears blurred her vision, her conscience called her the coward she was, and mocked her as she reached for the bottle.

* * *

Claire willed time to pass but allowed her mind to blur. It was too easy to give in to the sensation of floating, airborne in space, where nothing mattered.

No future. No past.

No nothing.

She kept the dogs with her in the den. The air had chilled with the predicted cold front, and she managed to light a fire. The flames warmed her, soothed her at first, but eventually retreated and left her to her raging thoughts. She tried watching a movie but couldn't focus.

Unable to sit still, too frightened of what memories lucid thought would bring, she opened another bottle.

* * *

"Claire. Claire, wake up." Somebody shook her, gently at first, then more insistently.

Claire stirred, rubbed her eyes, and sat up. James squinted down at her, his mouth drawn in a thin line.

She was still on the couch in the den. Still dressed.

"Wh...what time is it?" She pulled the soft blanket up to her chin and tried to recall the last few hours. Her eyes stung, and her mouth felt jammed with cotton. And she had a wicked buzz going.

"It's around ten-thirty. I called, but I guess you didn't hear the phone." He ran a hand over his face and crossed the room to the built-in cabinets. Claire heard the clinking of ice on glass and sat straighter.

She watched him down a hefty shot of her father's bourbon. And then he took another. Claire froze.

"Is she dead?" The words tumbled out, but somehow in the translation she heard the voice of a child. She drew her legs up to her chest and gripped her knees, pressing her fingers into her flesh through her jeans.

James put down the glass and looked back at her with that *are-you-stupid* expression she knew so well. "No, of course not. She's fine." He took slow steps around the room. The dogs followed at his heels, their tails slapping his legs.

"Jamie..." Claire could barely breathe. He looked so desperate. Defeated.

Stopping his march, he turned her way again. His face told her just how hard the past several hours had been on him. "You were right to stay home."

She nodded, feeling the fist prick of tears as he walked back to where she sat. With a sigh that said more than words, he sank down beside her, leaned into the cushions, and flung one arm over his face.

"Is Mel really okay?" Claire whispered.

"Yes." His voice was muffled. "They did a C-section. They've taken her up to a room now. The doctor says everything should be fine."

"Thank God. I've been going nuts."

He lowered his arm and opened one eye. "So I see."

The empty bottles sat on the square table in front of her in silent accusation. If she could have conjured up some trick to make them disappear, she would have. "The baby? Is the baby all right?"

James grunted. "She's fine." He got up and threw a couple of logs on the glowing embers. Flames sparked and heat soon filled the cold room. He sat down again.

"It's a girl?"

Her heart constricted as he inhaled and stared at her through bleary, wet eyes. "Yeah," he breathed out. "Mel wants to call her Jaclyn. After us."

"She what?" Claire screwed up her nose, watching the reflection of the flames dance in the gold band on his left hand.

"J A for James, C L for Claire. Jaclyn. Don't ask; that's Mel for you."

Claire lowered her head and let her tears fall. James moved a little closer and then drew her against him into his embrace. Back into the familiar place of safety she'd been running from for so long.

"I had no idea it would be this hard." He ran a hand up and down her arm, and she heard his own shuddering breaths.

"We should be happy," she told him, almost convincing herself. "Mel's all right, the baby is healthy. That's the important thing." She swiveled to face him and even managed a smile.

"I know. You're right." James ran a light finger down the side of her face, tucking a strand of her hair behind her ear. "But it reminded me of everything we lost."

The pain etched into his features was unbearable. Claire leaned against him again. "Have you seen her?"

"Not yet."

"I don't know if I can."

"I know."

Claire shifted, putting some distance between them, afraid of the depth of her emotions and what they might cause her to say. Or do. "I-I couldn't...stop." Her eyes went to the bottles on the table, the admission unnecessary but needed.

He let go a ragged sigh, his hand resting on her back. The warmth of his touch went straight to her soul and ignited feelings held dormant for too long.

She turned, almost afraid to meet his eyes. But when she did, her fear died and a familiar heat rushed through her and caused an odd fluttering in her stomach.

She'd always laughed at the notion of love at first sight. A shared look across a crowded room—soul mates from that moment on. The day Claire met James Ferguson turned her into a believer.

He was too close.

"Jamie, I..."

"Don't," he murmured, his eyes capturing hers, taking her back to a different place and time. Back to when things were good and normal and they were happy. "Don't say anything."

James cradled her face between his hands, threaded his fingers through her hair. And very slowly brought her lips to his. Claire melted into his kiss and let him pull her close. His tender embrace shook her senses and called her back from dark slumber. She allowed his kisses, too exhausted to think about what was really happening. Where this could lead if they let it.

After a while he pulled back. His lips grazed her forehead, and he gave his head a shake. "Are you...fully here, Claire?" Doubt simmered in his eyes.

She may not have been when he woke her, but she was definitely sober now. "If you're asking whether I'll remember this in the morning, the answer is yes." Claire wrestled with the deep need inside of her. She couldn't change the past, couldn't take away the pain. But maybe, for a little while, they could forget.

"Maybe I should go."

She pressed her hand against his wet cheek, light scruff bristling against her skin. "You don't have to."

His eyes locked onto her and told her what he wanted.

"Jamie…" Her arms came around his neck before she could think about what came next. She brushed her lips across his as he gave a low groan.

"Sweetheart, don't do this to me…" His lips found hers again with a new sense of urgency.

They should stop. Letting him spend the night wouldn't help. But his touch felt so good. So right. Like it always had.

Desire and emotion banded together and kicked aside reason.
Even as she pulled him closer and felt his hands slide lower, she knew it was too late for second thoughts.

* * *

Dawn's first light streamed through her bedroom window. Claire opened her eyes, stretched, and smiled. It was going to be okay.

She rolled onto her side and found the other half of the bed empty.

Claire showered, donned her sweats, and followed the aroma of coffee downstairs to the kitchen. James stood at the counter, already dressed in his jeans and crumpled white oxford shirt, untucked. His damp hair curled up at the collar.

A grin played with her mouth, and her stomach did a funny little flip-flop. "I'm glad you're here. I thought I was having a really good hallucination."

He turned quickly, tipped his head, and gave a wry smile. "Morning. You okay?"

"Yes. I have a bit of a headache, but I'm good." She hugged herself and watched the dogs playing on the lawn outside. The rain had stopped, and rays of sunlight poked through the thick grove that surrounded the property.

She pulled out a chair and sat at the table. "Are you going to work?"

"Maybe later." He handed her a steaming mug of coffee and took a seat opposite her. His eyes were restless, wouldn't settle on her. For a long moment he said nothing, just stared. "Uh…so, last night. That probably wasn't a great idea."

Claire sipped and tried to ignore the sudden sick feeling working its way upward. "Okay. Not sure what I'm supposed to say to that." She attempted a laugh that went nowhere. "We're still married. It's not like we did anything wrong."

"No, but...I shouldn't have let it happen. I'm sorry, Claire." He concentrated on his coffee instead of looking at her.

"Sorry?" A knife plunged through her, ripping out the happiness she'd felt moments ago. He was sorry. "Why? You..." Seeds of doubt took root. "...is there...someone..." She bit her lip, unable to speak it. Unable to fathom it, really, but under the circumstances she could hardly blame him.

James looked up and narrowed his eyes. "What are you asking me?"

Claire put down her mug and clenched her hands. The trembling started up again. "I guess I wouldn't be that surprised. After everything I've done and..."

"Claire, are you serious?" His brows shot skyward. "You think I'm having an affair?"

"We're separated," she whispered, studying the weaving grain in the oak. She ran a finger around a dark brown circle on the wood, her vision blurring.

"Do you honestly think I would do something like that?" His voice lowered. "Claire, look at me."

She raised her head, afraid of what she might see.

James reached across the table and took her hands in his. "I love you. You're my wife. End of story. But you're worrying me to death. I can see you're still not sleeping well. When was the last time you ate a proper meal? You're as thin as a rail. And this drinking..."

Claire shrugged off his acute observations and looked away, but his touch burned on her skin. She pulled her fingers from his grasp. "Don't worry about me. I'm fine."

James grabbed her hand again, forcing her to look at him. His eyes glinted in the soft morning light, capturing her own within them. She could quite happily lose herself in those eyes and pretend...

"No, Claire," he told her, his voice catching. "You're not fine; you're existing. There's a big difference."

"I don't know how else to get through it."

"You've got options. People who love you and want to help you. You've shut us all out. Me, Mel, everyone at church, they'd all be there for you in a second."

Yeah, right. That's why none of them had called or come to see her in months. She'd been silently excommunicated. But who could blame them?

Communion wine wasn't safe when she was around. "What do you want me to do?"

"I've told you." He sat back and folded his arms across his chest, resolute.

"Counseling. AA" Claire wiped her eyes.

James nodded. "I can't do this, Claire. I don't want to live with an alcoholic. You know what we went through with my father. I'm not going through it with my wife."

Claire blinked at his words, her hope fading. "Your dad's good now, though, right? I mean, I could be fine too. *We* could be fine." She felt about as fine as a patient coming out of brain surgery and the tremor in his hands told her he wasn't doing much better. "I mean, last night…"

He shrugged, pulling at the collar of his shirt. "One night together doesn't change anything. It doesn't magically solve our problems. You didn't expect it would, did you?"

Heat rushed to her cheeks, and she stared into her half-empty mug. "I wanted it to."

But life wasn't that simple.

"I don't know what I'm supposed to do." James pushed his fingers through his hair. "You've made it quite clear you don't want to be with me. But then you…you let me in again…you give me hope. It's confusing. I need to know what you want, Claire. What you're willing to do to save this marriage. Do you understand what I'm saying?"

The pain of their past stood in his eyes. Things longed for and dreamed of that would not now come to pass. The realization dragged her heart to her feet. She did understand. And he had every right to feel the way he did.

"Claire? Will you go to counseling, A.A? Come back to church with me?"

"Church?" And listen to how great God was? The same God who'd allowed her mother to wither away to a mere skeleton, struggling for her last breath, her eyes glazed with pain and morphine? The same God who'd snatched precious life from her womb as she slept, given no warning and no consolation after the crime had been committed?

A God who offered no comfort, no compassion, only condemnation each time she looked in the mirror?

Claire pressed her back against the chair and clenched her fists. "No." She watched a shadow creep across his face. Outside the dogs barked, probably chasing birds or the mail truck. "No. I'm not going back to church. God is …I don't know what to think anymore."

James scowled. "You're blaming God?"

"Why shouldn't I?"

He leaned forward, his eyes intent as they bore into her. "You can't blame God for your mother's death or the miscarriage."

Claire studied her husband, raw, blistering emotion oozing over the pleasure she'd found in his arms only hours ago. She remembered the look on his face the days following her return from the hospital. The unspoken accusation that ran between them reared its ugly head once more. The same one he consistently denied, yet she constantly felt whenever they were together.

"If it's not God's fault, then it's mine."

The seething silence that followed annihilated what was left of her heart.

Eventually he spoke. "So where do we go from here?"

"I don't know."

He pushed back his chair and walked across the room, opening the screen door to allow the dogs in. They raced to their water bowls. Claire listened to their lapping and tamped down dark thoughts.

She rose and went to where he stood. "I'm so sorry I hurt you, Jamie." Deep sorrow rolled in like a morning tide. Birdsong filtered in through the open window. A reminder of an ordinary day in which the sun rose and would set as usual, but everything in her world had already changed. "It's not that I don't love you. It was never that."

He emitted a faltering laugh and pinched his eyes shut with his thumb and forefinger. "If I didn't know you so well, I'd think you were playing games with me."

Claire fought against the insidious emotion that threatened to derail her at any second. Falling apart would serve no purpose. "I'm not."

"I know you're not."

The tears in his eyes brought Claire's hand to her mouth. James shifted slightly, turning from her. After a moment, he faced her again, cupping her face between his hands, his fingers cold as they pressed into her cheeks.

"I don't want to lose you. If I could change things, make it so it never happened, I would." The pain and regret in his voice only intensified her guilt.

Claire put some distance between them. "I know you would. And I know I'm not handling this well. But I can't seem to get through it."

"It doesn't seem like you're trying very hard." His blunt tone scared her.

"I don't know what life is supposed to look like anymore, Jamie. How do we just go on?"

"We don't have a choice."

Claire sat down again, wound her thumbs together, and glanced his way. "I'm scared."

He went back to stand at the door and shot her a sidelong look. "Mel told me you were talking about searching for your birth parents. You really think that's a good idea?"

"I suppose you don't."

"Well, you're not exactly the picture of stability right now, are you?"

Claire pushed her chair back and went to the sink, her eyes burning. Her mug slipped from her shaking hand and crashed against yesterday's dishes. "Maybe this is my way of moving on, Jamie. Maybe if I knew…"

"Claire, for the last time, it wasn't your fault." James gave a muted groan and covered his face with one hand.

Claire walked across the room, pulled his hand down, and met his startled eyes. "I need to know that for myself. I can't go on wondering or thinking you're wondering. I need to know. I need to find my birth mother."

"And how do you plan to do that?"

"I think she was from Maine. I was planning a trip there, to see if I could uncover anything." She explained her findings in her father's study, but it was almost as though he didn't hear her.

"You're going away." His eyes shone with disbelief. "When?"

"In a few weeks. Next month, the beginning of May."

"You know what next month is."

"Our anniversary." Claire moved around the kitchen. Her mother's prized violets, long dead, sat on the granite counter by the stove, mocking in silent witness to all the failures of the past year. "I already booked a room. But I can change it. If you want me to stay."

James tapped his bare foot against the hardwood. "And if I said I did? That would give you one more thing to hold against me, wouldn't it?"

"You're being ridiculous."

"Am I?" He raised an eyebrow. "I'm tired of you doing whatever you want, Claire. I'm always giving in, letting you have your own way regardless of how I feel. Maybe you don't even realize it. You've always lived that way. You snap your fingers and everybody jumps. Well, maybe for once, you should consider somebody else's feelings besides your own."

Claire shivered and rubbed her arms. "I'm only trying to get some answers. You don't know what it's like…not knowing where you came from or why you were given up."

"That's a load of crap, Claire. This has never come up before. Why now? I'll tell you why. You're running away. And you know it." James stepped back, challenging her to deny it. His hair fell over one eye, but he stared, unflinching.

"Have you lost your mind?"

"No, I think I've found it." His hazel eyes glinted in the sunlight streaming through the glass door. "I'm your husband, and I'm telling you to stay home. We're going to fix this marriage. You're going to counseling with me. You're going to quit drinking, get off the pills, and start taking responsibility for your actions. I'm not letting you go, Claire."

Claire opened her mouth to speak but shut it quickly. What she wanted to say would not go over well. "Get over yourself, Jamie. You can't demand I stay. You sound like some throwback husband from the fifties. I *need* to get away. I'm going to get the answers I'm looking for and maybe...maybe I'll be able to get over all this and put my life back together. I can't do that here."

He huffed out a sigh, and she watched defeat move over him like an approaching storm. "I think you're making a big mistake. I don't see what good can come of it."

"Now you're sounding like my father."

"For once your father and I agree on something."

Anger rushed in and brought more tension with it. James' low voice echoed around her and bounced off the wall she'd built around her heart. Part of her wanted to smack him, yet somehow she realized that some of what he'd said was true. She *was* running away.

He opened the door and went outside. Claire followed, pacing the back patio, trying to find some semblance of calm and searching for words that would help her explain how she really felt. James sat on the low wall that bordered the spacious courtyard. Leaves blew over the black tarp that covered the swimming pool.

"Would you please listen to me?"

He hunched over, tapped out a beat on his knees, and shrugged. "Go on."

Claire breathed in the fresh morning air and latched onto courage. "It's always been in the back of my mind—the unanswered questions, not knowing where I really came from. I just never talked about it. When I found out I was pregnant, I thought about it more. That baby was the first real connection I ever had to *me*. I wondered if she would have my nose. My hair." Claire exhaled, pushing back memories of happier days. "I've never known anyone that looked like me."

James gave a muted groan, put his head in his hands, and sat like that for a long while.

Claire found her voice again. "Maybe you can't understand that. And yes, it might seem like I'm running away, and maybe I am, but I know I can't stay here anymore. Not like this."

"What do you want me to say, Claire?" James stared up at her through haunted eyes. "What's it going to take for you to heal? Do you really want me to say I blame you? You're pretty convinced of it anyway. Do you want me to tell you that you probably didn't take good enough care of yourself, that maybe you worked too hard, ran too much, that you didn't deserve to have a baby...that maybe..."

"Stop it!" Claire put up a hand, as if that would stop the awful words assaulting her.

He jumped off the wall, marched over, and gripped her arms, his face pinched in fury. "Do you see how ridiculous that sounds? You didn't do anything wrong, Claire! You need to believe that." His expression switched from anger to deep sorrow in a matter of seconds, and Claire had to force herself to keep her eyes fixed on him. "But I can't make you," he breathed out. "Maybe you should leave. Maybe we're not ready to work things out."

Tension ran like livewire between them. Somehow, in the recesses of her muddled mind, Claire knew they'd come to the end of the road.

And she knew that he knew it, too.

James walked past her, opened the door, and stepped aside. "Go. Do what you need to do."

Claire was unable to move. "What's happening?"

He lifted his shoulders and let them fall. "I'm done. When you get settled, wherever that is, the ball is in your court. Call a shrink, call a lawyer—just don't call me until you know what it is you want."

This was it. That defining moment that changed people's lives.

There was no going back now to what they'd had. Their solid marriage, the perfect life they'd shared, all the things she'd taken for granted had been taken from them months ago—the night she'd awakened to bloody sheets and excruciating pain, and known something was horribly, dreadfully wrong.

9

Michelle ran a little faster, matching her pace to Kevin's. They jogged the circuit in Central Park, passing other runners. A slight drizzle wet her cheeks and cooled her heated skin. The sun's rays crested the trees and promised to chase the early morning rain away. After another lap, Kevin stopped at a bench to stretch. Michelle joined him and stretched out her leg muscles as Kevin chugged from his water bottle.

"Thirsty?" He held the bottle toward her, wiping sweat from his brow.

"No, thanks." She shook out her arms, made a half turn, and faced the small pond on the other side of the path. The squeals of children and their laughter floated across the park from the playground. Michelle watched a pair of swans glide effortlessly across the water and disappear underneath a weeping willow. *Swans mate for life.* She read that somewhere. Marveled at the beauty in the concept, wondered why birds could get it right when so many people couldn't.

"You okay?" He stood by her, bending over his knees.

Michelle drew in a breath of cool air and willed the tension out of her shoulders. "Sure. Just a cramp. Maybe I overdid it a bit."

Spring put on an extravagant display, blossoms bursting from the trees, crocuses and daffodils poking colorful heads through the dark earth. This was her mother's favorite season. She'd spend hours in the garden, planting, weeding, tending to her roses and vegetables and delighting in the new growth that happened each year without fail.

"All right." Kevin straightened, clasping his hands behind his neck. "You want to tell me what's going on with you? You've been agitated for weeks now. Unfocused."

Michelle folded her arms and met his searching eyes. There was no easy answer to give. Nothing he would understand or accept. She took his water bottle and drank what was left of it, then pitched it neatly into a nearby wastebasket.

"I knew getting involved with my boss was a bad idea." She gave a wry smile. "I've tried not to let it get to me, Kevin, but I guess I'm human after all. So, before I read it online, you want to give me the real story? Are you and Felicity getting back together? Are you moving back into the house?"

She watched his eyes narrow, then widen, but nothing else in his expression gave her any information.

"Are you serious?" His chuckle was low and deep.

Michelle stepped back, balling her fists. "It's not funny, Kevin. It's the hottest story out there at the moment, and everyone's calling *me* for information. Information I don't have. How do you think that feels? And don't tell me you didn't know this was going on. I'm not that stupid."

"I don't understand." He stared at her like she was suddenly spouting Finnish. "Yes, I've been spending more time with the kids, but as far as getting back with Felicity...since when do you listen to rumors?"

"When they have a direct impact on my life, that's when," she snapped, walking past him along the muddy path by the water. The stories had haunted her for weeks. Reporters were calling, wanting the scoop, asking if she and the senator had terminated their personal relationship. There were even pictures of Kevin and his ex-wife together, without the children.

"Don't walk away from me. Talk." He caught up with her, waiting.

Michelle glanced around, checking the surrounding area. An old man and his dog walked up on the pavement and a couple on bikes pedaled past. The last thing they needed was a reporter tailing them.

"All right. Look, I know when we started dating, we agreed to keep our relationship quiet. But back then I assumed your divorce was imminent. After you were elected, I figured it would happen. That was a few months ago. You haven't mentioned it since our conversation before Christmas." Michelle shrugged. "I feel like I'm being played, Kevin, and I don't like it."

"Stop." Kevin took hold of her hand. "Will you listen to me for a minute?" He brushed a strand of hair off her cheek, a smile sliding across his lips. "I wanted to tell you in a more intimate setting, over a nice dinner or something, but since you're so worked up...Felicity has agreed to it. She's filing for divorce."

The light in his eyes was so bright she almost believed him. Almost believed the moment she'd been waiting for, hoping for, and dreaming about had finally arrived. But she'd learned the hard way that dreams don't come true. She drew in a sharp breath ignored the pain his smile inflicted. "Now? You just took the Senate seat. Come off it, Kevin. I wasn't born yesterday." Michelle shook off his arm and continued down the path.

"Okay, so we'll have to wait a bit. But isn't that what you want, Michelle? For us to be together?" He blocked her path, taking her by the shoulders.

She met his eyes and waited a moment. Words wouldn't come. "I do. You know that. But I'm not convinced we want the same thing anymore."

"Of course we do. It will happen. I promise you." Kevin drew her close and placed his lips on her forehead. "Just be patient a little while longer."

Michelle nodded, catching a flicker of hesitation in his eyes. Forced laughter caught in her throat. "I'm sorry. I don't mean to sound like a shrew. I guess I overreacted." She pulled her arms behind her back, stretched, and let out a sigh. "Won't happen again."

"Good. You have nothing to worry about, Michelle. I need you. You're my life now, okay?"

Michelle smiled and stepped into his embrace. Everything was fine. His kiss gave her full assurance of that.

Kevin held her hands, his face glowing in the sunrise. "Why don't we take a drive up to Maine this weekend? I still haven't met your parents."

The momentary calm she'd found faded as his words jolted her. She held up a hand. "I think I told you some time ago that's not going to happen."

"Oh, come on." He put on his best little-boy grin. "What are you afraid of? They'll love me. I can be very persuasive." He slipped his arms around her once more, but she pushed him back.

"No."

"Why?" He jogged circles around her, his eyes teasing. "Are they some drugged-out hippie couple? Or maybe you were raised in the backwoods by Ma and Pa Clampett. Or no, wolves. You were raised by wolves."

"Stop it." Michelle laughed and pushed him off. "My parents and I haven't talked in years. I told you that. I have no intention of seeing them anytime soon. And, persuasive or not, I can assure you they would not approve of our relationship."

"Conservative?"

"You have no idea." She picked up her pace again and started a slow jog. Irritation goaded her. "Why the sudden interest in my family?"

"It's not sudden. We never talk about them, that's all."

"There's nothing to say." Michelle glanced at her watch and groaned. "It's almost 6:30. You're going to be late for your breakfast meeting."

He ran faster, swatting her on the behind as he passed. "I think you're keeping secrets, Michelle Hart. Have it your way, then. For now. See you at the office."

Michelle waited until he was out of sight before she sank onto the wet grass at the side of the path and pretended to stretch over her legs. Her breath came in spurts, her heart pounding far too fast to be the result of her brief sprint. She pulled blades of grass, one by one. She'd tempted fate by taking that trip to Connecticut with Belinda. The phone call from the DCF in

Hartford only a week later proved it.

Nausea rose and she glared at the pieces of grass in her hand. She'd been outraged, demanded to know how they'd found her. The woman said she'd simply looked her name up in the files, Googled her, and dialed her office number.

No, they hadn't called her parents.

Michelle blew air through pursed lips and pushed to her feet. She'd spent a long time burying her past.

It wouldn't catch up to her now. She'd make sure of that.

Keeping secrets.

Kevin didn't know the half of it.

* * *

Michelle woke with a start, sat up, and stared through the darkness. Sirens. They roared past her apartment building and off into the distance somewhere in the city. She sank back against the pillows and pushed her hair off her damp forehead. Her T-shirt stuck to her back. The clock beside her read 1:00 a.m. She closed her eyes and tried to go back to sleep, but her racing thoughts refused to allow it.

She jumped into the shower and put on fresh pjs, pulled on a robe, and padded down the hall to the galley kitchen. A glass of milk might settle her frayed nerves. She huddled on the couch in the living room with her laptop. Michelle frowned as she scanned her emails. Two from Kevin.

Hey, babe. Things going well here. Had good talk with F today, and I think we can work something out. See you soon. K.

Michelle hit the *Delete* key. Kevin's delusions were beginning to bore her. The sad thing was, he actually believed everything he said. Once upon a time, she had too.

The other email from him was all business, confirming another invitation list for a dinner he was hosting next month. And then he was going to spend June on the Cape with the kids. And Felicity.

Each week that passed snatched a little more hope from her.

Michelle finished her milk and gazed out the window at the city lights blinking in the darkness. A hard knot formed in her stomach, pulled tight, and threatened to evict her supper. One of these days she'd get out of New York. She'd quit her job and...

A deep sigh brimming with regret worked its way out of her. The approach of summer somehow managed to dump melancholy at her feet. The feelings she battled all year came back full force, and there was very little she could do to defend herself against them. She pinched the bridge of her nose and turned her attention back to the computer screen as her Skype conversation button beeped.

What are you doing up at 1:00 a.m.?

Belinda.

Michelle smiled and typed back. *Same thing you are, I guess. Couldn't sleep.*

Thinking?

Yeah.

Her birthday's coming up in a couple of months.

Michelle raised her eyes to the ceiling. *Yep.* Nobody in the world knew her as well as Belinda. Well, maybe one person did. Or had.

Hard to believe it's been twenty-seven years, Shel.

Yep. Michelle studied her polished fingernails. That aching, longing for God-only-knew-what started up again. *Some days it feels like yesterday.* She hit the keys harder than necessary.

I'm sorry. I can't imagine what you're feeling. Belinda tacked on a sad-faced smiley. And then, *Shel, why don't you try to find her?*

Michelle almost shut down her laptop. Honestly, this was just like Belinda, always out for that proverbial happy ending.

She pounded out her answer. *What for?*

Shel…

I'm tired. Going to bed. Call you tomorrow.

Michelle closed her laptop. What did Belinda expect? She let out a cry of aggravation and pushed all thoughts of the past out of her head. There was too much to do; she didn't have time to worry about long-forgotten mistakes. She reached for her leather dossier and pulled out the latest speech she was working on. It was a good speech so far, maybe even one of the best she'd written. He'd like it.

Michelle gave a wry smile. Now, if only she could make Kevin Harrison mean what he said beyond the podium.

10

The rolling hills of Connecticut climbed higher as Claire left her home state, crossed over into Massachusetts, up through New Hampshire and into Maine. Tall, lush pines of varying shades of green surrounded her on all sides. Blue lakes and spectacular views beckoned around every turn, but she didn't stop. She drove until she could go no further, hunger and exhaustion forcing her off the road for lunch at a roadside café. But she'd reached Maine, and in good time, less than five hours.

After a satisfactory meal, she focused on the road ahead and tried to ignore the devastation of her soul. She didn't deserve to be happy anyway. James would be better off without her. He'd see that soon enough.

Driving through the almost deserted streets of Bethel, Claire wondered if there had been a plague she hadn't heard about. Only a few people walked along the sidewalks and one or two cars passed her every now and then. As she slowed for the stoplight, she took in her surroundings.

Plenty of quaint shops seemed open for business. Angel's Antiques, Kathy's Knick Knacks, Bookends. Flowers of every description hung from baskets on the street lamps.

Driving on, she spotted the bank, library and post office. Not a Starbucks in sight. Claire slid a mournful glance toward her empty paper cup, grimaced, and continued on. She hadn't had anything else for two days. A pinch of pride brought a smile to her lips. Maybe she *could* do this.

But she'd left her husband, not cared enough to celebrate their anniversary. Self-loathing loomed, doubt hot on its heels. She knew as soon as she reached her destination, her self-imposed prohibition would more than likely become merely a fleeting memory. She'd brought a supply of wine with her under that exact expectation.

Claire forced her mind back to the reason she was heading north. She'd looked through the telephone directory when she'd stopped for lunch, but there were more than a few Kellys listed in the area. The owners of Tara's Place might not be her relatives, but they could have information that would help track down her birth mother. She'd find out soon enough.

She followed the directions they emailed her, hoping she was going the right way. Her car didn't have a GPS, and she'd forgotten to pick one up before leaving. James always drove wherever they went. He was a much better navigator.

Her SUV bumped along the unpaved road, rocks flying every which way. Thick forest lined the road on either side, the trees almost touching overhead in some areas. Claire slowed and let the car idle on the long gray road as the sun shot golden rays through the green leaves above. The tranquil scene resembled something straight out of *National Geographic.* The stillness overwhelmed her.

She leaned back against the seat, allowing the cool air from the vents to hit her face. Tears trickled down her cheeks. The whole idea was ridiculous. Going up to total strangers and asking them if they knew anything about a child given up for adoption twenty-seven years ago.

The temptation to back up, turn around, and head home was almost as strong as the urge to drink. Claire shifted, placed her hands on the wheel again, and strengthened her resolve. Her father was barely speaking to her. Her marriage was all but over. She had nothing left. But she wasn't a quitter. She'd come here on a mission, and she'd complete it. No matter the cost.

She gunned the engine and flew down the rest of the road, eager to catch a glimpse of Tara's Place. It had to be perfect. She knew it. Something had led her here. There must be something special about this place—besides the name *Kelly*—some reason the urge to come had been so strong.

Claire sucked in a breath as she drove through open wooden gates and onto the property of the main house.

A rambling mix of white clapboard and natural stone stretched out before her. The two-story house with green shutters sat pristine and proud. A wrap-around porch invited visitors; wicker rockers with chintz-covered cushions were positioned here and there across the length of it. Rose vines mingled with new ivy and wound their way around the thick front stone posts and clambered up the side of the house. A few pink buds poked through waxy leaves. Daffodils and crocuses dotted the lush grass around her. Beyond the house, the blue lake glimmered under the afternoon sun.

Claire had visited many places with her parents. She'd seen most of Europe, the Caribbean, South Africa, and Australia. But nowhere she'd been evoked such a strong, certain connection within her the way this place did.

There *was* something special about Tara's Place.

She pressed down on the gas pedal again and moved forward, peering out the side window of the car, searching for any movement inside the house.

The car jerked to a sudden stop and a horrible scraping reached her ears. Claire let out a yelp. She'd hit something.

She parked and got out of the car, her nerves shot. She almost couldn't look. Could barely breathe. *Not a deer, please.* She'd never hit an animal and didn't intend to start now.

A loud yell reached her ears, and she turned to see a man charging down the front steps of the house, followed by an elderly couple.

"What did you do?" He ran across the lawn, wild eyes fixed on her. Claire swallowed down fear and squinted at him through her sunglasses.

"Um, I don't know. I...might have...hit something." Fear slammed her at the roar he gave as he bent over and looked under her car. Maybe she'd hit a kid, his kid—oh, please, no... "What is it?" she squeaked, slowly making her way toward him.

He straightened, ripped a hand through dark straggly hair, and glowered. "Back up."

Claire did.

He raised his ink-blue eyes skyward and shook his head. "Not you. Your *cah*, sweetheart. Back it up. Slowly."

Claire looked across the lawn. The couple hadn't come any closer. Smart people. She gazed back at the man who towered over her and met his angry glare. "First of all, I'm not your sweetheart. Second of all, I'd like to know what I hit before I move my *cah*. And third, you could say *please.*"

A sound very close to a growl stuck in his throat. He brushed past her and, before Claire knew what was happening, he'd hopped in the driver's seat and reversed her car, revealing a large, tangled pile of metal. He unfolded himself from the inside of the vehicle, slammed the door shut, and strode to the front of it.

Claire clapped a hand over her mouth and stared at the wreckage. "Was that your bicycle?"

"No." He crouched before the metallic mess and poked at it. He lifted a piece, gray tinged with green, let out a long groan, and let it drop from his hand. Claire winced as it clanged onto the top of the pile on the grass. "Tha-at"—he pushed himself to full height, brushed dirt off the white button-down shirt he wore over a pair of dark jeans and sighed—"was a Rick Matthews original sculpture. *Swans by Morning.* It cah-an't be replaced." His thick Maine accent almost rivaled that of the gas-station attendant's she'd tried to get directions from about an hour ago. She'd kept asking him to repeat himself. He hadn't been too friendly either.

Claire gulped. She'd ruined an original sculpture. Great. But at least it wasn't an animal. Or a kid. "I'm sorry." Her feeble apology didn't appear to touch him. The groove between his eyes deepened.

The two observers approached, and she heard the elderly man chuckle. "I told you to put that thing closah to the house, son. You okay, Miss? You weren't hurt?" Blue eyes twinkled at her, and a friendly smile warmed her through and put her at ease.

Finally, somebody with manners.

Claire smiled, taking in the wrinkled face and almost white hair. She had few memories of her own grandfather, an austere, thin man with nothing good to say about anyone. The man in front of her resembled the grandfather she'd always wished she had.

"I'm all right, thanks." She laughed with relief and turned toward the other man. He looked to be in his forties, definitely not much older than fifty. Maybe he was an art dealer. "Look, I'm really sorry about the sculpture. Just tell me what I owe you. I'll write you a check."

He stared like she'd spoken in some tribal tongue. He tipped his head to one side and studied her. His bearded jaw twitched. "Are you deaf as well as blind? I said it cannot be replaced."

"Now, Rick." The silver-haired man stepped forward and gave him a thump on the back. "It was just an accident. She didn't mean to…"

Claire took off her sunglasses, her mind beginning to work. "Rick? Let me guess. *You're* Rick Matthews? You made this…thing. Correct?"

"Ayuh," he answered gruffly, folding his arms across a thick chest. His long hair played around a chiseled face, the breeze coming up from the lake tossing it this way and that.

Claire smiled triumphantly. "Then it *can* be replaced. Do another one. I'll pay for it." She turned her smile on the older of the two men and searched his face for any resemblance but saw none. "I'm Claire Ferguson. I have a reservation. I think." Perhaps she'd made a mistake coming here.

Rick Matthews turned on the heel of his cowboy boots and began to gather up his ruined sculpture. The warmth of the sun began to make her feel dizzy. Her stomach churned, and her hands trembled. Sweat dripped down her neck. "This is Tara's Place, right?"

"Yes, yes." The woman, a petite figure with a kind smile, hurried forward. She looked like the kind of grandmother any kid would want. A flowery apron sat over her ankle-length denim skirt. She wore a blue blouse under a thick red cable-knit sweater that she probably made herself. Her face didn't bear many lines, but Claire put her around the same age as the older man—late sixties, early seventies maybe.

"We've been expecting you. Why don't you come in, sit a spell?" She moved closer.

Claire nearly fainted from exhaustion, tension, and nerves. She tried to get a handle on her feelings and put her sunglasses back on. "I don't want to be any trouble."

"No trouble." The woman's brown eyes sparkled under the sun. Brown eyes. The same shade her own. Claire tried to focus on them, but the task proved impossible.

The woman spoke again. "I'm Jessie Kelly. This here's my husband, Mac, and that's Rick. Who I guess you already met." Her friendly laugh made Claire smile in spite of herself. "Come on in, and let me get you some tea."

"Tea would be nice." She hadn't enjoyed a cup of tea for a long while. Her mother-in-law, Margaret, loved the stuff and swore by it. In her Irish blood, she said. They'd spent many a long afternoon sipping tea and swapping stories. Hit by unexpected sorrow, Claire shifted, reached inside the car for her purse, made sure she took the key out of the ignition, and made some effort to pull herself together.

The two men were loading the pieces of the unfortunate sculpture into the back of a black pickup. She eyed them a little cautiously. "Should I leave my car here?"

"Eh?" Mac looked back over his shoulder and she repeated the question. He gave a snort and shook his head, laughter wheezing out of him. "I reckon you're fine there. I'll make sure Rambo here don't hit it on his way out."

"Okay." Claire ignored the way "Rambo" still glared at her, and followed Jessie Kelly into the house. A ruined sculpture—replaceable—two new friends who might know something about her birth mother, and one enemy. Not bad for the first day of her adventures.

11

The minute Jessie unlocked the door to the cabin, the smell of fresh paint and wood paneling reached her nose. Claire was pleasantly surprised with her new accommodations. The one-bedroom cottage was not overly large but definitely looked comfortable.

Dark green granite countertops shimmered under small glass lights that hung from the ceiling. It would be a shame to actually use the counters for anything. The kitchen was fitted with all new stainless steel appliances and, much to her relief, a microwave. Claire couldn't cook to save her life, but any idiot could throw a frozen dinner into a microwave. She'd survive quite nicely on Lean Cuisine, when and if she remembered to eat.

The bathroom was just as nice, tiled in travertine, with new faucets and one of those wonderful rain showerheads that Claire so enjoyed. James had installed one for her in their bathroom at home...but she wouldn't think about that.

The bedroom and small living area of the cabin were paneled in pine. The smell was rustic, soothing, and invited her to stay awhile. There was even a fireplace. She almost regretted the approach of summer. But this was Maine, after all. It might get cold at night.

Two days later, Claire opened her eyes to familiar cloying darkness.

Their anniversary. And they were both spending it alone.

Failure pounced and dug its claws in. Told her things would never get better. She'd made sure of that already.

She popped a couple of pills to calm her nerves and wandered the cabin aimlessly, waiting for the sun to rise. She clutched a small silver frame to her chest, not wanting to see James' smiling face. She missed him more than she could say but didn't have the courage to call and tell him that.

Claire sank onto the sofa, tears blurring her vision.

She went back to bed for a while. Got up, made some toast, then ventured outside.

Wrapped in a shroud of grief thicker than she'd imagined, Claire walked the property, not really enjoying the peace and quiet the way she hoped she would. Her thoughts turned to James and how he might be spending the day. Maybe she should call. But the possibility of awkward silence or another argument quickly changed her mind. She wasn't up for that today. The family would surround him. He'd be okay.

She, on the other hand...well, she only knew one way to get rid of the pain.

That afternoon Claire sprawled on a lawn chair by the crystalline lake, drinking her father's Château Rothschild Cabernet Sauvignon. She'd lugged a case of the expensive French wine up from the cellar and hauled it into the back of the car before she left.

She soaked up the sun, vaguely aware of the goings-on around her. Warm rays trickled through the tree branches and kissed her cheeks. Pine needles gave off scents of Christmas and reminded her of her mother. Memories assaulted her, unbidden, rendered her powerless to fight against them. She closed her eyes and turned up the volume of her iPod.

When she woke sometime later, Claire realized she was not alone. Rick Matthews moved in and out of her line of vision, eyeing her suspiciously while he applied a fresh coat of paint to the Adirondack chairs. When he went to work hammering new planks onto the dock, Claire gathered up her things and retreated to her cabin.

* * *

The next day she forced herself out of bed and vowed to get on with things. Enough was enough. She made a trip to the grocery store and picked up some necessities. Coffee, bagels, a few frozen dinners, and cheese and crackers. On the way through Bethel she'd spotted the Town Clerk's office. Claire figured that would be a good enough place to start. If her birth mother was from around here, there had to be some record of it. And as soon as she found enough courage, she'd confide in Jessie Kelly.

With only a dial-up connection, doing any research online would be a chore. Her cell phone didn't work, either, though apparently a new tower in the area was imminent. Jessie told her she could use the house phone whenever she needed it, but so far she'd resisted the urge to call home, too fearful of what her father or James might say to her. And she didn't really want Dad knowing where she was. Not yet.

When it started to rain in the afternoon, Claire wandered up to the main house. She poked through the various rooms. Nobody seemed to be around. She'd seen few visitors since her arrival.

She ran a finger along the old bookshelves in the long living room. Books and magazines were stuffed into every available space. Another shelf was packed with board games. On the far side of the room, a writing desk sat in front of a window. Claire walked over to it and sank into the chair. Her head pounded, and her stomach rolled. She hoped it wasn't the flu. Now was not a good time to get sick.

Her eyes went to an old black and white photograph on the top of the desk. Three children captured in motion as they raced along the dock, about to jump in the lake. She picked it up and stared at the girl in the picture. Long hair flowed about her face, her mouth open in a shriek. Claire frowned and stared harder. A strange sensation skittered down her spine.

"Can I help you?"

Claire snapped her head up and put the photograph back in place, almost dropping it. Jessie Kelly stood in the doorway with a curious expression.

Claire got to her feet and gripped the back of the chair. "Sorry. I was…um…hoping to get some aspirin or something. I've got a monster headache."

Jessie smiled, gave a nod, and turned on her heel. "Sure. Come on back here."

She followed Jessie down the hall into another room she hadn't seen before. It faced the lake, decorated in a more updated style than the other rooms in the inn. A sign on the open door read *Private.*

"Have a seat. Won't be but a minute." Jessie pointed to a comfortable couch and Claire sat, grateful for the soft cushions. She scanned the shelves and the mantle over the fireplace for any photographs, but there were none. Only knick-knacks and china vases.

Jessie returned a moment later with a glass of water and a bottle of aspirin. Claire helped herself and drank deeply. "Thanks. Sorry to be a bother."

"Not at all." Jessie seated herself in a chair opposite the couch. "You spend a lot of time in the cabin. Hope you're not coming down with something on your vacation."

"I hope not." Claire managed a smile, swallowing back another wave of nausea. She couldn't remember if she'd taken anything that morning. "Probably just a cold."

"Ayuh." The older woman seemed to hesitate, then tipped her head. "You expecting any company, Claire? Your husband, maybe?"

"No." Claire fiddled with the chain around her neck and focused on the painting above the mantle. She flinched as her stomach tightened again. "It'll just be me. I…needed some time…alone. You know."

Jessie's astonished expression told Claire she didn't know. Claire's cheeks burned, and she looked away.

"No matter," Jessie said quietly. "Hope you find what you're looking for here at Tara's Place."

Claire smiled and met the kind brown eyes. "Thank you. I'm not exactly sure what it is I'm looking for. But I'll know it when I find it."

"Yes." Jessie nodded, as though this time she knew exactly what Claire meant.

"You don't seem very full. Is it a slow time for you?" Claire regretted the question and the frown it brought to Jessie's face. Perhaps she shouldn't be so blunt. "I'm sorry. It's none of my business."

"Don't be afraid to speak your mind, Claire. Truth is always better than fiction, I say."

"Sure." Claire returned Jessie's soft smile, searching her face. If she told Jessie the truth, told her why she was really here, told her what it was she wanted, what would her response be? She clenched her hands in her lap and studied her sneakers.

"We started renovations last year," Jessie explained. "Didn't realize how much it would all cost. We're only able to have a few rooms open this summer. You're the first guest to get one of the new cabins. Do you like it?"

"Yes. It's great." Claire looked at Jessie again. "Have you lived here a long time, at Tara's Place?"

"Ayuh. A long while. This was Mac's family home. Tara was his mother's name. We decided to turn it into an inn about, oh…forty years ago now, I guess it would be." She emitted a low chuckle. "Time flies."

Claire sipped more water, her throat dry. "I think my parents might have stayed here. Maybe before I was born. Edward and Susannah Wiley."

"Wiley…Wiley." Jessie rubbed her chin, fixing Claire with a bemused expression. "Can't say the name sounds familiar. The old memory isn't as good as it once was. Maybe Mac would remember." She pushed herself up with a laugh. "Best see what them girls are doing in my kitchen. They burnt the potatoes last night. I used to do all the cooking myself, you know. But nowadays, with the arthritis, well…I still do what I can."

Claire stood also, unsure what to say next. She watched the older woman carefully, tempted to just come out with it, but there was a certain sorrow in Jessie's eyes that stopped her.

Jessie hesitated, settling her gaze on Claire. She fiddled with the cord of her flour-speckled apron for a minute, untying it and tightening it. "There's a guest book in the foyer. Goes back awhile. You're welcome to have a gander through it if you like. Hope you feel better, Claire." She stepped forward and patted her arm.

Claire stood motionless, watching the older woman take quick steps out of the room.

* * *

At the end of her second week at Tara's Place, Claire foraged through her purse and found the last bottle of pills. Half empty already. Or half full. She preferred that description. The latest doctor she'd found before leaving home was very empathetic. He'd probably even call in a refill for her up here if she needed it. She popped a small white pill into her mouth and went to the kitchen for water.

She let out a sigh and glanced at the clock on the wall. Three o'clock? In the afternoon? Impossible. Claire strode to the bedroom and grabbed her watch from the pine night table beside the double bed. It confirmed the time for her. Three o'clock. But that couldn't be.

Flopping down onto the soft mattress, she covered her eyes with one arm. The stomach cramps she'd been having started again and she groaned. For the past couple of days they'd been intermittent but getting worse. She crawled back under the covers and waited for the pain to subside.

Claire woke sometime later, groggy and disoriented, but managed to shower and pull on a pair of Juicy Couture sweatpants and a T-shirt. She ran her fingers through her wet hair, slipped into her brown loafers, and trudged up to the main house. Perhaps she could at least get a sandwich from the kitchen. Her supply of microwavable dinners was gone, and she hadn't had the strength to make the drive into town. She'd stopped drinking altogether a few days ago. She just didn't feel right, and that scared her. But she didn't have the nerve to go to a doctor. Admitting her failures to another complete stranger was not something she planned on doing anytime soon.

She stepped up onto the long back porch and admired the dazzling array of potted plants and flowers. Jessie clearly had a green thumb. Anything Claire ever tried to grow, apart from her roses, died the minute she laid hands on it.

No way were they related.

Inside the house, somebody was hammering and she heard some kind of machine coming on. Claire winced at the loud mechanical hum.

She pushed open the screen door and took faltering steps into a darkened dining room. About ten round wooden tables took up most of the space. At the far end of the room sat a long bar. Behind it, Rick Matthews perched on a ladder. Apparently the resident handyman around here, he was paneling the wall in fresh blond strips of knotty pine.

Each time he hit the nail gun, she flinched.

Claire grabbed a nearby stool and managed to position herself on it after a couple of attempts. She rested her elbows on the counter and put her head in her hands. Taking deep breaths, she swallowed back nausea and waited for a lull in the activity.

"Hi! Excuse me?" She had to raise her voice, which didn't help her aching head one bit. But on the third try he heard her.

Rick turned so fast she thought he might fall off the ladder. His dark eyes widened as he saw her. He climbed down two steps, jumped off, and shut down the machine. The room fell into blessed silence. He strode to where she sat, a scowl set in place. "Miss Ferguson. Coming up for air?"

She ignored the jibe. "I wanted to ask about dinner. I...the clocks in my room are all messed up. I think it's dinner time, right?"

He took a step backward. "Your clocks are working fine. I set them myself. It's Sunday morning."

Claire blinked. Disbelief crowded her senses. She'd fallen asleep yesterday at three in the afternoon? And just awakened now? He had to be kidding. "That's not funny."

"No, I guess it's not." He ripped off a red bandana from his head and wiped his face. "When did you pass out?"

12

Claire studied the black granite bar top. She pushed trembling fingers through her damp hair and tried to think, but her thoughts were muddled. Her racing heart gave her cause for concern. She heard him moving around, water running and ice clinking against glass, but she couldn't look up.

When she raised her head again, he placed a tall tumbler of ice water in front of her. Claire tried to hide her surprise with a cough. "Thanks. I'm just tired, I guess." She managed a smile and sipped. The cold liquid slithered down her parched throat and she grimaced, fighting nausea. She avoided his gaze and looked at the row of cupboards across from her.

"Mac and Jessie don't serve alcohol. You'll have to drive into Bethel if you've gone through your stash already. But, being a Sunday, you probably won't find much open. We're still pretty traditional 'round here."

Claire swallowed down a smart reply with another gulp of water. She was in no mood to defend herself. "I thought you were a sculptor or artist or whatever. What are you doing working here?"

Something close to a grin slid across his mouth and he smoothed a hand down his dust-covered Patriots sweatshirt. "I pitch in when I can." He leaned against the sink behind him and crossed his arms. He'd tied his dark hair at the nape of his neck, and Claire noticed a few flecks of gray in his beard. She wondered at his age. He wasn't as old as her father, that was for certain, but he was definitely older than her. Middle aged maybe, without the spread. He reminded her of an English teacher she'd had in high school—tough as nails and always pushed her to the limit.

"What are *you* doing here, Miss Ferguson?"

"Vacation. Not that it's any of your business. And it's *Mrs.*"

"That so?" He rubbed his long nose with his left hand and Claire noticed the absence of a ring—probably because no woman in her right mind would have him. The urge to vomit gripped her again, and she squeezed her eyes shut.

"You should eat," he said matter-of-factly. "Come on into the kitchen."

Claire followed him back through the dining room into a large well-equipped kitchen. She slumped into a chair at the kitchen table and finished her water, watching as he moved around with familiarity, pulling fruit from the fridge, peeling and chopping, and throwing things into a professional-looking blender.

In a few moments, he straddled the chair opposite hers and watched while she sipped the most delicious yogurt shake she'd had in her life. "Slow down, or you'll throw it up."

Claire rolled her eyes but lowered the glass. Her head throbbed and she couldn't stop shaking. She really hoped it wasn't the flu or worse. Making a visit to a hospital in the sticks wasn't on her to-do list. She took another breath and tried to focus. "Where is everyone?"

"Church."

Of course. It was Sunday. How had she slept so long, and not awakened once? Maybe Dr. Kay had been right about combining the pills with alcohol. She drank some more of the pink concoction and allowed it to soothe her stomach. "You don't go?"

He peeled off the skin of a banana and bit into it. "Not today." His blue eyes seemed fixed on her, taking in everything about her. She wanted to leave the room, but all she could do was sit there and endure his stare as another round of cramps came and went.

"What are you on? Valium? Anti-depressants?"

She snapped her head up and waited until his blurred image came into focus. His face remained impassive. There was no judgment in his tone. It was simply a question.

Claire shrugged. "A bit of both."

He raised a dark eyebrow. "When was your last drink?"

"This is none of your business." She pushed back her chair, anger rising. Who in the world did he think he was?

Rick grabbed her arm, preventing her from going anywhere. His steely gaze pinned her to the chair and she stared, open-mouthed.

"Mac and Jessie Kelly are two of the kindest souls you're ever likely to meet on this earth. I owe them a lot. I'm not about to let them wind up with some dead girl in their newly renovated cabin, so yeah, it is my business." His eyes flashed as he scowled, but then his expression softened. "Look, I don't know the first thing about you, but I can write a book on addiction. You're walking a thin line, Mrs. Ferguson. If you drove up here to kill yourself, may I kindly suggest you leave Tara's Place and find another venue?"

"Are you always this blunt?" *Abrasive* would be a more fitting adjective, but she didn't dare insult him.

"Don't know any other way to be." He released her arm, and Claire sat back. Tears stung her eyes, but she made no effort to wipe them away. He said nothing, just watched her cry.

"I don't want to kill myself," she whispered. "I only want to find some way to live without...feeling."

He pushed a paper napkin her way and gave a grunt. "No getting away from that one, I'm afraid. Only time and God can take away the kind of pain you're going through."

"You don't even know what I'm going through." Claire shook her head, mesmerized by the soulful eyes that seemed to reach past the door that held all her secrets behind it.

"I don't need to." He rubbed his chin. "Finish your shake. I have to get back to work. As you said, it's none of my business. If you can make it through tonight without taking anything, you'll feel better tomorrow. You'll probably be at some bar by noon anyway, and then you'll really feel better. But it won't last. And it won't fix your problems."

"I know that. I haven't had a drink in...four days." Claire looked back at him and wondered whether she actually could fight this despicable desire that had taken over her soul. "I'd like to quit. Everyone back home keeps telling me to. But I'm scared of...what it'll be like if I do."

"You're going to have to face it at some point, whatever it is you're running from." He stood and paused a minute. "But nobody can make you quit. You have to decide for yourself that you're done, that you don't want to live this way anymore."

Claire glanced around the homey kitchen. A child's drawings were stuck onto the large stainless steel refrigerator with magnets. Cheerful prints of kittens and flowers and picturesque scenes hung on the pale blue walls. She had imagined herself in such a place one day—in her own home, James out back playing with the kids, Crayola drawings stuck to the refrigerator.

"I'm not sure I'd know how to stop now," she admitted. "But I think I'm in trouble. I think I should try. I want to try."

Rick sat down again and gave a slow nod. "Okay. It won't be easy and you'll want to give up. And you might. But—if really do want to quit—if you're willing to try, I can help you."

Claire met his gaze and felt all the fight go out of her. "Why would you want to do that?"

Rick chuckled long and low as he moved his head back and forth. "I have absolutely no idea. You're a young woman. Surely you must have something, someone, to live for, Mrs. Ferguson?" He gave her one of the nicest smiles she'd seen in a long time. A sudden image of James brought more tears.

"It's Claire." She sniffed and wiped her eyes, not wanting to give in to the sorrow anymore. She'd been numb so long now she'd almost forgotten what life had been like before.

Forgotten what it felt like to be normal.

Depression and desperation choked her, but she pushed past it and felt the tiniest pinch of hope. "I'm not sure I do have much to live for anymore. But I guess I owe it to some people to stick around and find out."

* * *

The next few nights were the longest Claire ever endured. And when it was over, she couldn't remember much.

Of course Rick told Mac and Jessie of her sorry state. They'd shown up that evening, bringing food and supplies for her fridge. Instead of kicking her out, they seemed to take her on like some mission. *The Sobering of Claire.* It sounded like a bad B-movie.

They brought a doctor, but she refused to let them call James. As her system rebelled against the lack of alcohol and medication she had lived on for so long, Jessie, Rick, and Mac took turns sitting with her, getting her through the delirious hours, plying her with water and toast and standing guard whilst she slept.

The whole situation was so bizarre Claire wondered more than a few times whether she was dreaming it all. Here she was, in some miniscule town in the mountains of Maine, helpless in the hands of strangers. Being pulled back from the brink by people she didn't even know.

In moments of consciousness, Claire thought she heard Jessie singing hymns. A couple of times she'd opened her eyes to see the three of them huddled in a corner, murmuring. When Rick was there he didn't say much. Talked to his dog most of the time but occasionally wiped her brow and patted her on the hand.

The dog was a big black Lab he called Jazz, and Claire was glad he'd brought her along. She missed her own dogs and the animal's presence in her room gave her comfort. When Rick chose to speak, his words were filled with passion and conviction, and he promised her she was doing the right thing.

She would survive it.

Claire hoped he was right.

As the thick fog began to clear and her mind started to work properly again, Claire knew with everything in her that she was meant to be here at Tara's Place.

She'd been brought here, brought to this place by a force she wasn't yet willing to acknowledge. Why, for what reason, she didn't know, but, as she wrestled with her demons and dealt with the events that had brought her to this point in her life, she determined to discover it.

* * *

Claire stirred, opened her eyes, and the room came into focus. Somebody was watching her. A little boy stood at the foot of her bed. She blinked and rubbed a hand across her face. He looked real enough. His red T-shirt was stained, and his denim overalls were ripped in a couple of places and streaked with mud. His blond hair stuck out of his head in unruly spikes.

"Who are you?" she croaked.

The towheaded child still stood there, motionless.

Claire struggled to sit up. "What are you doing in my room?"

His face cracked into a mischievous grin and he chortled. Maybe he didn't understand English.

"What's your name?"

He laughed again and Claire pushed herself out of bed.

"Jackson! Jackson," a female voice called from outside the cabin. The child turned on bare feet and scooted toward the door. Claire tried to race after him but had to stop to catch her breath. When she reached the living room, a young woman stood just inside the doorway, the apparition hiding behind her.

"I'm so sorry. He shouldn't have come in here. I guess the door was unlocked." She looked more curious than apologetic. "Are you okay? I heard you were…sick." Dark eyes flecked with amber danced in a flawless pale face. Her thick hair—a mix of light honey and gold—hung straight, just touching her slender shoulders. She wore a gaily decorated peasant blouse over a flowing skirt. Her feet were bare, toenails painted the brightest pink color Claire had ever seen.

Claire crossed her arms across her Red Sox T-shirt and nodded. In her tattered pajama pants and tangled hair she probably looked more of a sight than the kid. She couldn't recall when she'd last showered. "I'm doing better. I think." She realized for the first time in days, she'd awakened without a headache.

"I'm Darcie Hart." Her visitor came forward and thrust out a thin hand. Several colorful braided bracelets were tied around her wrist.

Claire blinked as she shook hands with the girl who looked to be around her age, a few years younger. "Claire Ferguson." The oddest sensation came over her, although she couldn't say what it was. That feeling between sleeping and waking when you're trying to get your bearings and you can't figure out where you are.

"I'm not in the habit of barging in on guests, but I figured he had to be in here." Her eyes sparkled with humor. There was something about her, this Darcie, something in her easy smile and the way she carried herself that made Claire want to know her.

"This is my boy, Jackson." Darcie pulled the child from out behind her. "Who's going to apologize to you for invading your space." She gave him a prod, and he flashed Claire a wicked grin.

"I'm thorry. I just wanted to see what you look-ed like."

The sound of her own laughter took Claire by surprise. "Well, buddy, you should probably come back later, after I shower and put some decent clothes on. How old are you?"

"Four." He stuck out his chin. He had his mother's eyes, nose and grin. "How old are you?"

Claire smiled and glanced at Darcie, who shrugged and gave a dramatic eyeroll.

"He does have manners, I swear."

Claire sank into one of the wooden chairs positioned around the table.

Realization hit.

The heaviness she'd been cloaked in for months now had lifted. She took a moment to gather her thoughts, to see whether she might be imagining things, but no. It was gone.

She felt…normal.

Darcie tousled her son's blond hair. "Run out and play." He raced for the door and she moved forward, eyeing Claire a little warily. "You okay? You need something?"

"No." Claire sat astounded. "That's just it. I feel fine." She laughed at herself, feeling stupid, but Darcie didn't seem to mind.

She pulled up a chair, uninvited, and grinned. "My grandparents were awful worried about you. Jackson and I have been out of town the past month, visiting my dad in California. We just got in last night."

"You're Mac and Jessie's granddaughter?" Claire rubbed at a stain on her T-shirt. "Lucky you."

"Yeah." Darcie sighed and twisted her hands together. A faraway look crept into her eyes. "You don't know the half of it." She tipped her head to one side and fixed a scrutinizing gaze on Claire. "You can do it, you know.

Stay clean. Lots of people do."

Claire straightened and hoped her face didn't display shock. "Is everybody around here so forthright?"

Darcie's cheerful laugh rang through the cabin. "I guess so. No reason not to be. I don't have anybody to impress."

Claire frowned. Darcie looked more like a high-school kid. She couldn't be more than twenty-four, if that.

"I know what you're thinking. Yeah, I'm young to have a kid. I got pregnant when I was nineteen. It's kind of a long story." She turned to the door as Jackson raced through it, the screen door banging behind him. He ran to his mother and pulled on her arm, his eyes wide.

"Nana said I can play with the puppies now!" The little boy turned to Claire, hopping on one foot. "Didya know Uncle Rick's dog had puppies? He had 'em in Nana's laundry room while we were away. Come see!"

"Jackson, cut it out. Claire might not want to see the puppies right now." Darcie chuckled, but Jackson continued to tug on her.

"She does! Come on!"

"All right, all right." Darcie rose and shot Claire another grin. "Want to come? Not every day you get to see a *he* who has puppies."

"Sure. You go ahead. I'll be there in a sec." Claire watched the two of them run out of the cabin and up toward the main house. She'd grab a quick shower, change, and then go see what all the fuss was about.

She took a deep breath, let it out, and smiled. For the first time in longer than she could remember, she felt hopeful. Felt a little less scared. Felt like things might be okay.

For a brief moment, she closed her eyes and muttered a quick prayer of thanks. On the off chance God might still be listening to her.

It was good to be alive.

13

Michelle scanned the list of adoption registries on the screen. Her stomach churned, and she popped another antacid. There were so many websites she didn't know which to search first. But she had to start somewhere.

The doorbell jolted her from her quest. Ten a.m. on a Saturday. Typical. Her day off and she couldn't even be left alone. The door buzzed again, and Michelle crossed the living room to answer it.

"Who is it?"

"Who do you think? I left you a hundred messages. Let me in."

Michelle rolled her eyes at Belinda's breathless voice. She hadn't bothered to listen to the messages after the first two and didn't want to know whether she had any from Kevin. After their last disagreement, she didn't want to talk to him until she was good and ready. She pressed the entry button and opened her front door a couple of minutes later.

"About time. What are you doing?" Belinda pushed past her, her arms around a large brown box.

Michelle grinned, fished in the pocket of her jeans for a hair tie, and gathered her hair off her neck. "Not much. Antiquing again, Belinda? Don's going to have a fit."

"I know. Which is why you're keeping this stuff here until I can drive it to Connecticut." Belinda set the box down on a chair in the dining room and gave an impressive performance of someone on the verge of a heart attack. "This weighs a ton. I couldn't get a parking space out front, so I had to walk three blocks. But it was so worth it." She smiled like a kid in FAO Schwartz.

"You're an addict." Michelle went to the kitchen and opened two cans of diet soda, handing one to Belinda when she returned. "You need therapy, Lin."

"Therapy is for sissies." Belinda laughed, her sandals clicking on the hardwood floors as she walked through the apartment and sank onto the couch. She brushed dirt off her beige linen trousers. "Can you believe it's this hot in June already?"

"I know. I went for a run this morning and nearly died. I'll put the a/c on." She preferred fresh air, but Belinda liked to live in an icebox. Michelle walked back through the living room in time to see Belinda staring at the screen of her laptop. In her haste to answer the door she'd forgotten to close it down.

Wonderful.

She settled in an armchair across from her desk where Belinda sat, steeled herself against what was coming, and waited.

Belinda swiveled to meet her gaze, astonishment in her eyes. "You're looking?"

"Don't get too excited." Michelle set her can down on the glass coffee table and pulled her knees to her chest.

"You're kidding, right? I've been after you about this for years. Don't tell me don't get too excited!" Belinda scanned the screen again. "So? Why the sudden change of heart, Shel?"

Michelle groaned, choosing her words. "I wouldn't call it a change of heart." She stared out the window. "I got a phone call awhile ago. From the Department of Children and Families in Hartford."

"You what?" Belinda left the desk and plopped onto the couch, her shocked expression making Michelle slightly woozy. "When? Why didn't you tell me? What did they say?"

Michelle managed a small smile. "Actually the call came about a week or two after our trip to Connecticut. I must have angered the gods by going back there."

That, or the real God was punishing her big-time.

"And?" Concern filled Belinda's eyes. Michelle shrugged and mentally prepared herself for the conversation she'd been avoiding for days.

"Look, I don't want you to freak out, okay? I've dealt with it. It's over. DCF called to tell me that…she…she'd contacted them, filled out the application to request her non-identifying information."

"Are you serious?" Belinda's mouth formed a large red O. "So she knows who you are?"

Michelle glared, anger blindsiding her. For a minute she was pulled back in time, standing on the steps of her dorm building, facing the future alone. She'd called Belinda then, hysterical, but her friend never faltered. Rushed right over and told her everything would be okay until Michelle believed it. Blanketed her with words of comfort and offered wisdom where there was none. And somehow it had all worked out. Almost.

"Of course she doesn't know who I am. Do you think I'd let that happen? I'm not that stupid."

"Shelly…" Belinda's eyes narrowed. "What are you saying?"

"They needed my permission to give her the file." Michelle huffed out a sigh, her chest inexplicably tight. "I'm saying I refused. I told them I wouldn't allow them to release that information."

"You what?" Belinda's normally tanned face drained of color. "Shelly, what's wrong with you?"

"Nothing is wrong with me." Michelle studied her fingernails. The temptation to chew on them was strong, but she'd broken that habit years ago. Weariness dogged her. This was the last thing she needed. She lifted her chin and tossed Belinda a scowl. "Do you understand what this would do to me if this kind of a story ever came out?"

Belinda shook her head. "I don't think anyone would bat an eye. You made the only decision you could at the time. It's not uncommon."

Michelle sat on her hands to stop them from shaking. "I don't care. I'm not about to open my private life for the public to gawk at. It's bad enough with everything going on with Kevin. Besides that, I don't want anything to do with her. She'll get the point."

"Did you just say you don't want anything to do with her?" Belinda's stunned expression made her feelings clear.

"Are you hard of hearing?"

"Shel, this is…"

Michelle ground her teeth and counted to ten. She would not get into a shouting match over this. "No. Just stop. You are not going to sit there and give me some guilt trip. This is my decision, Belinda, my life. I've worked long and hard to get where I am. I'm well respected. People trust me. Kevin trusts me. If this came out, it would all be over."

"You're serious."

"Of course I'm serious," Michelle snapped. "Don't give me that look."

"But, Shelly, she's looking for you. She wants…"

"I don't care what she wants!" Michelle shot off the couch and paced the room. Sweat formed along her hairline despite the cool air blowing through the vents in the ceiling. "I made a choice, Lin. You're right. I did the best I could at the time. I've got a new life now, a career to consider. When I gave her up, I closed that door. Permanently. There is no point in opening it again. No point in rehashing the past. I'm not doing it."

"Then why are you looking at those registries?"

Michelle faced her friend, a slight twinge of regret twisting her heart at the disappointment in Belinda's eyes. "If you must know, I'm trying to see if anyone with her birthday left their name or any contact information. I want to make sure she's not still out there trying to track me down."

"Trying to track you down? Michelle, listen to yourself!" Belinda hissed. "You make her sound like some deranged psychopath. That's your daughter you're talking about."

"No!" Michelle shook her head, a beleaguered laugh sticking in her throat. Breathing was becoming a chore. "No, Lin. She's somebody else's daughter. Not mine." She stood in front of the window and watched the traffic creep by on the street below, and for the umpteenth time that week, questioned her sanity.

"I didn't realize you'd be so adamant about this." Belinda's tone softened, dripped with uncharacteristic melancholy. "Don't you think Darcie has the right to know she has a sister out there somewhere?"

"Absolutely not." Michelle whirled, pulling at her hair. She pressed her lips together and stared Belinda down. "She'd hold it against me for the rest of her life. Not that I think we'll ever have a good relationship anyway, but why add fuel to that fire?"

Belinda raised an eyebrow. Michelle looked down at her bare feet and willed her pulse back to normal. It was time for Belinda to leave. Perhaps there was an auction in the area she could send her off to.

"What about her, then, this girl? Don't you think she deserves some answers, to know where she came from and why she was given up?"

"No, I don't!" Michelle pinned her with a glare. Aggravation gave way to anger, tension tightening in her neck. "What gives her the right to start poking around, disrupting my life, damaging my reputation? Please. Don't start talking to me about rights. No. *She* doesn't need to know. Darcie doesn't need to know. Nobody *ever needs to know*, Belinda! Ever."

14

Claire wandered across the lawn, the little pup scampering along beside her. The summer sun kissed her face, and she pulled her hair up into a ponytail as she walked. "Hey, Chance. Come on this way." She snapped her fingers and coaxed him to follow her as she approached the fenced-in vegetable garden. She found it hard to believe it was almost the end of June.

Jessie crouched over the newly tilled soil, pulling weeds. The rich dark mulch permeated the air with promise of the crop to come. Tomatoes ripened on the vine, the large green blobs turning orange. Thick stalks bowed under the weight of the lush ripe fruit.

Claire inhaled the earthy smell and enjoyed it. She missed the long runs she and James used to take together. Missed staying up late, just talking. Missed him more than she could say. But she wasn't ready to think about that yet.

When she got all her strength back, she hoped to start running again, but for now she would enjoy long walks around the property. She used the time to think and figure out what her next step would be.

"Hi, Jessie. The garden looks great."

Jessie glanced up, and Claire caught her smile under the wide-brimmed straw hat she had on.

"One sec, honey." She patted down the soil with her gloved hand, rose, and brushed dirt off her jeans. "Looks like you found a friend there, Miss Claire." Her smile broadened as she stepped over rows of sod and let herself out of the wooden gate.

Claire picked up the puppy and gave the little chocolate Lab a gentle scratch on his tiny head. "We went for a walk down by the lake. I think when he's a bit older, he'll jump right in."

"Ayuh. Little scamp." Jessie pulled off her gardening gloves and smacked them together, sending dirt flying. The puppy gave a whine and opened its small mouth in a yawn. Jessie tickled him under the chin. "Come on up to the porch. I made some lemonade this morning."

Settled in what was now her favorite wicker rocker, Claire sipped the tart juice and watched Chance sleep in her lap. The runt of the litter, Jazz rejected the pup, she'd learned. At first, none of them thought the little guy would survive the night. But Jessie sat up with him, kept him warm, and tried to feed him through a baby bottle fished out from one of her cluttered kitchen cupboards.

The puppy lived, and they named him Chance.

And now he was Claire's. At least for as long as she was here, Rick was quick to add.

Claire leaned over and nuzzled the pup's soft fur. When she straightened, she found Jessie staring at her.

"What?" She grinned, pushing a stray strand of hair off her face. "Do I have something on my nose?"

"Nope." Jessie's mouth curled in a smile. "You mind if I ask you something?"

"Go ahead." Claire adjusted a blanket around the pup and rocked. The chair creaked back and forth. A gentle breeze filtered through the trees around the porch. Claire spied a lone sailboat out on the blue lake.

"What are you really doing here?"

The question jolted her, and she turned to look at Jessie in surprise.

The older woman smiled, her face creased in a tender expression of understanding. "I know you're on the mend, now, praise God. But people don't generally get themselves in a state like yours over nothing. Do you want to talk about it?"

Claire stopped rocking. She clenched her fingers over the wooden arms of the chair and stared down at the sleeping puppy in her lap. Silently she scooped him up and held him against her, seeking comfort from his warmth. Chance pushed against her, his pink tongue licking her arm.

"I don't mean to pry," Jessie said, looking contrite. "I was just curious."

Claire rested her head back against the cushion tied to the chair. Eventually she found her voice and faced Jessie. "It's okay. My...mother died. Last year. She had cancer. We thought she would beat it. But she didn't. And then, just after she died, I had a miscarriage. It was our first child."

"I'm so sorry," Jessie whispered. She reached out and placed her hand on Claire's arm, her eyes glistening.

"It's okay. I..." Claire faced the truth. "I went into a depression. Started drinking then. It helped. At least I thought it did. But I was really only trying to avoid dealing with everything I'd lost."

Jessie nodded. "I never lost a baby, but we lost our son. Jacob. He was ten. Went out on the lake one winter before it was fully frozen. We couldn't get to him in time."

"That's terrible." Claire swiped away her tears. "How did you get over it?"

She couldn't imagine it. A child you'd raised and watched grow, saw a future ahead of him, suddenly snatched away without warning. She couldn't imagine such a loss. Yet, at the same time, she could.

"You know, I don't know that we ever did." Jessie gave a half-smile and ran a hand over her gray head. "We focused on our daughter, Darcie's mother. Maybe too much. She always told us we were being overprotective. But she was three years older than Jacob, and she took it hard. By the time she graduated high school, she was pretty much doing her own thing."

"Does your daughter live around here?" Tiny needles pricked the back of Claire's neck. "You've never mentioned her."

Jessie's eyes hinted of sorrow. "No. I guess you could say we had a falling out. We haven't seen each other for a long time." She wound her hands in her lap and stared out across the lake.

"I'm sorry." Claire's heart melted at the sight of Jessie's tears. This wasn't the time to ask questions. "My mom and I used to argue, but most of the time we were pretty good friends." She coughed down the lump in her throat. Claire closed her eyes and stroked the puppy's head.

"Where's your husband, honey?" Jessie asked in a quiet voice.

Claire opened her eyes, surprised again. It was a logical question. After all Jessie had done for her, she had a right to know. "Back home in Connecticut. He didn't really understand what was going on with me. He thought we should just try for another baby. I couldn't. We're...separated. Another one of my many mistakes." She let go a ragged sigh and managed a grin. "You didn't bargain on such a sob story."

Jessie swatted at a fly and sipped lemonade. "We all have problems, Claire. But I don't believe there's any problem bigger than what God can fix."

Claire nodded. If she'd had it in her, she would have laughed. "My best friend, Melanie, would like you."

Jessie's face cracked with a smile and Claire returned it. Yes, Mel would like her very much.

"Would it be all right if I stayed here a bit longer, maybe until the end of summer?" She'd made her decision only a moment ago. "I'll write you another check."

Jessie's smile broadened, and she gave Claire's arm a squeeze. "Stay as long as you like, honey. The rate we're going you may be the only guest we have this season."

They sat in comfortable silence, rocking and drinking, and Jessie asked no more questions. Claire glanced at her watch. She'd be going into town tonight with Rick to their AA meeting. She'd gone for the first time last week and been pleasantly surprised. For what she imagined would be a mortifying experience, she'd come away feeling satisfied and humbled.

"Did you always live in Connecticut?" Jessie's sudden question pulled her away from her thoughts and Claire met searching brown eyes.

For weeks now, she hadn't focused on the real reason she'd come to Bethel. She'd been too busy fighting for her life. Now that she felt more in control, Claire knew she needed to decide how to proceed with her search. Or decide if she even wanted to. Maybe if she told Jessie why she was here, she could help unravel the mystery. Maybe, if her hunch was correct, Jessie was even a part of it.

"Yes, I've always lived there. I know I was born in Hartford. My parents adopted me when I was a newborn."

The older woman seemed to startle at her words. "That's interesting." Jessie sipped some more lemonade. "Do you know anything about your birth parents? You know they have these open adoptions nowadays. I saw something about it on *Oprah*."

Claire shrugged. "Mine was closed. I don't know anything, and I can't get my non-identifying information."

"Why is that?"

"My birth mother has to give the DCF permission. She refused."

Jessie sat in silence, a faraway look taking over her features. Claire studied her carefully and made up her mind. "Actually, I think that my birth mother came from Bethel. That's really why I came here. I want to find her."

"Really?" Jessie's eyes seemed too bright all of a sudden. "But you were born in Hartford."

"Yes. I may as well tell you. I don't know if it's a coincidence, but…" Claire felt her cheeks grow warm in the moment that could redefine her life. "I kind of went snooping through my dad's files one day and found the name *Kelly* scribbled on a piece of paper. And then I found a brochure for Tara's Place. That's why I thought my parents might have come here. When I saw your last name was Kelly, I wondered if there was a connection. I'm not sure what to make of it all." There. It was done. Claire breathed a sigh of relief, but the ashen look on Jessie's face alarmed her.

"Did you ask your father about it?"

"I did." Claire nodded, frustration bumping her again. "He wasn't very cooperative. I'm pretty sure he's keeping something hidden."

Jessie pushed herself out of her chair and walked to a potted rose near the porch railing. Spring being warmer than usual this year it had already begun to bloom in a bright display of pink buds. Claire watched Jessie pick off the deadheads and toss them far onto the lawn below.

"When were you born, Claire?"

Claire gave her the date. She was barely able to stand not knowing what Jessie was thinking.

For a long moment Jessie said nothing, just picked and threw. "Your birthday is next month."

"Yes." Claire needed to break the silence. "Do you...does any of this make sense to you?"

Jessie still remained silent. A strange sense of trepidation tickled Claire's spine. The feeling matched what she'd felt the first time she met Darcie. It was almost as though she kept stepping in the Twilight Zone.

If this kept up ,she'd start drinking again.

Jessie finally turned and met Claire's gaze, her face flushed, her eyes brighter than they had been a minute ago. "I don't believe in coincidences." She smiled, then looked down at her feet, clad in well-worn soft brown mules. "Let me think on this a bit."

Claire stared. "Do you know something? Something about my birth, Jessie? You have to tell me."

Jessie lifted a hand. "Patience, child." She gave Claire a long look and a brief smile. "I...uh...need to get inside. Better go check on that chicken if we're going to eat in time for you to make your meeting." Jessie moved past her and stopped to take Claire's empty glass from her. She rubbed the sleeping puppy's head. "Don't forget to feed that sweet thing."

As Jessie walked into the house, Rick ambled up the porch stairs. "Hey. Something smells good." He nodded toward her, and Claire raised a hand in greeting. The delicious scents from the kitchen had made their way out to the porch. Claire's stomach rumbled with anticipation.

"Roast chicken. And I think I saw an apple pie."

"Awesome. I'm always on the lookout for free food." He gave her a wink and lowered himself into the rocker Jessie had vacated. "You all right? You look a little spooked."

"I don't know." Claire looked down at the floorboards. Jessie did know something, she was sure of it. "I guess so."

"Hmm." Rick reached over and scratched the pup's head. "How's our Chance today?"

"He's worn himself out." Claire smoothed down the shiny black fur. "But he slept through last night. Didn't wake up until five."

Rick chuckled and stretched his long arms over his head. "Must be like having a baby."

An awful lump clogged her throat and took her breath away. He couldn't have known, but his words pricked her heart just the same.

He noticed. "What's wrong?"

Claire sighed, weary of recounting the story, but she wanted him to know. "You hit a nerve." She shrugged at his blank expression. "I just got through telling Jessie without breaking into hysterics so I may as well tell you." She blinked and waited for the tears to come. But strangely enough, they didn't. So she began again and finished with, "It was easier to keep drinking than quit."

Rick gave a muted groan. "I'm so sorry."

"You and the rest of the world."

He leaned over his knees and picked at a small hole in the faded denim of his jeans. Claire could hear Jessie banging around in the kitchen. Mac was probably still plastering one of the upstairs guestrooms. They'd accepted a few of their regular guests, but the place wasn't ready for full occupancy.

A breeze filtered up through the trees and cooled her face. Jackson waved to her from the swing-set down by the lake as Darcie pushed him high into the air. Claire smiled and waved back.

At first she'd tried to avoid the little boy. But his thousand-watt smile and mischievous eyes won her over, and spending time with him was something she now enjoyed doing. She was even thinking about offering to watch him this weekend to give Darcie a break. Claire didn't want to count on it, but she thought she was slowly beginning to heal.

"I had a kid once."

Rick's low voice made her turn in his direction and stare in surprise. "You were married?" Claire realized she knew very little about the man she credited for saving her life.

His eyes took on a sheen that tugged at Claire's heart. "No, not married. It was a long time ago. I don't know...ah." He pushed himself to his feet. "I don't want to talk about it."

"Okay." She wouldn't pursue it. Not today at least.

He leaned back against the white wooden railing, searching her face, as though unsure of what to say. "I was in town earlier."

"So? You want a prize?" Claire grinned as he shook a fist at her. They'd somehow fallen into an easy camaraderie. Same as she and Darcie had. Claire always considered herself a bit of a loner, Melanie being the only friend she really confided in. Since coming to Bethel, she'd discovered she actually enjoyed being nice.

"No, Miss Smarty Pants." He tossed her his trademark scowl. "Sometimes

I think you were easier to handle drunk. You didn't have as much to say." He chuckled as she stuck her tongue out, then he grew serious again. "Listen, I think you should know...some guy was asking about you. I overheard him talking to the owner of the art gallery where I show my work. He was asking him if he knew you, if you'd been into his shop."

Claire's heart sank. She hadn't contacted home since the first week here. And then all she'd gotten was Dad's answering machine. She'd left a brief message, letting him know she'd arrived in Bethel and that everything was fine. She planned on writing or calling again—soon. Soon was long gone. She hadn't called James either.

"Are you in some kind of trouble, Claire?" Worry niggled Rick's eyebrows, and he pulled at his beard.

Claire gave a short laugh but felt her throat constrict. "No, nothing like that. My family doesn't know where I am, though. They know I'm in Maine, but not exactly where." Guilt tightened its hold. She really should have made more effort to get in touch with them. But part of her had revolted against the life she'd left behind, and somehow she couldn't face their questions and concern.

"Claire! You've been here all this time and you haven't called home?"

She cringed under his look of admonishment. "I called my father once and left a message, told him I was okay. I should have tried again. But I've been a little out of commission if you recall. You didn't say anything to the man, did you?"

"Of course not. Who do you think it was? Your husband?"

"I doubt James cares where I am." Claire kicked her shoes together. "I'm a lost cause, you see."

Rick leaned forward. "You are not a lost cause, Claire Ferguson. You were put on this earth for a reason, like the rest of us. It doesn't matter whether you know what it is yet. You're going to find out."

"You sound so sure." She allowed a smile to lift her mouth.

He nodded. "I am sure. You've got a purpose here. You just got a little lost along the way. But you're going to be all right. And if your husband doesn't see what he's got in you, then he doesn't deserve you."

Rick put his back to Claire and she heard him muttering under his breath. A grin slid across her mouth. "Wow. That was quite a speech. Does this mean you forgive me for killing your swans?"

He swiveled on the heel of his boot and flashed an easy grin. "Maybe." He raised his arms and let them fall to his sides. "I see something in you, Claire. I don't get it, but something makes me want to help you. I know I'm a bit rough around the edges sometimes, but I do mean well."

"I know you do. I'm glad you took a chance on me." Claire laced her hands together and watched his face change.

"Somebody had to." He slid into the rocker again. "So, what are your plans? Seems like you've made yourself at home here now. You seem to get on well with Mac and Jessie, and Darcie likes you a lot."

"She's fun to be with." Claire gazed across the lawn and watched Darcie lift Jackson from the swing and pull him into a bear hug. Their happy laughter filtered upward on the wind.

Everybody had a story.

If only she knew whether hers would have a happy ending.

"I'm not sure how to go home, to be honest," she admitted. "Like I said, my husband and I have been at each other's throats. I thought a break was what we needed, but I'm not exactly sure where we stand now. And my dad and I had a huge fight before I left. I think he's probably still mad."

"What about? Did you steal his car?" Rick teased.

Claire laughed at his expression. "No, that's mine. I stole his wine, though. He probably hasn't noticed yet." She stretched her arms out in front of her and tilted her head. "We argued over my reason for coming here." She watched interest light his eyes and decided to tell him. "I was adopted. I've never really wanted to search for my birth family, but since…the miscarriage…I want to know."

"And your dad didn't want you to search?"

Claire nodded. "He was pretty adamant about it. Told me I shouldn't even consider it. But I did."

"So is that why you're in Bethel? To find your birth mother?"

"Yes. I have a feeling she was from around here. My dad at least intimated that much. I wasn't able to get my adoption papers, of course, or my non-identifying information, but I came across some things that led me here. I wanted to get away and figured this was worth a shot."

Rick eyed her in silence. Claire stared back at him, trying to read him.

"So what have you found?"

Claire hesitated again. Rick really didn't need to be involved. And if she shared her suspicions about Mac and Jessie, she wasn't quite sure what he'd do. "Nothing yet. Maybe I should have handled it differently with my father. I think he's afraid that if I do find her, she won't want to know me. Or she will."

"I'd say your dad probably doesn't want to lose you." Rick studied his scuffed boots. "Fear can make a man do stupid things."

Claire watched his jaw working and felt his sadness. She wondered what caused it. "I guess I should call him. He's probably hired a private investigator. I don't want him to worry."

Rick slapped his knees, shot her a grin, and stood. "Good idea. No father should have to spend his nights worrying about his little girl. Even if she is a brat."

She smiled at his teasing. Rick Matthews didn't sugarcoat anything and she respected that. Over the past little while, he'd come to mean a lot to her. If he hadn't confronted her a few weeks ago, Claire feared she might have done the unthinkable.

Claire got to her feet carefully, but Chance woke. He gave a whimper and regarded her with big puppy eyes. She crossed the floor to where Rick stood.

"Here, take him while I go get his supper ready. He probably needs to pee."

On cue, Chance did. Claire held him in midair and fortunately he missed her legs, but Rick's boots were in the direct line of fire.

Rick groaned. "Thanks, kid. Do I have *sucker* written across my forehead or what?" He took the puppy from her and held the little black nose up to his. "You pee on the grass, my friend. Not on my boots." He strode toward the steps, grumbling.

On impulse, Claire reached for his arm. He stopped midstride and turned to face her, surprise inching into his eyes. Claire smiled, got on tiptoe, and placed a kiss on his cheek. His eyebrows shot up a mile, and she laughed at his astonished expression. "Thanks. For everything."

Rick's face reddened, but she caught the beginning of a smile underneath the bushy beard. "You don't need to thank me, Claire," he answered gruffly, his dark eyes locking with hers. "Thank God."

15

At the end of the week, Claire returned to her cabin from her morning walk with Chance, made sure he had water in his bowl, and watched him lap. She was amazed how quickly the little dog was growing. She hated the thought of leaving him once she went home. Whenever that would be.

After he finished drinking, Claire put Chance into the dog crate Rick found at a yard sale and went into the kitchen. He began to whine at once. "Just go to sleep." She could do with another pot of coffee. She reached for the pot and her hand froze in mid-air at the sounds coming from her bedroom.

Somebody was in the cabin.

"Hello?" Claire crossed the kitchen and stepped into the hall. Fear gripped her and she glanced back at the front door, ready to make a run for it.

"It's just me!" Darcie's shout sent relief flooding through her. Claire entered the bedroom and found her new friend standing on a chair in her closet. Darcie turned and held up a long dark blue cable-knit sweater-dress that Claire had yet to wear. The tags were still on it. "This is so gorgeous. It's cashmere, right? But when would you wear something like this out here?"

Claire laughed and gave a shrug. "You never know. Maybe we'll convince Rick to have a show."

"I doubt it." Darcie snorted and hung the dress back on the rail. "Oh, I love this leather jacket. We're the same size, you know."

"No kidding." Claire rolled her eyes and flopped onto the soft bed. It had been awhile since she'd even thought about her wardrobe or gone shopping to needlessly add to it. Life in Bethel was blissfully uncomplicated.

The overhead fan whirred and sent a cooling breeze around the room. "What are you doing in my closet?"

"Grandma sent me over to change the light bulbs." Darcie buried her face in the clothes again and came up with a squeal. "I *love* these boots!"

Claire waved a hand and groaned at the sight of the high heels. "I don't know what I was thinking bringing those out here. You can have them if you want. I never really liked them anyway. Take the dress too."

"Really?" Darcie's eyes widened.

Claire nodded. "Sure. You can sell them on EBay for all I care."

"Oh, I wouldn't do that." Darcie jumped from her chair and flounced around the bedroom, pretending to waltz. Her face lit in an impish grin. "I'll find a hot date and get him to take me out to dinner someplace fancy."

"Good luck with that. Like you said, we're in Bethel." Claire yawned. She hadn't slept well last night. Thoughts of James infiltrated her sleep. The last time she'd driven into town she took her laptop with her and checked email at the café. He'd written her several messages, apologizing, asking if they could talk. She'd responded with a brief note telling him she was fine and that was about it. There was so much more she wanted to say now.

"Got any designer stuff in here I can steal?" Darcie skipped back to the closet.

Claire laughed and threw a pillow in her direction. Despite her country-girl looks, Darcie enjoyed fashion. She was forever poring over issues of *Vogue* and *People* magazines. If her life had been different, she'd probably be running one of them. "Where's Jackson?"

"Grandpa took him into town. Hey, these are awesome shoes…"

Claire groaned at the sight of the pointy Jimmy Choos she hadn't worn in months. She pushed herself off the bed. "Do you want coffee?" She didn't wait for Darcie's reply but escaped to the kitchen before having to face another reminder of her past.

By the time Darcie ventured out to the living room, the coffee was made. Claire was settled on the couch munching on Jessie's oatmeal cookies.

"Speaking of hot dates, please tell me this is your brother." Darcie flopped down beside her and waved a silver-framed photograph in Claire's face.

Claire took the picture and ran a light finger across the glass. "I don't have a brother." A smile tugged at her lips.

Darcie slapped her forehead, her jaw dropping. "If that fine face is your husband, then what are you doing up here in Maine without him?"

"It's complicated." Claire put down the photo of James and poured two mugs of coffee, handing one to Darcie. "Don't look at me like that."

Darcie stretched out her long bare legs and picked at the frayed ends of the denim shorts she wore. "Grandma told me your mom died. And about your miscarriage. I'm sorry."

"Thanks." Claire sipped, noting the way Darcie's eyes misted over. She supposed anyone with kids would react the same way. "Everything changed after we lost the baby. I might have been able to handle my mom's death better if it hadn't happened. I blamed myself. Things went downhill from there. I was pretty trashed when I got here. I guess I'm lucky I survived at all."

"But you did. I'm sure it wasn't your fault, Claire. Sometimes these things just happen. You shouldn't take on that kind of guilt." Darcie squeezed Claire's arm and gave a sympathetic smile.

Claire nodded, but the dull ache remained. She doubted it would ever go away completely. "I guess you're right. Coming here was good for me. Helped me put things in perspective. I was a mess for a long time. I didn't know what I wanted. I knew I had to get out of Connecticut, though. James and I kind of reached the end of the road. I'm still not sure where we go from here."

"You're going to have to face him at some point, you know." Darcie bit into a cookie and set her steady gaze on Claire. "I don't know what all went on between you, but I think you should at least try to work it out."

Claire inhaled and clenched her fingers around the warm mug. Darcie was right. She needed to talk to James. She had to face the past in order to move on to the future. "How'd you get so smart?"

Darcie screwed up her nose. "I'm not so smart. I've just learned things the hard way."

"I know what you mean." Claire looked over at the dog crate. Chance was curled up on the soft sheepskin, sound asleep. "I'll think about giving James a call."

"*He* doesn't have a brother does he?" Mischief shone from her friend's eyes.

Claire smiled. "He's got two. Actually his younger brother might find you interesting. Brian's going into medicine, studying at Princeton."

"Ooo, a doctor. Lovely." Darcie munched another cookie and wiggled her toes. Bright cotton candy colored polish sparkled under the overhead light. Claire wondered how many shades of pink she owned. "Maybe if I find myself a suitable husband my dear mother will start talking to me again."

Claire reached for anther cookie and raised an eyebrow. "Your mom doesn't talk to you?" Or Mac and Jessie either, apparently.

"Nope. Hasn't in years." Darcie gazed across the room with a hint of pain. "It's a long story."

"I love long stories." Claire smiled. "I don't have anywhere to go. If you want to talk about it."

Darcie grinned and swiveled on the couch, tucking her colt-like legs under her. "It's not a pretty one."

"I figured." Claire poked her on the arm and gave a knowing smile. Darcie's eyes were the exact shape of her own. It was the weirdest thing. "Speak. I command you."

"Yes, O Queen and giver of great clothes." Darcie's laughter petered out. "Well, let's see. My parents divorced when I was ten. My dad moved to the west coast. My mother...she's very career driven. Into politics and all that stuff. She worked a lot, and I started getting into trouble. By the time I was thirteen, I'd been kicked out of three schools."

"And your mother didn't understand your behavior?" Claire feigned shock.

"Hardly. Boarding school seemed to be the appropriate answer. My dad had remarried, and they just had a kid. His new wife didn't want a problem teenager on her hands. So off I went to the snottiest prep school they could afford. I got kicked out of that one too. I spent the summers with my mother, but we fought like banshees whenever we were together. When September rolled around, no way was I going back to another school, so I hit the streets."

"You ran away? How old were you?" Claire tried to imagine what Darcie might have experienced. She'd read stories like this, and none were good.

"Sixteen, almost seventeen by then." Darcie blew out a breath. "I did some awful things. Whatever they tell you in the media about runaways and life on the streets, it's worse. I don't know how I made it through, honestly. I don't remember a lot of what happened during that time. It's probably better that way."

"Why didn't you just come here, to your grandparents?"

Darcie shrugged, a sad smile lifting the corners of her mouth. "I didn't really know them. We never visited. They never called. I always got a birthday card, and money at Christmas, but I wasn't even sure where they lived. My mom and them still don't really speak. I have no idea why. Nobody will talk about it."

"Poor Jessie," Claire mused, remembering the sad look in the older woman's eyes when she'd talked about her daughter. "So how did you end up here?"

"When I found out I was pregnant, I knew I didn't have many options. My dad would have keeled over from the shock, and my mom...well, I wasn't about to find out what she would do. So I figured I'd give my grandparents a shot. I looked them up, blubbered on for about a half hour, and next thing I knew, they'd wired me money for bus fare to Bethel."

"What happened with your mother? Surely they must have called her."

Darcie glared into the empty fireplace. "They did. She drove up a few days after I got here. Told me what a loser I was, how ashamed she was of me for getting pregnant. There was quite a scene. Basically she told her parents to go to...uh, you-know-where...and take me with them."

"She did not." Claire refused to believe any mother would treat her daughter that way.

But Darcie nodded, her face impassive. "She did. It was pretty bad. I've never seen Grandma so upset." Tears stood in her eyes. "My mother is a very bitter woman. Trouble is, I have no idea why. Grandpa and Grandma doted on her when she was growing up, so they tell me. I know things with my dad and her weren't great when they were together, but still…"

"Jessie told me about your mom's brother dying when he was little. Maybe your mother has some issues with that," Claire suggested. "People have different ways of dealing with tragedy."

"Maybe. But that really has nothing to do with how she treated me." Darcie took the box of tissues Claire offered and blew her nose. "I don't get how you could just turn your back on your own kid like that, you know? Now that I'm a mother, I know there's nothing I wouldn't do for Jackson. He could murder a hundred people in cold blood and I'd still love him."

Claire smiled at the dramatic analogy. "I've wondered that too. How a mother could forget her own child. It's something I've thought a lot about lately. I was adopted."

"Really?" Darcie brightened at the change in topic. "Did you just find out?"

"No. I always knew. Can't remember not knowing. But I've only recently decided to search. I need to know where I came from. I want to make sure there wasn't some genetic abnormality I'm carrying that caused my miscarriage."

But that wasn't her only reason for searching now. The more Claire thought about her adoption, the more questions she had. Since considering it again, a new feeling sparked within, something she hadn't felt before—a fierce longing to know the woman who gave birth to her. She could no longer deny it. "I want to know who gave me life. I want to know why she didn't keep me. I just want the truth."

"Wow." Darcie gave a long whistle. "Is that why you're in Maine? Do you think she was from around here?"

"Might have been." Chance gave a yip and Claire went to retrieve him. She sat down again, scratched his little head, and took a moment to gather her thoughts. She wouldn't tell Darcie the whole story. She wasn't sure of anything yet, and there was no point in speculating.

"I'll help you if you want. Whatever you need me to do."

"Thanks." Claire smiled, not in the least bit surprised. "But this is one journey I think I have to make alone."

Darcie fell silent, gazing at Claire through thoughtful eyes. "As much as I complain about my mother and how nasty she is, I can't imagine not knowing where I came from. Did you have an awful life?"

"No, not at all." Claire couldn't help laughing at Darcie's forlorn expression. "Quite the opposite. My parents loved me very much. I sort of feel guilty for searching. Like I'm betraying them."

Darcie shook her head. "You shouldn't. Everyone deserves to know the truth about who they are."

"I'm beginning to believe that," Claire said quietly, sorrow infringing on her thoughts again. "But as much as I want to find her, I don't think it will change who I am. Who I used to be, and the person I'm becoming. Being here has helped me see that."

"How so?"

"I guess everything I went through, dealing with losing my mom, the miscarriage, my marriage falling apart, then getting through my addictions— it's all made me stronger somehow. In a weird way I think it was meant to be."

"God has a way of bringing it all together when we least expect it." Darcie's smile was warm, and her eyes shone with sincerity.

The peaceful look on Darcie's pretty face was something Claire didn't understand. Maybe it wasn't so much that she didn't understand. Maybe it was more that she was afraid to. Mac and Jessie, even Rick, talked the same way. Their faith was like a beacon shining bright on a fog-filled night. Something to come home to.

Claire was beginning to long for a safe harbor.

"Why don't you come to church with us on Sunday?" It was almost eerie the way Darcie could read her mind.

Claire rolled her eyes at the invitation. "Thanks, but I don't do so well in churches. Too many boring hymns and hypocrites for my liking."

Darcie's laughter pealed around the room. "Oh, our church isn't like that. Trust me. Come see for yourself. I dare you." Challenge sparked from her eyes and laced her tone.

"You dare me, huh?" Claire wrinkled her nose but gave in to a grin. "All right, Darcie Hart. Maybe I will."

16

"Ms. Hart? You have a call on line one."

Michelle cursed under her breath at the interruption. She scratched out the last sentence she'd written, pushed the flashing button on the telephone keypad, and glared at the stack of notes on her desk. "Who is it, Sharlene? I told you I didn't want to be disturbed. Senator Harrison needs this speech as soon as possible."

Silence. Were the phones on the blink again? Michelle tapped her fingernails on the mahogany desk and made a mental note to tell Sharlene to book her for a manicure. She could do with a whole day at the spa but didn't have time for that. "Sharlene, are you there? I don't have all day. Who is it?"

"Um, Ms. Hart? She says she's your…mother."

Michelle felt all air leave her chest. After how many years? She sat back against her leather chair and closed her eyes. Impossible. She wouldn't call here. Unless…

"Put her through." Michelle's heart raced, but she took slow, controlled breaths. She could handle this. "Hello?"

"Shelly, is that you?"

She was rendered speechless at the sound of her mother's voice. Memories and thoughts of home slammed her. She inhaled and scowled at the painting on the wall. The familiar scene served as her only reminder of the place she'd left so long ago. Left and banished from her mind and heart.

The artist had captured the lake at sunrise, mist rising from the water. If she allowed it, the memory of that morning would return in an instant.

She should have packed it away with all the others—the painting and the memory.

"Shelly?"

"Of course it's me. Is Dad okay?" A pause on the other end gave Michelle a chance to breathe and get her rambling thoughts under control.

"Yes. He's fine."

"And…you…you're fine?"

"I'm doing okay." Mom's soft voice cracked and Michelle blinked, her pulse picking up speed again. If they were both in good health, then it had to be something else.

"Darcie? Is she…?" Michelle couldn't voice her thoughts. Had it really been five years since her parents had taken on that wild child? Five years since Michelle had spoken to any of them?

Having to take a few weeks off work to deal with Darcie's infraction back then had almost cost her her job. Michelle made her position clear—she'd send money, but she wanted out of the picture. Darcie was on a path bound for destruction at her own choosing. The pregnancy was the last straw. She washed her hands of her daughter and let her parents take over.

"Darcie and Jackson are fine too. This isn't about them." Her mother spoke quietly, quickly, as though she didn't want to be overheard. "I'm sorry—I didn't want to upset you by calling—but I…Michelle, I need to ask you something."

"Okay." She almost let out a sigh of relief. They probably needed money. Tara's Place had been falling apart the last time she'd seen it. Michelle grabbed the cordless phone and pushed herself out of her chair. She took slow steps across the room and stood at the long window.

Madison Avenue teemed with activity, people coming and going, jostling for space on the crowded sidewalks. The tall trees spread out long branches thick with green leaves, providing shade under the blistering heat of a New York summer. "Can you hurry it up, Mother? I'm busy."

"Michelle, what happened to the baby?"

The question roared in her ears even though her mother's trembling voice barely cleared a whisper. Nausea rose in her throat. Michelle stumbled back to the desk and reached blindly for her chair.

It was a conspiracy.

God and the rest of the world were clearly out to get her.

"Michelle? Did you hear me?"

"I heard you." The words raked her throat. She rested her elbows on the desk and leaned heavily into the receiver.

Time rewound in slow motion. For a moment she was nineteen again—scared and pregnant, with no place to go. No place to run and hide, and everyone she loved turned against her.

She pursed her lips together. "You want to talk about this now, Mother, after how many years? What's wrong? The guilt finally got to you?"

"Shelly, please…"

"No, Mother. You please…please *stop*. I don't know what game you're playing, but I don't want to be a part of it. I'm hanging up now."

"Shelly, wait! Tell me, I beg you. Did you…did you have an abortion?"

Michelle opened her eyes and checked again that the door to her office was closed. She trusted Sharlene not to be listening on the other end, but there were other people around that she didn't trust.

Her heart thudded against her chest, and she made a fist with her free hand, opening and closing it. "No. I didn't have an abortion. I couldn't go through with it. After I left Bethel, I went to stay with a friend's family in Connecticut, and I gave the baby up for adoption."

Had she ever said those words out loud, to anybody?

"Do you know…did they tell you if you had a boy or girl?"

"It was a girl." Michelle gulped air and blinked, tears clinging to her lashes.

Do you want to hold her, Miss Kelly?

No. Take her away…

Her mother was torturing her, and probably on purpose.

"Where?" Anxiety rang through her mother's tone. "Where did you have the baby?"

Michelle tapped her pen against the desk in sporadic rhythm. "Some hospital in Hartford. I don't remember the name of it. What's this about? Why the—why are you asking me these questions?"

"When was she born, Shelly?"

Twenty-seven years ago next week. Michelle squeezed her eyes shut. "I don't remember. July something. It was hot."

"Try. It's important."

"No!" Michelle shot out of her chair and marched across the room, locking the door. "Are you out of your mind? Why would you do this to me?" Her voice rose to a shriek and she put a hand to her mouth. *Please let Sharlene have already gone for lunch.*

"I'm not trying to hurt you." Mom was crying. "But there's…there's a chance…I think she might be here, Michelle."

"Who? What are you talking about?" Michelle sank into her chair again and kicked off her black high-heels. Her racing heart forced her to take extra breaths. She'd give a lot of money for a cigarette right now, and she hadn't smoked in years.

"Your daughter. I think she's looking for you."

Michelle leaned over her knees. *No, no, no.* She had to make this go away. Had to make this day, this hour, this moment, disappear.

"It was a closed adoption. No names were recorded on the papers I signed. There's no way she'd ever be able to find me even if she wanted to." It sounded good in theory, but Michelle was beginning to suspect it was not the truth.

"Maybe so, Shelly, but I think she's here anyway."

"Where? In Bethel? You're not making any sense, Mother."

"She's staying here, at Tara's Place."

"What?" Michelle hissed. Disbelief pounded her. This was not happening. Could the DCF have given out her information without her permission? It was the only answer that made any sense. "Dear God, am I hearing this? She's staying with you? And you think she's looking for *me*? Mother!"

"Calm down. She doesn't know much. She's pretty sure you came from Bethel. And she thinks...well, I guess the name *Kelly* was written down by someone, maybe her father, at the time of the adoption. She's already asked me if I thought there was a connection."

Her heart plummeted, and Michelle paused to gather her raging thoughts. "What did you tell her?"

"Nothing. I-I wasn't sure what had happened. But now..."

Michelle gripped the back of her neck. This was *not* happening. "Mother, be rational." She talked as much to herself. "I'm sure I wasn't the only girl from Bethel to give birth that month. I think it's highly unlikely that this person is my...her."

"I don't know, Shelly. I had a feeling about her from the minute I laid eyes on her. She looks more like you than Darcie does."

Michelle pressed a hand to her forehead. She was going to throw up. She walked across the room to the bar on the far side and poured a glass of water. If she didn't have a meeting to get to, she'd have opted for something a lot stronger.

God, please, no. Not this.

Not now.

Not ever.

"What should I do, Shelly?"

"What should you do?" Michelle's hands began to tremble. She bit back the only reply she could think of, returned to her desk, and put down the glass. Perspiration soaked into her blouse. There was no way to deal with this. Only one answer to give.

The past was signed, sealed, and...delivered.

Across the room, an extravagant floral arrangement sat on a wooden cabinet. The heady scent of white roses and Stargazer lilies permeated the air. Kevin's flagrant attempts to convince her of his true feelings were wearing her down. *If he were to get wind of this...*

Michelle made a fist and watched her knuckles turn white. "If you ever loved me at all, Mother, then forget all about this conversation. Get rid of the girl, whoever she is, and let's not talk about this again. Ever. Please."

Michelle heard her mother's reticent sigh but refused to acknowledge it.

"She has a right to know where she came from."

The almost whispered words jarred her. Was the woman deluded? *Maybe she has Alzheimer's.*

"No, she doesn't!" This would be the catalyst to finally drive her insane. Michelle glanced at the clock on her computer screen. She had a meeting in twenty minutes and she hadn't finished the speech. "Look, whether you think this girl is the child I gave up for adoption or not, you need to leave it alone. I *gave her up*, Mother. I want nothing to do with her. Do you understand me?"

"But...she could be my granddaughter."

"No. She *could have been* your granddaughter. You and Dad made your position on the matter perfectly clear. Or have you conveniently forgotten that? You can't go back and fix the past. *Please*, don't do this. Don't tell her anything. I need your word on that. If this got out..."

"Is that the problem?" Her mother's voice turned cold. "You're worried about what people will think? How it would affect your career?"

"Yes, I am." Old bitterness rose around her and wrapped Michelle in the thick cords she believed she'd cut loose from years ago. "Sound familiar?"

The silence that ensued allowed unwanted memories to flood back. Memories she'd thought she had so carefully locked away and forgotten. Cruel words, shouted through the dead of night, broken promises, and a legacy of rebellion.

"She's gone through a lot," her mother said quietly. "I think it would mean the world to her if she could just talk to you."

"We've all *gone through a lot*, Mother. The answer is no." Michelle made a big dark X on her legal pad, scratching the paper so hard she made a hole. "I have a meeting to get to."

"We made mistakes, Shelly. Surely you can give me this one thing. A chance to put things right."

"I don't believe in second chances." She had to get off the phone. Another minute and she'd lose it. "I don't suppose you'll honor my wishes and keep your mouth shut. But don't expect me to attend the welcome home party. She's dead to me. You got that, Mother? Dead."

17

After a lengthily phone conversation with her father, Claire promised she'd drive down to Connecticut and spend her birthday with him. She wasn't sure she was ready to stay for good, but she knew she couldn't stay away forever.

She arrived late the night before her birthday, and the next day he took her to her favorite restaurant for lunch. Then they took a walk through the park.

"Are you really all right?" Dad took her arm and led her to a nearby bench.

Claire rubbed her palms over her jeans, met his anxious gaze, and nodded. "I am."

His eyes grew brighter almost at once.

Claire smiled at the relief she saw flooding over him. "I'm not drinking, and I've stopped taking the pills. I wasn't sure I could do it at first. But I've been going to AA and, with any luck and a lot of prayer, I'll stay on track. I guess I let it all get control of me, Dad. I'm sorry." She pushed up the sleeves of her cardigan, the sun warm.

"Now, Claire." He took her hand in his, patting it like he used to when she was little. "You've been through so much, honey. It's only natural that you would react the way you did."

"No." Claire grinned. "Getting high on pills and alcohol to avoid pain isn't natural, Dad. It's stupid. I'm lucky I didn't kill myself."

"I'm grateful you were able to get help when you did. These people you're staying with up in Maine, can we repay them somehow? Do they need anything?"

"You mean, can you write them a big check? No." Laughter caught in her throat, but a wave of sorrow chased it away. "They wouldn't take it. I think they took on saving me like some mission from God. They're very religious in a nonreligious kind of way. I mean, they don't bash you over the head with the Bible or anything, but you feel good when you're around them."

"Oh, boy." Dad groaned and rubbed his hands down his face. "You're not going to turn into one of those holy-roller types are you, sweetheart?"

"You never know." She shot him a wink. "I guess I'm keeping an open mind. Okay?"

"As long as you're healthy and happy, you can become a Tibetan monk for all I care." His laughter told her he teased, but Claire knew he'd never had much of a faith.

"I think everyone needs something to believe in, Dad." She hesitated, hoping she wouldn't upset him.

Claire held her breath as Dad leaned back against the bench, put his hands behind his head and set an amused gaze on her. "How's that?"

"Well, I felt guilty for a long time about the baby, my marriage. But maybe I was too hard on myself. I'm not so sure God deals in guilt. If anything, I think He deals in forgiveness."

At least that's what Rick kept telling her. But for all his talk, Rick Matthews had his secrets. Claire knew he harbored deep emotion over something in his past and still battled his own pain. Maybe he'd received forgiveness from his Maker, but she doubted he'd tried giving out much of it to himself.

Dad looked thoughtful. "Maybe so, Claire." He pinned her with an enquiring gaze. "So, how is that husband of yours?"

Claire balled her fists and took a breath. "I'm not sure. We haven't talked much since I left. A couple of emails here and there."

"I hope you're going to work things out." Dad raised a bushy eyebrow.

Claire snorted. "Since when are you on his side?"

"He's a good man. He loves you very much."

Claire folded her arms and surveyed her surroundings. She and James had taken many walks through this park. Just across the pond, under the weeping willow, he'd dropped to one knee, pulled out a black velvet box, and proposed. It had been the happiest day of her life.

"I'm going to go see him. I don't know what will come of it, I'm not sure I'm ready to come back here. I'd like to spend the rest of the summer in Maine. But we do need to talk."

"Good. I hope it goes well. I only want the best for you, sweetheart."

"I know." Claire smiled. White clouds floated across the clear blue sky. She waited for the tension that would stiffen her neck and shoulders at the thought of being back here for good. But it didn't come.

"I hope, at the end of the summer, you'll come back home. You belong here, honey, with us." He put an arm around her shoulder, pulling her in tight. "Claire, I need to apologize. For two things—first of all, I shouldn't have sprung the news about Eleanor on you like I did. She and I talked, and we're not going to rush into anything. She's got her own place in town and we're…dating. So, when you're ready, we'd like to get together with you. But only when you're ready."

"Oh, Dad." Claire shook her head. She was tired of ruining people's lives. "I probably said some stupid things. It was a shock, yes. But if you're happy, that's all I care about. Honest. Make some plans for the fall. I'll look forward to meeting her. And I'm sorry for acting like a brat."

"Nonsense." Dad planted a kiss on her forehead, removed his arm, and swiveled so he was directly facing her. "Now, the other thing."

"You want another case of wine?"

Dad chuckled and shook his head. "I'll let that one slide. This time. But listen…"

Claire swallowed down nerves at the serious expression he took on. His eyes came to rest on the locket around her neck and a brief smile touched his lips. Claire reached for the gold heart by habit. He'd given it to her on her sixteenth birthday.

"About your adoption…"

Claire raised a hand. "We don't need to talk about it. I know I upset you. I'm sorry."

"No. It's your birthday, and I'm sure you're thinking about it today."

"I always do," she admitted somewhat reluctantly, not wanting to ruin their perfect day.

"I'm sorry." His eyes glistened, his face more serious than she'd seen it. "I wasn't willing to see things from your side, how much it meant to you, knowing where you came from."

"Dad, it's okay. Really." Claire twisted her hands together. "I'm beginning to think the whole thing was a waste of time anyway." If only Jessie had told her something tangible, something she could use. A stricken expression was hardly proof she was related to the Kellys.

"Did it really bother you, not knowing?" Dad almost whispered the question.

One of the adoption search websites she found had a saying, "*You existed before you were adopted.*"

Claire mulled that over for a very long time, and it stuck. What bothered her the most, tugged at her very core, latched on and refused to let go, was that, according to everyone else, she didn't. She didn't exist. All the days after her birth, before her adoption, she was simply the baby with no name, the baby nobody wanted.

Claire turned back to her father. "Please don't think my wanting to search had anything to do with the way you and mom raised me. You were

114

the best parents a girl could want. I just..." Claire blinked against the first sting of tears and lowered her gaze.

Her father's hand closed around hers. "Don't apologize. You want answers. You want to know why you were given up."

Claire snapped her head up. New understanding shone from his eyes.

"Claire, your mother and I were devastated when we learned we couldn't conceive a child. Then, when we decided on adoption, we had to wait so long. Some nights she'd cry herself to sleep wanting a baby so badly. I would have done anything to help her, but I knew there was nothing I could do. All we could do was hope and wait."

"We got the call from a woman at Social Services in Hartford. She said that a young girl had come down from Bethel. Was staying with friends and went into labor. She'd given birth at Hartford Hospital. She wasn't married and she wanted to give the baby up for adoption. Were we interested?" He choked on his laughter and Claire sniffed.

"Of course we rushed to the car and drove straight over there. I was lucky I didn't get pulled over for speeding. You were a beautiful baby. The most beautiful baby I'd ever seen. Perfect in every way. As soon as I laid eyes on you, I knew you were meant to be our daughter. It never mattered to me that you didn't belong to us biologically. You were ours in every other way, Claire. And always will be."

Claire leaned into her father's embrace. Although she'd heard the story before, she'd never really *felt* it. An intangible sorrow settled in her heart, yet it also brought a certain freedom. Her cheek rested against his chest and she released a shuddering sigh. "I know, Dad. I feel the same way about you and mom. You were meant to be my parents, and I'll always love you, no matter what."

She pulled back and wiped her eyes. "But it's hard, knowing that somebody gave birth to me and gave me up. I want to know why. Maybe it shouldn't matter, but it does. In a strange way I feel like I was abandoned, that somehow I wasn't good enough for her. I can't deny the need I have to know where I came from, who I look like, what I inherited from them." She managed a smile. "Dad, you'll always have first place in my life. Nothing will change that. But I thought that if I were able to get those answers, I might find some peace."

Claire sat back and allowed her own words to sink in.

Maybe that's what she *had* thought when she first started this journey. But she'd found peace anyway, even without those answers. The realization surprised her.

Dad blew his nose and nodded, his expression grave. "I never really tried to understand your feelings. I thought that if I allowed it, encouraged it, actually told you the truth, I might lose you."

Claire gave a soft laugh and leaned into him again, putting her arms around his broad frame and hugging him tight. "That's never going to happen. I think you're stuck with me, Daddy."

"I'm glad." He rested a hand on the top of her head and kissed her. "Now listen, I need to get going. But I'd like to tell you something. And I'm sorry I kept it from you before. Like I said, I was scared." He straightened, giving Claire a sheepish smile. "You asked me the day you called, before you left for Maine, if the name *Kelly* meant anything to me."

"Yes. You said no."

"I lied."

Claire nodded, inhaled, and watched him struggle with the truth.

"When we met with the lawyer to sign all the papers to finalize your adoption, he left the room to take a call, and I happened to glance at his notes. I wrote down a name. I don't know why, really. I guess in the back of my mind I thought one day you might want to know."

Claire stared at him, her pulse racing as he took her hands in his.

"I'm sorry for keeping this from you. I pray you'll forgive me, Claire. I was angry that you didn't want to meet Eleanor. And I was scared to death of losing you."

"Dad, I know. Just tell me."

He cleared his throat. "I wrote down the name of your birth mother. Just the last name, but I saw her given name too. It was Michelle. Michelle Kelly."

The name said, spoken out loud, changed everything.

Dad coughed and looked around, ill at ease. "Later, I did some investigating. I was curious, I guess. I wanted to know where you had come from. I found out her parents had a hotel or something up there in Maine."

"Tara's Place." Claire sat numb, the truth in all its finality settling over her at last.

"You've seen it?" Surprise inched into his voice.

Claire rested her head in her hands. "I'm staying there."

* * *

She pulled up outside the old Victorian home just a few blocks away from the house she and James owned and put the car into park. Her heart thumped out a slow rhythm, but Claire forced her hand to open the car door. She moved slowly up the walkway, took the four steps up to the porch, and waited outside the green front door.

Maybe she should have called.

Right as she was about to knock, the door flung open and Melanie stood there, her face lit with a smile. "Claire!"

Too late.

"Surprise." Claire managed a grin before her friend pulled her into a tight embrace. "Um, a little air, Mel."

"Sorry." Melanie laughed and brushed away tears. "What are you doing here? Why didn't you call? Are you back?"

Claire grinned, her joy at seeing Mel looking so well and happy overwhelming speech. Then, she managed, "Maybe you could let me in first?"

As she stepped into the foyer after Melanie, Claire caught a glimpse of the white bassinet in the corner of the living room. Her throat tightened but she gathered her strength and smiled at Melanie. "How's Jaclyn?"

"She's good." Fresh tears filled Melanie's blue eyes.

"Don't start with the blubbering. Show her off already." Claire took slow steps into the room. The smell of baby powder tickled her nose and brought an unfamiliar longing. "Is she sleeping?"

"No, she's awake; I just put her down." Melanie hurried toward the bassinet, bent over the pink bundle, and glanced Claire's way. "Are you okay?"

Claire nodded. Surprisingly enough, she was.

Melanie picked up her daughter and Jaclyn turned big blue eyes on Claire. A gurgle stuck in her throat and her rosebud lips moved into the tiniest smile.

Claire let out her breath. No shaking. No noose around her neck. Only...peace.

"Oh, Mel. She's beautiful." She reached out a finger and stroked the baby's soft cheek. "Can I hold her?"

Melanie cradled the baby in one arm and reached out to give Claire's hand a squeeze. "Absolutely."

Claire sat on the couch with Jaclyn while Melanie went to the kitchen. She studied the baby's features, talked to her in low whispers ,and marveled at her shock of thick auburn hair.

"Wait until you're older, and you and I are going to have some fun," Claire put on a mock whisper as Melanie came in with their tea. "I'm going to take you shopping and buy you whatever you want."

"We'll see about that." Melanie's face glowed, but at least she wasn't crying anymore. "I can't believe you're here. Happy Birthday, by the way."

"Thanks." Claire laughed as Jaclyn made a face. "I came down to see my Dad. We had a nice lunch. I might stay another night. I wanted to come see you before I left for Maine the first time, Mel, but..."

"It's okay. I know it was hard." Melanie poured their tea and set Claire's down on the coffee table beside the couch. "So. Tell me everything."

Claire took her time going over the events of the last few weeks, letting it all sink in as she laid it out for Melanie. "So that's where we are. I'm actually staying with my biological grandparents. Only they don't know it. At least I don't think they do."

"Sounds like you have quite the conversation ahead of you," Melanie said. A small smile lifted her lips. "I'll pray for you."

"Thanks, Mel. That will definitely help." Claire laughed at the astonishment that raced across her friend's face. "What?"

Melanie shook her head. "It's so great to see you. You're looking really good, Claire. I'm so proud of you. Did you tell James you were coming?"

"No." Claire smiled as Jaclyn squeezed her finger. "Do you know where he is? I didn't think he'd be in the office on a Saturday so I drove past. I went by our house too, but I didn't see the Jeep."

"Oh. Well..." Melanie sipped her tea and nibbled on a brownie. When she veered her gaze, Claire's stomach lurched.

"Mel? Is something wrong?"

"You should come home, Claire. For good." Melanie turned to face her again. She wore such a serious expression that Claire almost didn't want to ask.

She looked down at the baby again, her mind filling with unthinkable scenarios. "What's going on?"

"Nothing, really, I'm sure. It's just...here, let me take her." Jaclyn had started to fuss and Claire gave her up reluctantly. Melanie sat down again, patting the baby's back. She glanced at the clock on the wall. "He's been helping out a lot with the youth group. They're having a drop-in tonight, with a light meal. He's probably down at the church setting up." She gave a smile, but Claire saw right through it. Her friend was worried.

"Okay. So..." Claire rubbed the soft denim of her jeans. "Should I go down there?"

Melanie nodded, her smile gone.

18

Claire walked through the hall of the recreation center of the church she'd once attended with James, her hands in the pockets of her denim jacket. Kids passed her and acknowledged her, but she didn't recognize any of them. Not that she would.

She pushed open the doors to the gym and scanned the beehive of activity. Music blared from the overhead speakers. Tables were being set up, chairs moved around. A couple of older boys were shooting hoops at the far end of the court. A few people were putting up decorations.

James was easy to spot, his tall figure standing out among the crowd. He and another guy were lugging a table across the room. James had his back to her and she didn't know the man who could see her. They set the table in position and Claire moved in a little closer, her sneakers squeaking on the wood floor, nerves hammering.

A sudden shriek drew her attention toward a young woman on a ladder. "Somebody help!" She lost her balance as her foot slipped out of the rung, and she fell backward with another shriek, right into James' waiting arms.

Claire watched in disbelief as he set her down, his face full of concern. "Are you okay?" he asked, disentangling himself from her.

The blonde swung her hair over her shoulders, gave the fakest laugh Claire had ever heard, and threw her arms around his neck. "My hero."

Hero? She'd practically fallen on top of him. Probably on purpose.

When she stepped back and gave Claire a good view of her face, Claire's suspicions were confirmed. *Susan Dawson.* She should have known.

"Are you sure you're okay?" James ducked out of her embrace and took a step back. The girl was still close enough to brush bits of confetti off his shirt.

Claire set her jaw, her heart slowing to an unsteady rhythm. Melanie had been trying to warn her, trying to tell her something without actually saying it out loud.

An older man came over and sidled in between the two of them. "Susie, Lucy's in the kitchen. She needs your help. You should take a break, James." He nodded in Claire's direction.

Claire recognized him then but couldn't remember his name. She tried mental telepathy to get the guy to ignore her, but it didn't work.

Her husband turned her way and stared. "Claire." He stood motionless, frozen in time.

Susan saw her too and smiled, inching a little closer to James. Claire narrowed her eyes and took a step forward. Susan raised a hand, wiggling ridiculously small fingers. "Good to see you, Claire. I'll ah...just...go find Lucy."

"You do that." Claire watched her go and gave James a caustic glare that she hoped conveyed her opinion of the scene she'd witnessed.

"Claire."

"Yup. It's me." She vaguely wondered if the fact he had seemed to lapse into a state of catatonia was a good enough reason to slug him. In a church.

"Wha...wow. What are you doing here?" His deer-in-the-headlights expression wasn't exactly the welcome she'd been hoping for.

"I'm not sure." *Anymore.*

James gave a shrug and began to walk toward her.

Claire backed up. She wasn't ready for this after all.

"Didn't mean to disturb you. I'll get out of your hair." She dodged the arm he extended to her and bolted for the door.

"Claire, wait!"

She ran until she reached the parking lot, stopped at her car, and fumbled with her keys. This had been such a bad idea. Probably one of the worst ideas of her life.

James caught up to her and grabbed her wrist. "Would you hold up a second? Talk to me!" He leaned up against the car door so she couldn't open it. "You practically disappear off the face of the earth with barely any contact, show up here out of the blue, and now you're running off like I have the plague. What's with you?"

Claire shook her head, hating the tears that stung her eyes. It had been such a good day. Until about five minutes ago. "I guess I should have called to tell you I was coming. You could have made sure your ex-girlfriend was out of sight first."

Surprise flashed across his face and a tiny grin lifted one corner of his mouth. "Don't be ridiculous."

"Don't be ridiculous?" Claire pushed the strap of her purse up onto her shoulder and stared, mouth open. "I'm sorry, were you not in that room when she was hanging all over you? I was, Jamie. You know, at least you could have the decency to..."

"Stop." He grabbed her arms and pierced her with a look that withered her anger in seconds. "Don't you dare come breezing in here with no warning, take one stupid incident, and turn it into an indictment against me. You don't have the right to do that."

"I don't have the right?" Claire shook free of his grip, hating the mask of sorrow he wore. "Unless you filed for divorce while I was gone, citing spousal abandonment, then I think we're still married. So don't tell me I don't have the right."

He let out a frustrated growl, stalked around the car, braced himself against the trunk, took a few deep breaths, then came back to her. "What are you doing here?"

"You asked me that already," she whispered. Tears clouded her vision and clogged her nose. She fumbled in her purse and pulled out a Kleenex. "I came to see my dad. And then I went to see Mel. And then I…"

"You saw Mel?" James straightened, his arms drooped to his sides, and he took a step toward her. His expression softened. "And the baby?"

"Yes. I spent the afternoon with them. She even let me hold her." Claire sniffed and drew a shaky breath. "She's cute. Looks like Mel, thank God."

Relief lifted his features, and he gave a broad grin. "I won't tell Steve you said that."

Claire managed a smile, but her hands began to tremble. The familiar longing to erase the gnawing pain made its presence known.

No. She could do this. She would do this.

She would get through this day without a drink.

She had to.

"So." She gave a shrug and eyed him carefully. "I guess maybe I stayed away too long."

James stepped closer, his eyes intent on capturing hers. "Claire, I don't know what you think you saw in there, but nothing's going on between me and Susan. You know that, right?"

"I don't know. She was looking pretty protective when she saw me." The day had turned gray and cold. She stared down at the tarmac and watched a few spots of rain darken the blacktop. "You dated her for almost a year before you and I started dating. She's never married. I think she would have you back in a second. If you don't realize that, then you really are an idiot."

"Good to see how much you trust me." His mouth formed a thin line. "What do you want me to do, Claire? Lock myself in the house? You're the one spending all your time in another state. You left me, remember?"

She jangled her keys, threw back her shoulders, and unlocked the car. "I need to go."

"That's it?" His face darkened to match the sky above them. "You need to go?"

"Yes. I have to get back tonight. I'm not staying."

"Are you sure you should be driving?"

Thunder rumbled off in the distance.

Claire narrowed her eyes, her heart racing again. "Actually, I haven't had a drink in weeks. Thanks for the moral support."

James scowled. "I meant because you're upset. I didn't mean to…"

"No. I know what you meant." Claire took in the circles around his eyes. His T-shirt seemed loose, his jeans baggier. "You look tired."

He scratched his chin and kicked at some pebbles. "Been busy, I guess. With work."

"How's it going?"

"Good. It's steady. Steve's happy."

"And the designer that took over from me?"

"She's all right. My clients seem to like her. I don't think she's got your eye, though." A light breeze lifted his hair as more drops of rain splattered around them.

Claire fought against the fierce emotions that churned in her, her mind a whirl of irrational thought. "That's good. I'm glad it worked out."

Stilted conversation between strangers.

She brushed a hand across her cheek and stepped toward the car.

"Claire, don't leave. Let's go someplace and talk. Please." He reached for her hand, but she pulled away.

"I can't. I have a long drive ahead. I-I have some things to take care of up there."

"Like what?" Anger moved across his face and flashed a familiar warning. "What could possibly be more important than fixing our marriage?"

Claire flinched and looked beyond the cars in the parking lot to the field behind the church. A few black and white cows were making their way toward the gate at the road. "My dad just gave me my birth mother's name. Probably the weirdest birthday present he's ever given me, but there you go. I guess you must have been so *busy* you forgot what today is."

"No, I didn't forget. I know it's your birthday." He sighed. "You might want to check your cell phone. I left you five messages."

"Oh." Any happiness she'd felt earlier in the day had fled. All she wanted to do now was put all this behind her, crawl under the covers. And never come out.

"So what are you going to do?" James glanced over her shoulder and Claire turned slightly. People were starting to come out of the building.

"Go back to Maine, ask some questions. I need to finish what I started."

"Yeah, I guess you do." He rolled his eyes skyward and rocked back and forth. "Once again, it's always all about you, isn't it, Claire?"

"This is important, Jamie." Her voice shook as fear inched up her spine. "You are too, I know that, but I have to do this. Actually, I was going to ask you if you wanted to come back there with me."

"What, up to Maine?"

"No, to Disneyworld."

"I can't take time off work right now."

"Of course not." Claire pushed past him and opened the car door. "Well, I want to beat the storm."

He placed a hand on her arm. "I'm in the middle of a big project, a new build in East Lyme. I can't just up and go with no warning. Maybe in a week or so...I...Claire, don't look at me like that."

"Like what, Jamie?" she spat, the words bitter on her tongue. "What am I supposed to think, huh? Yes, you're right, I left you. I went to Maine even though I knew you didn't want me to. But I never said I wasn't coming back. Now I'm beginning to wonder if I have anything to come back to."

"Fine." He glared at her, smacked his palms together, and stepped backward. "If you honestly think so little of me, if you think the vows I took with you, before God, mean squat, I'm not going to stand here and argue the point. You go on, go back up there and do what you have to do. When you're ready to be rational, give me a call."

Claire brushed her hair off her damp cheeks, tried to muster calm, and met his eyes. "All right. I'm sorry."

"Yeah. Whatever." His stubborn streak won out over anything else he might have wanted to say.

Claire lifted her shoulders and let them fall. "Okay. Well. My cell phone doesn't always work up there. If you need to get hold of me for any reason, my father has the number." She turned toward the car.

"Wait..."

"What?" Claire looked back and met his eyes.

James moved closer, ran his hands down her arms, then drew her into a tight embrace. Claire squeezed her eyes shut and leaned against him, hearing the beating of his heart against his chest.

"I'm sorry." He stroked her hair and kissed her forehead. "Baby, I'm sorry. I love you," he whispered. "Don't ever doubt that."

She raised her head and watched desperation settle into his features. She placed a hand against his cheek and managed a weak smile. "I know. And I know I've hurt you, Jamie, but I want to work things out. I do. I need you to believe that. If you can get some time off, I'll be waiting."

He traced the curve of her face with his finger. "I'll talk to Steve. Don't...uh...don't go running after some lumberjack up there, okay?"

Laughter stuck in her throat as she drank in the sudden sparkle in his eyes. Maybe there was still hope for them. Maybe one of these days, things would actually be okay. "I'll stay away from the lumberjacks if you stay away from Elvira in there."

"Deal." He threaded his fingers through her hair, drew her close, and pressed his lips to hers in a lingering kiss that gave her strong incentive to change her plans and stay. "Are you sure you want to leave?" He read her mind, and she flushed under his grin.

"No, but if I don't leave now, I'll lose my nerve and never go back there." Claire smiled, kissed him back, and reluctantly stepped out of his embrace. "I'll see you, Jamie."

Her husband kissed her again and held her close. "Not if I see you first."

19

Rick stood back to examine his latest creation. The bronze sculpture still glowed red in places. He gave a nod of satisfaction at the replica of the swan statue he'd made for Mac and Jessie and ripped off his gloves. A metallic odor lingered in the air of the warm studio and tickled his nose. Rick wiped his damp brow with the back of his hand, tipping his head slightly. It wasn't exactly the same as the one Claire had plowed down, but it wasn't half bad.

It would do.

As he cleaned up his workspace and swept the floor, the distinct crunching of tires over gravel filtered through the open window. Jazz rose from her position by the door with a loud bark. Rick clenched his jaw as he stomped across the dusty wooden floorboards and hooked a couple of fingers through the dog's collar. He was half-tempted to let her go.

People who showed up unannounced deserved to be slobbered on.

He locked the door to the small log studio from the outside and strode down the path, catching a glimpse of the shock of red curly hair as the driver unfolded himself from a red Jaguar convertible.

Angus Clermont.

Rick let Jazz go, grinned, and waited.

Angus barely had time to stretch before the big lab hurtled herself on him. "Ach away!" He pushed Jazz off, but not before a couple of pats, brushed fur off his khakis, and lumbered toward Rick. "Don't tell me, they cut your phone line. If you need money, Rick old boy, you should say so."

"My phone works, Angus, I just screen my calls."

"Ouch." Angus staggered back, hand over heart. "A fine greeting for your oldest and dearest friend."

Rick chuckled and shook the hand extended toward him. "Come on in."

"Good thing I remembered how to get here for the few times you actually let me near the place." Angus huffed up the stairs, shrugging out of his long black raincoat.

Rick couldn't argue with that. The ten years he'd lived in Maine had passed in a self-imposed solitary confinement. When his grandfather willed him the cabin, Bethel was the last place on earth he intended to return. But familiar images from childhood crept into his dreams, and he knew he couldn't up and sell without at least visiting one more time. And then he'd stayed.

Angus stood on the porch and surveyed the scenery, a bemused look on his face. "You got cable out here? High speed?"

"Nope." Rick pushed open the front door and let Jazz inside. Thunder rumbled across the lake and the dog circled his heels. "Have a seat, Angus. You want coffee?"

"Coffee?" Angus gave just the reaction Rick hoped for.

"Don't have anything stronger."

"No. Of course…" Angus got a little flustered, reaching into the breast pocket of his cotton shirt. He pulled out a silver cigarette case and raised an eyebrow. "You mind…yeah, okay." He slipped the case back into his pocket and looked around, his sharp eyes taking everything in. "You've done a lot of work since I was last here."

"Yep." Rick lost count of the cash he'd spent renovating the old cabin. It looked rustic enough from the outside, but inside, the modern three-bedroom house gave testimony to the time and effort spent on it.

Pine-paneled walls displayed many of his paintings. Two bronze sculptures stood near the huge stone fireplace, one of a couple in each other's arms, the other the Blue Heron he'd come across in a marsh one day. If he could work solely in bronze he would, but it was time consuming, not to mention expensive. He'd need to make more of a name for himself before starting that venture.

"What brings you up to the backwoods, Angus?" Rick kicked off his boots. Rain pelted the roof now and put a chill in the summer air. Thunder rolled in across the lake, increasing in volume. Jazz trailed him around as he checked for open windows.

"Do I need a reason to visit an old friend?"

Rick grunted at Angus' innocent tone, threw a couple of logs on the fire and lit it, wiped his hands on his jeans, and went into the spacious kitchen and made coffee.

Soon the scent of burning balsam filled the room and the flames warmed the cabin.

"I know you didn't drive all the way up here from New York just for the fresh air. I could kid myself and say you really wanted to see me, but something tells me I'd be wrong. So, what's up?" Rick settled into his favorite recliner, drank his coffee, and waited for Angus to come clean.

"Here's the thing." Angus leaned forward, placing his hands on his knees.

His eyes shone with secrets waiting to be spilled. "The Alexander Gallery in New York wants to show your work. Sculptures and paintings, isn't that great?"

"No." Rick almost laughed at the hope in his friend's eyes. "When?"

"Two weeks. Is that enough time for you?"

"Angus, I think you're even pushier than you were back in college."

"Just doing my job. Looking out for my best client."

Rick made a face and drained his mug. "I never asked you to be my agent, Angus, remember? You took that on all by yourself. And if I'm your best client, maybe you should consider another profession."

Angus waved a hand, a chuckle rumbling out of him. "Humor me. One show. If you bomb, I'll leave you alone, I swear to the good Lord above us. You'll never hear from me again."

"Promises, promises. You don't even believe in God." Rick stared at the flickering flames. "Angus, I don't want to get into that scene. I've sold plenty to folks out here. I get enough work on commission. I'm happy showing at the gallery in town. I wish you'd get that through your thick head."

"Don't be such a putz. This is huge, Matthews. The Alexander is very highly respected, crème of the crop clientele. Just do it."

"I know The Alexander. Or did you forget I used to live in New York?"

"Don't get me started." His friend wagged a thick finger at him. "I know you keep telling me how much you like it up here, that you've found peace, yadda, yadda, but I gotta tell you, Rick, moving to the sticks was the worst thing you could have done for your career." Angus wheezed out a loud breath and sent himself into a coughing fit.

"You need to quit smoking."

"Don't change the subject." Angus went to the kitchen and came back with a glass of water. He thudded into his armchair again and nailed Rick with his shut-up-and-listen-to-me look. "You're good, Rick. Much better than you give yourself credit for. I've let you sit around up here mooning over your past, and have I said a word? No. But enough is enough. Life goes on, my friend. The world continues to revolve. And you need to jump back on the ride. It's time."

"It's New York." Rick glowered.

"It's a big town. Besides, I already told them yes." Angus' tone began to resemble Jackson's when he wasn't getting his way. "Please don't make me go back there and look like an idiot."

Rick raised his eyes to the ceiling.

The truth was, he *had* been thinking about doing a show. Not that he'd share that with his friend. Angus was right. He couldn't hole up here forever, fixing up Tara's Place and pretending the rest of the world didn't exist.

"Two weeks, huh?" It wasn't that he couldn't be ready. The thought did hold some appeal. Who was he kidding? His heart was already racing.

A show at The Alexander would be the jumpstart he needed.

It was just…New York.

"If you're hesitating because of her," Angus said in a low tone, "don't waste your time. I hear she's getting married."

Rick studied his faded jeans, picked a thread from the small hole started on his knee, and watched the hole get bigger. "So?"

"'Course he has to get divorced first, so you know…but that's the word on the street."

"Great. Ever thinking of doing your own talk show, Angus?"

"No need to get snotty. But I thought you might be interested."

"I'm not." Rick exhaled and rubbed his temples.

Angus sat in silence for all of five minutes, his heavy breathing taking up all space in the room. "I saw her once. After you took off for California."

"That right?" Rick met his old friend's eyes, aching at the sorrow in them.

"Why didn't you ever tell me, Rick?"

Rick lifted his shoulders and let them sag. "There was nothing to tell. I left. She told me what she intended to do; that was fine with me." The truth galled him now. He hadn't thought of that terrible night in a very long time.

Angus took out a cigarette and rubbed it between his thumb and forefinger. "See…that's the thing, Rick. She changed her mind. Said she couldn't go through with it. I don't know what happened after that; she left school. I thought she might have gone home."

Rick pressed his back against the chair and took deep, measured breaths. "She didn't go home. I know that much."

"Sorry, man. Maybe I shouldn't have brought it up." Angus stood, his knees cracking. "Going outside for a smoke. Let me know what you want to do about the show."

She changed her mind.

"The show is fine. Set it up." Rick ran a hand down his face, his heart thumping.

His hand trembled as he put down his mug on the side table and rubbed his jaw. He was getting a little tired of the beard. He'd worn it for years, never really cared for it, but couldn't bring himself to shave it off.

He still wasn't ready to face the man in the mirror.

"You sure?" Angus didn't believe him. "You won't bail on me last minute?"

"No. I'll do it." Perhaps living out here in the middle of nowhere had finally turned him mental.

"Brilliant." Angus put on the Scottish brogue his father still spoke with and rolled his l's with a dramatic flourish of his hand. "Well, this was worth the drive. Say, I stopped in at that place down the hill you're always yammering about. Tara's Place. They serve dinner?"

"Sure." Rick smiled. The small dining room and home-cooked meal would hardly be Angus' style. This might be fun. He reached for the phone on the table beside him just as it began to ring. He checked the caller ID. "That's Mac now."

"Rick, can you get down here?"

Rick sat up at Mac's anxious tone. "What's going on? Is Jessie okay?"

"Jessie's fine. It's Darcie. She's collapsed. We've called an ambulance."

20

laire drove back to Tara's Place, her mind a mess. All she could think of was the information her father had given her.

Michelle.

She couldn't remember Mac or Jessie saying their daughter's name. Darcie hadn't told her what her mother's name was, she was pretty sure of that. But with her father's news, there was no room for doubt.

Mac and Jessie's daughter was her birth mother.

It was too late to go in and see them by the time she pulled into the parking lot. The lights were out anyway. Mac and Jessie went to bed early.

Claire spent a restless night and rose with the sun, eager to talk to Jessie.

She walked up to the house and frowned at the empty driveway. The old Ford station wagon was gone. That was odd. The older couple didn't usually go out on the weekends, but maybe they had some errands to run. Mac's truck was still in the garage, though. The sun was just starting to crest above the mountains across the water, casting a pink hue across the lake.

"Hello? Anybody up?"

Silence greeted her as she pushed open the screen door and walked through the empty dining room, went down the hall, and knocked on the door to the den. Nobody answered. Claire opened the door and stepped back in surprise. Rick sprawled on the couch, his eyes closed, Jackson asleep beside him covered with one of Jessie's colorful quilts, his head on Rick's leg.

"Rick?"

The instant he stirred and met her eyes Claire knew something was wrong. He put a finger to his lips. Slowly he lifted Jackson's head, placed a cushion under it, and moved off the couch in slow motion.

"What's going on?" Claire hissed, shocked at the dark circles under his eyes, as if he hadn't slept at all. "Where is everyone? What are you doing here?"

He took her elbow and led her out to the hallway. Jerking his head toward the living room, he said, "Come sit down."

Claire followed him into the spacious room and sat on the edge of a wingback, her pulse racing. "Are Mac and Jessie okay? Did something happen?"

"Mac and Jessie are fine." Rick sat opposite her on the chintz-covered couch. He wound his hands together. "It's Darcie. She collapsed yesterday afternoon. Her fever was through the roof. They called an ambulance when she wouldn't respond. They've admitted her to the hospital, and they're running tests. Nobody's said anything yet. I spent the night here with Jackson. He got up early but fell asleep again."

"Darcie? That's crazy." Claire shook her head. Darcie couldn't be sick. Darcie was young. Healthy. "I know she wasn't feeling that great this week, but she thought it was the flu. What kind of tests?"

Rick shrugged and pulled at the collar of his white T-shirt. "I don't know. Could be food poisoning, some nasty flu bug…they don't know yet." His eyes veered to the mantle where the family portraits sat. Darcie looked down at them from behind the glass, her trademark grin set in place.

Emotion crashed over her with the force of a tidal wave. "You think it's serious, don't you?"

Rick turned to face her, pulling at his beard the way he did when he was worried. "She didn't look too good when they left here, no." The phone on the desk across the room shrilled and he pushed his lanky frame off the couch. "Maybe that's Mac."

Claire slipped into the chair and waited while he took the call. When he hung up, he stood for a long time with his back to her. Occasionally he'd raise a hand to scratch his head, messing with his ponytail. His deep sighs were worrying, not to mention annoying. Claire willed him to turn around but was half afraid of what he would say.

Rick took slow steps back to where he'd been sitting and sank down. When he met her eyes, she knew it wasn't good.

"Darcie has Hepatitis."

"Hepatitis? What is that? Like cancer?" Claire allowed Rick's words to sink in as he relayed their conversation. Claire vaguely remembered learning something about it in high school and wished now she'd paid more attention in health class.

"No. It's a blood disease. Darcie has Hepatitis B. She's probably had it for a few years. It's something that can be contracted through dirty needles, unprotected sex. I guess those years she spent on the streets have taken their toll." Rick stared down at his sneakers.

"Is she going to be okay?"

Rick lifted his head, his blue eyes misty. "She'll recover for now. But the doctors say she has a high chance of developing complications later. The disease affects the liver, could cause cirrhosis of the liver, and sometimes people can get liver cancer."

Words wouldn't come. Darcie was so young, her whole life ahead of her. A mother.

"Jackson will have to be tested," Rick spoke quietly, as if almost afraid to voice his feelings. "We can just pray she didn't pass it on to him, which would be a miracle." He coughed and looked at his watch. "I'd like to go to the hospital to make sure Mac and Jessie get home okay when they're ready to leave. Do you mind staying with him?"

"Sure. I'll stay here. Call me when you get anymore news." Claire stood and went to him as he got to his feet. She tried to find a smile but couldn't. Rick gave her a quick hug, an odd gesture for him, but Claire found it comforting.

"She means a lot to you, doesn't she?"

Claire nodded. "I don't want anything to happen to her," she whispered.

Rick squeezed her on the shoulder. "She'll be okay, Claire. You have to believe that."

Claire turned from him and the words he spoke. "You know, I was just beginning to see some good in the world. Even beginning to believe again. But this isn't fair. Why would God allow this?" She faced him again, angry and wanting answers.

"I..." He took another step back, and his face lost a little color. Claire watched him take a deep breath, but then he shook his head, giving her a sheepish grin. "Sorry." He shrugged. "I don't know, Claire. I don't have all the answers. I wish I did. I'm sorry." He grabbed his denim jacket and pulled it on. "Listen, answer the phone if it rings. Jessie's been trying to get hold of Michelle since they left for the hospital."

Claire stood motionless, her feet unable to move. Blood rushed from her cheeks and she had to close her eyes as realization surged through her. Rick walked back to her and snapped his fingers, concern marring his features.

"Claire? Did you hear me?"

"I heard you. Michelle?"

"Darcie's mom." He grunted. "Not that she gives a care, but you know how Jessie is. Had to let her know. Okay, I'm outta here. You sure you're all right?"

"Fine." Claire watched him go with a heavy heart. Fine as the prize turkey the day before Thanksgiving.

She took faltering steps back to the den and gingerly lowered herself down beside Jackson. In slumber, his rounded face was perfectly peaceful. Long eyelashes almost touched his cheeks, pinked by the sun. A smattering of freckles rambled over his snub nose. Claire put a hand on his warm head, his hair damp with sweat.

The little boy stirred and Claire smiled down at him. "Hey, buddy."

He rubbed his eyes and yawned. "Where's my mommy?"

"Mommy's in the hospital. She got sick. But they're going to try and make her all better, okay?" Her voice caught and fresh tears came as he sat and looked up at her through bleary brown eyes.

Brown eyes that were identical to her own.

* * *

The phone never rang. Claire spent some time with Mac and Jessie after they returned from the hospital and they seemed encouraged. Darcie was feeling better, but she needed to stay in hospital for a few days. Claire knew the timing wasn't right to talk about Michelle. Not yet.

After another restless night, Claire woke early, showered and dressed, and planted herself on the back porch of the main house before the sun rose.

A fine mist hung over the lake. Every now and then a loon called out, its mournful cry echoing across the glass-like water. The call was returned from somewhere along the shoreline. A lone canoeist appeared from the west, pushing through the water, breaking the stillness with methodical strokes that sent ripples across the lake.

The peace Claire thought she'd found here in this magical place was shattered. Just as she'd started to get her life back, the revelations she'd uncovered sent her spinning again. Her thoughts were muddled, and she didn't know where to turn or who to talk to.

"Claire? For heaven's sake! You're up awful early for a Sunday." Jessie pushed open the screen door and Claire got to her feet, picking up the cushion she'd been sitting on. Chance yipped and tried to scramble up the stairs but slipped on the damp wood. Claire scooped him up, placed him at the top of the stairs ,and he raced to Jessie.

She gave him a pat, then tightened her thick purple flannel robe around her waist and padded over to where Claire stood, her slippers slapping against the wet porch. "How long have you been sitting out here?" Her face showed genuine concern and Claire felt the trembling start again. All night she'd fought the familiar craving, but she was determined not to give in. She could do this.

She shoved her hands into the pockets of her fleece. "I...told Darcie I'd go to church with her today. Figured I should go anyway." Hot tears pricked her eyes and Claire looked away. Jessie would think she'd lost it for real this time. "I didn't know what time to be ready."

Jessie gave a soft chuckle. "Not at six in the morning, to be sure. Come on into the house. Mac's making breakfast."

Claire followed Jessie into the kitchen. Jackson was perched on a stool at the counter. He turned when they entered the warm room.

"Clayah!" Jackson put his arms out, a delighted smile lighting his face. Claire picked him up and held him close, needing his tight hug.

"Action Jackson! What's up?" She planted a kiss on the blond head and plopped him back on the stool.

He played with the zipper on his red footie-pajamas, faded from many washes. His pjs displayed an image of his favorite Disney movie, something about cars, she couldn't remember now. "Papa's making pancakes, see?"

"Really, Mac? I didn't know you could cook." Claire straddled a stool beside Jackson and grinned at the look Mac gave her. Jessie laughed and excused herself, saying she needed to get dressed.

"Ayuh. I was a cook in the army. Made the best grub in Vietnam." Mac poured batter into a fry pan. The sizzle and tempting aroma of pancakes and sausages soon made Claire's mouth water.

"Sure smells good."

"Ayuh. You're up awful early, ain't ya?" Mac chuckled and winked at her.

Claire laughed, pulling a stray thread off Jackson's pajamas. "Figured I'd tag along to church with you, if you don't mind."

"Yay!" Jackson gave a whoop. "We gotsa walk, though. It's far."

"No, it's not. Just up the road a stretch." Mac put two plates down in front of them, a small helping for Jackson and three huge pancakes for Claire, with a side of sausage and bacon. "Coffee?"

"Please. Oh, I don't think I can eat all this."

"No matter." Mac poured two mugs of coffee and juice for Jackson. He settled across the worn counter with his own meal. Claire picked up her fork, but then hesitated. Jackson had smothered his food with syrup, but he hadn't started eating yet so she decided to wait. Claire had been invited to eat more than a few meals with them and knew they prayed before eating. Maybe they did it at breakfast too.

Mac closed his eyes and gave a heavy sigh.

Claire watched Jackson shut his eyes tight and clasp his hands under his chin while his grandfather prayed.

Mac prayed for Darcie, prayed for Jessie and Rick and Jackson and even for her. Claire couldn't stop a smile as she Jackson opened one eye to see whether his grandfather was close to finishing. Mac was.

"Geesus is name, amen." Jackson speared a piece of pancake and shoved it in his mouth. Claire burst into giggles and Mac's tired eyes lit with a smile.

"Dig in, Claire. Nice to have you here." He kept his gaze on her for a moment. and Claire felt heat rise to her cheeks.

"Thank you." She and Mac hadn't spoken much since she'd come to Tara's Place. He seemed to keep to himself. Claire sometimes got the feeling he wasn't exactly thrilled with her presence here. Since her first thoughts about searching for her birth mother, Claire was becoming well acquainted with the feeling of being unwanted. She lowered her gaze and focused on her food.

They ate while Jackson entertained them. The child enjoyed his food, but he also liked to talk. Mac scolded him more than once about speaking with food in his mouth. Eventually he finished his plate and was sent upstairs to get dressed.

"Looks like you were hungrier than you thought." Mac nodded toward Claire's empty plate.

Claire stared in surprise, almost embarrassed. "I guess I was."

"It's good for you. You need some meat on those bones."

His eyes came to rest on her again and Claire shifted. "Have they said when Darcie might be able to come home?"

"Maybe sometime this week, long as they get rid of the fever." He gave her a warm smile. "You and Darcie got the same spirit. She'll pull through just fine, same as you. Don't you worry 'bout our girl."

Claire balled up a paper napkin, his words resonating. They had the same spirit all right. The same mother too, given what she now knew. "Will Darcie's mom come to see her?"

Mac's steady gaze faltered for an instant. He began to stack the plates. "I doubt it."

"Has Jessie spoken to her yet?"

"Not that I know of." He walked across the kitchen and put the dirty dishes in the sink.

Claire rose and grabbed the ketchup and syrup, going toward the fridge. "I'm sure it would mean a lot to Darcie if she came. And you and Jessie too."

"Oh, sure. But..." Mac let out a weary sigh and turned to face her. "We don't get on. There's good reason for it. and I don't blame her for staying away. But I don't wish for the impossible. Not like your...Jessie."

Claire drew herself up and inhaled. Did Mac and Jessie have their own suspicions? She couldn't ask him. Not now. Didn't have the nerve.

"Well, now." Jessie breezed into the kitchen, pretty in a peach-colored pantsuit. Claire rarely saw her dressed up and couldn't help smiling.

"That's a good color on you."

Jessie grinned and smoothed down the linen fabric. "Ach. This old thing. I really should get into town and buy a couple of new outfits. Darcie's always after me about that."

Claire glanced down at her jeans and light cotton blouse. "Should I go change? I didn't know what to wear."

"Oh, no. You're fine. Our church doesn't stand on ceremony." Jessie went to the sink and shooed Mac away. "You go on and see what Jackson's doing."

"Thanks again for breakfast, Mac," Claire said as he made for the door. He looked over his shoulder, shook his head, and flashed an almost shy smile.

"My pleasure." His voice sounded thick, and he hurried away. Claire wondered if she should say anything to Jessie. There was no way for her to know whether Mac and Jessie knew their daughter had given a child up for adoption. She would hate to be the one to break it to them if they didn't know. Still, they were her grandparents. They needed to know the truth.

And maybe, just maybe, that's why she'd been brought her here.

21

They hiked up the beaten path together. Jessie walked in step with Claire, Mac just aways ahead, with Jackson on his shoulders. When they rounded yet another corner and the church came into sight, Claire sucked in her breath.

The round wooden structure sat at the crest of the hill surrounded by pine trees. A metal cross was secured in the middle of the gray slate roof. She recognized Rick's handiwork at once. The cross was simple enough, but hung around it, carved out of bronze now green with age, was something that looked like a cloth.

"Coming, Claire?" Curiosity made her stare longer than she'd realized, and Jessie's voice startled her. She nodded and hurried to catch up.

About ten people stood around in groups of two or three, chatting. Claire didn't know any of them but they all smiled and greeted her warmly. She managed her own greeting and went into the church with Mac and Jessie. There were more people inside and soon they were surrounded, everyone enquiring after Darcie.

Jackson ran off with a group of children his age and older. Claire looked for somewhere to sit. There were no pews or regular chairs. Hollowed-out tree trunks carved into benches or individual chairs were placed around the circular room. The homey smell of pine permeated through her. Brightly colored rugs lay on the floor, beautiful banners hung on the walls ablaze with color. Some were quilted, others embroidered, some made from flannel. They held messages like *Jesus Saves* and *God is Love.*

Where was the one that said *Exit?*

Three men sat on stools toward the front of the room strumming on guitars and singing.

"This is a surprise."

Rick's low voice made her turn. He nodded her way and she smiled. "I was supposed to come today with Darcie." Sudden tears burned her eyes. She should invest in the Kleenex Company—they were making a fortune on her consumption alone.

He returned her smile and stepped toward her. "So what do you think of our place?"

Claire laughed. "It's not like any church I've ever been in."

"That's kind of the point." Rick chuckled and rolled up the sleeves of his blue cotton shirt he wore untucked over jeans, "Mac and a bunch of us built it a few years ago. We don't have a pastor or any of the traditional 'church' type things you'd expect to find. Come have a seat."

Claire sat beside Rick in one of the tree chairs, which were surprisingly comfortable. She wound her thumbs around each other and wondered what would come next. After a moment the others sat, some around them, some on the floor. A middle-aged man made his way up to the front of the church.

"Welcome friends. Let's pray."

* * *

Claire sat rigid through most of the singing. She didn't know the words but she liked the music. When Mac got up to speak, she about fell out of her chair. She listened intently to his every word. By the time he'd finished, she had a feeling he was talking directly to her.

Mac closed his Bible and nodded. "I've made some terrible mistakes in my life. Most of you know our story. We founded this very church on God's promises of restoration. We clung to the hope of forgiveness and pressed on after Him, seeking His truth and His love. I'm still holding on to those promises. I don't know how to explain things like cancer, babies dying, and families being torn apart. But I do know we all have choices to make."

He cleared his throat again, his face turning a deeper shade of red. Tears stood in his eyes. "We can choose to blame God when things go bad. or we can choose to praise Him, and trust that He loves us, even through the hard stuff. Through the things we don't understand. Even when we're not all that sure He exists. Oh, I don't have all the answers and I don't pretend to. Not anymore. What I do know is this: My God loves me." He thumped his chest and gave a hoarse chuckle. "*No matter what.*" Mac's eyes came to rest on Claire. She held his gaze, but her jaw trembled.

He *was* talking to her. And it was entirely possible, perhaps even probable, that God was talking to her too.

She stood on the edge of a precipice, not knowing whether to jump or step back and return to the safety of solid ground. Every word reached down into her soul and soothed her, pouring a healing balm on raw skin.

Claire wasn't sure what Mac said after that. She lowered her head and allowed her tears to fall. The only thing she was aware of was Rick's gentle hand on her shoulder.

"It's going to be all right, Claire." He leaned in and whispered in her ear. "Just let it out."

Agonizing sobs ripped through her as every awful memory of the past year of her life flooded back.

Her mother dying.

The miscarriage, sirens screaming through the night.

James' awful silence afterward.

Every harsh word they'd said to one another and all the things they hadn't said.

She heard Jessie on the other side of her, and then Mac. Claire allowed the pain to surface. There was so much of it and she'd been fighting it, holding it at bay for far too long.

It was time to let go.

"God, please...help me." She barely recognized her own voice.

Eventually she raised her head and wiped her eyes. Only Mac, Jessie, and Rick were remained, all the others gone. A peace and a sweet blessed release she could not explain filled her soul. Claire smiled and basked in the luxury of it. Slowly she met Jessie's eyes and unspoken words passed between them.

Claire reached for Jessie's hand and squeezed it tight.

Jessie smiled and placed her other hand on Claire's cheek. "Let's walk back. We'll get some lunch. Then, later, we'll talk."

* * *

Claire sat with Mac and Jessie on the back porch. Rick took off after lunch, saying he had work to do at home. Jackson was down for his nap. Claire had read him a story and at last his little eyes closed and he fell asleep. They planned to take him to see Darcie later.

Claire fiddled with the beaded bracelets on her arm that Darcie had made for her. Nobody said anything for a while. Claire half hoped one of them would speak first, tell her they knew she was their long-lost granddaughter. But it didn't happen. Eventually she looked over at Jessie, suddenly nervous.

"I have something I need to tell you." Claire forced herself to look at them. Her voice came out soft and shaky and feared she might break down again. Jessie and Mac exchanged a worried look but still didn't speak.

She pulled at the gold chain around her neck, found her courage, and went on. "You know I went down to Connecticut for my birthday, the day Darcie was taken to hospital. I had an interesting conversation with my father. We talked about my adoption."

She clenched her fingers around the sides of the rocker she sat in and told them everything. "My dad only wrote down the last name, but he memorized my birth mother's given name as well. It was Michelle. Michelle Kelly."

The afternoon sun bled through the thick pines around the lake. Squirrels chattered and birds chirped, but all Claire heard was the thumping of her heart. She settled her gaze on Jessie and waited.

The silence was broken every now and then by the birds. Tears slipped down Jessie's cheeks. Mac patted her arm every now and then, his forehead creased as he glanced from her to Claire. Then Jessie stood abruptly and went into the house.

Claire stared at Mac, worry wrapping around her. "Where is she going?"

"Don't know." He was quiet, thoughtful looking, studying Claire as though seeing her for the first time.

Jessie hurried back out onto the porch, her eyes lit with sure excitement. She held out a silver-framed portrait and placed it in Claire's hands.

Claire stared at the image and sucked in her breath. "Is this your daughter? Michelle?"

Jessie nodded, eyes shimmering. Further explanation wasn't needed. The face in the picture was almost identical to Claire's. Jessie held Claire's chin between her thumb and forefinger. "I knew who you were the minute I laid eyes on you. Oh, he didn't believe me," she shot her husband a grin, "but I knew. I prayed for you every day, my dear. I prayed that one day God would bring you back to us. And He has."

Tears blurred her vision, but Claire managed to get to her feet. Jessie enfolded her in a tight hug and held her as they both cried.

"I'm so happy," Claire breathed out, staring at Jessie in delight. Her grandmother's smile was wide, but all she could do was nod.

"You think I might get one of those?" Mac asked gruffly as he ambled over to them, wiping his eyes. "Welcome home, honey."

Claire laughed and threw her arms around the big man. "I can't believe you're my grandparents." They took their seats again and Claire examined the photograph she still held. Michelle at her high-school graduation, beaming, her eyes filled with the promise of the future. "She's beautiful."

"You look just like her." Jessie reached for Claire's hand. "Are you all right?"

"I think so." Claire brushed the tears off her cheeks. "So you knew about me? I always wondered what happened. Why I was given up for adoption."

Mac sat forward, his eyes connecting with Jessie's for a moment. "We knew Shelly was pregnant with you. It's a long story, and some of it's not ours to tell."

Jessie nodded. "We hope you'll understand, Claire. Until Shelly comes around…"

"Comes around?" Trepidation needled her. "Have you spoken to her?"

Jessie looked away for a minute, her mouth drawn. "I had my suspicions about you, like I said. But we…things were such a mess when Shelly came home from college and told us she was pregnant. She was beside herself, and we were furious. She ended up leaving…and I…we never knew what happened. Until the day you drove up here and knocked over that silly swan." Jessie chuckled, winding her hands together. "After I got to know you better and you told me you were adopted, I called Shelly. Asked her if…where she'd had you. She told me Hartford."

Claire sat very still. So her birth mother, Michelle, knew that in all likelihood, the daughter she bore was here in Bethel, staying with her parents.

And she had stayed away.

"She doesn't want to know me, does she?"

"She doesn't know what she wants," Mac interjected. "Never did."

Claire looked to Jessie for verification, all hope fading. "I'm right, aren't I? She doesn't want anything to do with me."

Jessie gave her an agonized look. "Maybe in time, Claire. After all these years, it's a shock. I'm sure she never expected that you'd look for her."

"And she never wanted me to. She never looked for me, did she?"

"We don't know." Anguish was stamped on Jessie's face. "You have to understand, this tore us apart. We don't have a real relationship with her anymore. We never talked about the baby. Ever."

Claire's mind whirled in a frenzy of desperate hope and reluctant acceptance. "Should I contact her? Call or write to her? Tell her who I am? Ask her if…"

"I don't think that's such a good idea right now." Jessie's soft eyes clouded, her sorrow speaking more than words. "And we're going to have to ask you not to say anything to Darcie."

Claire closed her eyes. "But she…we're…sisters." Thick cords of bondage wound around her, choked her, reminding her once again that her life was not her own. Decisions made before her birth still ruled beyond reason.

"Darcie doesn't know Michelle had a child before her, does she?" Claire knew the answer but asked anyway. "Nobody knows. That's what you're telling me? That all these years I've been this big secret, right? My birth mother gave me up and went on with her life, pretending it never happened. And I'm supposed to just accept that?"

"Claire..."

"No, Jessie!" Claire shook off the woman's hand and got to her feet. "You don't know what it's like. To not know why your own mother didn't want you. I don't want to be somebody's carefully buried secret. Do you understand that? I want the truth. I want to know what happened. All of it!"

"Sweetheart, listen." Jessie went to her and clasped her arms. "If we could tell you all of it, we would. But we can't right now. Let me try to talk to Shelly again. Please, be patient a little while longer."

"I guess I don't have a choice." Claire tried to pull herself together, anger simmering.

"That's right." Jessie drew her into another hug. "We have to wait it out. We have to trust God in this. God doesn't ever start anything He doesn't intend to finish. But I'm very glad you're here, Claire Ferguson. My granddaughter."

Claire's crumpled in Jessie's arms and let the older woman comfort her even as anguished thoughts tore at her soul.

* * *

Rain pelted the roof as Claire and Jackson ate spaghetti and meatballs in front of the television. Mac and Jessie were back at the hospital with Darcie. They'd taken Jackson for a brief visit earlier. Darcie's fever was up, and she wasn't having a good day.

Claire picked at her food. She wasn't hungry, but she tried to finish it. She couldn't very well scold Jackson for not eating if she wasn't going to. Somehow she managed to pretend everything was okay and kept smiling for him. Inside her heart was screaming.

Jackson fell asleep at last, and Claire paced the living room. She couldn't focus on the television, didn't want to read. All she could do was stare at the photograph of Michelle. Jessie told her she could keep it, said she had plenty more, even though Claire had never seen a single one.

So many unanswered questions.

Claire shuddered as a bolt of lightning ripped across the sky. She'd tried calling Rick, but he wasn't answering his phone. She wasn't sure what, if anything, he knew of this story, but she needed to talk to someone. Melanie's line was busy. She'd even dialed James' cell but hung up. She didn't want to worry him.

When the phone rang out, she jumped. It sat on the desk in the far corner of the room. Claire knew Jessie didn't have an answering machine on their private line, so she walked toward it. She hesitated a minute longer, then picked up the receiver. "Hello? Kelly residence."

Silence. Claire frowned. Thunder rolled, and another gust of wind sent rain pelting against the window. Maybe the line was dead. "Hello? Is anyone there?"

"I'm calling for Jessie," a woman's voice said at last. "Who is this?"

"Claire Ferguson. Jessie isn't here right now. Can I take a message?" It was probably one of their church friends. Claire sat in Mac's old leather chair and reached for a pen and paper.

The line crackled and for a second Claire thought the caller had hung up. Then she heard her swear softly. Claire raised an eyebrow. Definitely not one of Jessie's church friends.

"I can take a message if you like. They're at the hospital," Claire tried again, watching rain streak the window in long slashes.

"Darcie's still in the hospital?"

"Yes. Her fever spiked again."

Another colorful word carried down the line.

Claire sat straighter, suddenly realizing what was going on. "Is this Michelle?"

"Yes, it is."

An interminable silence threatened Claire's composure. She tried to still her pounding heart, but it would not obey.

What did one say to the person who gave them life?

Darcie. Focus on Darcie. This was *her* mother. Claire drew in a breath and went on before she lost her voice altogether. "The...um...doctors have started her on medication, but they say she could be up and down for a while. And they're running more tests to check for liver damage."

"Liver damage? What is she, an alcoholic now?"

"Darcie has Hepatitis B. They say she could be fine, but there could also be complications. Mac and Jessie...said you might call. They asked me to tell you what's going on. They thought you might want to come."

"It's that serious?" She swore again, then fell into silence. "You're the person my mother told me about, aren't you? The one who's staying there?" Michelle's tone softened and brought unwanted tears to Claire's eyes.

"Yes. I'm watching Jackson for them. Well, he's asleep but..."

"So it's true then? You think I'm your birth mother?"

Claire tried to summon rational thought. "The facts line up. And there appear to be physical similarities."

"When were you born?"

"July sixth."

"Where?"

"My papers say Hartford Hospital."

The pause that followed gave Claire time to catch her breath. Time to think of a thousand things to say, but she lacked courage to speak them. The silence dragged on and again she thought Michelle had hung up.

"Why did you want to find me?" She finally spoke. "Does the fact that I gave you up not tell you all you need to know?"

Claire recoiled at the cold, clipped words and shrank back in her chair. "No. Not really. I wanted to know who you were. Where I came from. I wanted...I want to know why you gave me up."

"Because you were a mistake! Does that answer your question? I was a stupid college kid who didn't know any better. That's all there is to it. You had a good life, didn't you? I was told your parents were very wealthy."

"I had a good life, yes," Claire replied, almost whispering. "My parents loved me very much. But I always wondered."

"So you figure you have a right to mess with my life just to satisfy your curiosity, is that it?"

"No. I...I'm sorry. I didn't think about it like that. I thought you...I thought you might..."

"Well, you thought wrong. If I wanted you in my life, I would have looked for you. I didn't. I kept my end of the bargain."

Claire gripped the receiver and fought the urge to hurl it against the wall. She couldn't speak. Couldn't even move. A pain mirroring the one she'd fought so hard to overcome burrowed deep into her soul once more.

"I'll tell Jessie you called." She slammed the phone down and buried her face in her hands. She wanted to sob, but emotions remained out of reach, leaving her numb with disbelief.

Claire made her way upstairs to check on Jackson. He slept soundly, so she went back downstairs. Her mind replayed every word of the terrible conversation and her stomach rolled like she'd just come off a roller coaster. Claire leaned against the counter in the kitchen and watched Chance lap from the large water bowl in the kitchen.

Angry tears finally came, and she made no effort to wipe them away.

Slowly she walked across the room to where the telephone hung on the wall. She dialed the number and waited as it rang.

After a while the answering machine clicked on and she heard her own voice. *"Hi. You've reached Claire and James. We can't take your call right now..."*

Claire closed her eyes against another onslaught of grief. The machine beeped, and she let go a ragged sigh. "Hi, Jamie, it's me. Claire. Well, duh. I…" She sank against the wall and slid to the cold tiles beneath her. Chance bounded over and put his paws on her chest. His pink tongue licked at her tears. "I was just calling to…say…" Her voice cracked and she pressed the off switch and let the phone sit in her lap.

Then she picked it up again and dialed Melanie's number. It rang twice before Melanie answered.

"Hey, Mel. It's me."

"Claire! I'm so glad you called. You've been on my mind constantly the past few days. I tried calling you, but your cell wasn't working. Are you okay?"

Fresh tears sprang to her eyes at the sound of her friend's voice.

"Claire? Are you there?"

"I'm here." Claire fumbled for a tissue and wiped her nose. Chance found a ball and dropped it in her lap. She rolled it across the floor and the pup chased after it with an excited bark. Tremors overtook her again, and Claire held the phone with both hands as she tried to speak. "But I'm not okay."

22

Claire drove back from town chugging coffee. She hadn't slept all night, only tossed and turned, Michelle's hateful words echoing in her mind. Part of her wanted to call the woman back and tell her exactly what she thought of her. Another part of her wanted to crawl into a dark hole and never come out. It was that part she listened to as she made her purchases that morning.

Claire parked, reached for the large brown paper bag in the backseat, and locked the car. She shuffled down the path toward her cabin, casting a wary glance toward the house. No sign of Mac and Jessie. She hadn't said much to them when they got home last night. Only managed to blurt out that Michelle had called. Jessie asked her how the conversation went, but Claire could only shrug and gave some lame excuse about having a headache. They let her go without pressing.

The rain had stopped, leaving the air crisp and fresh. Normally she would have taken deep breaths, maybe even gone out for a run. But today she had other plans.

"Hey, Claire." Rick sat on the steps of her cabin, tapping his boots on the gravel as she approached.

"What are you doing here?" Claire pulled her lips together and tightened her arms around the bag.

"Waiting for you, obviously." He lifted his chin, his expression grim. A knowing look crept into his eyes.

The man possessed an uncanny ability to read her mind, and Claire was getting a little sick of it. "Move."

He didn't, so she sidestepped him and pushed open the front door.

Rick got to his feet, his joints cracking. "Jessie told me you spoke to Darcie's mom last night."

"Not exactly. She did most of the talking. It wasn't what you'd call pleasant conversation." Claire turned at the door, not about to let him in. "Was there something you wanted?"

"What's in the bag?" He folded his arms across his chest, his eyes drilling her.

Claire bristled but stayed put. "Groceries." She took a step back and watched his jaw twitch.

"What else?"

"Nothing. Look, I'm tired. If you want to chat, make it another time. I'm going back to bed."

"Claire, give me the bag. You don't want to do this." Rick stretched out a hand.

"I don't know what you're talking about." Claire inhaled and glared at him. "Go away and leave me alone."

"No can do, kid." He stepped forward and tried to grab the grocery bag from her.

Claire pulled it back, her heart pounding. "Stop it. Just leave me alone. You don't know what's in here anyway. You don't have the right to come in here throwing accusations at me. You can't tell me what to do." She stalked to the kitchen and banged the paper bag onto the counter. The clinking of bottles together reverberated around the room and made their own ugly accusation.

Tears of shame stung her eyes, and she put her back to him.

"Claire, I only want to help." Rick's low voice settled her wild thoughts and calmed her. "I had a long talk with Mac and Jessie while you were in town. I've got a pretty good idea how your conversation with Michelle went. I know what's in that bag because years ago I would have done exactly the same thing." He paused and she heard his shaky intake of breath. "And I can sort of tell you what to do. I hear it's a parent's prerogative."

Claire drew in a breath and let his words sink in. Her pulse was suddenly so erratic she feared it would stop altogether. That or she might pass out. She made a slow turn and locked eyes with him. "What did you say?"

Rick appeared just about as shell-shocked as she felt. He lifted his broad shoulders and let them slump. "Remember I told you I had a kid?" His eyes misted over and he scratched at his beard.

"Yes, but…" Realization flooded over her like a warm bath after an afternoon of skiing. The room began to tilt as the blood drained from her face.

"You should probably sit." He took her arm and propelled her toward the couch. Claire thudded onto it and stared up at him. "You're serious. You're my birth father? You and Michelle…"

"Yeah." Rick paced the small room, stopping in front of the fireplace. "It's a long story. Not one I'm proud of." He lifted a wooden duck, examined it for a moment, and put it down. He laced his hands at the back of his neck and emitted a long, battle-weary sigh.

Claire's throat constricted as he moved past her and went to the kitchen. She watched him rifle through the bag and pull out the bottles she'd purchased. When he unscrewed the cap on the first one, she gave a shriek.

"Don't!" Claire bolted across the room and tried to take the bottle from him, but he held it high above his head. "If you drink that, you'll regret it. Seriously, Rick, don't do it."

His deep chuckle broke the tension between them. "I wasn't going to drink it." He took the few steps needed to reach the sink and poured the liquid down the drain. "Give me the other one."

Claire held the bottle of liquor in her hands. Her pain had been so intense she'd forgone her usual penchant for wine and gone straight for the hard stuff. She looked at the dark liquid inside, tipped the bottle back and forth in her hands.

"Do you want it?" Rick watched her, caution written over his face. When he ran his tongue over his bottom lip, Claire saw something in him she hadn't recognized before.

He was just as vulnerable as she was.

The glass felt cold against her skin, inviting. She could almost taste what was inside of it. None of this would hurt quite so much…

"What do you do when you're tempted?" She met Rick's eyes and held the bottle of liquor toward him like it was a weapon.

"Pray."

Claire nodded, tried to smile, but couldn't. She was so used to handling things herself, dealing with things her way, she'd already forgotten God. Guilt choked her, and she endured another dose of shame.

He took the offending object, opened the lid, and poured the stuff away. "Got any more in the car?"

"No. That's it." The battle over, Claire began to shake. She didn't want to break down. She needed to stay strong, to hear what he had to say, to…

"Come here." Rick put a hand on her shoulder and turned her toward him. "You don't have to go through this alone."

Claire moved into his arms and began to cry.

They sat together on the couch for a long time. Finally she sat up, her eyes burning. "Why was she so awful to me? Is it so wrong to want to know where I came from? She made me feel like I was committing murder or something."

Rick rubbed her back and gave his head a shake. "She's scared. My guess is she thought she'd be taking this secret to the grave. I didn't even know if she'd had you. The last time we spoke she…"

He didn't need to say it. Mac and Jessie had alluded to the same. The realization that her very existence had hung in the balance made her sick.

Claire sat back and crossed her legs under her. "Can you talk about it?" She placed a hand on his arm and saw his fear when he lifted his eyes to hers. "It's okay if you don't want to."

He leaned back against the cushions and turned toward her. "No, I'll tell you. I owe you that much, Claire."

"You don't owe me anything. You saved my life. If it weren't for you…"

He let out a frustrated groan and pushed himself up. Claire watched him pace the room like a caged animal, his eyes almost as wild. "Don't put me on a pedestal. I'm not perfect. Far from it. Shelly will be the first to tell you that."

He slumped down beside her again. "I still remember the day she and I met. I was about nine or ten, I guess. My grandparents had just bought the cabin and we were visiting. I was on the beach. I'd made this huge sandcastle, spent hours on it. It even had a wooden drawbridge you could pull up and down. She came racing down the beach, some kid chasing her, and knocked it right over. Actually fell right on it."

Claire clapped a hand to her mouth and tried to suppress a giggle. "And I bet you let her have it."

"Oh, I started to." Rick chuckled, his blue eyes dancing. "But then she fixed me with those big brown eyes…and I was done for. Haven't been the same since." He reached out a hand and gently brushed the side of Claire's cheek. "You have no idea how much you look like her. I didn't really see it until now."

Claire smiled, still processing it all.

Rick Matthews, her birth father. Unbelievable. Apart from having a knack for interior design, she didn't possess a whole lot of artistic ability, but it certainly explained her temper. "So you grew up together?"

"I lived further away, Bar Harbor. But my grandparents lived here, in the place where I live now. I spent summer vacations here. Shelly's parents had moved here that year. She and I spent every hour of every summer together. We were best friends. I don't think there was anything we didn't talk about. Of course by the time she turned fourteen she decided it wasn't cool to have a guy friend."

"Well, duh." Claire rolled her eyes and laughed at the face he made. "Obviously she changed her mind at some point."

A soft smile touched his lips, and he seemed transported to another place and time. "My folks decided to move to Bethel after my grandmother died. Gramps wasn't doing so well living on his own. So I enrolled in the same high school Shelly went to. She wasn't too thrilled to see me, or so it seemed."

"What did you do?"

"What do you think? Dated every girl who'd go out with me, of course."

"And she was jealous?"

"I guess." He gave a shy smile.

Claire poked him in the ribs. "What? You can't stop now. Tell me everything."

"Argh." He covered his face with his hands. Then he set his gaze on her once more. "She was dating some jock. A quarterback with a brain worth...well, you know. There was this big party after one of the games. I'm not even sure why I was there. The jerk got wasted out of his mind, got a little too fresh with her after she told him to knock it off, so I put him out of his misery."

"You punched him?" Claire tried to conjure up that particular image. She couldn't.

Rick chuckled and nodded. "Sent him flying. First and last time I ever threw a punch. Shelly just stood there, in shock. I took her home and...that was the beginning of us."

"And I was the end."

Rick pinched the bridge of his nose and inhaled. The room grew warm as the midday sun infiltrated the pine paneling. Claire reached for the a/c remote and clicked it on. She listened to the mechanical hum, her thoughts reeling.

Rick sat in silence, winding his thumbs round each other. Claire went to the kitchen and came back with two sodas. He popped the lid on his and took a long gulp, settling his gaze on her once more.

"After she finished high school, she was accepted to the same college I was at in Boston. She wanted to study Journalism, and I was doing Fine Arts. I was a sophomore and she was a freshman. My roommate left for the weekend. Sleeping together wasn't something either of us intended. Both of us were pretty grounded in our faith and wanted to wait." His eyes pleaded with her, begged her to believe it. "We swore it wouldn't happen again. But I guess we weren't as strong as we thought we were. We talked about getting married in a year or two, as if that made it okay."

"Everybody makes mistakes." Claire hoped her smile covered the pain. She didn't want to think of herself as a mistake, but the facts were there for her to see. Michelle had spoken the truth.

Rick rested his head in his hands and muttered something under his breath. When he turned to look at her again, his eyes were red and moist. "When Shelly told me she was pregnant, I was furious. I was angry at myself, at my own weakness, and I took it out on her. All I could think was, what would people say? Her parents, my parents and grandparents. I was twenty years old, nowhere near ready to have a child. And there she was, pregnant and expecting me, *trusting* me, to have all the answers." He choked on the words and fell silent again.

Claire's tongue stuck to the roof of her mouth. She couldn't stand to see him so torn up, but she couldn't stop it. She needed to hear this.

Rick gave a hoarse laugh. "I think Shelly figured I'd propose right then and there. We'd get married, have the baby, and get on with life." He glared into the empty fireplace. "I loved her with all my heart but, God help me, I didn't want to marry her. Not yet. I wanted to finish my degree. I wanted to travel, maybe go to Paris. Become a famous artist. So..." He faced her again, his eyes hooded. "I took off. Packed up my stuff, got in my yellow VW, and hightailed it across the country. And I didn't look back."

"You left her." The dull ache got stronger. "Where did you go?"

"California. I transferred to Berkeley and stayed out there. I buried my shame and pain at the bottom of a Jack Daniel's bottle. I wasn't sober a whole lot during that time. I guess I kind of hoped my mistakes would stay buried too, so I'd never have to deal with them. Looks like God had other plans."

"How did you end up back here?"

"My grandfather died about ten years ago. Left his place to me. I had settled in New York and didn't want to live here. I was going to sell it, but something made me come back one last time." He chuckled. "I ran into Mac in town. I walked circles around the aisles of the hardware store, hoping to duck out before he saw me, but I wasn't quick enough. I thought he was going to cuss me out right there in front of half the town, but he didn't. He asked me up to the house for dinner."

"Sounds like Mac." Claire smiled but Rick shook his head. Something flickered in his eyes that she didn't understand.

"Not the Mac I knew. But that's for them to tell. Suffice to say we made our peace, and they talked me into staying. I decided to give it a shot, got into AA, got my life back, and here I am. Hiding out in the backwoods of Maine."

Claire tried to think of something appropriate to say, but came up empty. The awful truth invaded her heart like a disease with no cure. He hadn't wanted her. He'd run as far from his responsibility as he could.

And that left Michelle.

"Do you think...she really did want me?"

Rick's lip curled in a half-smile, and a tear rolled into his beard. He tucked a strand of her hair behind her ear. "I know she did. She's angry now, and bitter, but that's because of me, not you. Believe me, the Michelle I knew would have gone to hell and back for you."

The ensuing silence said perhaps she had.

Claire swiped at her tears and scowled at him. "Why didn't you come back to her? You could have changed your mind…you could have…"

"Claire." Tenderness brought new light to his eyes. "I know. I'm sorry. I don't know why I did what I did. I've lived with that regret for twenty-seven years. But you can't play the what-if game. Life doesn't work that way."

Claire stood and marched to the mantle. "I really hate that you were such a jerk." She nailed him with her eyes but he stared back, unflinching.

Rick raised his hands, gave a slight shake of his head, and lowered them again. "You wanted to know what happened. It's not the romantic fairy tale they make movies about, is it? Some stories are best left untold."

"I don't know if I believe that." Claire stared into the fireplace.

Hard as it was to hear, to accept, it was the truth. Truth she'd been seeking her whole life. She'd asked for nothing less.

Claire made a slow turn, not quite ready to face him. Tears slipped down her cheeks, landed on her lips, and inched their way into her mouth. "Would you have cared if she'd had an abortion? Did you ever wonder what happened to me? I was your child too."

In two strides Rick stood in front of her. "Claire…" His eyes shone as he cupped her face with his hands. "Yes, of course I wondered. I've thought about you every day since the moment I left her. I prayed that somehow you were spared, and that one day I'd get up the nerve to find Shelly and ask her about it." He shook his head. "That day never came. You don't know what it's like to live with that kind of guilt, that kind of shame. I don't expect you to understand, but I hope you can forgive me." Rick let her go and stepped back, his eyes never leaving hers.

Claire pressed her lips together, unable to speak. She moved away from him and went to stand at the window. The lake shimmered under the sun's glare. Happy shouts and the sound of splashing reached her ears. Other people living other lives, oblivious to the pain she was drowning under.

The hard truth of her entrance into the world fell at her feet. She'd had a good life, raised by two loving parents who'd given her everything. God had protected her, blessed her even. Was there any point in laying blame or casting judgment? She was hardly qualified to do either.

Claire walked back to Rick and gripped his hand. "I *do* understand. And I do know what it's like to live with guilt. I've been consumed with it. Blaming myself for my miscarriage and the way I handled things with my husband, wishing I could turn back the clock and do things differently. But you're right, life's not like that." She smiled and felt a rush of affection for him. "We do the best we can and move on."

Rick nodded, scars of the past marring his face.

Claire sighed. "I almost wish now that I hadn't started this. I didn't mean to hurt you or Michelle. I never stopped to think about how this would affect her. I've dredged it all up again, haven't I?"

"Oh, no, you don't." Rick placed gentle hands on her shoulders. Sternness crept into his eyes. "Believe it or not, you don't have the market cornered on guilt, Claire Ferguson. That's my territory. You haven't done anything wrong. Don't think that for an instant."

Sorrow overwhelmed her, and he gathered her into his arms. She heard his shuddering breaths. A different kind of grief crept in, and she cried for the pain they'd suffered, these two people responsible for her life. And here she was, the very cause of it, bringing it all to the surface.

"What do we do now?" She drew back, searching his face for answers, but knew he had none.

"You're asking me?" Rick gave a wry grin, his voice thick. "Heck if I know. But I'm not going to stand here and tell you I'm sorry this happened. I'm glad you found me—found us." A slow smile slid across his mouth. "'*You shall know the truth and it will set you free.*' So maybe that's where we start, huh? I've wished a thousand times over I'd made different decisions back then, but I can't change the past. All I can do now is do my best to make up for it."

"I already have a dad." Claire watched his eyes widen. "Sorry. I'm not...I'm not trying to be mean."

"It's okay. I know you and your dad are close." His smile faltered. "Look, before today, I'd have said you and I were already friends. So maybe...if you want...we can just take it from there."

"Maybe." Claire's heart thumped against her chest. This discovery would take some getting used to. She had to forgive him first. She angled her head. "You might get more than you bargained for, though. I'm a tad stubborn, have a wicked temper, and don't know when to keep my mouth shut half the time. I have a feeling the traits are genetic. Probably from my father's side."

"Probably so." Rick's grin brought out her smile.

Claire moved closer. "I'm not the overly affectionate kind either, but if it'd be okay with you, I'll take another hug."

"That I can do." He opened his arms and she stepped into them, one part of the puzzle of her life gently falling into place.

23

Rick made sure Claire was asleep before he left her. Poor kid had been thrown for a loop in the last twenty-four hours. But then hadn't they all? And she only knew his side of it.

He paced the porch of her cabin, memories pounding him. What must Shelly be thinking right now? He couldn't imagine.

Almost didn't want to know.

After the initial verbal assault he hurled at her when she'd told him of the pregnancy, he'd calmed down some and they'd agreed to go home for Thanksgiving, decide what to do, talk to their parents. Rick was supposed to pick her up outside her dorm. He could still see her—Shelly standing on the steps, bag in hand, snow coming down around her, landing on her long dark hair and red wool coat. As he turned the corner, he knew he couldn't do it. Couldn't be a husband. A father. He'd taken a sharp right, driven around the block slowly, then sped off, tires screeching, hoping she hadn't seen him.

Somehow he knew she had.

Rick sank into one of the two rockers and closed his eyes. No matter how hard he tried to forget, that memory remained vivid in his mind.

He'd snuck back to his room like a deserter dodging the draft. While he was throwing his things into a duffel bag, the phone rang and kept ringing until finally his answering machine clicked on. He could still hear her voice, questioning, then crying, then screaming, letting him know what she thought of him and what she planned to do…

"I pray to God I never lay eyes on you again, Rick Matthews!"

He'd made sure she hadn't.

He didn't blame her for giving Claire up. He'd left her with no choice. But he knew she'd buried her secrets well. If this came out, she would suffer. They would all suffer.

But they couldn't run from this anymore. They shouldn't have even tried.

Rick walked across the deck and whistled for Jazz and Chance. The puppy and its mother had forged a new relationship now that Chance was older.

The few guests Mac and Jessie had taken on were lounging on chairs on the beach. The animals ambled back through the trees at his call, but something diverted Jazz, and Rick watched her bound toward a man who seemed to be headed for Claire's cabin, Chance hot on her trail.

The stranger bent over the dogs, patted them, and looked up, as if getting his bearings. He held a duffel bag in one hand, and was dressed casually in a cotton button-down shirt, sleeves rolled up, over khaki shorts. Although he looked the typical tourist, Rick didn't recall Mac and Jessie saying they had another guest coming.

The man gave a nod as he got closer. When he started up the steps, Rick blocked his path. "Can I help you?" He realized his tone wasn't altogether friendly, but then he hadn't meant it to be.

The man dropped his bag and took off his shades, revealing a pair of hazel eyes. "They told me Claire Ferguson was staying here. Do I have the wrong place?"

"Who wants to know?" Rick noted they were almost the same height, but the guy was pretty thin. He could take him if he had to. The man's face darkened, and Rick was tempted to back off but remembered the guy in town asking questions about Claire and stayed put.

The visitor, whoever he was, didn't seem too impressed. "Look, buddy, it's a simple question. Is Claire here or not?"

"She's sleeping. You can come back later."

The guy raised a light eyebrow, his lips twitching. "Mind telling me who you are?"

"Matter of fact I do. Was going to ask you the same thing." Rick clenched his fists, his pressure rising.

The guy only shook his head and brushed past him, making for the front door.

"Hey!" Rick grabbed his arm, ducked at the first punch that came his way, and nailed the jerk right on the jaw. He stared up at him in surprise and Rick matched his expression.

Apparently he still had a pretty good right hook.

"What in the world?" Claire opened the door, staring at him through bleary eyes. Then her eyes swept over the man struggling to his feet. "Jamie!" She flung herself at him and he lifted her into his arms, his deep chuckle echoing her delighted squeal.

Rick rubbed his chin and felt all the air go out of him as Claire stepped back and assessed the damage.

"Did you hit him? Rick!" Her eyes flashed, and she turned back to the guy. "Are you okay? What are you doing here? Where are the dogs?"

"I'm fine." He rubbed his jaw, which was turning a lovely shade of scarlet. Then he pinned Rick with a gaze that could have frozen the afternoon sun in a millisecond. "The dogs are at Mel's. And as to what I'm doing here, I would hope that's pretty obvious. You mind telling me who your bodyguard is, babe? Or would you rather not?"

"Hey!" Claire gave him a push and looked ready to slug him herself.

"Whoa, there." Rick put up a hand and stepped forward, confusion lifting. "Is this your husband?"

"Yes!" they answered in unison, both glaring at him.

"Well, you could have just said so." Rick ran his tongue over his bottom lip and a grin started. Then he chuckled. Once he started laughing, he couldn't stop. He didn't want to and he knew he really shouldn't, but he couldn't help himself.

"Way to make a first impression, jerk," Claire muttered. "Would you stop?"

"Sorry." Rick tried to sober, but when he caught the thunderstruck expression on the guy's face, he doubled over again.

"When you're ready, Maverick."

Ouch. Who told her his real name? Rick acknowledged Claire's pointed tone and conquered his laughter. Claire gave a satisfied nod and slipped her arm through her husband's, who looked as bewildered as a farmer in Times Square. Rick covered his mouth to hide another grin and bent to pick up Chance for something to do.

"James, this is Rick Matthews. Rick, this is James. My husband." She took a deep breath, and Rick felt his heart lurch as he watched her eyes soften when she looked into James' eyes. She drew in a breath and cast another glance his way. "You're probably not going to believe this, Jamie, but Grizzly Adams over here is...my...birth father."

"Say what?" James frowned and took a step back, ogling Claire like she might finally have slipped over the edge. Her sudden giggle didn't do much to help the assessment.

Rick offered his free hand, holding the squirming pup under one arm. "'Fraid she's right. Nice to meet you, James. Sorry about the jaw."

"No problem." James shook his hand and turned to Claire, his eyes wide. "*Are you kidding me?*" he mouthed.

Claire laughed harder and shook her head. "I have a lot to tell you."

"I'll say." He faced Rick again with an affable smile. "Okay. Well. Rick." He rubbed his bruised jaw and picked up his bag, slipping his free arm around Claire's waist. "Do you mind if I take my wife inside now? Seems like we have a bit of catching up to do."

No harm done, apparently. Rick breathed a silent prayer of thanks. "Don't mind at all." He swallowed down emotion at the joy shining from Claire's eyes. "You kids go on inside. I'll take Chance up to the house and catch you later."

"Thanks. Come for dinner," Claire called over her shoulder. The door to the cabin slammed shut and Rick was left to stand there with only the dogs for company.

* * *

Claire let James shut the door and clenched her hands at her sides. Her initial excitement faded as she reminded herself that she and James had been apart for quite some time and still had things to work through. Her nerves kicked in, and she shifted from one foot to the other.

"Nice place." James dropped his bag in the corner of the room, gingerly prodded the side of his jaw, and made a face. "What is he, a pro-boxer?"

Claire smothered a grin. "He's an artist. Do you want some ice?" She hightailed it to the kitchen and busied herself putting some ice into a dishcloth. When she returned to the living room, he was sprawled on the couch. "Here." Claire sat beside him and pressed the cold cloth to his cheek.

"Easy there, Florence." He grunted but a twinkle crept into his eyes as she dabbed at the bruise. A surge of fresh joy swept through her. He really was here. "What are you smiling at? I just got decked."

"He didn't know who you were. He was protecting me." Her smile broadened and his scowl deepened.

"I thought that was my job." James' hand came over hers and he met her eyes, uncertainty creeping across his face. "At least it used to be."

"Oh, Jamie." Claire sighed, still so much pain between them.

James took the cloth from her, stood, and went to the kitchen. In a moment he returned and sat with her, tipping her chin upward.

"Mel called and filled me in. I got your message on the machine this morning. I didn't bother calling you back. When I heard your voice...how upset you were...I didn't think about anything other than getting up here as fast as I could."

His words brought another wave of emotion that Claire couldn't contain. James put his arms around her and pulled her close, placing a gentle kiss on her forehead. "I'm sorry, babe," he whispered, his voice catching. "I've been the biggest jerk in the world. I should have come back up here with you when you asked me to. Can you forgive me?"

Claire sat back in amazement. "Of course. And you had every right to be mad at how I was acting." She realized, then, how far she had come since leaving home. "I was way out of control before I came here, Jamie. I just didn't realize how much. But everything's different now." She smiled and moved that lock of unruly hair away from his eyes. "It's so good to see you. I was afraid to ask you again…"

"I would have dropped everything if you had."

Claire nodded. There was no room for regret. "Coming here was the right decision for me, though. I was able to get a handle on things. It wasn't easy, but I gave it all up, Jamie—the drinking, the pills. Rick, Mac, and Jessie were so supportive. I couldn't have done it without them. I'm so sorry for everything I put you through." She rested her palms against his chest and felt the steady beating of his heart as he leaned in close and touched his forehead to hers. His shaky sigh told her what he couldn't.

Claire sat back and met his eyes again. "There's something else you need to know." She gathered her thoughts and managed a smile. "I know that everything I went through, losing my mom, the miscarriage, brought me to this place. I don't understand it, but…there it is. I'm healing, Jamie. Slowly, but I feel it. I'm getting a second chance."

James wiped her tears with the base of his thumbs. His eyes shone with new light. "You're back."

"If you want me." A hint of doubt pricked her as she searched his face, but the smile he wore told her she didn't have to worry.

"Always." When he lowered his head and brushed his lips against hers, she melted into his embrace. His mouth moved against her neck and sent shivers through her entire body as his hands wandered down her back. "You need reminding?" Before she could answer, he swung his legs off the couch and stood, taking her with him.

With her arms tight around his neck, Claire recognized the love and desire in her husband's eyes and felt the depth of her own. "Yes, please."

24

"Claire, stop hovering." Darcie lowered her magazine and took the glass of iced tea Claire brought out from the kitchen. "I've barely been home a week, and you haven't left me alone for a minute. I'm not dying."

"Of course you're not. Don't say that." Claire flopped into a lounge chair beside Darcie and sipped her own cold drink. They sat on the grass behind the house, watching the activity on the lake. "Did you get enough to eat for lunch? Do you want some zucchini bread?"

"Claire. Cut it out." Darcie's eyes flashed, and she made like she was going to chuck the magazine at her. Claire grinned at her fierce expression. It was good to have her back. Yet there was so much she wanted to tell her, so much she couldn't say. Having to stay quiet about their true relationship was proving more difficult as each day passed.

"Sorry. Just trying to be helpful."

"I know." Darcie shielded her eyes as she squinted across the lawn. "Looks like your husband found a new best friend."

"I think he has." Claire watched Jackson tagging along beside James as he pushed a heavy wheelbarrow toward the newly built cottages beyond her own. Mac and his small crew of three had finished one already. New guests were arriving next week. She was pleased for Mac and Jessie. She'd been pondering a way to help them but knew they wouldn't take a dime from her.

"I thought he was supposed to be on vacation," Darcie said, frowning as she looked at James and Jackson.

Claire laughed at the comment. "Oh, he is. You don't know James. His idea of a vacation is finding as much to do as possible so he doesn't ever have to sit still."

"Okay." Darcie's lips twitched with the beginnings of a smile. "And how did you two end up together?"

"Shut up." Claire stuck out her tongue and pretended to pout.

Darcie returned the gesture, then grew serious. "I'm glad he came. You seem so happy together. Is everything okay now?"

Claire sat back and clasped the cold glass, thinking about the question as she watched her husband. James stopped on the path by the area needing more gravel. He shoveled the small rocks onto the ground, letting Jackson help with his small plastic beach shovel. The little boy's incessant chatter could be heard even from here. Every now and then James' laugh drifted across the lawn and made her smile.

"We're getting there. I'm determined to do whatever it takes to get our marriage back on track. When we get home we're going to counseling. I'll continue with my AA meetings as well."

"I hate the thought of you leaving." Darcie sighed wistfully. "It feels as though you've always been here. Like you belong here somehow."

Claire nodded and took a deep breath. She did belong here.

In two weeks' time, she and James would be on their way home. Only God knew how the rest of this story would play out.

"Anyway," Darcie went on, "I want you to know how grateful I am. I know you really pitched in with Jackson while I was in the hospital. Grandma told me you and Rick were a big help."

Claire lifted her shoulders and shook off her sorrow. "I was happy to do it. I wish I hadn't had to, though."

"Yeah." Regret slid across Darcie's face. "I know I can't turn back time, Claire, but I really wish…well…I guess there's no sense in wishing, is there? I made poor choices, and I have to live with the consequences."

Claire placed a hand on Darcie's slender arm and tried to smile. "You're going to be fine, Darcie Hart. You'll be a walking miracle, defy all the odds. You watch."

"I'm praying for that." Darcie fiddled with the vast array of bracelets on her wrist. "Some days I have more faith than others. It's hard not to feel guilty, especially when I think that Jackson might have it too."

"Jackson is going to be fine." Claire set her jaw, convinced.

Darcie's wide smile broadened and she tipped her head back in laughter. "Oh, Claire. It's so good to see you happy."

Claire smiled back. "Maybe, if you're feeling up to it, we could go to church on Sunday. I want Jamie to come too. What a place they built, huh? What's the story behind it, do you know?"

Darcie placed her glass down on the plastic table between their chairs and yawned. "Not really. You should ask Grandpa. I think I'm going to take a nap. Hey, is that…" Her mouth fell open and she pushed herself up in the chair. "Rick? Oh my word."

Claire turned in the direction of the house and saw Rick walking toward them. Except the man didn't look like Rick. Not the Rick she knew anyway.

She almost fell off her chair.

Dressed in khaki trousers and a dark blue cotton shirt, Rick Matthews looked more respectable than she'd ever seen him. But most surprising was the absence of the long hair and beard. Claire bit her bottom lip to prevent a giggle as he approached.

"Hello, ladies. Lounging by the lake today, are we?"

Darcie scrutinized him as she extended a hand. "I'm sorry, have we met? Claire, do you know this man?"

Claire screwed up her nose. "I'm not sure. He looks kind of familiar…"

Rick swatted Darcie's hand away. "Brats the pair of you." He flashed a grin, sat on the edge of Claire's chair, and shot her a wink. "What do you think?" He ran a hand over his thick dark hair and made a face. "Too short?"

Claire tilted her head and studied him. "Hmm. No, I think it's fine. You just look…different." Years younger and way too good-looking to be anybody's father, least of all hers. Visions of having to deal with his and her dad's love lives flashed before her and made her feel slightly nauseous. "New York will never be the same."

"You're going to New York?" Darcie perked up. "Nobody told me that. What's in New York?"

"Art show." Rick's cheeks darkened, and he glanced at his watch.

"At The Alexander." Claire turned to Darcie, unable to keep the pride out of her voice. "It's a very prestigious gallery. They're showing his sculptures and paintings."

"What?" Darcie sat straighter, staring at him like he'd won the lottery. "That's amazing! We have to go with, Claire. Come on…" She slid one leg off the chair and Claire grabbed her arm.

"You're not going anywhere. You're under strict instructions to take it easy. Rick doesn't need us tagging along. He'll be fine. Won't you?"

"Yep. I'll be fine." He looked more like someone headed for a triple bypass, and Claire suddenly wished they *could* go along for moral support.

"My mother lives in New York." Darcie's enthusiasm died. "Did you ever meet her, Rick?"

Claire sucked in a breath and studied the chipped nail polish on her toes. Michelle's location was news to her, but not, she suspected, to Rick. She didn't dare look his way to confirm it.

Rick cleared his throat. "We…uh…knew each other. A long time ago."

Darcie's laugh was laced with bitterness. "I saw her on television while I was in the hospital. Can you beat that? Haven't seen her in years, I'm there sick as a dog, and all of a sudden there she is at some political rally. Made me want to puke all over again."

"Darcie," Claire chided. Darcie rolled her eyes but said no more. Claire's curiosity was piqued, though. "What was she doing at a political rally?"

Darcie waved a hand and looked disgusted. "She works for some senator—I can't remember his name, but he just got elected. Big whoop. You think the least she could have done was send flowers or something. I told you she didn't care about me."

"She called." Claire hadn't meant to say it. The memory pained her, but when she saw the surprise in Darcie's eyes, she was glad.

"My mother called? When?"

"Um...a couple of days after you went into hospital. I took a message. Sorry I didn't tell you; it slipped my mind. She said to send you her love and that she'd talk to you soon." Claire avoided Rick's piercing gaze and studied the rings on her finger.

"Oh." Darcie clasped her hands in her lap. A smile touched her lips, and she seemed satisfied with that information.

Rick got to his feet. "I better get going. Long drive." He went to Darcie and gave her a peck on the check. "Behave yourself."

"Don't I always? You better behave *yourself*, Mr. George Clooney lookalike. Don't you be coming back here with some floozy on your arm."

Rick chuckled long and loud. "Oh, I'd say the chances of that are fairly slim, kid. See you next week."

"I'll walk with you." Claire pushed herself out of the chair, stepped into her loafers, and they walked up the path together. When she was sure they were out of Darcie's line of vision, she slipped her arm through his. "You knew Michelle lived in New York, didn't you?"

Rick's silence and the twitch of his clean-shaven jaw conveyed the answer. There was also a dimple in his left cheek she'd never noticed. She had an identical one. "You're going to see her."

Rick let out his breath and leaned against the side of his black truck. His blue eyes scanned the property and eventually landed on her. "I'm thinking about it. I doubt she'll let me within ten feet of her, but I'd like to at least try. It's time."

"I'd say good luck, but I have a feeling you'll need more than luck."

His mouth curled in the beginnings of a smile and he patted her cheek. "We'll see how it goes."

Claire caught his hand in hers. "I just wish she and Darcie...well, I guess it doesn't matter what I want. But I'd like to see Darcie get some closure, you know? It still hurts her so much, what happened between them. When I think about it, knowing that Michelle went through exactly the same thing Darcie did, being pregnant so young…and she had the nerve to be so hypocritical, it just…"

"Save your breath, Claire." Rick pulled her into a brief hug. "Believe me, I've asked the same questions a million times over, and I can't make any sense of it. It's one of those things we're going to have to ride out. There's a lot of healing that needs to happen in this family."

"I'm starting to see that." Sorrow weighed upon her again. There were so many dynamics, such far-reaching emotion, and so much hurt. When she thought of the veritable Pandora's box she'd unknowingly flung open, Claire wanted to hop on the next plane to Kenya and throw herself to the lions.

Rick knit his brows together. "What did I say about those guilt trips?"

Claire laughed and gave him a push. "Go on. Have a great show. I hope you sell everything and make a million bucks."

He pulled open the door and climbed into the truck. "I'll be happy if I can make it through opening night. I really hate these things."

"Your parents are going to be there, though."

"Yeah. And my brother."

"I didn't know you had a brother."

"Yep. Landon. Well, we're not really brothers. He was a foster kid who came to live with my parents when I was already in college. Unfortunately we never got that close, but I still think of him as a brother."

Claire wanted to ask more, but there wasn't time. "I'm sure they're all so proud."

Rick hid behind a pair of shades, but his grunt conveyed nonchalance. He lifted the shades and seemed to hesitate. "If the opportunity comes up, I'd like to tell my family about you. Is that okay?"

"Sure." Hope lifted her spirit and she felt the warmth of his smile as she nodded.

Claire stood in the driveway and watched Rick drive away. Her skin prickled and she rubbed the back of her neck. It was almost like a sense of foreboding came over her, but she couldn't say why. No matter what happened, she knew that from here on in, their lives would never be the same.

She'd released the deadbolt and opened the door to the past, and they all had to walk through it. Whether they wanted to or not.

25

Rick paced his hotel room, tapping a pen against his palm. The events of the past few days weighed on him, making his sleep intermittent and his mind run on overdrive.

He had a daughter.

A smile tugged at the corners of his lips and he gave in to it. He stood at the long window and watched the Manhattan traffic move along the street at a crawl. Pedestrians strode past each other deftly, well used to the race. The tourists were easier to spot with their maps and cameras and the way they stopped to stare up at the buildings, slack-jawed. He could hardly believe he'd once enjoyed living here.

"What are you doing up so early?" Landon strolled out of the bedroom, pulling a T-shirt over his head. Rick slumped into a chair by the window. Angus had surprised him by booking two suites. No doubt the lavish treat was an effort to make up for practically forcing Rick into this. His parents were in one room, and he and Landon were sharing the adjoining one.

"It's going onto eleven, hardly early." Rick yawned anyway, Landon's tousled appearance and sleepy expression almost making him consider going back to bed.

Landon fiddled with the coffee machine on the bar, soon had it going, and the promise of caffeine began to fill the room. "That was quite a bombshell you dropped on us last night, man. I don't think Mom and Dad will ever recover." Landon set his piercing gaze on Rick and raised an eyebrow.

Rick smiled. "I thought they took it quite well, all things considered." Once Mom stopped crying and Dad picked his jaw up off the floor, they'd actually had a decent conversation.

"I'm sure it will take them awhile to process it." Landon poured two cups of coffee and handed one to Rick before he sat down. "Why didn't you ever tell me about you and Michelle?"

Rick sipped the lukewarm liquid and thought about it. "No point. I thought it better to just move on and forget about it."

Rick met Landon's eyes, and a connection he hadn't felt in years sparked.

He'd tried to be there for Landon as much as he could, despite the age gap between them. But they didn't see each other nearly as much as Rick would have liked. Life got in the way. "You doing okay, Landon?"

"Sure." Landon shrugged, cradling his mug between his hands. "So…how'd this girl find you anyway? I thought adoptions were sealed up like Fort Knox back then."

Rick noted the change in subject. "Her father wrote down Michelle's name. I guess there's a lot on the Internet nowadays."

Landon's brow furrowed. "I don't really remember Michelle. We might have met once at a Christmas thing, years ago. But you never forgot her, did you?"

Rick scratched the tip of his nose with the pen he still held and frowned. "No, I didn't forget—her or any of it. It became a nightmare I just lived with."

"I'm sorry. It can't have been easy."

Rick sighed and closed his eyes. "I think I got the better end of the deal compared to what she must have gone through."

"Probably. So what's she like, this daughter you never knew you had?" Landon flashed a grin.

"She's…hard to describe." Rick smoothed down his hair. "Stubborn, smart, funny, sarcastic, likes to get her own way…"

"Sounds like a chip off the old block if you ask me." Landon snorted and gulped the rest of his coffee.

His tanned skin and clear eyes showed he was taking care of himself. He'd even put on a bit of weight to balance his muscular build. He looked healthier than Rick had ever seen him. But shadows in his eyes hinted of trouble beneath the surface.

Landon's mouth curled and he narrowed his eyes. "You're still as transparent as ever, Maverick. I saw you spying on me last night at dinner."

"I wasn't spying on you." Rick coughed and swallowed down irritation. "I didn't know it was illegal for me to care."

"It's not." Landon glanced downward. "Sorry for snapping. I'm just a little tired of being under the magnifying glass, you know. I'm okay, seriously."

Rick nodded. "Good. I, uh, heard what happened at work, what you went through."

"Mom and Dad told you." The fatigue in Landon's normally rigorous gait wasn't hard to miss, nor was the tension etched across his forehead.

"You didn't seem like yourself so I asked. Do you want to talk about it?"

Landon rolled his eyes and stretched his arms high above his head. "Let's just say the last operation went south and leave it at that. There's going to be an investigation, and I'm out until it's over."

Rick's pulse jacked up a notch. "Were you hurt?"

"Nah. Just a graze. Overnight in hospital." Landon rested his head against the back of the couch and closed his eyes. "My partner wasn't so lucky."

"I'm sorry."

"Yeah."

"Nothing says you have to go back, you know. You're not married to the DEA."

Landon held his gaze for a long moment. "It's what I do, Rick. Leave it be." He got to his feet and headed back to the coffee maker.

Rick ran a hand down his face and uttered a silent prayer for patience. "You know, Landon, whatever you're going through…whatever it is that drives you to rid the earth of all evil even if it kills you, you're never going to be satisfied. Trust me, I know what I'm talking about."

Rick waited for the groan but it didn't come.

"It's not an easy life, but it's my life. I'm living it the best way I know how." Landon's voice thickened, and he didn't make eye contact.

"We just worry, that's all."

Landon's eyes shimmered. "I know. Thanks." He gave a sheepish smile. "Anyway, back to your shocking revelation. Have you talked to Michelle?"

Rick stood and went to the window again. He put one hand in his pocket and closed his fingers around the piece of paper he'd scribbled on hours ago. The office building wasn't far from here.

"No, I haven't talked to her." The thought of doing so terrified him, but he vowed to get it over with before leaving New York. Rick glanced at his watch. "Why don't you take Mom and Dad out for lunch? I need to go over to the gallery for a meeting. I'll check in with you later."

"Sure. Hey, I wanted to ask you something."

Rick turned, curious.

Landon smiled and lifted broad shoulders, looking suddenly younger than his twenty-nine years. "Since I can't go back to work until after the investigation, I was wondering…" He pulled at the back of his neck and hesitation twitched his mouth. "Well, if it was okay with you, I wondered if I could come stay with you awhile."

"Are you serious?" Rick tried not to keel over from shock, but a chuckle escaped before he could stop it. He felt a stab of guilt at Landon's dejected expression. "Of course you can stay with me. As long as you do your share of the cooking and pick up after yourself. If I remember correctly, you always were a bit of a slob."

"I'll be on my best behavior." Landon's smile was genuine, one Rick hadn't seen in a long time.

Rick chuckled as he donned his faded denim jacket. "Okay. Well, I'll see you later then."

"Rick?"

He turned at the door and glanced back at Landon. "What?"

"Good luck." He came forward and placed a hand on his shoulder. "I know where you're really going. I hope it works out."

Rick inhaled and managed a smile. "I don't think it's going to be quite that easy, but thanks."

* * *

Once inside the towering glass office building, Rick found her floor with relative ease. To his relief, the desk outside her office seemed unoccupied.

Rick inched toward the door with her name on it. It was slightly ajar, and he scanned the room undetected.

Michelle sat at an angle behind a large wooden desk. She frowned at the computer screen in front of her, bending her head every now and then as she wrote furiously on a legal pad.

Her long dark hair was swept up in some fancy style. Her finely sculpted face didn't look a day older. She wore a silk blouse, patterned in aqua, red, and brown circles. Not colors he would normally put together, but it worked.

Twenty-seven years slipped away in the time it took for him to take his next breath.

"Can I help you?" Michelle glanced up from her work.

Already sweating and more nervous than he'd been the night he'd first kissed her, he moved into the room. Captured once more by those amazing dark eyes, his breath left him with the speed of the subway train he'd just ridden on.

She was as beautiful. No, more beautiful than he remembered.

Recognition inched across her face. "Get out."

And just as livid.

She pushed her chair back and stood, her eyes glinting. "I don't want you here. Leave. Now."

Rick raised a hand, his mouth drying up. "This won't take long."

She marched around her desk, brushed past him, and stuck her head around the door.

"There's nobody there."

"I can see that." She slammed the door shut and leaned against it. "What do you want, Rick?"

"To talk." His shirt was already sticking to his back.

Michelle curled a finger around the string of pearls she wore. "We haven't 'talked' in twenty-seven years. What makes you think I'd have the slightest interest in doing so now?"

The nerve he'd found to step into the room withered under her scathing glance. But he was tired of running—tired of feeling like a coward. Tired of covering up his mistakes of the past and pretending they didn't exist.

Rick balled his fists and summoned fresh courage. "Please. Just hear me out. You know why I'm here." He willed his heart to stop thumping and tried to formulate a sentence that actually made sense.

Michelle lowered her eyes. Anger flared in her cheeks when she finally looked at him. "She found you, too? Wonderful." She strode across the office and stood at the window, her back to him.

Rick shrugged off his jacket and sat in one of the chairs opposite her desk. Somewhere in the cool room, a clock ticked. "She didn't exactly find me. I live in Bethel now, in my grandparents' house. Which is right up..."

"I know where it is. I knew I couldn't trust my mother." A soft curse slipped from her lips. "If you had any idea what this is doing to me, you wouldn't be here."

Rick leaned forward and pinched the bridge of his nose.

Please, God...

"Shelly, I didn't come here to hurt you." His voice cracked, and she turned his way, her face pale, still tight with anger.

She put one hand on her hip and tossed her head. "No, that's been done. Tell me something, though. Did you ever once, in all these years, think of anyone other than yourself?"

"I'm sorry." Shallow, meaningless words.

She stared in clear disbelief. "You don't get to be sorry, Rick." Michelle sagged in her chair and stared up at him through cold eyes. Her anger seemed to fade, replaced by something he could only liken to resolute acceptance. "I spent a lot of years hating you." She gave a shrug and pressed her fingers against her temples. "But in the end I decided you weren't worth it. I got on with my life. I don't need this now. I didn't ask to be found. I'm not interested."

"I don't believe that." Rick startled at the words he spoke.

"I don't care what you believe."

"You wanted her, Shelly. If I'd done the right thing, you would never have given her up."

"Well, you sure didn't *do the right thing*, did you?"

168

There was no answer needed for that one. "Why did you tell me you were getting an abortion?"

"Because I was." She placed her elbows on the desk and hid her face in her hands. Then lowered them and pinned him under her gaze once more. "Just get out of here. I'm not having this conversation."

Silence crept around him again and threatened his sanity. "I know you don't want to talk about it. I know it's hard. But we have to. I have to. We've lived with this for twenty-seven years." His voice cracked again. Rick shifted and raked his fingers through his hair. "I didn't know whether my child was alive or dead, and I didn't have the guts to pick up the phone and ask you. The biggest regret of my life is sitting up there in Maine on your parents' back porch."

Eventually she spoke, her eyes softer, but void of real emotion. "I thought I could go through with it," she whispered. "I couldn't. But I also knew I couldn't raise a child alone. I had no money, no support. I wanted her to have two parents who loved her, who could provide for her. I thought if I gave her up, she'd have a chance."

His gut tightened as he watched her wrestle with the pain of a past he was only now beginning to comprehend.

"I carried her for nine months. I talked to her, felt her grow inside of me, and I promised her a good life. I...even named her." Michelle gave a thin smile. "Stupid, huh?"

"What did you name her?" Rick's eyes burned. The effort it took to hold himself together and not break down in front of her was almost suffocating.

"Beth. I wanted to call her Beth."

"Claire's middle name is Elizabeth." He choked on the words.

Michelle stared at him for a long time. He wished he could know what was going on inside her head, wished he could read her thoughts. But maybe it was better that he couldn't.

"I know."

"You know?" Trepidation skewered him. "How?"

He could almost see the wall coming up around her heart as she set her jaw. "I was curious. Sue me."

Rick suddenly wished he hadn't shaved off that beard. Smiles were too hard to hide now. "What else do you know about her?"

She drummed her pen on the desk and lowered her gaze. "Not much. Just what was on the Internet. I know of her family, the Wileys. Her mother was a Dupperault—they own a cosmetics company, very wealthy. She hasn't wanted for much, apparently."

"Just answers."

Michelle shook her head and scratched a hard black line on her notepad. "Why? Is it not enough for her to know that I gave her life? I don't want to relive the past. It was hard enough the first time around."

He couldn't argue with that.

"I have a picture if you'd like…"

"No." Certain fear took hold of her features as she held up a hand.

"Shelly, I'm sorry." Rick leaned closer to her and waited until she met his gaze again. "I'm not here to persuade you to meet Claire or even talk to her. That's completely up to you. I came here to apologize. What I did was unconscionable. I know that. You have every right to hate me. I don't expect you to forgive me, but you have my apology."

She gave a small shrug and looked away.

Rick couldn't tear his eyes from her. All his well-submerged memories surfaced and floated over the still waters of his soul. As young as they had been, he'd loved her. Completely—with all his heart and mind and soul.

Looking at her now, he knew he'd never gotten over her.

Probably never would.

"Are you done?" Her eyes became chips of ice once more and told him their meeting was over.

Rick stood and pulled on his jacket. Her chair scraped against the hardwood floor. He turned to go and his eyes landed on the painting on the wall adjacent to him. A fresh flood of memory cascaded over him and almost forced him back into his chair.

"You still have that." He made a slow turn.

They'd sat snuggled under blankets for hours, watching the sun come up while he painted. He'd told her he loved her that morning. And he'd meant it.

Michelle moved swiftly, snatched the painting off the hook, and crossed the room again. "Take it with you when you leave." She thrust it at his chest.

Rick let out his breath and placed the painting down against the side of her desk. "No. It's yours. If you don't want it, take it down to The Alexander. They're showing my work this week. I'll make sure you get a good price for it."

Her mouth formed a reply, but a knock on the door smothered it.

"Michelle, ready to go?" A well-dressed man strode halfway into the room before he pulled up short in front of Rick. "So sorry. I didn't know you were in a meeting."

"I'm not." She fumbled at her desk and made a good attempt at looking busy.

Rick hesitated. He recognized the Ssnator. The last thing he wanted to do was put Shelly in the awkward position of having to explain his presence. He needed to leave, that much was clear, but the man blocked his path. He couldn't very well push past him.

"Is everything all right?" The guy gave Shelly the once-over and then his gaze lingered on Rick. "Say, aren't you Rick Matthews? I was at your show the other night. Impressive stuff."

"Thank you, Senator." Rick cast a glance at Michelle. She sat at her desk, head down, as though concentrating on the notes on her pad.

"Is there anyone in the world you don't know, Kevin?" she muttered.

Her boss chuckled and extended a hand. "Kevin Harrison. Congratulations again." He pulled at his striped silk tie and loosened his top button. "I was just reading an article about you, Matthews. I recognized you from the picture. You're from Michelle's hometown, right? Are the two of you friends?"

Wads of cotton formed in Rick's mouth as Michelle met his questioning gaze.

She rounded the desk and gently moved the senator out of Rick's way, her face impassive. "Acquaintances. He just popped in to say hello, and we had a bit of a chat. Told me his grandparents had died. I was close to them at one time."

"Oh, shame. Sorry to hear that." Harrison's apology was lukewarm at best, his smile officious.

"Thanks." Rick inhaled and avoided Shelly's gaze. The excuse given for his visit rankled him, but what had he expected from her? The truth?

"Hey, why don't you join us for drinks later? I need Michelle now, I'm afraid. We're already running late."

Michelle shook her head. "Can't do drinks. You have an early dinner appointment. Rick was just leaving. He's late as well."

"Oh, sorry." Harrison jumped out of the way, looking almost relieved. Rick didn't fail to notice his arm slip possessively around Michelle's slender waist. A sudden intense dislike for the man crept out and pounced on him like Jackson would after winning a game of hide-n-go-seek.

"Nice to meet you." Rick forced a smile and chanced a fleeting glance at Michelle. "Thanks for seeing me." There was nothing more he could say now, yet years of conversation sat on his tongue.

She stood very still, stoic and immovable. "Good-bye, Rick."

26

Michelle paced herself, splashing through puddles as she rounded the corner of the last block before she reached home. She weaved in and out of pedestrians enjoying the Saturday afternoon now that the rain had stopped. A humid heat rose from the wet pavement and seeped through her pores. She slowed and jacked up the volume of her iPod, the pounding beat of Nickleback quickening her speed.

Fury ripped through her again and urged her on.

How dare he! Her hatred for Rick Matthews intensified as she replayed their meeting. Who did he think he was, waltzing back into her life after all this time, offering an apology? As if she'd ever forgive him. Or her parents.

She breathed in the muggy city air and swiped sweat off her face. At least Kevin was out of town this weekend. She wasn't up to another inquisition. Thankfully he didn't dwell on the subject of her and Rick's friendship for long. She'd mastered the art of distracting him when need be.

Kevin had been pushy lately, though. The break would do them good. Her living room was filled with more elaborate flower arrangements she planned to get rid of today. The lilies made her eyes water—their heady scent overpowered the apartment. She didn't even like lilies. She'd told him that a million times. Gerber daises. Big, bright Gerber daises, all colors. That's what she liked. But Kevin never listened.

Michelle slowed to a jog as she approached the front steps of her apartment building and turned down the music.

Her neighbor was coming out the door. "Afternoon, Ms. Hart."

"Hey, Mr. Rosenburg. How are you today?" She raised her voice enough so he'd hear her but not loud enough to make him think she was shouting.

"As fine as a pickle on rye and pastrami." The older gentleman stepped spritely down the steps and flashed her the toothy smile she'd grown so fond of over the past few years. "You were out longer than usual. Do an extra lap around the park?"

"Four extra laps." She stretched out her legs on the cement steps and grunted, her muscles screaming louder than the music she'd been listening to. At this rate she might even have a heart attack.

Thank you, Rick, the cause of my early demise.

"Got men trouble?" He waved his walking stick in the air. "I told you, honey, I'd marry you tomorrow. Just say yes and it's a done deal. You wouldn't have a care in the world." His wrinkled face cracked as he tipped his head back in raucous laughter.

"Oh, boy." Michelle let her own laughter come. Tugging at her ponytail, she retied it in a bun at the back of her head. "I don't think I could keep up with you, Mr. Rosenburg."

"No, you probably couldn't. Well, I'm off to my chess game. You take care, honey."

"You, too. Oh, watch out…" He stepped onto the curb and nearly barreled into a man hurrying past their building. Michelle moved down a step in case he needed help, but the two narrowly missed colliding. The man stopped to apologize, and Michelle's heart stopped right along with him at the sound of his voice.

Maybe she was being punished.

She'd always believed God had a rather warped sense of humor.

Her eyes shot to the front door of her building, and she attempted a dash before being spotted.

"Shelly?"

Not fast enough. She turned and locked eyes with Rick Matthews again.

Surprise showed from his eyes, and he smiled briefly. "You live here?"

She scowled. "Genius."

His smile broadened, and Michelle's heart beat a little faster. How was it possible for him to look as handsome as he'd been when they were kids? In tight fitting jeans and a white cotton shirt, open at the collar, he didn't look a day over twenty-five.

She inhaled. Who cared what he looked like? He was pond scum. Attractive pond scum, but pond scum nonetheless.

Michelle tugged at her damp T-shirt, hovering between two steps. "What are you doing here? Please don't tell me you found out where I lived and…"

"Don't shoot." He raised his hands, a grin curling his mouth. "The Alexander is on this street. I was heading that way. It's my last showing tonight."

Okay, she couldn't deny that. The gallery was right around the corner. At least he wasn't stalking her.

She gathered her scattered thoughts. "Congratulations. I hear you're the talk of Manhattan." She could be civil.

Kevin had shown her the article he'd read. It sang Rick's praises. Art dealers were flocking to see his work. Kevin wanted her to secure him one of

Rick's paintings for his office. She almost offered to give him hers.

"Yeah, well." Rick's smile faded, and he ran a hand over his hair.

It was as thick and dark as she remembered, without a strand of gray. Another reason to hate him. He'd probably never run a day in his life either, didn't have to work out three times a week to keep that fine physique.

"You must be pretty pleased with yourself." Michelle's cheeks grew warm as the telling words popped out. "I mean, with your show." She really hoped it wasn't obvious she was checking him out. But the way one eyebrow quirked as a grin settled on his lips told her it probably was.

A faint pink hue tinged his cheeks. "It's not that big a deal, really."

Michelle took two steps down and folded her arms across her chest. "Of course it is. Is your family in town?"

Rick's chuckle swept over her like a cooling breath of air. Her eyes began to sting, the odd sensation taking her by surprise. She lowered her head, kicking at a stray piece of newspaper.

If he noticed her emotion, he didn't let on. "Yeah, even Landon. Flew in for the show. I don't know if you ever met him. He came to live with my folks when I was in college."

"I think I might have once." Michelle tried to smile as she met his eyes. "I didn't go home much...after. So, how is he? Married, kids?"

Rick shook his head. "Nope. He lives in DC, works a pretty tough job. He's taking some time off. Wants to come back to Bethel with me."

Michelle snorted. "Not much to do there."

"Yeah, well, maybe that's what he needs." His smile reached right through her and jangled the chains around her heart.

She backed up a step. "Well, I need to go. Shower."

"Say, uh, we're having a thing...drinks and whatnot afterward tonight. Maybe you and the senator want to come?" He gave a hesitant glance in her direction.

Michelle drew in a breath. Did he know she was involved with Kevin? Of course he did. Kevin didn't hide the relationship. He used it to its full advantage. Rumors of his divorce and their pending engagement had been running the wires for weeks.

"Kevin's out of town." She'd have gone with him too if he hadn't been visiting his mother. But there was no love lost between her and Jessica Harrison. Michelle pulled at the waistband of her running pants and turned off her iPod.

Rick shrugged. "You could always bring the old guy. I saw the two of you talking before he almost barged into me. Is he your neighbor?"

174

"Yes." Michelle sighed, desperate to escape the deep blue eyes she thought she'd long forgotten. "He'd probably love that, but he goes to bed around seven. Sorry."

A slight breeze whispered through the trees and lifted his hair. Her mother had said Claire looked just like her. If they'd had a son, she'd bet...

Rick scratched the side of his jaw. "Okay, I get it." His face tightened and the humor left his eyes. "If you change your mind about Claire or ever just want to talk, my number is listed."

"Don't hold your breath." She blanched at her sharp tone. "Sorry, it's...difficult. I wasn't expecting this. I don't know how to deal with it."

"I know. Me either." He moved a little closer and captured her gaze. "She just wants to meet you. Wherever it goes from there is up to you."

"Don't push it, Rick." Michelle shielded her eyes from the sun. "You don't understand. I've moved on. That part of my life is over. I don't think anybody has the right to demand anything of me. I don't want to do it and that's that."

His laughter wrapped around her like a favorite sweater. She drew herself up and hugged her arms. "There's nothing funny about this."

Rick tipped his head, raised an eyebrow in question, and set his gaze on her. "You always were as stubborn as a herd of cows."

"And you always had such a way with words." She glared and watched the color disappear from his cheeks.

He ran a hand down his face, clearly aghast. "I didn't mean that you...you know...I wasn't comparing you to a cow or anything."

She wanted to let him wallow in his misery, but laughter bubbled out of her before she could do a thing about it. He joined in, that deep familiar chuckle penetrating her soul again, reminding her of past pleasures.

Michelle caught her breath and leaned against the concrete arm of the stairs. "Do you remember that time when we cut through the Jensens' field and left the gate open?" She smiled at the memory, and Rick laughed harder.

"Cows all over Main Street," he spluttered. "And we sat in school and pretended like we had nothing to do with it."

"Yeah. But my dad figured it out. You sure did have a way of getting me in trouble, Rick Matthews."

Their laughter petered out like a stone skimmed across the lake, finally sinking beneath the dark depths. He veered his gaze, and the weight of her words fell heavy around them.

Michelle shifted. The safety of her apartment called to her, but his bleak expression made her stay. "So, uh, this girl...Claire. Is she going to stay in

Bethel?"

Rick's eyes got brighter as he looked her way again. "No, I don't think so. She and her husband are due back home the end of next week."

Michelle pulled her arms behind her and worked a kink out of her shoulder. "They have children?"

"No." Rick rubbed his eyes. "They had a miscarriage awhile back—about a year ago I think it was. Claire had just lost her mom. Took it pretty hard."

For some reason, his words shook her. Like someone had shoved her finger into a light socket. Michelle turned from him and pulled her hair free, ran her hands through it and shoved old memories away.

Claire had lost a baby.

Michelle knew that kind of pain. Knew that kind of loss.

The kind you never quite get over, no matter how hard you try.

Rick was right. She couldn't run anymore.

"What am I supposed to do?" She faced Rick again. "I can't go back there. You don't know..."

"I do know." Understanding settled in his eyes. "Your parents told me the whole story, what happened when you came home. Shel, they're sorry. I know they'd give anything to change things; so would I. But we can't. All we can do is forgive and move on."

"No." Forgiveness wasn't an option. Not now. "I can't be the person everyone expects me to be, Rick. That girl is long gone. If you knew me now..." Michelle shook her head at his curious expression. "You wouldn't like me very much."

"Try me." He moved toward her.

Michelle knew they were creeping toward dangerous territory. She raised a hand. "I can't do this. Please. I don't expect you to understand, but that's just the way it is. I know why you came to see me, and I hope it helped. But I can't tell you what you need to hear. I'm sorry."

His blue eyes shimmered. "I didn't really expect you would. But thanks for listening anyway." He offered a meager smile. "It was good to see you again, Shel, in spite of the circumstances."

"I can't say the same."

He nodded, gave a slight smile. She hadn't intended to hurt him. Or maybe she had. Either way, the look in his eyes said she succeeded.

She clenched her jaw. If he came any closer, she'd probably throw herself into his arms. "I really have to go. Have a good trip home."

She raced up the stairs and fumbled with the locks, only looking back once she was safely inside the foyer.

Rick Matthews was already halfway down the block.

And he didn't look back.

* * *

Just as she dumped the last of the offensive flowers into the garbage chute at the end of her floor later that afternoon, she spotted the florist's delivery guy making his way down the hall. Michelle took slow steps in his direction, waiting to see where he would stop.

Right outside her door.

Great. *Give it up, Kevin. Please.* She was all out of allergy medicine.

"I'm coming." She quickened her pace, not wanting to keep the kid waiting. Fishing a couple bucks from the pocket of her jeans, they swapped.

"Thanks, Miss Hart."

"See you later, Joey." She hoped not.

Michelle unlocked her door and set the arrangement down on her dining room table. It appeared smaller than Kevin's usual over-the-top attempts at cajoling her into doing whatever it was he wanted. Gingerly she peeled back the thin pink tissue paper.

Michelle blinked at the array of color sitting before her. Bright yellow, pink, and red Gerber daises sat in a crystal bowl, white baby's breath tucked in between their large petals. Green fern set off the arrangement. A card fluttered to the floor.

She gave a tiny groan and slit the envelope. Her eyes scanned the neatly penned words and she recognized the writing at once:

"The first time ever I saw your face"...remember that song? Still feels like yesterday even after all this time. Again, I'm sorry for everything. I hope you'll change your mind and come tonight. Rick.

Alarm shot through her. Michelle slapped the card face down on the table and walked to the kitchen, her heart pounding.

What did he think he was doing?

"The first time, ever I saw your face, I thought the sun rose in your eyes..."

Their song played in her mind and brought old memories along with it. It was already years old when they first heard it playing from an old record her mother had saved. The moment those soft words reached her ears and Rick's arms drew her close, she knew it was written just for them.

They had a fort, an abandoned cabin in the woods. Rick claimed it and fixed it up some when they were younger. As the years went by, it became their special place. Always the collector, he had an old turntable there, an antique even then she supposed. They created many memories there, listening to those old records and sharing secrets, experiencing the wonder and joy of falling in love.

Michelle pushed the memory away and chugged Perrier, choking on the fizz. It wasn't possible to still have those feelings. They were long dead and buried, and not about to be resurrected.

She kicked off her shoes and flopped onto the couch, staring at the dazzling display that had succeeded in sending her mind into a tailspin.

Okay, so he sent flowers. It meant nothing. She grimaced and clenched her fists.

No, flowers with no note meant nothing. That note…she let out a cry of frustration and glared at the black television screen across the room.

Rick's artistic side dominated his emotions. He always acted first and thought later. Always. She'd hated that about him. So what if he was sorry.

She brought her knees to her chest and drew in a deep breath. As angry as she was, there was no denying the impact of seeing him again. The cute boy she'd fallen in love with had matured into an extremely handsome man. Even so, the boyish grin she remembered still played on his lips. He had been her best friend first, the love of her life later.

And what was he now? Trouble. With a capital T.

She'd put away all thoughts of Rick Matthews a long time ago. No way would she jump into those waters again.

Unbidden, his smiling face flashed before her and Michelle groaned. If the fluttering of her stomach was anything to go by, she hadn't eliminated *all* memories of their past. It was insane. Absolutely, ridiculously insane. She refused to consider what Rick Matthews once meant to her.

He'd broken her heart. Put her through the unthinkable.

But he'd apologized.

The agonized expression he wore that day in her office still prodded at her, made her believe that perhaps he really did mean what he said.

The flowers were just his way. He was probably only being nice. God knows he needed to be.

Michelle covered her face with her hands. She should have gone to Boston with Kevin. Playing bridge with Jessica Harrison would have been far better torture.

27

Michelle slipped into the crowded gallery and swore at herself for the tenth time that evening. She'd lost her mind. Completely. She didn't even have Belinda to talk to, since she was in Europe for the next month. But Lin would have forced her into going anyway and come along for the ride.

It took an hour of changing in and out of the simple black dress she'd finally stepped into before she knew she really was coming. The more reasons she found to stay home, the greater the desire to go became.

What could it hurt? She'd always loved Rick's work. Maybe she'd buy something for Kevin. There would be so many people around, perfectly safe. No room for any intimate conversations.

She tucked her hair behind her ear and accepted a glass offered to her by a passing waiter. Conversation sparked the air, the room electric with excitement, as often happens when something or someone new and exciting hits the scene. Never in a million years would she have dreamt that Rick Matthews could cause such a stir.

She'd been to so many of these soirées now, and frankly they bored her.

Nodding to a few acquaintances, Michelle strolled the room and allowed his paintings to mesmerize her and capture her heart.

Again.

The vivid colors and images drew her back to times and places she hadn't thought of in years. The urge to guzzle down the champagne and grab another glass was tempting, but she tamped it. When she rounded the next corner, Tara's Place jumped out at her from a larger painting on the wall and her hand flew to her throat.

The pristine white house was just as she remembered it—ivy and roses creeping up the walls. How she'd loved living there, right on the lake. Able to swim and sail all summer, ski in winter. Dad was more into winter sports, and the two of them would drive to the ski resorts, stay a couple of nights and come home sore but satisfied with the black diamonds they'd conquered.

She and her mother waited patiently all year for blueberry season. Then they'd disappear into the woods together for hours, picking the best berries, sharing secrets and girl talk. More hours would then be spent baking pies. Her dad and Rick would prowl the kitchen like hungry lions waiting for their next meal. An unexpected memory of Rick's laughing face, covered in blue sauce, skittered across her mind.

"Do you miss it, Shelly?"

For a moment she thought she imagined the soft low voice behind her—she'd heard it so often in her head over the years—even when she didn't want to.

No polite greeting and small talk, Rick cut to the chase. But then he always had. His honesty had been only one of the things she'd admired about him.

Michelle swiveled on her high heels and clutched the stem of her glass. She managed a whisper of a smile, her heart too full for more. "Your work is amazing. Really."

"Mmm. Thanks." Vague amusement settled on his face, no doubt caused by her dodging the question. The habit always drove him crazy.

He shook hands with an elderly couple walking past and took a glass of sparkling water one of the servers brought him.

"No champagne? You should be celebrating." Michelle sipped her drink as they walked through the impressive display of paintings and sculptures.

He gave a short laugh. "I'm afraid I celebrated a few years too many. Just the soft stuff for me now."

Something about his tone dragged her eyes to his face and made her stomach tighten. When she caught the regret in his eyes, she looked away.

She stopped again when they came to a large oil painting of the lake. Another album of memories spread open before her, and she needed to stop and compose herself. Coming here was such a bad idea.

Rick cleared his throat. "Your folks asked me to please give you their love if I saw you."

"Oh." She willed her hands to stop shaking. Her eyes moved of their own accord, taking in everything about him. Tonight he wore a black suit, a light blue shirt, and royal-blue silk tie. And he wore it well.

Too well.

Rick gave a sudden grin and scratched the back of his neck. "Can't wait to rip this tie off. I feel like I'm going to a funeral."

Michelle tossed her hair over her shoulders and laughed, eager to break the tension. If Rick felt half as awkward as she did, it was going to be a long night. "You look very dignified. I think the last time I saw you in a suit was at prom. If I recall correctly, you weren't too happy about it then, either."

"Nope." His eyes sparkled under the glow of the small fluorescent bulbs.

"I had to buy this monkey suit for the showing. Angus talked me into all this by the way. He's around here somewhere. I live in jeans most of the time, spend most days working in the studio or helping your dad around the property, so..." He rolled his eyes like he regretted his words.

Michelle's high heels began to pinch. She placed her empty champagne flute on a tray as a server passed. "Why did you move back to Bethel, Rick?"

"I don't know." He looked down at his feet, then back at her, his stare intense. "Well, that's not true. If you really want to know, your parents had a lot to do with it."

"How so?"

"Ah." Rick scratched his head and gave a sheepish grin. "Let's just say I needed some help back then. They've been good to me."

"How nice for you."

"Shel..."

Michelle drew her lips together. "How are they?"

Rick's steady gaze settled on her again and she braved it. "Great. Getting older like the rest of us. They've taken a real shine to Claire, though." He flinched and shook his head. "Sorry. This isn't going so well."

Had he expected it would? Michelle mustered a smile. "I got the flowers."

A faint blush darkened his cheeks but he nodded, guiding them along the room, his hand at her elbow. He stopped to place his glass on a nearby table, then turned her way, his eyes piercing under the stark lights. "I probably shouldn't have, but I saw them on my way back to the hotel, thought of you, and couldn't help myself. Look..."

He pulled her into a deserted corner of the room and took her hands in his. "The thing is, Shel, I've spent a lot of years trying to forget you. It hasn't worked. The minute I laid eyes on you again, I knew I'd never get over you. I know you're still angrier than a swarm of hornets, but you're here. Why?"

"You misunderstand." She lowered her gaze. "I only wanted to see your work."

"Not me?" His finger grazed her chin and tilted her face upward. "Be honest. We don't have time for anything else. I know what I'm feeling. I also know there's talk of you getting married to Mr. Politics. But if there's the slightest chance that you might forgive me, that we might start over, get to know each other again, I'd jump at it."

Michelle stared at him in disbelief. "Are you crazy? You don't know me anymore, Rick. I don't know you. You're just caught up...in the past." She brought a hand to her mouth. She'd never been more blindsided and, for the first time in years, Michelle had to scramble for an appropriate response.

"Look, let's not get carried away. We shared a lot, and we went through a lot. But we were kids. It's over. I have a career, a life here in New York. I'm sorry, but I don't believe in second chances. Life doesn't work that way."

"Sure it does." He stepped closer and cupped her face in his hands. He was close enough for her to feel his breath on her cheek. Her flight instinct kicked in, but her feet sealed themselves to the floor. All she could do was stare into those amazing eyes and wait for the moment his lips brushed hers.

That didn't happen. He let her go and stepped back. Paling, he cleared his throat—an uncomfortable sound that made her nervous.

Michelle turned to see what caused such surprise, no, shock, to flit across his face.

The moment she saw the two young women making their way toward them, Michelle knew she'd been set up.

28

Claire watched Rick's face drain of all color as soon as he spotted them. She stopped walking, her feet suddenly cemented to the floor.

She should have told Darcie no, should have insisted that they not surprise Rick. But it was too late now. There was no waking from what was turning into a nightmare spiraling out of control.

"What's wrong?" James slipped his arm around her and she leaned into him. If the elegantly dressed woman standing with Rick was who she thought it was, she might faint.

"What in the world is my mother doing here?" Darcie muttered. Annoyance laced her tone, but she maneuvered her way through the noisy crowd. "Hey, Rick. Surprise!"

Rick was clearly more than surprised. He was doing a fabulous imitation of a deer caught in the headlights of an oncoming tractor-trailer. Claire thought he might pass out before she got the chance.

She forgot about making an exit plan and allowed herself to study the woman who stared at them as though they all held high-powered rifles pointed in her direction.

Michelle. Her birth mother.

"You're not going to believe this," James whispered in her ear. "I've met her before."

"You what?" Claire stiffened, ready to bolt. "How?"

"She came into the office with one of my clients. I thought she looked familiar, but I figured it was just because I'd seen her on the news or something. Weird."

"Really weird." Claire hung back, glancing at James as fear gripped her. "I knew this was a bad idea. What am I going to do? Darcie has no clue."

"Just be cool. Stay calm, okay? We'll see what happens."

"What *is* she doing here anyway?" Claire glanced back over her shoulder and wondered if they could slip out the front door again. But Darcie waved them over, and she knew they had no choice but to stay and let this nightmare play out.

"Hi, Mom." Darcie's timid voice tore at Claire's heart. "You look nice."

"Hello, Darcie." A brief smile touched Michelle's lips, and she tugged on her hair at the exact moment Claire did the same to her own. "What a surprise to see you here. Both of you."

Claire watched Darcie's face change, her smile fading and a look of utter confusion claiming it. Had the room been silent, Claire figured she would have heard the wheels turning inside her sister's head. Michelle obviously assumed that by now one of them had told Darcie the truth.

If she'd ever needed a miracle, it was now. But none came. The floor didn't open up and swallow her. A bolt of lightning didn't rip through the sky and cause a blackout.

She was stuck.

"Do you know Claire?" Darcie's eyes widened as she looked at her mother and then at Claire. And then her gaze settled on Rick.

Claire's heart pounded, but she couldn't stop staring. Nobody bothered to make any introductions. None were needed, but Darcie didn't know that.

A younger man joined their silent group and slapped Rick on the back. "There you are. Only you could pull off a disappearing act at your own show. Hey…"

Claire figured it was probably Rick's brother, Landon, and by the look on his face, he clearly knew who she was. His handsome grin broadened as he looked from her to Michelle.

"Michelle, right? I haven't seen you since I was what, twelve? How are you?" He gave her a peck on the cheek. When he stepped back, Claire knew she was next.

Please, no. Don't say anything. Just go away, Claire pleaded with him in silence. Her eyes met Rick's, but he only shook his head, looking more frantic than she was sure she did.

"And you have to be Claire. Wow. You look just like your mother, huh?" Landon chuckled and nodded toward Rick. "Good thing, too, with his ugly mug." He pulled her into a hug before she could protest. "Nobody told me we were having a family reunion tonight. Pretty cool, huh?"

"Landon." Rick's low voice held clear warning, and Landon took a step back, his tanned face turning a lighter shade. He rubbed his jaw, his eyes locked on his Rick's.

"Why do I get the feeling I'm about to get shot?" He gave a half laugh, but nobody joined in.

"Landon," Rick said again, louder this time.

Landon drew in a breath, his eyes narrowing as the lights came on. "Oh. Crap. Sorry. Okay, then. I should just…um…go." He fled into the far end of the gallery.

Claire clutched James' hand so tightly that she saw him wince.

Darcie's translucent gaze moved over all of them, her eyes troubled. "What's going on here?"

"Darce, just calm down…" Rick moved in to put an arm around her.

She shook him off. "Would somebody please tell me what that guy was talking about?"

Michelle shot a scathing glance at Rick. "I knew I shouldn't have come here. You are not someone to be trusted, Rick Matthews. You never were." She pushed past the small group and Claire caught her breath as she stopped and fumbled in her purse. Turning back to Darcie, she handed her a business card. "Call me later, please." She took quick steps in the direction of the door, then stopped again and walked back to where Claire stood.

Claire's pulse raced as she locked eyes with the woman who'd given her life. The feeling was unlike anything she'd ever experienced. She wanted to laugh and cry at the same time, but tears trumped.

Michelle mirrored her pained expression. She glanced at James and shook her head. "Mr. Ferguson. Small world."

"Something like that," he replied in a quiet voice.

She placed a hand on Claire's arm, her dark eyes glistening. "I'm sorry. I just can't talk to you right now."

And then she was gone.

* * *

Rick raced down the sidewalk, bumping into people and jostling his way around couples holding hands as they walked. "Shelly, wait!" How could she walk that fast in heels? "Would you stop? I'm going to have a heart attack."

That got her attention. Rick leaned over, trying to catch his breath. He heard the quick click of her heels coming his way and he looked up to meet her eyes as she stopped in front of him.

Her eyes flashed daggers. "Good. I hope you die right here on the street. Really." She turned and picked up her pace again. "Stop following me, or I'll scream for the cops."

Rick ignored the irrational threat, managed to catch her this time and grabbed her arm. "I had no idea they were coming! I'm not lying to you. They wanted to surprise me. It was Darcie's idea. I would never have planned that, Shel, for you to meet Claire that way…come on. Give me a break here."

"Why should I?" Michelle's voice rose to a high-pitched shriek as she yanked her arm out of his grip. He wondered if he should call a doctor or something because she looked on the verge of a nervous breakdown. "I'm sure I just got through telling you how difficult this has been—what a nightmare I lived through after you left—and then there she was. I...can't...deal...with this." Low sobs strangled her words until they took over completely.

Rick gently guided her across the street to a park bench. Michelle crumpled in his arms and sobbed. He suspected she hadn't really cried for a very long time. The aloof, career-driven professional she had become was a stark contrast to the young girl he'd left behind all those years ago.

He held her against him for what felt like hours. He didn't know how long. He didn't trust himself to speak.

All he could do was hold her and utter silent, urgent prayers.

* * *

Michelle allowed Rick to take her home, but she'd said good-bye at the door and sent him back to the gallery. She took a hot bath and downed half a bottle of wine. She hadn't felt so out of control in years. And she hated it.

It hadn't taken Darcie long to call. Her daughter wanted answers. Michelle didn't blame her, but she wasn't in any state to talk. She'd stupidly assumed her parents would have told Darcie the truth by now. The stunned expression Darcie wore after Landon's faux pas had quickly set her straight.

Michelle tossed throughout the night, seeing Claire's stricken face before her every time she closed her eyes. She needed time alone. Time to process everything and figure out what to do about it, and how to make it go away.

As if.

She called Darcie back early the next morning and asked her to come over. She wouldn't be going to work. Kevin would live without her for a day. Or a few days. There was no putting off the inevitable.

If it were as easy as telling Darcie everything and being done with it, she'd have some peace. But there was no getting around what she'd done. How she'd treated her own daughter.

The exact same way her parents had treated her.

And she wasn't sure Darcie needed to know that.

Sins of the fathers. How many generations would suffer the same mistakes?

The doorbell jangled and Michelle buzzed her in. Darcie walked into the apartment, looked around, and made for the couch. Michelle shut the door and took a seat opposite her daughter.

Darcie appeared thinner, more mature than she'd been five years ago, the last time Michelle had seen her before last night. A pang of guilt twisted around her heart. "Are you all right?"

"Do I look all right?"

Michelle winced. "Can I get you something? Coffee's made."

"No." Darcie's eyes were red-rimmed, her pale face splotched. Fresh tears formed as she pinned Michelle with an angry glare. "It's really true? Claire is my sister? Rick said he's her birth father."

"Yes. He is. She's your half sister."

"I don't believe this." Darcie pulled tissues from the pocket of her shorts. "Rick took me back to the hotel last night and told me the whole story. He said you and Claire hadn't met. That you were still thinking about it all and hadn't made up your mind what to do. Is that why you didn't tell me?"

Michelle shrugged. "No. When I saw you together last night, I assumed you already knew. Darcie, I wouldn't have wanted you to find out that way."

"You didn't want me to find out at all." Darcie drew in a deep breath. "Do my grandparents know who Claire is?"

Michelle nodded and hoped Darcie would leave it at that.

"This is insane." Her daughter pushed to her feet and paced the room, her eyes wild. "I know we don't exactly talk, Mom, but you might have told me I had a sister! How long have you known who Claire was? Just how long has everyone been lying to me?"

"Nobody lied to you, Darcie. Your grandmother called me a while ago and told me she thought Claire might be the child I'd given up for adoption. Claire put two and two together around the time you went into hospital. I asked Jessie not to say anything to you yet because I wasn't sure what to do. I didn't count on Claire ever finding me."

"Am I the only one who sees the irony in this situation?" Darcie hissed, her face pinched with accusation. "You tore me to shreds for getting pregnant, Mom. Do you remember that? Do you have any idea how you made me feel?"

"Yes. I do." Michelle brushed tears off her cheeks, her hands trembling. The memory of that time, the things she'd said to her own daughter, made her ill. "I'm so sorry for that, Darcie. My harsh reaction was uncalled for. I didn't want to see you end up like me. When I got pregnant with Claire, I was young and alone, and I made the best decision I could at the time for my baby. If I could have saved you that pain…"

"You caused that pain!" Darcie's voice rose. "You turned your back on me, remember? I had nowhere to go. Thank God for my grandparents, because without them who knows where Jackson and I might be right now? I love my son, and I'm not ashamed of him. I made mistakes, and yes, I'm paying for it.

Maybe he'll end up paying for it too, but you could have supported me. Could have shown even a shred of caring. You...you walked in my shoes, Mom!" Darcie's sob plundered Michelle's heart, but she rode out the waves of pain. She deserved every bruise they caused.

"Did you even make that connection?" Anger fading, Darcie swiped at her tears and studied Michelle with disdain. "Or had you forgotten about Claire completely by that point?"

"I never forgot her."

"Really? Is that why you want nothing to do with her?" Darcie sank onto a chair. Her breathing slowed, and Michelle saw her gulp air. "Darcie? Are you all right?" The last thing they needed was for this to land her back in the hospital. Michelle went to the kitchen and returned with a glass of water.

"I'm fine. I'm..." Darcie waved her away, tears streaming down her cheeks. "I'm having a hard time processing this." She sipped from the glass and finally spoke again, calmer than before. "My whole life I only wanted to please you. Nothing I did was ever good enough for you. I wasn't pretty enough because I didn't wear makeup or have the right haircut. I needed to lose weight. Even when I got good grades, you told me I should try harder, do better. You always pushed me one step further. I finally realized I was never going to make you happy. In the end I gave up trying."

Darcie's words stunned her. Shocked her and delivered another box full of mistakes. Mistakes she could not now go back and fix.

"I'm sorry," Michelle whispered, clutching a throw cushion to her chest. "I didn't realize. Darcie, I never meant to push you like that. I was so angry with myself, with all the mistakes I'd made." She acknowledged the truth at last. "I never got over losing her. Losing my baby. After Rick left me and I was on my own, I knew I couldn't raise a child alone. I believed placing Claire for adoption was the best thing for her, but it hurt me more than I would have believed. They told me I'd get over it, that I'd move on and make a new life for myself. I wasn't sure I'd ever be able to do that. I knew my baby wasn't dead, but it felt like it. And something inside me died too."

She held Darcie's gaze and summoned the courage to go on. "Some days I thought I'd never get through it. Then I met your father and we married, and you came along. I wanted to be a good mother to you, truly I did. I just didn't believe I could be."

"You never gave yourself a chance." Darcie wiped her face with the bottom of her shirt. "Rick told me his side last night. I know he was a jerk, and I know he hurt you, but you let that dictate how you lived the rest of your life, didn't you?" She gave a brief, sad smile. "After all these years, I think I've finally figured you out. You could never love my father properly, fully, with all your heart, because he wasn't Rick. And you could never love me the way I needed you to, because I wasn't…I wasn't Claire." Darcie lowered her head and stifled a sob.

Michelle let her daughter's profound words settle deep within her soul and acknowledged them, accepted them, as truth. Truth she could no longer deny. "You're right, Darce. Yes."

Her daughter looked unsure, as though she'd said too much and might now be punished. A sudden reminder of the day she'd told Darcie she was sending her to boarding school flashed before her. At the time she'd believed it was the right thing, but truthfully, Michelle knew she was merely shirking responsibility. The same way she had when she'd learned of Darcie's pregnancy. "Darcie, I'm so sorry. I'm sorry for everything. Please, can you forgive me?"

Darcie turned away, her shoulders shaking.

Michelle wanted to go to her, take her in her arms and tell her it would all work out. But she couldn't. It was too late to make empty promises.

The silence of the room suffocated her and told her what she already knew. There were no second chances.

After a while, Darcie slowly walked to where she sat. Her eyes hardened, but then the softness returned, giving her an almost serene look.

Michelle held her breath while Darcie sat down and took one of her hands in hers. Tears stood in her eyes, but a smile touched her lips. "No matter what happened, what went on between us, you're still my mother. Of course I forgive you."

Michelle took a moment to let the words resonate. She ran the back of her hand down Darcie's pale cheek. "Thank you." And then she drew her into a hug, one she hoped told Darcie all she was unable to say.

Eventually Michelle drew back, wiping her eyes. "Can we start over? Or is it too late?"

Darcie's smile broadened. "We can start over. I'd like nothing better. My son needs to know his grandma."

Hope surged through Michelle, and she smiled for the first time that day.

Perhaps there was redemption to be found in the ashes of her life.

29

Claire sat in the living room of Tara's Place with James beside her, a strong, silent presence she didn't know how she'd ever thought she could live without. Crickets chirped outside, and a cool breeze fluttered through the open window.

The sun had long been down, and Jackson slept peacefully upstairs. Mac had asked them all to come in here after supper, saying he had something he needed to share.

Darcie sat on the floor opposite Claire, leaning up against the other couch. Jessie paced the room, wringing her hands. Eventually Mac looked from her to Darcie.

"I'm sorry for what you've been through the past few days. I know you're both hurting. So is Shelly, I'm sure. But we need you to know...want you know, what really happened all those years ago."

"Grandpa, we already know." Darcie sounded tired. In the two days since they'd returned to the lake, she'd spent most of her time with Jackson. She and Claire hadn't really talked, and Claire wondered if their relationship would change now that Darcie knew the truth. "I can't believe you would all keep the truth from me. All this time you knew I had a sister and..."

"No." Jessie shook her head, her eyes bright. "That's just it, honey. We didn't know."

Darcie narrowed her eyes. "You didn't know my mother was pregnant?"

"Oh, we knew that all right." Mac pushed to his feet and poured a glass of lemonade from the trolley in the corner of the room. He downed the small glass in one chug. "Your mother, God bless her, didn't tell you the whole story when you talked, I'm afraid. But we want you to hear it. It's time for truth now."

"What are you talking about?" Darcie wiped her eyes and stared at Mac. "Mom told me everything. She got pregnant, Rick took off, she had Claire, gave her up, and moved on with her life. What else is there?"

Claire wondered the same thing. Rick had alluded to problems between Michelle and her parents, but she never knew the extent of it. She glanced at James, trepidation pricking her. Whatever Mac was about to share, she had a feeling it wouldn't be easy. For him or them.

Mac leaned over his knees for a long moment. Eventually he raised his head. "The year Michelle went off to college marked my tenth anniversary serving as pastor for Bethel's largest church. You see, my dear," he went to Darcie and extended a hand. She rose and they sat together on the couch. "Your mother isn't the only who's been keeping secrets."

"You were a pastor, Grandpa?" Skepticism crept into Darcie's eyes.

Claire raised an eyebrow. This was news to her as well.

"Oh, yes." Mac gave a chuckle.

Jessie nodded in affirmation.

"I was a very different man back then, girls. My belief system consisted of black and white. Good and evil. There were no gray areas in our house. God was to be feared, and the fires of hell were just a mistake away." He studied them through serious eyes. "Shelly was a good girl, a good student. A little headstrong at times." Mac shot Claire a wink and she smiled, her eyes burning.

"After we lost our son, Shelly was all we had," Jessie put in, twisting a paper napkin in her hands. "I know we were overprotective, but she never seemed to mind too much. We watched Shelly and Rick over the years." The creases in her forehead deepened. "As they got older and grew closer, we worried about where it would lead. But we liked Rick. Trusted him. When Shelly went off to college, we assumed they'd be getting engaged eventually."

Mac grunted. "Imagine our shock when Shelly came home that Thanksgiving and told us she was pregnant."

"Everyone makes mistakes," Darcie said quietly, her eyes on her grandfather.

Claire blinked back moisture and thought of Jackson sleeping upstairs.

Mac nodded, knitting his thick brows together. "Yes, honey. We know that now. But at the time..."

"At the time we reacted the only way we knew how. We were furious." Jessie's voice shook and Mac raised a hand.

"No. *I* was furious. Mortified. My first thoughts were not for my daughter and what she must be going through. I was more concerned about what people would think. Here I was expounding on purity and holiness from the pulpit each Sunday, and my own daughter was going to have a child out of wedlock. The shame was almost unbearable."

"It didn't take long for people to find out," Jessie said quietly. "Shelly didn't go back to school, and soon the phone started ringing."

"Judgment came down pretty quick from the deacon board. They wanted me to resign." Mac pushed fingers through his hair. "Made it pretty clear that if I didn't, well...I'd be fired."

"What? That's ridiculous." Anger flashed in Darcie's eyes.

Claire agreed with her but Mac and Jessie only shrugged.

"It was what we'd expected," Jessie said. "But it was humiliating. We didn't bother to hide our anger from Shelly. Our home became a battleground." Jessie wiped her eyes and leveled her gaze on Claire. "One night, when it all got to be too much, there was a terrible scene. We screamed, she yelled. Oh, we all said things we shouldn't have, and she ended up leaving."

Mac nodded, his eyes wet. "Yes. I told her how ashamed I was of her, and that every time I looked at her and her child, I'd be reminded of my failure as a father. I told her God would punish her. Punish all of us. She left here that night and never came back."

Claire sagged against James, allowing his quiet breathing to comfort her. Darcie sat in silence, tears trailing down her cheeks.

"We didn't understand things like we do now." Jessie's tearful explanation pulled at Claire's heart and sent a shudder through her. "It wasn't until years later that we realized how wrong we'd been. About everything."

"That's when you started Church on the Rock, isn't it?" Darcie asked, a bare smile touching her lips.

Her grandfather nodded. "We found we weren't alone. There were others who'd been hurt, misled, and misunderstood."

"We've seen a lot of healing up there on the rock." Jessie smiled, a twinkle in her eyes chasing off sorrow. "We've moved past those dark days. But Shelly, well…she's a different story. I'm not sure she'll ever get over it. Or forgive us."

Mac blew his nose and coughed. "We tried to contact her over the years, to talk about what happened and ask for her forgiveness, but she never would come to see us. We had minimal contact. We knew she'd married and of course she told us when you were born, Darcie, allowed us to send cards and gifts to you, but she never came back to Bethel."

Jessie stood behind Mac and placed her hands on his shoulders. "I desperately wanted to know what had happened to you, Claire, whether she had you or…oh, I prayed she hadn't done the unthinkable, angry as she was."

She moved around Mac's chair and perched on the couch next to Claire, took her hand in hers, and smiled. "One day, not too long after the time you must have been born, I had a dream. I saw a baby lying in a crib, wrapped up in a pink blanket. And she was crying. Crying with all her might. She was alone, abandoned. You could hear the pain of rejection in her cries. I felt it in my spirit. And I knew then this wasn't over. That one day I'd see you again.'"

Claire stiffened, all the hairs on her arms rising. Warmth unlike anything she'd ever experienced flooded through her being as she concentrated on Jessie's kind face. Her grandmother's smile lit the room.

"The very day you showed up here at Tara's Place, Claire, I had that same dream. I'd almost forgotten it. But I took a nap later that afternoon, after I got you settled, and it came back to me." She laughed, wiped her tears, and clapped her hands together. "God hadn't given me that dream for no reason. Oh, girls, He always keeps his promises."

"That's amazing." James whispered—the first words he'd spoken that afternoon.

Claire nodded, the powerful image capturing all speech.

"What about my mom?" Darcie's voice shook, her eyes wild. "How will she get over this?" Darcie broke then, deep, silent sobs shaking her thin frame. Mac took her in his arms and hushed her.

Claire shifted, suddenly uncomfortable. "Maybe once I'm gone, she'll come back. It's me she doesn't want to face."

"Claire, no." Darcie managed to get a handle on her emotion, crossed the room, and crouched before her. She gripped Claire's hands in hers. Her warm smile displayed her true feelings, her cheeks red, eyes shining. "It's not about you, Claire. It's not about any of us. She's running from herself. I think seeing Rick again, whatever he said to her, softened something in her. I know deep down she wants to meet you, Claire, get to know you. I'm sure she wants to forgive Grandma and Grandpa. I just think she doesn't know how yet."

Darcie rose, still holding Claire's hand. Her eyes shone with new light as she smiled at Jessie and extended her other hand to her. "You're right, Grandma, God does keep His promises. We're all here today to testify to that. And I believe Mom will come home. That's what we'll pray for."

30

Michelle sat in her apartment and watched the sun come up. Traffic on the street increased in volume. The alarm clock in her room went off, and she traipsed down the hall to silence it. She'd already been awake for hours.

After a meager breakfast of coffee, half a bagel, and more coffee, she settled on the couch. She was worn out and desperate for answers. She'd even tried praying, but soon gave up. Why would God listen to her now?

Nightmares plagued her. She'd made it through the last few days operating on automatic pilot. Written speeches, made appointments, booked dinner reservations, all the while trying not to allow her mind to wander back to the place she'd run from so long ago.

Back to Bethel.

Claire was probably back home in Connecticut by now. Darcie had said Claire's husband's vacation was ending soon.

Michelle gazed around her pristine surroundings. The apartment was sparsely decorated with a few pieces of furniture, but there was nothing that would give anyone a glimpse into her personality. No colorful paintings on the wall or family photographs displayed. The place seemed almost empty.

Like her life.

Darcie called the other night to see how she was doing. She'd put Jackson on the phone, and Michelle spoke to her grandson for the first time. She smiled at the memory of his little voice. He sounded adorable, such a chatterbox. She'd promised to come and see him soon.

Michelle gave a sigh and pushed herself off the couch. She glanced at the clock and picked up the phone. It was early, but she didn't care.

He answered on the third ring. "I had a feeling I'd be hearing from you."

"Yes. I'm sure you know why I'm calling." She clutched the receiver and willed her hands to stop trembling.

"Have you seen her, spoken to her?" He sounded older, but as in control as ever.

"I saw her briefly the other night. We haven't really talked."

"But you want to."

Michelle nodded, unable to speak. Tears slipped down her cheeks into the receiver. "I wasn't sure what…if…you'd told her…I don't want to say the wrong thing."

His low chuckle surprised her. "I didn't think you political types were big on grace."

"I've never really been a political type," Michelle admitted, the revelation startling and sad. "Just a wannabe."

He gave a short sigh and she heard him sniff. "If you're calling to ask me for advice, Ms. Hart, I'm not sure you're going to like what I have to say."

"Go ahead." She waited, stretching out her legs on the chair across from her.

He paused. "I think you should tell her the truth. She's gone through enough. She deserves to know the whole story. All of it."

"But you…this could damage your relationship. I'm sure she already thinks I'm a real piece of work, so I don't have much to lose. But you…you're her…father."

"I am, yes. But I'm not perfect. What you and I did was wrong, no doubt, but I think if you have any thoughts at all of establishing a relationship with her, you need to lay it all out on the table from the get-go. I'll deal with my side of it when the time comes."

"So you haven't told her then?" Michelle narrowed her eyes. *Take your own advice, buster.*

"I'll talk to her when she comes home. When will you see her?"

"I'm not sure. I have some things to sort out here, with work."

He gave another heavy sigh. "May I offer you another piece of advice, Ms. Hart?"

"Sure."

"Life is short. Don't waste any more time. You've waited twenty-seven years for this. Go see your daughter."

* * *

Kevin let her in and strode through his apartment ahead of her, his face buried in the morning paper. He was always in a hurry, never able to sit still more than a moment. Michelle entered the lavish penthouse suite and glanced around. She'd once dreamed of living here.

The view of Manhattan was expensive, but well worth it. The rooms were elegant and spacious, filled with fine furniture, over-priced window treatments and Persian rugs. They'd hosted many a dinner together around the long mahogany table.

The only thing about the place that appealed to her now was the front door.

"Is this going to take long?" Kevin refilled his coffee mug, offered her some, but she shook her head.

"I'm not sure how long it's going to take. I told you we needed to talk, Kev. You said it was fine."

"It is fine." He loosened his tie and smiled. "Sit." She didn't fail to notice the way he pushed up his sleeve to glance at his watch.

Michelle sat on the black leather couch and studied her sneakers. For the past couple of days all she'd worn were jeans, T-shirts and Nikes. She'd never been more comfortable.

"What's going on with you, Michelle? You haven't taken a day off in all the years I've known you. You look terrible. Are you having some kind of breakdown?" His pale blue eyes shot through her, his mouth twitching like he'd swallowed a piece of moldy bread.

She stared, unbelieving. But then she smiled. "No, Kev. I'm not having a breakdown. But after what I have to tell you, you might be."

By the time she finished her story, he'd traded his coffee for Scotch.

"Let me get this straight." He paced the long room and set his crystal tumbler down on the dining table. Liquid sloshed over the sides. He blinked a couple of times. "You're telling me that you had a child with Rick Matthews twenty-seven years ago? That you gave up for adoption?"

"Yep." She couldn't stop a grin at the horror and disbelief on his face. She'd never seen Kevin Harrison at a loss for words. It was almost enjoyable.

"And you want to meet this girl? Talk to her, let her into your life maybe?"

"Maybe."

Kevin slumped into a chair and scratched his forehead. She wracked her brain and tried to remember if he had any important meetings today, although she had no idea why she was worrying. Kevin drank hard but could sober up quicker than anyone she knew when he needed to.

He sat in silence for a long moment. "Okay. I'm shocked, of course, but it's not the end of the world. We can make it work. It's not like *I* had a bastard kid or anything, God forbid. If the story gets out, we'll just spin it. People will feel sorry for you, being apart from your child all those years. You know," he leaned forward, eyes gleaming, "this could actually work in our favor."

Sudden anger ripped through her. "What do you mean?"

Kevin went to her and took her hands, pulling her to her feet. "You know I've been thinking of throwing my hat in the ring for the next election. People love a good tear-jerker, sweetheart. Think of it—the two of you reunited after all these years. She can even make a few appearances with us. The press will be clamoring."

Michelle yanked her hands from his and put as much space as she could between them. And the really sad thing was, he wasn't kidding. "My life is not fodder for the press, Kevin Harrison. Nor is it at your disposal to sway the public in your favor. What is *wrong* with you? I've just told you something only a few people in this world know about. The last several weeks have been a living hell for me. I've been in torment, Kevin, but you haven't noticed. You're too busy focusing on your career, aren't you?"

"And you should be as well," he snapped. "It is, after all, what I pay you for."

"Not anymore." Michelle grabbed her purse off the couch and marched to the door. Oh, she'd been blind, but her eyes were wide open now.

"Where do you think you're going? We're not done here," Kevin shouted. His voice took on the tone she recognized and warned of what might follow. Michelle swiveled and watched his face contort with anger. She'd put up with his violent outbursts too many times before but wasn't about to do so today. She glanced at the door, ready to run if he came toward her.

He made an honorable effort to control himself, even managed a smile. "What about us, Michelle? I thought we had something going."

"So did I." Michelle shook her head, aware her eyes were dry. "I guess if you consider that 'something' as someone who looks good on your arm, someone who says and does all the right things, and maybe at some point, someone with whom you might have a marriage of convenience, then yeah, we did have something going. But I don't want that, Kevin. Not anymore."

He pulled a hand over his ashen face. "Then what do you want? Enlighten me."

In a few years she'd be celebrating her fiftieth birthday. And what did she have to show for it? What *did* she want?

Tears came then, but they weren't for Kevin.

"I'm not sure what I want yet. But I know I'm not going to find it in New York."

"Well, you won't find it in some hick town up in Maine either," Kevin scoffed. "You'll die of boredom up there."

"Oh, Kev." Michelle let out a tired sigh and moved across the room to stand before him. "I used to believe that too. But I think I might have been wrong. I pray I am."

"You're really serious?"

"Yes." She walked toward the door again, smiling.

"You're throwing it all away, Michelle! You're throwing your life away."

Michelle turned one last time to look at him as his front door opened. Felicity Harrison and the kids wandered in, stopped when they saw her, and stared.

Michelle squared her shoulders, gave a brief nod, and somehow managed not to laugh at the astonished expression Kevin's wife wore, a perfect match for her husband's. "No need to worry, Mrs. Harrison," she told her, shooting Kevin a last scathing glance. "I was just leaving."

* * *

The white house came into view as she rounded the corner, the setting sun throwing a pink hue over the wooden walls and the lake beyond. Michelle slowed her car to a crawl and pulled into a vacant spot. She drank in the scene.

Home. At least it used to be.

Now that she was here, she wasn't sure what to do.

Her eyes came to rest on a large bronze sculpture across the lawn, a fair distance away from the parking bays. Two swans were about to take off from the lake, the piece of art firmly anchored onto a large cement slab. A smile tickled her lips. She'd recognize that artist anywhere.

Off to the right of the old house, two newly constructed cabins could be seen through the trees. A child's laugh reached her ears as she stepped out onto the gravel drive. Michelle peered across the lawn to where the old swing-set used to be. It was no longer there, a newer wooden play-set having taken its place.

Darcie stood behind the swings, pushing a tow-headed child high into the air.

Jackson.

He squealed in delight as she pushed him higher. Michelle allowed the unexpected rush of feeling and embraced it. She fought the urge to race across the lawn to join them, instead settled her gaze on the front door of the house.

With faltering steps, she reached the door, gripping the leather strap of her purse. Maybe she should have called. Brought flowers.

Not come.

The door flung wide and her mother stepped out onto the porch, squinting through her bifocals. "Shelly?" Michelle couldn't stop a laugh at the face Mom made as she pulled her glasses off. "Never can see a body with these things on! Oh. It *is* you..." Her face cracked, reddened, and she took a step

198

back, hand to her mouth.

Michelle could only nod.

Her mother looked older. Her hair had grayed, pulled back off her face, and many more wrinkles marked the passage of time. But her serene smile remained the same and those kind dark eyes sparkled as they always had.

Michelle inhaled and waited a moment before she trusted speech. "I should probably have called. But I...I didn't know...what to say." She met her mother's eyes and felt all the years, all the pain, slip away in an instant.

Tears shone in Mom's eyes as she came forward and grasped her hands, smiling and nodding. "No need to say anything, Shelly, girl. No need at all." She turned and yelled into the house, "Mac! Come quick, honey. Shelly's home!"

31

Claire placed the last item of clothing into her suitcase and closed the lid. In a few hours she and James would be on their way, leaving this place and the people she'd come to love in such a short space of time. She couldn't wait to see Melanie again, her dad and the dogs, but part of her dreaded going back to Connecticut.

So much of her heart would remain here, at Tara's Place.

Male laughter filtered into the bedroom through the open window. James didn't have much to pack, and he and Landon sat out on the porch. They'd all risen early, gone to church together, and afterward Mac and Jessie laid on an enormous brunch. She didn't know where Rick had gone after that. He'd taken to pulling disappearing acts. His time in New York seemed to have had an adverse affect on him.

He'd been spending hours alone in his studio, even with Landon around. He took long walks with Jazz and moped around the property with a haunted look that tore at her heart. She wasn't sure what Michelle's presence at the art show that night meant, but she knew the evening hadn't ended well.

Thanks to her.

Claire lugged her case off the bed and carried it out to the front door, dropping it beside the other bags James had already left there. She took a long lingering gaze around the cabin, then stepped outside and breathed in the fresh air. It was hard to believe she'd been here so long, yet part of her felt she'd never been anywhere else.

"How's my gorgeous niece today?" Landon squinted at her over the top of his shades.

Claire grinned and positioned herself on the swinging chair beside her husband. "Quit calling me that. It's weird. You know you aren't that much older than me. I hope you don't expect me to call you Uncle Landon."

"No, don't you dare." He chuckled and sipped from a soda can. "At least not in public."

"Where's Rick?" Claire checked her watch. James didn't mind driving at night, but she didn't want to get home too late.

Landon shrugged. "Not sure where he went. Poor guy seems really torn up since talking to Michelle. I was hoping he might get some closure, but I don't think he realized the extent of what she went through before now."

"I know." Claire entwined her fingers through James'. "He's always telling me to stop blaming myself. Maybe he needs to take his own advice."

Landon gave a yawn and stretched his muscled arms over his head. "That would be a first. Don't you know you got your stubborn streak from him?"

Claire smiled. "Really? He told me it came from Michelle."

"Right." Landon pushed to his feet and waved as Jackson and Darcie rounded the corner from the main house. The little boy raced down the path toward them. Jackson skipped up the steps and Landon swept him into a bear hug. "Hey, tiger!" From the moment Landon set foot on the property, the two were literally inseparable.

"Jackson!" Darcie ran after him, breathless. "Quit bothering Landon. How many times do I have to tell you?" She let out a frustrated breath and made her way up the steps. "Sorry." She reached for Jackson, but he held on to Landon's neck and shook his head, jutting out his chin.

"We're going fishing. Landon said."

Claire hid her smile with her hand. The stubbornness definitely came from both sides.

"If that's okay with you," Landon put in, pushing his sunglasses onto the top of his head, his dazzling blue eyes sparkling.

Darcie's flushed face deepened a shade. Claire smiled as she watched her sister open her mouth, then shut it again. That was new. Landon was definitely one attractive man and apparently Darcie had noticed.

Why did she have to leave just when things were starting to get interesting?

"Okay, fine, but not too long. It'll be dark soon."

"Best time to go," Landon said, giving a wink.

"Best time. Yep." Jackson's grin was wide.

Darcie muttered something under her breath and turned to Claire. "You'll never guess who's here." She wiped her forehead and slumped on the edge of the porch step.

Landon chuckled and took a seat again, Jackson perched on his lap. "Barbara Walters wanting the scoop on the big family reunion?"

"Oh, please." Claire rolled her eyes at Landon's proclamation.

"Nope." Darcie seemed to recover from her speechless state and flashed a grin in Claire's direction. "It's my mother. *Our* mother."

"What?" Claire's skin prickled and she stared at Darcie in disbelief. "Really?"

"Yep." Darcie's eyes were bright. "She's in the house, talking to Grandma and Grandpa. I think she plans on staying. There were a lot of bags in the back of her car."

Landon let out a long whistle that Jackson tried to imitate. "Well, now. Isn't that interesting? What time are you leaving, Claire?"

Claire turned to James and searched his face. He gave a shrug and ran a finger down her nose. She knew he'd promised Steve he'd be back in the office tomorrow. Claire let out a sigh. "We were planning on going in the next hour or so, but maybe we should leave now."

"Claire!" Darcie voiced her disappointment. "You don't need to skip out just because she showed up. Who knows why she's here? The fact is, she hasn't set foot on this property in years, and now she's here. Maybe God is answering our prayers after all, huh?"

"She's got a point, babe." James rubbed Claire's back, the action soothing her. "If you want to stay, we can."

"I don't know." Claire wrestled with what Michelle's arrival meant. If she'd come to make amends with Mac and Jessie, that was great, but Claire didn't want to get in the way.

She was still unwanted.

Jackson slipped off Landon's knee and stood in front of Claire, leaning on her, his eyes big. "Auntie Clayah, why do you hafta go? I want you to stay hereah, with us."

Claire smiled and cradled his little face in her hands. Mournful brown eyes stared up at her. "I know, buddy." She kissed his forehead and wished there was some way...

"Hey, I think I hear those fish biting. What do you say, Jacko?" Landon got to his feet and took Jackson by the hand. His eyes came to rest on Claire, his expression serious. "Don't take off without saying good-bye."

Claire stood with a sigh and planted a kiss on his rugged jaw. "I won't. Have fun. Don't forget his life jacket."

"Yes, ma'am." Landon winked again, and he and Jackson headed down the steps toward the boathouse.

"Maybe I'll go with them." James yelled to Landon to wait up. "We won't be that long."

"Okay." Claire watched him go, hands shoved in his pockets, whistling as he jogged down the path. She'd never get over how blessed she was to have James in her life. And to think she'd almost thrown it all away.

Darcie gave a long groan and put her head in her hands. "I shouldn't have let Jackson go."

"Why?" Claire went to sit beside her and draped an arm across Darcie's slender shoulders.

"Because. Jackson doesn't need to get close to him. Landon's only going to up and leave in a few weeks. Poor kid's upset enough that you and James are leaving."

"I know." Claire pulled a tissue from her shorts pocket and blew her nose. "I wish we didn't live so far away."

"He's a good guy, your husband." Darcie sounded wistful.

Claire met her eyes and nodded. "He is. You'll find somebody just like him, Darce. I know you will."

Darcie gave a sigh that smacked of regret. "I'm not so sure. Sometimes I get scared, you know? I think this disease is going to get the better of me." She swiveled to face Claire and reached for her hands. An earnest expression chased off her usual happy smile. "I want you to know how glad I am that you're my sister. I always wanted one. It was a shock at first, but I wouldn't change it."

"Neither would I." Emotion tightened Claire's throat and made it hard to speak.

Darcie stared at her for a minute without speaking. Then she lowered her gaze. "If something happens to me...if I get worse or I don't make it..."

"Stop it, Darcie," Claire squeezed her hands. "You're going to be fine."

Darcie raised her head, her eyes wet. "But if I'm not...will you and James...will you take Jackson? I know he's happy here, but Grandma and Grandpa are getting on. I think he should be with you. Would you?"

"Darcie, of course we would, but..." She gave a shaky laugh and pulled her sister into a hug. "This is crazy talk. I don't want to lose you. I just found you."

"I know." Darcie laughed and drew back, her trademark grin making an appearance. "I'm not planning on going anywhere either, but you know, it's best to say things while you think of them."

"Will you come to Connecticut to visit me? You and Jackson?"

"Every weekend, sister. You know it." Darcie laughed. "In fact, we might just move in with you. Do you think James would mind?"

Claire gave her a push but couldn't help laughing. "He probably would. I wish we could stay here."

Their laughter faded.

Claire picked at a weed growing through the wooden steps, wishing for time to stand still.

"Mom's coming." Darcie's soft words broke the silence between them.

"What?" Claire lifted her head, anxiety racing through her.

Darcie got to her feet and Claire did the same but moved to stand a little ways behind her sister.

Darcie glanced over her shoulder. "Chicken."

"You got that right."

Michelle slowed when she reached the bottom step of the cabin. Dressed in jeans and a red T-shirt, her dark hair pulled back into a ponytail, Claire thought she looked very young and pretty. But dark circles framed her eyes, and it wasn't hard to tell she'd been crying.

"Hey, Mom." Darcie moved down and extended her arms, giving her mother a hug. "This is a surprise."

"Yes, I suppose it is." Michelle drew back. She smoothed down Darcie's hair, worry in her eyes. "How are you? Feeling okay?"

"Oh, sure." Darcie laughed and shrugged. "I'll be fine. Hey, you just missed Jackson. Landon took him fishing. They'll be back in a while, though."

"Good. I can't wait to meet him."

"You talked to Grandma and Grandpa?" Darcie gave a hesitant smile.

"Yes. It was long overdue." Michelle's eyes inched upward toward Claire. "A lot of things are long overdue." She gave a firm nod. "Hello, Claire. I wasn't sure you would still be here."

Claire attempted to find her voice, sweat prickling the back of her neck. "We're leaving today. Soon." She checked her watch. "Very soon. Well, I'll...uh...get out of your way," she mumbled, making a half-turn to head toward the door. She'd hide under the bed if she had to.

"Actually, I was hoping we could talk."

Michelle's soft voice, so much like her own, brought Claire to a halt. She caught her breath and turned around.

Darcie slipped past her mother. "I've got some things to do at the house."

She left Claire to stare at Michelle, desperately trying to come up with something sensible to say.

Michelle smiled and tipped her head toward the door. "Shall we go inside?"

"Okay." Claire fought a sudden wave of panic but pushed open the door to the cabin. She uttered a furtive prayer for help and peace and hoped she wouldn't pass out.

"Wow." Michelle looked around, her eyes widening. "This is really nice."

"Yes. They're building four more just like it. Actually my husband was talking about bringing a crew up here to help Mac. And Rick's been a huge help. They uh..." Claire stopped her flow of words and stared down at her feet. "Sorry. I tend to yammer on when I'm nervous." She suddenly felt like a five-year-old on the first day of school.

Michelle's laughter washed over her. "Maybe we should sit."

"Okay." Claire tried to ignore the pulsing in her temples. She'd have a migraine by the end of this. She took one of the chairs and let Michelle have the couch.

For a long moment, Michelle just stared at her. And then she smiled, a genuine smile that lit her face and radiated warmth. "You really do look like me."

"Yes." Claire forced the word out. "Look, I want you to know that I'm sorry. When I started my search for you, I never really thought how it would affect you. I just assumed that my birth mother...that you...would want to hear from me. I never imagined what a painful time it must have been for you. I guess I just wanted answers. I was selfish. I'm sorry."

Michelle clasped her hands together, the exact way Claire always held hers. "No. Please don't be sorry. I...I'm the one who should be apologizing. I was awful to you that night on the phone."

No kidding. Claire fiddled with the rings on her fingers. *Grace, grace, grace.* She ran the back of her hand across her eyes. "It must have been a shock for you, to find out I was here."

"Of all places, yes." Michelle leaned back against the couch and breathed out. "How did you end up here anyway?"

Claire shrugged, unable to stop a smile. "Google and God." She laughed at Michelle's look of surprise. "It's a bit of a long story. I'm a pretty good sleuth when I want to be."

"Apparently." Michelle leaned forward and rested her head in her hands for a moment. Claire felt the weight of her sorrow. When Michelle raised her head again, her eyes held fear in them. "I need to tell you something, Claire, and I'm not sure how."

Claire clenched her fists and forced herself to breathe. "You don't have to. I'm not expecting anything to come from this. I mean, you know, if it's okay with you, I'd like to keep in touch with Darcie and your parents, but...you and I don't have to keep in touch or anything. The last thing I want to do is force myself on anyone."

"No, it's not that." Michelle shook her head, looking suddenly ill at ease. "You're part of the family now. They wouldn't have it any other way."

She rose and took slow steps around the room. Finally she turned and faced Claire again. "You already know Rick's story. I'd like you to hear mine."

"Are you sure?" Claire hesitated.

Pain marred Michelle's face, and she didn't want to put her through anymore. But Michelle nodded.

"I'm sure." She flashed Claire a tiny smile and went on. "The day you were born, there was a horrible storm. It rained buckets—thunder, lightning, howling winds. I lay in my room afterward—they'd already taken you away—and I watched the lightning slash across the dark sky. I prayed for it to come right through the window and slash through me." She brought a fist to her mouth and put her back to Claire.

Claire took deep shallow breaths and waited for the pain to pass. For both of them.

At last, Michelle looked her way again, her face pale and drawn. "I didn't know how I was going to go on. How I would live without you. But I wanted the best for you. I gave you up because I wanted you to have a proper home, a mother and a father who would love you, take care of you. Do you understand that?"

"Yes." Claire's voice shook.

Michelle went back to the couch and slumped into it. "The papers that I signed said I had six months to change my mind." She struggled to compose herself. Claire almost didn't want to hear what might come next.

"I went into an awful depression afterwards. I stayed on in Connecticut with a friend's family, got a job as a waitress, and tried to figure out what to do with my life. But I couldn't stop thinking about you. I kept dreaming you were dead. I had to know if you were okay. My friend's father was a detective and he made some calls. I don't know how he did it, but he managed to find out where you were."

Silence thickened the air and Claire stared at Michelle. No words would come. Michelle shrugged and looked away.

After a while she reached for the box of tissues on the coffee table and blew her nose. "I called your father, Claire. I called Edward. I knew I wasn't supposed to, but I was desperate. I had to know if you were okay. I...I was even thinking I might...well, I guess it doesn't matter now."

"You spoke to my dad?" Cold hands snaked around her throat as Claire tried to make sense of it. And then the truth of what Michelle was saying hit her, slammed her with the force of a sumo-wrestler, pinned her to the ground, and held her there. "You wanted me back, didn't you?"

"I did." Michelle exhaled and offered a meager smile. "I was twenty years old. I had no money, no plan for the future, but...yes. I realized I'd made a mistake giving you up and I wanted you back. I thought I could do it."

"What happened?" It wasn't hard to figure out. Overcome with sudden nausea, Claire doubled over, waiting for the feeling to pass. She lifted her head and locked eyes with Michelle. "He paid you off, didn't he? My father paid you to go away and never contact them again."

Michelle sat in silence, tears rolling down her cheeks.

"I can't believe this." Anger rushed out of her. Claire couldn't sit still. She paced the room, her heart hammering.

"He was desperate. Claire...they loved you so much. He didn't want your mother to suffer, to have to go through giving you up. And I...I was young and stupid. I thought the money would give me the start I needed. I could go back to school, get on with my life. I thought it would help me forget about you."

Horror gave way to numb, blinding pain. "Did it?"

"No." Michelle's hands trembled.

"This is crazy."

"Don't be angry with him, Claire. I called him the other night, before coming out here. I wasn't sure he would have ever told you, and I didn't want to tell you. I know how it looks. But he...he wanted me to. He said you should know the truth. All of it."

Claire blew air through her lips. Her mind swam with thoughts that dragged her down and seeded bitterness. "Great." What was worse, knowing your father bought you or your mother sold you? She struggled for air, wishing she had the nerve to walk out. "How much?" she whispered, glaring at Michelle's stricken face. "How much was I worth?"

"It doesn't matter." Michelle's voice cracked, and she turned her head.

Claire's pulse raced as she forced down another wave of anger. "He wanted me to know the truth, so tell me. How much?"

"He gave me fifty-thousand dollars. At the time it was..."

Claire slumped into her chair and shook her head. It was almost too much to comprehend. Too sickening, horrifying, yet at the same time, completely understandable.

"I shouldn't have taken the money." Michelle pulled at her hair, her eyes pleading with Claire.

"My father can be very persuasive."

"I spent years afterward convincing myself it was okay. I've spent a lifetime trying to forgive myself. Even after I married and had Darcie, it haunted me."

"It's done," Claire told her quietly, wishing it were so.

"I suppose it shows you what kind of person I really am, doesn't it?" Michelle's tone was thick with self-loathing. "If I could change it, I would. All I can say is that I'm sorry and that I hope you'll forgive me, Claire."

Claire grunted, unable to do more. The tension in her neck forced her to move, but she didn't want to. She just wanted to sit, be still, and pretend none of this was real. But it was too late for that.

"That necklace..." Michelle pointed to the locket around Claire's neck, her dark eyes wide.

"What about it?" Claire reached for it instinctively. "My father gave it to me for my sixteenth birthday." She studied the floor, her stomach rolling. Any minute now she'd have to rush to the bathroom.

"Did he...say anything about it?"

Claire somehow managed to meet Michelle's eyes. "He told me it was to remind me how very much I was loved."

"Yes," Michelle whispered after a while. "That's exactly what I said to him when I asked him to give it to you."

"You?" Claire could barely get the words out. "You gave me this?"

Michelle smiled, her face brightening for an instant. "It was my friend Belinda's idea. I stayed with her family for a while, before I had you, and after. Maybe you'll meet her someday. She thought I should leave something for you with your dad. I never believed he'd actually give it to you."

Claire pressed down anger and fumbled with the clasp of the chain. Lies upon lies. She held the locket toward Michelle. "Here. Take it back. I don't want it."

When Michelle didn't take it, Claire let it slip from her fingers. Tears blinding her, she walked with unsteady steps to the door and held it open.

Michelle bent to pick up the necklace, pocketed it, and moved toward the door. She stood just in front of Claire, her face flushed. "If it means anything, I never did forget you. And I...I'm glad you found me. I...I'll be staying here for a while, if you..."

"I'm leaving." Claire blurted the words out and stiffened at the flash of sorrow that passed across Michelle's face. But she would not be moved.

What goes around comes around.

Michelle lifted her head, met her eyes, her gaze steady, and nodded. "I see. Well, thank you for listening anyway. Good-bye, Claire."

32

"I'm out." Michelle scowled and pushed back from the table. Landon gave a crow of victory and gathered his Monopoly winnings. She shot him a glare. "You cheated, Mr. Marsh, and if I had anything left to bet, I'd put it all on the fact that your brother taught you everything you know."

"Mom." Darcie's eyebrows rose.

Michelle walked behind the bar and grabbed a couple of sodas from the fridge. "Coke?" They both nodded so she had to make a second trip. Rain pelted the roof of the house and beat against the windows. The guests still in residence had long since called it a night, and her parents always retired early.

Once seated in the lounge area, Michelle flicked through yesterday's newspaper.

"Man, it's pouring." Landon strode around the room like a caged tiger. "Can we wake Jackson up?"

"No, we can't wake Jackson up." Darcie's laughter flooded the room. "You get bored far too easily, Landon. Why don't you read a book?"

Michelle glanced up in time to see the bemused expression Landon wore. She laughed too. "Books. You know—these things? With writing inside the covers?" She waved a hardcover at him.

"I know what a book is." Landon stuck out his tongue and flopped onto the couch opposite her. "It's just been a while since I read one." He stretched out long legs and studied his fingers.

"Why am I not surprised?" Darcie stood and began to pack the game away. "What is it that keeps you so busy, Mr. Marsh?"

"This and that." Landon tossed Darcie a grin as he watched her. Michelle straightened, trepidation inching around her at the interest in his eyes. Landon Marsh was checking out her daughter.

Rick had finally told her that Landon worked for the Drug Enforcement Agency. She'd watched the younger man over the last few days, seen the way he interacted with Jackson, the long looks he gave Darcie when she wasn't paying attention.

Michelle cleared her throat and he met her eyes. The look she sent him erased the need for speech. His resulting blush made her feel sorry for him.

"Heard from Claire?" He threw her pointed look right back at her.

She didn't feel sorry for him anymore.

"Nope. You?"

Landon shrugged and smothered a yawn. "No. Rick's tried to reach her a few times, but she doesn't return his calls. What about you, Darcie?"

Darcie sat cross-legged on the rug and played with the laces of her moccasins. It took her a minute before she looked at them, and Michelle saw hesitation cross her face. "We've talked a few times. She's doing okay."

Michelle picked up the paper and pretended to read again. Since her talk with Claire, her emotions were all over the place. Telling Claire the truth had probably been a mistake, but she couldn't take it back now.

The back door slammed and she shot her head up as a bolt of lightning lit the room. "Anybody home?" Rick called from the porch.

"We're in here." Darcie rubbed her arms and pulled on the sweater she'd discarded earlier. "It's cold tonight. Maybe we should light the fire."

"I'll do it." Landon jumped up, apparently in need of something to do other than stare at Darcie.

"Good. Make yourself useful for a change." Michelle still hadn't forgiven him for spilling the beans the night at the gallery. He hadn't even apologized.

Rick entered the lounge shaking droplets from his dark head. "Evening, all. I should have brought my boat."

Landon threw a few thick logs into the fireplace and turned his way. "I hope you drove here. I walked down."

Rick snorted. "'Course I drove. I'm not as stupid as you."

"That's debatable." The words shot out before Michelle could stop them. She buried her face in the newspaper, her cheeks burning.

"Nice to see you too, Shel." She didn't have to look up to know he was grinning.

"Hey, she accused me of cheating."

Michelle raised her head, a smile pinching her mouth at Landon's whine.

Landon finished with the fire and rose, pointing toward the game table like a petulant child. "And she said you probably taught me all I know."

"I did." Rick rounded the bar and grabbed a towel, drying his wet head. "Glad to see you were paying attention." He flashed Michelle a wink that succeeded in turning her insides out. "Anybody heard from Claire?"

Michelle folded the paper, stood, and tossed it into the orange flames. She watched as it crackled and burned, the fire eventually consuming it. If only the mistakes of her past would vanish just as quickly.

Her heart pounded against her chest. She'd told Darcie and her parents the extent of the conversation she'd had with Claire, but Rick had no idea. She'd almost been afraid to tell them, but after Claire left that afternoon with barely a word, not even waiting to say good-bye to Rick, Michelle figured they deserved an explanation. To her relief, they hadn't judged her, only given her the love and support she so desperately needed right now.

Part of her wished she'd found the courage to come home years ago.

The reason she hadn't stood just behind her.

"I've talked to her." Darcie's quiet voice pushed Michelle's emotion to the edge. More tears welled as she thought of the years she'd missed with her daughter.

"And?" Impatience laced Rick's tone. "Why'd she leave so quickly? And why won't she return my calls? What did you say to her, Michelle?"

"Excuse me?" She made a slow turn to face him. If the vase on the coffee table hadn't been full of flowers, she might have thrown it at him.

"Oh, look, *People* magazine." Landon's easy chuckle filled the room. "Did you sneak this in here, Darcie? Hey, Rick, you might be in here some day. You know he's almost famous now, right?"

"Oh, leave him alone," Darcie scolded. "Rick, take this man home. He's too much of a nuisance."

Michelle prayed Rick would do just that.

"Answer me, Shelly. What did you say to Claire?" Rick was ignoring everyone but her. "You were the last person she talked to. Then she just took off. Didn't even say good-bye to me."

Michelle dragged her hands down her face and stormed past him. She wasn't about to put up with a temper tantrum from Rick Matthews. "I don't answer to you."

She fled the room and made her way down the hall to the small sitting room. She fell onto the couch and buried her head in her hands.

A few minutes later, Rick thudded into the room. He still walked like an elephant. "Go away." Michelle smothered her face in a cushion.

"I want to know what happened."

"It's none of your business, Rick. Go away and leave me alone." Michelle bit her bottom lip and somehow refrained from giving him clearer directions. She'd been trying to break the habit of resorting to bad language when angered, especially around her parents. If he opened his mouth again, she'd gladly pick it up again.

"She's my daughter too," Rick growled. "That makes it my business."

Michelle sat up, hurled the cushion onto the floor, and met his eyes. "She's your daughter, too? Is that right? Remind me again, where were you when I was lying in a hospital bed, twenty-seven years ago, having *your daughter?* Huh, Rick? Because as far as I recall, you sure weren't there with me!"

She spat words at him and watched him recoil. "No. You were too busy doing your own thing, living your own life. You didn't claim her then, did you? What gives you the right to come in here and judge me now?" Her breath came in spurts and she prayed for calm.

Michelle stared at the photographs on the mantle. She didn't have the energy to rise. The grandfather clock out in the hall ticked in steady rhythm with her pounding heart.

"You're right. I'm sorry." Rick's low voice pulled her eyes toward him. He sank down onto the easy chair just across from her. His face was drawn and pale. "I don't know what else I can say. You're right. I wasn't there for you, Shelly. If I could go back and change it all, I would. But I can't. All I can do now is thank God I have another chance with Claire. A chance to get to know her—be a part of her life. Since she left, I'm beginning to wonder if that's gone."

The desperation in his words branded her. Was there any way past this pain? She doubted it.

Somehow, she needed to find the courage to walk through it.

Rick stared at her through haunted eyes, eyes she could hardly bear to look at. He didn't know what he was asking of her.

"She's not angry with you. It's me she doesn't want to talk to. You were right. After what I told her, I doubt I'll be hearing from her again."

He leaned forward and reached for her hand. "Can you tell me?"

Michelle nodded, released a deep sigh. "My life hasn't exactly been a walk in the park. It might look that way, but I've lived with a lot of hatred—toward you, my parents, myself. If Claire hadn't come back into our lives, I'm not sure I'd be sitting here right now. My parents and I are starting over, and I'm getting to know Darcie again, and my grandson. I was hoping Claire would fit into that picture too."

Michelle let his hand go, pushed to her feet, and crossed the room. Her father's writing desk lay open where she'd sat hours earlier, trying to compose a letter to Claire. She hadn't been able to get past the first two words. She pulled her cardigan around her shoulders. Slowly she turned to look at him. Rick watched her in silence, his mouth drawn.

And then she told him. Told him all of it. From beginning to end.

Leaving nothing out.

Rick rubbed his face. "You told Claire this?"

"I had to. I spoke with her father again before I came out here. I didn't know what to do. He told me I should tell her the truth."

"You took the money." Rick sat with his head in his hands.

"Yes." Tears trailed down her cheeks.

It was done.

He could do with it what he liked.

"I don't blame her for hating me," she whispered. "I've lived with this guilt her whole life. I still can't believe I did it."

Rick said nothing for what felt like an eternity. "I didn't leave you with much choice, did I?" He raised his head, his eyes full.

Amazement crept over her, but she shook her head. "This has nothing to do with you. It was my decision. I was intimidated. I could have refused to take the money. I was within my rights to take Claire, but I didn't know that. If I'd gone through proper channels…"

Rick put up a hand, his expression grim. "You were barely an adult. How would you know your rights?" His tone hinted at the pain this caused him. "He shouldn't have offered to pay you off in the first place. It's despicable."

Michelle could only shrug, weariness settling over her soul. "I'm sure he didn't see it that way. In his world, money, power, those things get you whatever you want. Fifty grand was probably a drop in the bucket to him. I tried to rationalize it—I didn't know anything about babies. I couldn't have raised her on my own with no money and no home to go to—I told myself she really would be better off with them. They loved her. I never doubted that." She gave a muted groan and covered her face for a moment.

Rick stayed quiet.

"So I moved on. I created a life for myself, got married, tried to raise a child." Bitter laughter rose. "I failed miserably on all three counts." Michelle lowered her hands and took in his look of pity. "I've learned the hard way that the best things in life are the things you convince yourself you can live without."

Rick nodded and leaned back against the couch. Shadows circled his eyes and told her he hadn't been sleeping any better than she was. Sudden empathy for him took her by surprise.

Forgiving her parents was one thing, but…forgiving Rick?

"So, that's what happened. That's why Claire left so quickly. I'm sure she'll call you soon." Michelle recognized her clipped tone and instinctively reached for the pearls she no longer wore. In their place sat a tiny gold heart on a chain.

He nodded, not looking at all convinced. "Thanks for telling me."

"You would have hounded me until I did." She managed a smile and met his penetrating gaze.

"I guess I was a little overbearing." His hard look softened. "I'm sure Claire will come around eventually. She probably just needs some time. She's kind of stubborn. Gets it from her mother."

"Right." Michelle set her gaze on him. He scratched his head and looked across the room for a moment. Then he looked straight back at her, his eyes locked with hers, and Michelle felt the room spin.

She pushed aside trepidation and gave in to curiosity. "Did you...did you ever marry?"

He chuckled, his sorrow lifting and a new light creeping into his eyes. "Nope. I came close once, but...fortunately I realized it wasn't going to work out before we got that far."

"What was wrong with her?" Michelle wrapped her arms around her knees. The chill in the air permeated her skin, but the smile Rick gave her warmed her in an alarming way.

"Nothing. She just wasn't you."

Michelle bit her lip and looked down at her jeans. She knew that tune. "Is it my imagination or have you been keeping your distance?"

His face deepened a shade, but another smile lifted one corner of his mouth. "I guess I've been keeping my distance. I figured you needed some time with your folks and Darcie. Didn't think you'd want me hanging around."

His knowing look eased her racing pulse, and Michelle returned his smile. "I suppose I have given that impression."

Rick's smile faded and he opened his mouth as if to speak, but closed it the next instant.

"What?" She didn't know what made her ask and she regretted doing so at once. His chuckle sent her pulse racing again.

"Well, I guess I'm just wondering how long you plan on staying in Bethel. I thought you had some big fancy job to get back to, among other things."

"Ah." Michelle watched the dimple in his cheek dance. "No, actually. No job. I quit."

His dark eyebrows rose, but he said nothing. She stood, stretched, and moved to the other side of the room, feeling lighter than she had in years.

A selection of Rick's paintings hung on the wall, and Michelle studied them. She recalled the older ones and admired the ones she hadn't yet seen. Maybe one day she'd summon the nerve to visit him in his studio.

"What are you planning to do then? What happened to you and the..."

"Senator?" She swiveled to face him and quirked an eyebrow. He sat against the couch, one long brawny arm draped over the back of it as he tipped his head in her direction. "He...wasn't...good enough for me."

A shadow passed across his face and his eyes left hers. "Seems to be going around."

Michelle pushed her fingers into the pockets of her jeans and sucked in a breath. As much as she wanted to reply to that, tell him what he wanted, needed, to hear, she couldn't.

Not yet.

33

"Rick called again. And your dad." James walked across the deck, Chance skittering after him, his nails clicking on the redwood. Their other dogs raced around the back lawn. Claire stretched out on a lounge chair, enjoying what was left of an Indian summer. She'd been trying to read, but the book held no interest.

Claire shielded her eyes from the afternoon sun and watched the pup scramble down the steps to join his elders. They'd accepted him almost at once. She'd been a bit worried about bringing him back to Connecticut but couldn't bear to part with him.

"Claire? Did you hear me?"

"I heard you." She picked up her book and flipped pages, having no idea where she'd left off. After coming home, she prayed daily for release of the pain that had returned to shroud her, yet it intensified. Eventually it bowed to bitterness and Claire had no idea what to do with that.

"You can't ignore everyone for the rest of your life." James' insistent tone made her put down her book again. He sat forward, his eyes intent on capturing hers.

Claire made a face. "Why not?"

A smile slid across his mouth and he shook his head. "Because they love you. They're human—they made mistakes. I'm not saying any of it was right, but it was years ago. Let it go."

"I can't." Claire stood and went to the edge of the deck, gripping the warm wood railing. Shouts and splashing from the pool next door floated on the air. Tall trees, wild rose, and holly bushes flanked their garden. James had mowed the lawn that afternoon and the smell of freshly cut grass still hung in the air.

The gurgling stream at the edge of the property normally soothed her. She even enjoyed hearing the kids having fun. Soon she'd be seeing the school bus drive past their house, and the neighborhood would fall into that eerie silence for the majority of the day.

Jackson was getting ready to start Kindergarten. Darcie was a wreck, but Jackson couldn't wait. When they'd last talked, he'd described his new *Cars* backpack in full, very lengthily detail.

Claire gave way to a sudden grin. Months ago she couldn't have imagined she'd be standing here in her own home, her heart aching for a family she'd only just met, missing people she hadn't even known existed. People who'd somehow managed to infiltrate every part of her, given her life new meaning.

She jumped as James came up behind her and wrapped her in his arms. Claire leaned back against him and inhaled the familiar scent of his cologne. "I guess I should talk to my dad," she conceded. "He's torn to pieces over this. You're right. It was years ago. I can't say I wouldn't have done the same thing in his shoes. I'm not sure I want to talk to Michelle, though."

Claire watched a flock of birds rise from the trees. Their strident tribute to the day filled the air as they flew off, a cloud of black disappearing into the horizon. "I thought things were supposed to be easier once you let God take the wheel."

"I think you're watching the wrong channel, babe." James' soft chuckle soothed her and coaxed a smile.

Claire turned in his embrace and slid her arms around his neck. "I love you."

He grinned and kissed the tip of her nose. "You better."

She waited a moment, just in case she changed her mind, but then she broadened her smile. "I'm ready, Jamie. I want to start trying for another baby."

His eyes lit and filled with tears at the same time. He hadn't pushed her since they'd gotten back together. Only waited patiently, as always. "Are you really sure?"

"Very sure." A long-forgotten joy slowly entered her heart once more, and she laughed with the thrill of it. "So? What are you waiting for? A gold-embossed invitation?"

"Now?" A wicked grin claimed his face, and Claire's laughter intensified.

"No time like the present, Mr. Ferguson."

"Well, in that case…" He lifted her into his arms, yelled for the dogs, and took her inside, up to their bedroom.

Where she belonged.

* * *

"You are more stubborn than a mule at the bottom of a mountain." Melanie stirred her tea and glared at Claire from across the table.

Claire bit into a chocolate-chip cookie and glared back. "I didn't ask you to come over here and be rude."

"Since when do I need permission?" Melanie flashed the grin Claire had missed so much during her time in Bethel, but it reminded her of Darcie and her smile was short-lived. She picked up the latest drawing Jackson sent in the mail and traced the brightly colored house with her finger. He'd drawn the entire family, including *Gramma Shel,* and a big circle around an empty spot labeled *Clay-uh.*

Darcie seemed to be doing well, and they were all elated with the news of Jackson's test results. He showed no signs of Hepatitis whatsoever.

Melanie flicked through the stack of photographs Claire showed her earlier and gave a soft laugh. "I still can't get over this. Darcie looks so much like you. So does Jackson. He's adorable. Don't you have a picture of your mom?"

"She's not my mom." Claire tightened her hold around her mug and lowered her eyes.

"Claire."

"Well, she isn't." Claire lifted her head and glowered at Melanie's surprised expression. "You can call her Michelle or my birth mother. Anything else just feels wrong."

"Fine. Michelle, then. Do you have a picture of her?"

"No."

"Just asking." Melanie pushed the stack toward her with a smile. "I can tell you miss them a lot."

"I guess." They were the first thing she thought of each morning, the last before she went to bed and night. Claire went to the sink and started to stack dishes in the dishwasher. September had given way to the red and orange October leaves that scattered her driveway. She'd felt a distinct chill in the air as she went outside for the paper that morning.

"Do you think she told her parents what happened?"

"She did." Claire plunged her hands into the soapy water and blinked. Across the street, two young mothers pushed strollers. A secret smile stretched her mouth. Just like last time, it hadn't taken long. They'd gone to the obstetrician last week. Everything was fine, and she told them to just relax. Claire didn't intend to relax until this child was forty. Probably not even then.

"Explain to me how you're talking to your dad, Rick, Darcie, and your grandparents, but not Michelle? Claire, that's really not fair."

Claire dried her hands and faced Melanie, her eyes burning. "How is that not fair, Mel? I don't have anything to say to her. She took money in exchange for me and walked away. It's the worst thing anybody could do. If somebody offered you a pile of money for Jaclyn, would you have taken it?"

"So you agree with what your father did? Paying Michelle off so he could keep you is fine, but her taking the money isn't?" A sly smile flitted over Melanie's mouth.

Claire sank into her chair again and groaned. She went round in circles with it until nothing made sense. "I don't know, Mel. I guess it's just easier to forgive someone you've known your whole life. I know my dad loves me—not that what he did was right, but I can understand his motives. Hers…I don't understand."

"She probably doesn't, either." Melanie's sigh sounded sad and filled with regret. "Oh, Claire. You must have some idea of what Michelle went through, losing you. Think of how she must have felt, knowing she'd never get to see you, hold you, or watch you grow up. And the guilt of what she did on top of it."

"Stop it, Mel." Claire clenched her fists on the table and studied cookie crumbs. She wouldn't be coerced into feeling sorry for the woman. Michelle didn't deserve her forgiveness.

But she'd asked for it.

"You're the one who wanted to find her," Melanie pointed out. Claire's face burned as she held her tears at bay, but she forced herself to meet her friend's gaze. Melanie went on. "We agreed you had no way of knowing what you were walking into, that you'd just have to accept whatever you found, remember?"

"Yes." Claire did remember. But there was something else, something that bothered her no end, something she'd never expressed to anyone. "Do you think all of this was God's will, Mel? I mean, I just kind of jumped into this, you know. I didn't pray about it, I never asked Him if I should do it. Maybe all the pain and heartache I'm feeling now is because of that."

Melanie shook her head. "I don't believe for a minute that anything we do surprises God. Look at the circumstances. Sure, your story isn't an easy one to accept, but look at all the good that's come out of it."

Claire couldn't deny that. A smile brightened her spirit for an instant. "Yes, I guess you're right."

Melanie seemed to hesitate. "I found a Bible verse, not long after we first talked about you searching. I wanted to share it with you before you left, but I knew you weren't ready. Can I tell you now?"

"Sure." Claire sat back and waited.

Melanie quoted from memory, in a clear voice that held conviction: "'*Can a mother forget the baby at her breast and have no compassion on the child she has borne? Though she may forget, I will not forget you!*' It's a verse from the book of Isaiah."

"Thanks, Mel." The verse spoke volumes. Mel was right. God *had* been there from the beginning, and He would not abandon her now.

Jaclyn's happy chortles carried through from the den where James and Steve were watching the afternoon game. The baby was crawling at high speed, pulling to stand every now and then. She'd definitely be walking before her first birthday.

"I feel like I caused them all so much pain, Mel." The admission, once said, was strangely freeing. She'd needed to say it for a while. "As much as I want to be part of their lives, at the same time I wonder if it's better that I'm not."

Melanie put out her hand and Claire took it. Shouts from the den ensued as the Red Sox got a home run. Normally they would be in there watching too, but today Claire needed time alone with Mel.

"If you hadn't searched, you wouldn't know your grandparents. You wouldn't know you had a sister, or a nephew. You wouldn't have Rick." A grin squished her nose and lifted her freckles. "Oh, Claire, do you think for a moment that any of them wish this hadn't happened?"

Did she? Claire remembered Rick's panicked messages at the end of August, after she'd returned to Connecticut. It had taken her a couple of weeks to call him back. When she had, he'd almost cried with relief at the sound of her voice. Of course in the next breath he was chewing her out for not calling, but you couldn't have everything.

Darcie wanted her to come to Bethel for Thanksgiving. Jessie and Mac mentioned it too, each time they spoke. Not in a pushy way, but in a way that told her she was loved.

Wanted.

"I do miss them, Mel. So much." Grief choked her and made further speech impossible. In the secret place in her mind, where she allowed her dreams and memories to live, Claire thought about a house on the lake.

"You know," Mel looked thoughtful as she played with a spoon, "Steve and James are always talking about expanding the company. I've been thinking that Maine seems like a pretty good place to set up a new branch."

Her friend's perceptive smile told Claire she'd been mind-reading again. Only two people in this world could read her mind.

Rick Matthews and the fiery redhead across the table.

Claire pretended to shrug off the idea. With her father's wedding planned, she had wondered at the possibility but dared go no further than her daydreams.

Dad and Eleanor planned to travel extensively once they were married. James' family was always busy, but they'd definitely protest their moving. Maybe. Still, Maine wasn't that far. But leaving Connecticut would mean leaving Mel...

Guilt pricked her at the sight of the tears in Melanie's eyes.

"You should talk to Jamie," Melanie said softly. "If you put off moving until after the baby comes, I'll never let you go."

"How did you know?"

Melanie stood and rounded the table until she was beside her and hugged her tight. "How could I not know? You've been wearing that goofy grin for the past two weeks." She kissed the top of Claire's head and stepped back. "Besides, my brother never could keep a secret."

"The rat." Claire got to her feet, already battling nausea. She pulled Mel into another long hug. "Pray as hard as you can, Mel. I know this pregnancy is right, but I'm scared."

"Don't be." Melanie smiled through her tears and somehow managed to look reassuring. "I have a feeling it's going to be just fine this time."

"Yes." Claire felt the agreement in her spirit—warmth that flooded her completely. Liquid gold. That still small voice that whispered in her ear and told her to cast aside all fear and just believe.

And she did.

34

Michelle trudged through the crisp leaves even as more swirled from the high branches of the trees that shrouded the sandy path she walked along. As she climbed higher, lush pines presided over the area. They scattered cones on the ground and filled the air with their heady scent, reminding her that Christmas was only a couple of months away.

This year would be so different.

Her breath rose in a fine mist around her as the trail narrowed and there were more rocks to climb. Michelle pushed her gloved hands further into the pockets of her fleece.

It had been many years since she had walked this way.

She stopped in her tracks and took in the sight of the new home before her. The ramshackle three-room cabin she remembered Rick's grandparents owning had been replaced by a sprawling two-story structure constructed of thick pine logs and smooth round stones. Long windows were framed in green shutters. The spacious front porch displayed a couple of his swan sculptures. Two large urns filled with bright Gerber daises, still blooming, sat at the top of the stairs. And two Adirondack chairs, one blue, one red, were positioned around the side that she knew faced the lake. Jazz lay just outside the front door.

The dog lifted her head as Michelle approached. Brass chimes hung from the rafters and gave off a welcoming sound.

Smoke swirled from the stone chimney and told her he was home. Jazz left her position at the front door, emitted two short barks, then padded down the front steps, her thick black tail wagging.

Michelle laughed as she bent over the dog. "Some watchdog you are, Jazzy. You're supposed to be protecting the place."

"Do I need protecting?"

Michelle straightened and drew in a breath. Rick leaned against the doorframe, arms folded across his chest. He was barefoot, in jeans and a black T-shirt, over which he wore a white apron splattered with all sorts of different colored stains. The barest of smiles toyed with his lips.

"Not from me."

"You sure about that?" His eyes sparked with mischief.

As she stepped closer, delectable aromas wafted around her. "What are you making?"

Rick scratched his jaw and gave a low chuckle. "It's supposed to be some kind of Mediterranean stew. But I'm not sure I'm doing it right."

His hair was longer now and it lifted in the breeze, giving him that boyish look she remembered so well. Amazing how twenty-seven years could change a person so much, yet not at all. The times she'd spent with him since coming home made her wonder if they'd ever been apart.

Of course she hadn't told him that.

Michelle smiled but didn't dare get any closer. "It can't be that bad. Smells good."

"Oh." Relief washed over him, followed by a scowl. "Do you know what coriander is?"

"It's a spice. Haven't you got any?"

"Don't think so."

"Well, maybe it won't matter too much. How about parsley?"

"Got that." He held up a band-aid covered finger. "Had a little run in with the chopper."

"Ouch." A giggle stuck in her throat at his befuddled expression. "Sounds like you might need a little help, Mr. Matthews."

"You offering?" He walked out onto the porch as she took the steps one at a time.

Michelle almost laughed at the ridiculous way her heart pounded when she raised her eyes to meet his inquiring gaze. Insane. Perhaps she'd truly slipped over the edge of reason.

She wrestled with the fierce urge to turn tail and run but embraced the moment and lifted her shoulders. "Maybe."

She stood less than a foot away from him and felt her knees buckle. It was all she could do to take her next breath. Rick moved quickly and took her by the arms, waiting while she steadied her breathing.

His clear eyes moved over her, and she saw his hesitation. "What are you doing here, Shel?"

"I..." Tears formed as she stared up at him. How she'd missed that face. Even when she hated him, she'd never stopped loving him. Not really.

Something she'd read once, a long time ago, came back to her then—a quote from Winston Churchill. After going back to college, she'd taken history and political science. She loved Churchill: *Never give in! Never give in! Never, never, never, never -- in nothing great or small, large or petty. Never give in, except to convictions of honor and good sense.*

Michelle ran a light finger over his thick eyebrows and down the side of his face. He gave a slight shudder but kept his eyes fixed on her.

"I came to tell you that I...I forgive you."

Her heart aching, she took the final step needed to bring her fully into his embrace. Slowly she slipped her arms around him and held him tight. He released his breath in a haggard exhale as he pulled her against him.

Michelle didn't know how long he held her. Didn't have the slightest clue what either of them would say or do next. But she didn't care.

She was home.

Finally Rick drew back and cupped her face in his hands, his eyes moist but his smile brighter than she'd ever seen it. "I love you," he whispered hoarsely. "I don't know what that means to you or what you think about it, but that's the way it is. The minute I saw you again, I knew it. There's never been anyone else for me, Shel. I know I was a fool, and I'll regret that until the day I die. But, if you're crazy enough to give me a second chance, I swear you won't be sorry." His eyes sought hers and she saw the fear in them.

Fear had no place in their lives anymore.

Michelle placed a finger on his lips. "You always did talk too much. I didn't walk all the way up this mountain for nothing, Maverick."

He tipped his head, a grin bringing out his dimple. "Thought you didn't believe in second chances."

"Maybe I changed my mind."

"Lucky me." He rested his forehead against hers and tightened his hold. "Do you have any particular plans for the rest of your life, Miss Kelly?"

Laughter caught in her throat as she shook her head. "It's kind of up for grabs at the moment. Did you have a suggestion?"

"Possibly."

His face was so close she could barely bring it into focus, but she felt his breath on her mouth and longed to be reminded of his kiss. "Are you going to stand here making small talk, or are you going to kiss me?"

"Um...I think my stew..."

"Forget your stew." Michelle grinned and pulled his head down to hers, claiming his lips with her own.

It was all the incentive he needed.

35

As Tara's Place came into view, Claire shifted in her seat, her excitement building. James laughed as he parked the truck off to the side of the house. "We can always turn around."

Claire tossed him a grin as she scrambled out and let the dogs out from the back. They catapulted out of the vehicle, all of them barking at once. So much for surprising everyone.

"Leave the bags. Let's just go in." She waited for James, and they headed up the front steps together. The door swung open before they reached it, and Jessie stepped onto the porch, beaming. She opened her arms wide and Claire ran to her.

"You didn't tell anyone we were coming, did you?" Claire drew back, unable to stop her laughter.

Jessie joined in as she held Claire's face between her hands, her brown eyes sparkling. "Just Mac. Oh, it's good to see you! Where's your father?" She looked past Claire and James with an enquiring gaze. Claire smiled at her enthusiasm and loved her all the more for it.

"He and Eleanor are coming tomorrow. In time for a late lunch, if that's okay? They'll get an early start." Claire pushed back nerves again and took comfort in Jessie's reassuring smile.

"Wonderful. We're just about ready for tomorrow. It's going to be the best Thanksgiving ever. Hello, dear." Jessie went to James and drew him into a long hug.

Jessie had somehow convinced her to invite Dad and Eleanor, and they'd jumped at the idea, much to her surprise. Claire had no idea how Michelle or Rick would feel about it but suspected they'd all done a much better job of letting go of the past than she had. They would all get along just fine.

"Can we go in already?" Claire stamped her feet, suddenly cold.

"After you, O, impatient one." James held the door for them, and Claire breathed in the familiar smell of the place as she stepped into the warm house. Furniture polish, potpourri and apple pie.

It was good to be back. Where she belonged.

She followed the sound of Jackson's chatter to the den, where she found Mac, Darcie, and Jackson sitting at the table working on a puzzle. Mac held his gray head at an angle as he watched his great-grandson decide where to put the piece he held in his little hand.

Darcie looked on, her eyes shining with pride, waiting to see what his decision would be. A couple of times she pulled her hand back to stop herself from helping him.

Claire tried to contain her laughter at what the next moment would bring. "Boo."

They all looked up at the same time. Mac's face cracked first and he released a knowing chuckle. Darcie's mouth hung open as she stared at Claire, while Jackson gave a whoop and shot out of his chair, barreling toward her.

James was quick to step in front of Claire and lift the little boy high into the air before he could hurl himself on her. "Easy there, bud. How are you?"

"Good." Jackson gave him a quick hug and reached for Claire, his eyes shining. "Clay-uh! You're here! I prayed last night you would come for Thanksisgiving!"

"Well, I guess God answered your prayer." Claire pulled him into her arms and gave him a squeeze. "I missed you, buddy."

"Okay, my turn. *What* are you doing here?" Darcie jumped from one bare foot to the other, her grin wide. Claire drew her into a long hug. Darcie shot Jessie a look as she stepped back. "Did you know about this?"

Jessie's delighted laughter was answer enough. Mac harrumphed behind them and Claire turned to receive his bear hug. She'd missed them all far too much.

While they greeted James, she took a moment to catch her breath.

"Is Rick here?" Claire asked a little hesitantly. "I saw his truck outside."

"In the kitchen with Mom." Darcie flashed a grin and pushed her wild hair off her shoulders. "Just follow the shouting."

Claire raised an eyebrow. "Shouting?"

"Oh, yes," Mac laughed and waggled his eyebrows. "Them two can't hold a civil conversation for nothing. Never could."

Jackson gave a dramatic eye roll and slapped his hands against his legs. "It's kissing and shouting, shouting and kissing."

Darcie let out a squeak and clapped her hand over his mouth. "Hush, you."

Claire gawked. "Kissing? What have I missed?"

Darcie giggled and tipped her head toward the kitchen. "Go on. You'll see."

James came to her and took her in his arms. "Go. You'll be fine," he whispered.

226

Claire pulled at her thick sweater as she walked down the hall to the kitchen, and willed her heart to quit pounding. She felt sick enough already without nerves getting the better of her.

Michelle and Rick stood at the long wooden counter, their backs to her. Michelle appeared to be peeling potatoes while Rick...Claire strained her neck...she couldn't really see what Rick was doing, other than giving instructions that were not welcomed. Every now and then he jostled Michelle with his shoulder and she yelped.

"If you're not going to help, go away," she told him in a teasing lilt.

"I am helping. I already chopped the onions for you. Hurry up, already. At this rate we'll be having your stuffing at Christmas."

A good kick in the shins from Michelle, and it was Rick's turn to yelp. "You can be uninvited from this dinner very easily, Mr. Matthews."

"You'd never do that." He moved behind her, working his fingers into her neck as she peeled. Michelle's low groan wavered between annoyance and appreciation, but Claire didn't intend to find out which would win out.

"Wow. Is it just me, or is it really warm in here?"

Both jumped and turned, astonishment stamped on their faces.

"Sorry," Claire giggled. "Didn't mean to interrupt the love fest."

"Hey, brat." Rick's face cracked into the biggest smile she'd seen on him as he strode across the room and swept her into his arms. "What are you doing here?" His laughter resonated through the kitchen and settled on her like an old familiar blanket from home.

"Hey, jerk." Claire hugged him hard before he set her down. "What do you mean, what am I doing here?" She took a step backward and pushed up the sleeves of her sweater. "It's Thanksgiving. Families are supposed to be together. Didn't you get the memo?"

He pinched her nose between his thumb and forefinger and grinned. "Better make more stuffing, Shel. You haven't seen anyone eat like this one."

Claire swatted his hand away and made a face. The aroma of onions and sausages was already making her want to run for the bathroom.

Michelle washed her hands and dried them with a tea towel. She kept her distance, hesitation written all over her face. Claire couldn't blame her.

"No offense, but I'm probably not going to be eating much this year." She locked eyes with Michelle and gave a shrug. "I was pretty sick last time too."

"What?" Rick's mouth opened, and she could have sworn he paled. "Claire...are you..."

"She's pregnant, Rick, not dying." Michelle laughed and inched a bit closer. "That's wonderful. Congratulations."

"Thanks." Claire took one look at Rick's face and dissolved into giggles. "What's the matter with you, Grandpa?"

"Nuh uh." He raised his hands and backed off. "No way. I am not old enough to be anybody's grandfather. Seriously, Claire." He looked so alarmed she only laughed harder. Michelle joined in and walked to where he stood, slipping her arms around Rick's waist.

"You have a few months to get used to the idea, Maverick. When are you due, Claire?"

"End of June." Claire smiled at both of them, grandparents her child would never have to live without.

Rick studied her, worry in his eyes. "Are you okay?"

His concern brought fresh tears and Claire nodded. "Yes. We're both very happy. I'm trying not to be nervous."

Rick pulled her in for another hug. Claire released a long sigh and silently thanked God for this moment. "By the way, my dad's coming tomorrow."

"Whoa, what?" Rick stared down at her, his eyebrows shooting skyward. "You're kidding, right?"

"No." Claire ran her hands down her face and laughed. "Jessie called him herself. He and Eleanor are really looking forward to meeting everyone. So, you think you can handle that one, Maverick?"

"Depends on whether he can handle us." Rick chuckled and scratched the back of his neck. "It's not exactly the Park Plaza around here."

Claire waved a hand and rolled her eyes. "He's not like that. Just don't discuss politics and you'll get along fine."

"Oh, we don't. Ever." Michelle grinned, her face flushed and prettier than Claire remembered. In fact, she looked years younger. Tara's Place had worked its magic again.

Claire managed a smile, shooting Rick a pointed look. "Maybe you could help James with our bags."

"You have bags?" Rick gave a dramatic groan and pressed the back of his hand to his forehead. "I'll get the forklift."

"Shut up." Claire gave Rick a push as he left the room chuckling. She met Michelle's eyes. "You seem very happy."

"We are." A faint blush crept into her cheeks. Claire nodded. This was how it should be.

How it should have been.

She fiddled with the rings on her fingers and cast a glance around the room. Beyond the kitchen on the other side of the hall was Jessie's sewing room. "Can we talk?"

They crossed the hall and Michelle sat on one of the rocking chairs. She pulled one of Jessie's brightly colored afghans to her chest. Claire wandered around the room and tried to organize her thoughts. It was hard to know where to begin. Or how.

Finally she turned and met the eyes she'd longed to see again for weeks. "When I was growing up, I had this fantasy of what you'd look like. Every time I looked in the mirror I wondered…did I look like you? Sometimes, before I fell asleep at night, I'd think about where I came from. I always felt guilty about it, though, like I was betraying my parents by wanting to know. It was hard to get beyond that." She lowered herself into the rocker opposite Michelle's. "But even now, despite everything, I don't regret it. I'm glad I found the truth. I'm glad I found you." The confession hung in the air and Claire tried to gage Michelle's reaction.

"I know you didn't want me to find you, but I think in some way I was supposed to. I still don't understand it all, but I know everything happens for a reason. I think we were all part of a bigger plan. Bigger than any of us could imagine."

"Yes," Michelle dabbed at her eyes with a tissue, "you're right. We all needed healing, Claire. If you hadn't come here, hadn't looked for me, I'd probably be making another mistake of graphic proportions right about now."

Claire grinned, the somber mood lifting. "You weren't really going to marry that stuffed suit, were you? Rick said he was awful." She regretted the words as soon as they were out, but Michelle only laughed.

"Oh, he was. But I didn't think I deserved any better."

"You were wrong."

"Yes." Her eyes lit up, and Claire saw how much the last few months had changed her.

"Well." Claire blinked and looked away for a moment. "All that to say…I…I don't have the right to blame you for anything you did, Michelle. None of us are perfect. We all make mistakes. You certainly didn't have to tell me the whole story. You and my Dad could have kept it to yourselves, but you didn't. But it really doesn't matter anymore." Claire nodded, the words striking a chord deep within.

It *didn't* matter.

"When I started this search, I was curious, but afterward…once I knew who you were, it became more than that. I felt like I was getting a second chance, getting to know the family I might have had. And I wanted you to be a part of that. We all did."

"I was scared of you, Claire," Michelle whispered. "But I never meant to hurt you like I did. I was just terrified to face my past, face what I'd done. I didn't want you to hate me."

Claire shook her head, bewildered. "I don't hate you. How could I? You gave me life."

"I'm so sorry, Claire. For everything."

Claire moved to crouch before her, taking her hands in hers. Michelle's eyes flew wide. "I know you are. But what I'm trying to say, probably not very well, is that I forgive you. And, if you're still interested, I'd like very much for us to get to know each other."

Michelle placed her hands around Claire's face, wonder and tears shining in her eyes. She kissed the top of Claire's head. "Since you've come back into my life, I've been given a second chance—with my parents, Darcie, Rick, and with you—I never believed that was possible, but...here we are."

"Here we are."

They stood together and Michelle took Claire's hands in hers. "Can we start over, Claire?"

Claire's heart was full as she squeezed Michelle's hands. "I'd like that. Do you want to go first?"

"Okay." Michelle's face shone with the light of restoration as she held Claire's hands tight and tipped her head toward her, her smile wide and filled with promise. "Hi. I'm Michelle—your birth mother. It's nice to meet you."

Claire held her gaze and savored the moment. "Hi. I'm Claire. And I've wanted to meet you for a very long time."

A new sensation tugged at her heart. A feeling that went far beyond initial curiosity and hinted at the chance of a real relationship. Claire drew Michelle into a hug and embraced it.

When she stepped back, her eyes came to rest on the locket she'd noticed around Michelle's neck the minute she'd turned to face her in the kitchen. Claire smiled at the sudden hesitation in Michelle's eyes and pointed to it. "I think you have something that belongs to me."

Michelle gave a soft laugh and reached behind her neck. She undid the clasp and held the chain in her hands. "May I?"

Claire turned and lifted her hair, waiting while Michelle fastened the necklace. When she could face her again, she swiveled, reaching for the charm that now meant so much more.

Unshed tears stood in Michelle's eyes. "To new beginnings, Claire?"

Claire nodded, peace and joy like no other flooding through her. "To new beginnings."

Author's Note

Dear Reader,

I hope you've enjoyed *Hidden in the Heart*. For me, this is a very personal story on many levels. While it is not exactly *my* story per se, Claire's journey is loosely based on my own experiences.

When I was about two or three, perhaps younger, my parents read me a story. It was called *The Chosen Baby*. They explained to me then how I was special, I was chosen. God had made us a family. While all that remains true, it was only later, as an adult, that I came to know and understand all the complex dynamics and emotions that go hand in hand with being adopted.

Making the decision to search for my birth family was very difficult, and not one I undertook lightly. I had no idea what doors I was opening, and who, if anyone, would open them.

My search was not difficult in terms of the time it took, but it was emotionally draining and definitely took a toll on my family and myself at various stages of my journey.

Fortunately, I can say I have no regrets. God blessed me greatly with new people to call family, new relationships to foster, and He gave me all the answers I needed. There are still things along the way that did not turn out the way I hoped. But everything happens for a reason, and I believe I have all I need now.

If you are an adoptee with a desire to search, please make your decision very carefully. If you do, however, decide to proceed, there are many resources available to you. Here are just a few I recommend:

Books:

Gathering The Missing Pieces In An Adopted Life, by Kay Moore (Hannibal Books, January 2009).

Lost & Found: The Adoption Experience, by Betty Jean Lifton (Harper Perennial, March 22, 1988).

Journey of the Adopted Self: The Quest for Wholeness , by Betty Jean Lifton (Basic Books, May 6, 1995).

<u>Internet:</u>

International Soundex Reunion Registry (ISRR)
http://www.isrr.net/about.shtml
http://www.childwelfare.gov/adoption/
http://www.adoption.com
http://www.adoptionvoices.com
Adoptees Christian Fellowship, Jody Moreen—jodymoreen@gmail.com

May God bless you on your journey!

Catherine

Questions for Reflection and Discussion
For individual or group use

1. As the story opens, Claire is at a very dark time in her life. She feels guilt for things over which she had no control. Have you ever felt "illogical guilt"? In what situation(s)? How did you deal with it?

2. Claire struggles with the fact that nobody seems to understand her pain and, as a result, withdraws from those who love her. Do you think she was misunderstood? Or do you believe she misunderstood other's responses to her? Have you ever been in a situation where you and a loved one "misunderstood" each other? Has the situation been resolved? If so, how? If not, how might you take the first step?

3. Claire's losses cause her to question God and blame Him for her suffering. When bad things happen, do you tend to blame God, yourself (or your past), or others first? Why? What experiences in your past and present are you currently struggling with?

4. Many adoptees feel as though someone who is not adopted cannot understand their need to know where they came from. If someone asked you, "What's your definition of adoption?" what would you say? How do you view

the birth mother? The adoptive parents? The adopted child? In what way(s) do these views influence your view of someone who tells you, "I'm adopted"? Or of being adopted or being an adoptive parent yourself?

5. When Claire begins the search to find her birth mother, she runs up against many brick walls and feels as though she simply does not exist. Have you ever felt this way? As if you're alone in the world? As if no one really knows you or cares? How have you handled that feeling in the past? How might you handle those feelings in a healthy way in your present and your future?

6. Inability to forgive creates estrangement between Michelle and her parents. Have you struggled with forgiving someone? If so, why was forgiving that person particularly difficult? How did you finally seek resolution (if you have)? If you chose not to forgive, how has that impacted your relationship with that person since then? How has it influenced the way you feel about yourself and the way you approach new and existing relationships with others today?

7. Rick chooses to help Claire through her addictions, rather than judging her. When you see others in a tough spot, are you tempted to gossip about them and judge them? Or is your first response one of compassion, help, and understanding? What in your past influences the way you respond to others? What does it say about yourself? Think of a current situation in which someone is facing a hard time. How might you actively help that person?

8. What parallels do you see between Claire's and Michelle's lives? What parallels do you see between Michelle's and Darcie's lives? What feelings, emotions, and life experiences do they share?

9. The mother/daughter relationship is explored within a variety of circumstances throughout the story. How does this put your own relationships in perspective? In what areas do you need to choose to forgive? Choose to move on? Choose to discuss so that you might make things right in your relationship?

10. Psalm 139; 13-16 is quoted at the beginning of this book. What does this verse mean to you? How might it practically affect the way you see others? Yourself? God? The world around you? The subject of adoption?

yesterday's TOMORROW

CATHERINE WEST

She's after the story that might get her the Pulitzer.
He's determined to keep his secrets to himself.

Vietnam, 1967.

Independent, career-driven journalist Kristin Taylor wants two things: to honor her father's memory by becoming an award-winning overseas correspondent and to keep tabs on her only brother, Teddy, who signed up for the war against their mother's wishes. Brilliant photographer Luke Maddox, silent and brooding, exudes mystery. Kristin is convinced he's hiding something.

Willing to risk it all for what they believe in, Kristin and Luke engage in their own tumultuous battle until, in an unexpected twist, they're forced to work together. Ambushed by love, they must decide whether or not to set aside their own private agendas for the hope of tomorrow that has captured their hearts.

A poignant love story set amidst the tumultuous Vietnam War

Website: http://www.catherinejwest.com
Facebook: https://www.facebook.com/CatherineJWest
OakTara Website: http://www.oaktara.com
Blog: http://www.thisisablogaboutbooks.wordpress.com
Trailer for Yesterday's Tomorrow:
http://www.youtube.com/watch?v=vVQUMRlYhkM

About the Author

CATHERINE WEST is an award-winning author who writes stories of hope and healing from her island home in Bermuda. Educated in Bermuda, England, and Canada, Catherine holds a degree in English from the University of Toronto. When she's not at the computer working on her next story, you can find her taking her Border Collie for long walks or tending to her roses and orchids. She and her husband have two college-aged children.

Catherine is a member of American Christian Fiction Writers and Romance Writers of America, and is represented by Rachelle Gardner of Books & Such Literary. Catherine loves to connect with her readers and can be reached at Catherine@catherinejwest.com.

For individual reflection and group study and discussion questions, go to: http://www.catherinejwest.com.

Website: http://www.catherinejwest.com
Facebook: https://www.facebook.com/CatherineJWest
OakTara Website: http://www.oaktara.com
Blog: http://www.thisisablogaboutbooks.wordpress.com
Trailer for Yesterday's Tomorrow:
http://www.youtube.com/watch?v=vVQUMRlYhkM

CPSIA information can be obtained at www.ICGtesting.com
Printed in the USA
LVOW041515011012

301035LV00006B/31/P

9 781602 903296